Misadventures of A Motor Home Driver

Misadventures of A Motor Home Driver

Lyle E. Meyers

Writer's Showcase
San Jose New York Lincoln Shanghai

Writer's Showcase
an imprint of iUniverse.com, Inc.

For information address:
iUniverse.com, Inc.
5220 S 16th, Ste. 200
Lincoln, NE 68512
www.iuniverse.com

ISBN: 0-595-16029-8

Printed in the United States of America

A big thank you for the help and advice is given to the following persons:

Arleen Bervig, Park Rapids, Minnesota

Leonard L. Meyers, Prescott Valley, Arizona

Lynn Wingert, West Des Moines, Iowa

Brad Meyers, Des Moines, Iowa

This story is dedicated to one special group of people
—all of the motor home drivers, wherever you are.

Contents

CHAPTER I

In The First Place

Before telling a story, it is advisable to obtain as much information as possible relating to the subjects involved, to consolidate the pertinent facts in detail, and to promote accuracy as the uppermost value in presentation. This won't happen here. Accumulating facts and listing information are relegated to the trash bin, substituted instead by the fleeting memories that occasionally tiptoed through the caverns of my mind concerning events involving myself, other drivers, and ordinary common people. This tale is true and reputable, but with a little exaggeration tossed in. Many of the so-called "adventures" could be considered little more than a series of driving repetitions, repeatedly repeated over and over again. Perhaps such a statement is not entirely accurate, because a driver cannot tell when unexpected events may change tranquillity into sudden excitement or even horror. One must find himself always alert, since flashing red lights may appear in the rear view mirror at a moment's notice, gusts of wind can wrench the steering wheel from his hands, and times of extreme crisis may cause fainting spells to overcome even the most brave hearted when attempting to dodge the dead bodies lying along the road side, some of which are human.

Maybe you think I am some rich guy with nothing more to do than to drive some fancy motor home wherever my whims may lead or my wife dictate. Nothing could be farther from the truth. In opposition, motor home driving in my experiences proved to be a means of occupation, albeit only part-time. It must be understood that this undertaking, albeit only part-time, provided employment for this humble driver, originating from a factory delivery point. My duty was to drive recently constructed vehicles from this factory to dealers throughout the nation and beyond. Such vehicles were then sold, rented out, or in extreme cases, destroyed by a car crusher.

This part-time employment (moonlighting to be more exact) actually played second fiddle to my primary occupation, which the city folk so crudely designate as "dumb farmer." Being categorically classified in such a despicable, detestable manner causes an abhorrent resentfulness to rise within my breast, resulting in a vehement maliciousness aligning against those who so callously display those demeaning attitudes. The effrontery provokes inappropriate calculations, dispelling any possible forgiving appropriation whatsoever. Attaining a high school diploma may have caused greater resentment, while including a college education intensified the condition (even though the college part only lasted six weeks). A vacancy, created when my uncle's tenant up and left just ahead of planting season, provided the opportunity to enter the farming sector. So it came to pass that on bended knee I was able to beg my uncle's favor, with the provision that enough money could be borrowed from the First City Bank in Otoonga to purchase the necessary machinery and equipment. After quitting college, the illustrious career of farming began to take shape, while the acquisition of a $60,000 debt also became noticeable. This life-changing event meant moving the family from our apartment in Otoonga to the farm five miles east of the city. A short time later, motor home delivery driving intruded into our lives, along with the dire consequences thus entailed.

It may be a puzzling concept to you why this narrative is being written in the first place. There is a very good reason for this, an ennobling announcement that will bring enlightenment to all who pay attention. This is to be a warning which cannot be over-emphasized. Apparently there is no other source from which this information can be obtained.

The news media completely ignore it. Heretofore only by word of mouth has any knowledge been brought forth, and this by a minute minority who have been caught up in a Draconian obsession. These words are given in hopes that those thus informed will harken to the principles involved, and that from the college graduate to the lowliest laborer, all may understand and profit thereby. This proclamation is hereby given: PEOPLE OF AMERICA WAKE UP! DON'T EVER DRIVE MOTOR HOMES! Involvement in this activity leads to disappointment, pessimism, poverty, and degradation. Such an atrocious habit surpasses that of gambling, drugs, alcohol, and even sex. If this revelation can be made throughout the confines of our great nation, if even one of our sons or daughters can evade such dangerous entrapment, and those already hooked can somehow escape a lifetime of failure, then my duty would be fulfilled and my life will not have been lived in vain.

Why should such a warning need to be issued in the first place? Well, I am going to tell you why such a warning needs to be issued in the first place. You must understand, there are multiple dangers and perils when driving motor homes. It cannot readily be imagined the difficulties, trouble, and life-threatening situations continually facing those who are unwary. Because the average happy- go-lucky person does not believe what is being told, an explanation of this warning is to be followed with a partial listing of the horrifying complications that entangle careless individuals who go merrily on their way, staring death and destruction squarely in the face. It can be compared to the child playing with matches while the house is burning down around him, or like the fisherman reeling in a big minnow with water up to his armpits while the boat is sinking. Yes, prevalent are the many dangers of motor home travel.

To begin, there are constant weather problems of all descriptions: head winds, side winds, dust storms, sand storms, blizzards, hail, sleet, icy roads, rain deluges, hurricanes, cyclones, typhoons, fog, smog and bright sunshine. Weather dangers are constant threats.

Even normal driving conditions provide a continuous series of hazards: construction sites, detours, potholes, single lanes, and barricades. Road hogs are dominant, cars won't dim their lights, accidents are the norm, and law violations are recognized by the excellency of the written tickets presented. Gas station attendants excel in cheating, plumbing is shut off at rest stops, road signs point in the wrong direction, and drunk drivers run rampant. Animals run loose on the roads: birds, cows, dogs, rabbits, coyotes, horses, buffalo, skunks, and armadillos. Deer can be seen congregating in the ditches, deciding which one would be the next to make the supreme sacrifice.

If such obstructions listed above are not enough to curtail motor home driving, then consideration of illness striking should be made. Periods of nervousness, headaches, eye strain, indigestion, vomiting, arthritic pains, muscle fatigue, heart palpitations, strokes, and sneezing. Perhaps worst of all are those twin curses of the road, diarrhea and constipation, both of which may occur at any time without prior warning, sometimes intermittently and sometimes simultaneously.

Accidents happen in a moment's time: running into ditches, bumping into light poles, dropping into potholes, sideswipes, facing hit and run drivers who hit and run, and hub caps being dented by little boys who throw stones.

Yet to be mentioned: volcanoes, mud slides, fires, earthquakes, bomb threats, explosions, and falling meteors. There are threats of muggers and thieves lurking around every corner, drunks and beggars appearing at all hours of the day or night, prostitutes and homosexuals vying for your attention, while the most serious obstacle of all is apt to take control—a lackadaisical attitude that says "who cares?"

And there are places in our nation that must be avoided if at all possible. South Dakota, where rattlesnakes crawl up your pant legs while pumping gas. Arizona has tarantulas, scorpions, fire ants, violin spiders, and jumping cactus…all of which can cause instant death when provoked. Florida is even worse with cobras, pythons, and crocodiles in every pool of water. There are Reds who are on the warpath, Blacks who monopolize welfare, Yellows confiscate our businesses, Browns take our jobs, Muslims terrorize our very existence, and Jews swindle away our money. And we poor white boys are outnumbered, out-maneuvered, and outsmarted by them all, while sadly, our government encourages these conditions.

There are bosses who we delivery drivers must contend with, grouchy dispatchers and know-it-all inspectors. Highway rules and regulations defy all reason. Our government controls our roads with an iron fist, seeking some poor innocent motor home driver who is insulted, slapped with fines, and given jail sentences right and left. If a delivery driver is lucky enough to finally arrive at his destination, in spite of all of the obstacles previously mentioned, he would discover dreadful encounters with dealers who are impossible to please, harbor unreasonable expectations, and display superior attitudes and surly dispositions.

This is not the end of the matter. When, by the intervention of fate and providence, a driver is to safely deliver his vehicle, he is confronted with yet another perplexing problem. How will he get home? Some smart-aleck drivers pull a small car behind their vehicle, believing they are striking it rich. But if the pay doesn't cover the expenses and the car begins to fall apart, how are they to survive? Some of the more advantaged drivers, who are employed as drivers just for the fun of it, are able to board a plane to make their return. Only the rich, retired, and on Medicare can afford to do this. Some return to home base by taking a train, but then must hire a taxi for the last hundred miles to get back to Otoonga. Many of the more incompetent and unfortunate, myself included, must humble themselves by riding a bus all the way home. Hitchhiking is very dangerous and should only be undertaken as a last resort. Walking home, while being the most economical method, is usually not worth the time or concerted effort.

It must be understood that only a few of the driving perils have yet been mentioned. Many are the other problems that defy evaluation, are enormous in dimension, and horrible in consequence. I have listed many of such dangers to inform the uninformed how some of these troubles will invariably occur on every trip. In the very worst case scenarios, all may be faced, and possibly more than once.

In spite of all the fiendish consequences, motor home driving proved to be a very pleasant activity. Abounding were constant episodes of freedom and excitement. One was able to experience the wonders and vast complexities of our wonderful country, to be enthralled by the scenery, and overwhelmed by its greatness. How thrilling it was to pass through the great cities encountered, although appreciation is somewhat diminished when no parking places can be found. How interesting it was to meet people from all walks of life, ignorant and wise, slim and fat, grouchy and irritable. You are able to visit parks and historical sites, attend fairs and celebrations, experience sporting events and races, and to discover the natural majesty of mountain, plain, and valley. Yet this was not always enjoyable when traveling in the dead of night or in a freaked-out condition. Such appeal is curtailed when plagued by periods of sleepiness and exhaustion, when horrendous traffic jams are encountered, or when cursed with illness.

But I was lucky. I had the best of two worlds. I could plow corn and pitch manure during farm duties while being allowed to drive motor homes in my spare time, on weekends, and at night. To obtain such a wonderful moonlighting job as this did not require a great amount of brain power or physical strength. No book learning, college degree, or mental dexterity were necessary. What kind of employment could fit this lucky farm boy better than this? Being a happy-go-lucky, devil-may-care person like myself melded everything together to advance the situation. It did so happen that there was a certain attribute that became the essential ingredient. A newly acquired talent intruded in a sneaky sort of way suddenly without warning, with no prior consideration, or with any malice aforethought. To the psychologist or the intellectual of the community, it would not be burdensome to discover just what this necessary qualification proved to be. For you see, the primary motivation that so efficaciously inserted this enlightenment in a forceful manner, striking with lightning speed, could be described in one word: jealousy.

This does not proclaim that jealousy was the only reason leading to this employment, but it did become a cause and effect, more or less, so to speak, by and large. It was jealousy of my best friend that sparked the outcome of the cause and effect, you might say. This contributing attribute was visibly enhanced after I had cleaned out the hog barn and was in the process of spreading the ingredients out on the field. Along the roadside at the end of the lane appeared the most beautiful, magnificent, dazzling vehicle ever seen by the eyes of man. It had pulled to a stop adjacent to the road fence. The horn could be heard honking as my tractor approached the end of the field. Out of this beautiful, magnificent, dazzling vehicle stepped Eddie, waving his arms and with a big grin on his face. I stopped the tractor, disengaged the spreader mechanism, and climbed the fence to where the vehicle was parked.

"Hi, Myle. How's things in the farming business?"

"O.K. with me I guess, Eddie. What are you doing driving that big thing?"

"You know what?" he asked with a widening smile.

"What?"

"I quit my job at the rock quarry and got me a new one. I got hired on at the Otoonga Trailer Factory as a driver, and I'm taking this baby to Portland, Oregon."

It was at this point in time that the first haunting specter of resentfulness unceremoniously made its first approach. I was tired and hungry, and with little flecks of waste material clinging to my clothing, caused by a contrary wind blowing across the spreader. Now Eddie was making a triumphant entry, lording it over me with a new job, a bragadocious attitude, and with a beautiful, magnificent, dazzling vehicle to throw in my face.

"How in the world did you pull off a trick like this?" With twitching eyes I continued, "You don't have enough brains to know where you're going, and nobody in their right mind would trust you to drive that thing five miles." I was trying to hide my envy as much as possible while hoping that the tone of my voice wouldn't give it away.

"The boss must have thought I would do alright. Anyway he hired me right on. Since the road to the freeway goes right by your farm, and when I saw you out on the tractor, I decided to stop."

"I can't believe this, Eddie. You never drove one of these things before?"

"No, but they need drivers at the factory real bad right now, so I got hired in no time."

"You mean you ain't had no training or nothing?"

"That's right. All I needed was a driver's license, a Social Security card, two good hands and at least one eye."

"This don't make sense, Eddie. With your kind of records in and out of jail, how you could get hired is more than I know."

"The boss just liked my looks maybe. You know, Myle, I'll get to drive this kind of critter all over the good old U.S.A. No telling what all I'll get to see. I'm gonna have the time of my life."

"That's great, Eddie. I sure wish I had a job like you got."

"You probably can. That's if you can break away from all that haulin' of fertilizer posies." This was said with a smirk on his face.

"You never know. Maybe I'll try and do the same thing."

Suddenly Eddie changed the conversation. "Myle, I can only stop for a minute. Got to keep moving you know. I would invite you inside to have a look around this baby, but you're smelling so bad, some of it might rub off on the furniture. I can't waste my time talking to you all day. I plan to make it out to Portland by Friday and fly back Sunday. Got to do a little sight seeing while I'm out there you know. I'll get in touch when I get back. Don't work too hard and be sure to keep that fertilizer flyin.'"

After these words were spoken, he stepped back in the beautiful, magnificent, dazzling vehicle and started it in a burst of speed and a cloud of dust, leaving me in an envious, stunned condition. I walked back to the tractor, climbed up to the seat, and slowly bumped my way to the building site, muttering all the time.

"Myle, how can this be?" my Bad Self asked. "Your friend Eddie doesn't even have a high school education. Yet he's traveling in a brand new motor home, living like a king. Look at yourself! What are you accomplishing? You're nothing but a slave! Cleaning out hog houses like a coolie in China."

The wind at my back, blowing the odor toward me, didn't offer much condolence. You see, I talk to myself during conflicting situations, especially when I'm by myself. Most of the conversation is more like an argument.

Good Self then started to introduce advice. "Myle, take a close look at the good life you have on the farm. You are able to spend your time in the great outdoors, have freedom to come and go as you please, can be your own boss, and are lucky to have a kind, considerate landlord. You are also blessed with a wonderful wife, five and one-third happy kids, and are only $75,000 in debt."

"Yeah, freedom to what?" Bad Self replied. "Freedom to work seven days a week? And Azailia is always nagging about something. Besides, six kids are too many, each with a mouth to feed. We should have quit at five like I wanted to. Abortion is against her religion, and it is mine too, until now. That landlord, even if he is my uncle, is never satisfied no matter how much I work or how good the crops are. And at the rate I'm going, I'll never get out of debt."

"Now, Myle, just because that bugger Eddie has hit the big time is no reason to blame yourself or complain about your problems. There are other things in life worthwhile besides an easy living and traveling all over the country, making big money."

This argument continued all the way until the tractor was parked in the machine shed. It would seem that Bad Self had won the fight, since my mind was being made up to get a driving job like Eddie, if at all possible. It would be a dream come true to deliver motor homes for the

Otoonga Trailer Factory, which would result in riches, adventure, and notoriety. Bad Self had whispered in my ear that with all my talent there would be little to prevent this intention from being fulfilled. Only one obstacle appeared to stand in the way…Azailia's approval, which could be insurmountable at first glance.

While doing chores that evening, discussions were bandied about between Bad Self and Good which offered numerous ideas how to satisfy the decision. Thoughts were running rampant while filling the hog feeders with ground corn, cleaning out the six pens with a pitch fork, throwing eight bales of straw from the barn mow, bedding the six pens with the eight bales of straw, filling the waterers with a hose, and attempting to make 234 pigs comfortable for the night. Intensive improvision, in conjunction with multiplying mental augmentation, was inducing a radical departure from normal procedure, thus enhancing a negative outcome. Chore completion meant that it was time for supper and completion of another work day.

Supper time around the kitchen table wasn't the best time to make a presentation regarding new employment possibilities. The boys seemed to be at their very worst behavior, kicking each other under the table, fighting over who would get the biggest piece of cake, and throwing crumbs at each other when their mother wasn't looking. All of this caused Azailia to be extra grumpy. Some of the grouchiness spilled over to my shoulders since I had come for the meal late. The lateness caused the pork to be slightly overcooked. Burnt to be exact. So it wasn't a very appropriate time to make my presentation. Yet I boldly spewed forth my intentions. Her reaction didn't offer my ego much enthusiasm.

"Azailia, honey, you know we need the extra money with Christmas coming on in a few months. And I would like to buy you a new dress and other things around the house you like. The boys need new overalls and we should be buying things for the new baby ahead of time. I would only be gone a few days at a time during each trip."

"I don't like the idea, Myle," she replied. "You would be galavanting all over the country and I'll be left to take care of the boys alone. And all of those pigs, too."

"Honey, there's one less to take care of now. One died last night. Pigs I meant. Anyway I am going to get Old Barney to work the hog chores for you."

"Barney? That old guy? And him being drunk all the time?"

Everyone called him "Old" Barney but he was only about fifty years of age. He was the neighborhood bachelor who lived down the road east a mile and a half, who owned several farms which were rented out to other farmers, and who was available to help out his neighbors with their farm work. It was well known that young women were hired out to do his own house work and cooking. This was another cause for jealousy, if stray thoughts persuaded too much concentration, which I tried mine not to. He wasn't much of a threat to my own wife because at fifty years of age he wasn't old enough to be a dirty old man yet.

"Myle, if you think we need more money, why don't you try to get a different job than this? One where you can be home nights and won't have to hire anyone to do the hog chores."

"There aren't any jobs available this time of year except maybe at the rock quarry. Who would want to work at that back- breaking place?"

"I can't do all the housework, take care of all the boys, and still have the responsibility of feeding all those hogs. Another thing, I don't feel good a lot of the time, with the baby growing more and more."

"Honey, this would only be a part-time job, you know. It would be a good way to get out of debt. We could really live the good life."

"Maybe you could, but what about the boys and me?"

Nothing went in my favor. She had an answer for every question. Sleeping that night for me was evasive. A rebuff had been made to each argument. Both Bad Self and Good had been silenced. The awesome possibilities of driving were prominent in each dream sequence and during each devilish nightmare that erupted in the night-time hours. I broke out into a sweat while contemplating the enormous potentialities in travel and advancement.

Like a meteor flashing across a moonless sky, a grenade exploding in a foxhole, or a cannon ball crashing through a barricade, a decision was reached. Bad Self had again won a victory. His profound utterance was, "Go for it, Myle. You remember what the preacher said from the pulpit last Sunday don't you? He said man is head of the house, so that is what you better go by. Assert your authority and go for it! After all, you're the boss in this house. And you can't let that bragging Eddie get ahead of you, can you?"

By four o'clock in the morning a final decision had been reached. This very day I would go to the Otoonga Trailer Factory to make application for the job of driving motor homes. Little did I realize what all this would entail, what horrible consequences would result. This downward pathway would lead to untold anguish, lethargy, frustration, dissipation, bondage, austerity, friction, grumpiness, consternation, withdrawal, hysteria, impuissance, nyctophobia, rancor, rebellion, repudiation, sarcasm, disillusionment, bickering, bereavement, antagonism, diabolism, denunciation, suffering, humiliation, estrangement, illness, sorrow, regret, loneliness, degradation, remorse, exasperation, failure, poverty, fear, dread, dismay, injustice, insults, retaliation, shame, foolishness, perplexity, instability, bitterness, apprehension, misfortune, condemnation, dissension, agitation, ignominy, disgrace, deception, viciousness, and disgust.

The culmination of all this was inception of ulcers, baldness, senility, gluttony, hemicrany, hernia, neuralgia, nervousness, xanthochroia, lunacy, hallucinations, delirium, abuse, weariness, palpitations, hemiopia, psoriasis, and twitching eyes. Yet during such catastrophic times I was able to experience periods of light- heartedness, frivolity, laughter, and enjoyment (but not very often).

CHAPTER II

What For Did I Do This?

A loud blast of the alarm clock at six o'clock provided me the opportunity to fix my own breakfast consisting of two fried eggs with broken yolks, a piece of toast black on one side and cold on the other, and topped off with a lukewarm cup of sugared coffee. Hearing my wife begin to stir and the younger boys begin to whine caused an early exit to the hog house. Filling the self-feeders, adding to the water tanks, and bumping my head three times on the swinging top door, were the usual procedures to begin another day of farm life. Only this time, changes were to take place. After hog chores were completed I jumped in the pickup and was off to Otoonga, where the route just happened to lead past the employment office of the Otoonga Trailer Factory. Feed purchases were made at the Hog Kitchen Store prior to the upcoming dreaded encounter.

Backwardness, nervousness, and apprehension accompanied my approach to the office. "What if they won't hire me?" was Good Self's inquiry.

Bad Self replied, "Nonsense. If that good-for-nothing Eddie can get a job here, then anyone can."

With a sudden burst of super-charged ego, I climbed the long flight of stairs where my fate was to be determined. The window on the office door bore the words "W. L. Hummer, Dispatch Officer." Underneath his name, but in smaller letters was another name, "Miss Missmossmus, Secretary."

"I-I-I would like to try up for motor home driving," was my stammering exclamation to the matronly secretary seated at a desk inside the office. She greeted me somewhat cordially and presented a questionnaire, the contents of which probed my past in every phase. Time was spent agonizing over the forms in attempt to make the best impression possible with only a minimum amount of lying. She asked to see my driver's license and other identification papers. I waited in trepidation for an interview with the employment officer, but that didn't happen. Instead, this same secretary summoned me back to her desk with the words, "Mr. Hummer phoned that he won't be back in the office for the rest of the day since he is out playing golf with an important client. But since we are in dire need of more drivers, he said to go ahead and hire you. Where would you like to go on your first trip?"

To say that I was stunned, shocked, and bewildered would be a vast understatement. Was I to be sent out on America's dangerous highways with no instruction whatsoever? Somehow I was able to choke out a reply. "Maybe I should take a short trip since it will be the first."

"Let's see," Miss Missmossmus remarked in contemplation, "we have a 24-foot unit going to Tulsa, Oklahoma. Would that be alright? It's only about a 600-mile drive."

"Yes, I guess so, since it is short." Wow, 600 miles to Tulsa, Oklahoma! I hadn't been that far away from home in my life.

She presented me with a huge packet consisting of travel documents, identification and insurance papers, destination memos, a ring of keys, packing sheets, and other printed instructions too numerous to mention. It must be understood that this undertaking began many months ago before the time of ICC exams, driver's tests, multitudes of governmental regulations, log books, and the multiple employer requirements that are in vogue today.

"Your assigned unit will be located in Section 22, Lot 3, over by the Wheel & Rim Building," she continued. (In the language of the upper echelons in the Otoonga Trailer Factory, motor homes were called units.) "You won't have any trouble finding it. After you have checked the unit to make certain that everything is in perfect running condition, be sure to stop at the Parts Department Office in the Radiator Stop Leak building in Lot 9. Find out if there are any parts that are to be shipped along to the dealer in Tulsa. Be careful, good luck, and have a safe trip. Any questions?"

"No, I guess not." I had a million but didn't know where to start.

Leaving the office, the dazed expression on my face was best concealed by a forced smile. Proceeding to Section 22 about 2000 feet to the south, I began to scan the millions of motor homes parked in rows and sections. The search proved fruitless until discovery was made that I was looking in Lot 2 when it should have been Lot 3. By using the same scanning procedure as in the preceding lot, and by finding the numbers on the windshields of the various units, success finally prevailed at last. There it was! My very first motor home to drive! A beautiful, magnificent, dazzling vehicle! But when one got a closer look, a slightly different opinion was obtained. It wasn't very beautiful because it was slopped with mud and covered with dirty spots from one end to the other, paper and chalk marks were in abundance on the windows, and it was parked in the midst of a group of units that were much larger, brighter colored, and more shiny than this one. This signified to me that magnificent wasn't a good way to describe it either. It certainly wasn't dazzling, for about that time a fog and mist began rolling in, completely nullifying what little admiration there formerly had been. This caused a churning of the thought processes which slowly worked downward to the stomach regions, causing instant indigestion which in turn made a return visit to the brain, imposing the question that Good Self interposed, "What kind of a mess are you getting into, Myle?"

To all you ignoramuses who don't know what a motor home is, I will attempt to describe it. It is something like a house trailer that you pull down the highway behind your car, except in this case you sit inside it and try to guide it from the front. You place the car behind it, just the opposite, and pull the car instead. A motor is located someplace inside the unit that enables a driver to force it anywhere he wants it to go. Well, to a lot of places anyway, providing he can keep it out of the ditch. Most of the units have two wheels in front, one on each side. There are supposed to be four wheels in back, duals directly opposite and in exact alignment with the ones on the other side, but you can't prove it by me. The unit I was to drive to Tulsa had only one door which was located on the passenger side. This door was called the "entry door" by those in the know, but a few of the more sarcastic drivers called it the escape hatch. Each big unit looks a flying box drifting down the highway, causing little compact cars to be breathless trying to keep up. Just think, people actually live in these boxes for months on end, rarely making an appearance until the batteries run down.

The problem that first concerned me was, out of a group of 53 keys on the ring, how does one know which one was the door key? After many attempts by trial and error, the correct key was found, permitting my feet to enter this beautiful, magnificent, dazzling vehicle which would be in my care until delivery was made in Tulsa. Once inside, my first impression allowed Bad Self to utter, "Wow, how are you, Myle Heyers, ever going to drive this big monstrosity for 600 miles without wrecking it on the way?"

Directly in the front of the unit was a huge dashboard filled with gauges, gadgets, lights, signals, buttons, numbers, switches, levers, knobs, and warnings all mixed together, a radio that actually worked, a heater control, and a motor air conditioner. Protruding from left center was what was called a steering wheel which we were expected to use with a calm disposition and a nonviolent attitude. The immense drivers seat was positioned directly behind the steering wheel like most of them are supposed to be. The seat was covered with plastic, revealed arm and head rests, and was equipped with both a backward and sideways adjustability. Behind the drivers chair was a Formica-covered table lined on both sides with benches topped with plastic cushions. The front passenger seat also had a matching plastic covering similar to the rest of the decor. Behind the passenger seat and directly across the aisle from the table was a mini-kitchen containing a stainless steel sink, tiny half-size refrigerator, and a two-burner gas stove. None of these appliances were to be used by any delivery drivers. One of the cardinal rules issued from the dispatch office was: NO FOOD OR DRINK IS TO BE CONSUMED IN THIS UNIT. Yet I fooled them all one time by drinking a can of pop and eating a bag of potato chips, and they never found out about it either.

Perhaps the greatest miracle of all about a motor home is that each one has its own bathroom. This unit provided a stool, sink, and shower enclosed in its own little private domain, and included lights, mirrors, curtain, and exhaust fan. We drivers were commanded not to use this room either. Instead we were forced to stop at gas stations, rest areas, or under a tree. Neither were we allowed to use the generator, air conditioner, or television, which this cheap economical unit didn't have anyhow.

Along the back wall was a couch that would fold into a bed that we drivers were permitted to use, providing we had sleeping bags or blankets. Much of the time the bed didn't do us any good. Sleeping was many times out of the question because of all the noise and commotion in the parking areas, and from nervousness while driving, having faced adverse weather conditions, motor problems, and accident potentiality. This unit had a rear view mirror but it couldn't be used because there was no rear window. Instead, there were outside rear view mirrors on each side. A farmer like myself who is used to looking straight ahead down the corn rows has a difficult time squinting at those little outside mirrors, trying to keep from getting rear-ended. By the time a driver has been on the road for ten or twenty years, he can usually get the hang of it. Since this unit was one of the smaller, less expensive ones, there was cheap linoleum tile on the floor while the luxury models contain soft, thick carpets, you know.

According to the manual instructions, before attempting to start the motor, we were ordered to check the oil, water, and lights, while looking for any thing else that might hamper good driving conditions. We were also supposed to scrutinize the entire machine, seeking to find some damage that careless assembly workers may have caused for which we drivers could be blamed. A lengthy search allowed me to discover where the hood latch was located. It took another ten minutes to find the oil dipstick. Under the hood was the most amazing mess of objects to be seen. Exposed to the naked eye were hoses, pipes, wires, metal pieces, plastic tubes, plugs, containers, rods, switches, caps, batteries, iron frames, and bird feathers. Underneath the entire conglomeration was something that looked like a motor.

Placing myself gingerly in the driver's seat, I tried to find the correct key for the ignition, and I did. Turning the key caused a mighty explosive roar. Being a pessimist by nature, I was afraid the motor might not start at all, and then what would I do? With courageous effort the gearshift was placed in forward motion which permitted a slow easing out of the parking area. From there it was manipulated to the blacktop drive, and finally on to the main highway. It wasn't long until this momentus momentum was interrupted by Mr. Good Self who yelled out, "Myle, you idiot! You were supposed to stop at the parts office!" There we were, the motor home and I, going in the wrong direction the very first thing. The nearest gas station provided the opportunity to reverse directions. By cramping the wheels as far as possible and using great mental agility, the unit was able to somehow miss the gas pumps, the parked cars, and all the pedestrians milling about. Backtracking to the dispatch location, I parked the unit near the parts department. Nervous moments continued while waiting on the lazy parts workers to provide the essential items to make the accompanying journey.

"This must be my lucky day and yours too, Joe," said one of the workmen. "You've just got this one little old apple to take along. Just you hustle this little old release paper down to door #35 and pick it up. And be careful, don't drop it."

You want to know what the little old apple was? A complete generator, the kind that operates the lights and air conditioner when the motor isn't running. It took the clerk at door #35 and myself to muster all our strength to carry it out to the unit, squeeze it through the entry door, and place it in the hallway. It was soon noted that several grease spots appeared on my pant leg from this episode. This caused fear that some of this grease might be transferred to the furnishings. Another direct commandment from the manual read: EACH UNIT IS TO BE CLEAN INSIDE AND OUT WHEN DELIVERED. Cleanliness was yet another obstacle to overcome in this dreadful occupation.

Again the unit was started, slowly inched across the parking tarmac, and cautiously moved onto the road previously encountered. It appeared that traffic was soon backing up in my rear, since the speedometer was only reading 25 mph. However, as I gradually increased the speed, a braver, more confident feeling took control, and my outlook acquired a series of brighter advancements. Since the unit was not required to be delivered until Thursday, my decision was to drive to my home, stay overnight, and begin the trip early the next morning. Turning on to the gravel road that led homeward, a horrible predicament was to unfold the very first thing. Ahead in the distance was a cloud of dust. Out of this cloud of dust appeared a swiftly moving object. This swiftly moving object turned out to be the largest, ugliest semi this side of Detroit, and it was headed straight for me on this narrow gravel road. Panic was rising, fears were approaching, and eyes began twitching. Bad Self sounded the alarm, "Now what are you going to do, Myle? You're dead meat!" Thankfully, my Good Self had a ready answer, "Pull over to the edge of the road as far as you can and park it." The reason for this advice was that if there was going to be a collision, it would be the truck that hit me, not the other way around. The opposing monster wasn't slowing down at all. It roared past my shut eyes with a terrific burst of power, showering my poor unit with mud and dust and stones. Somehow it had avoided striking my vehicle completely. In the aftermath of confusion, a tiny rock chip appeared on the windshield. My first accident, only four miles from the factory. Why did this have to happen? It wasn't my fault!

While driving into the farm yard, another problem was taking root. This could prove to be the biggest obstacle of all. Bad Self asked, "What is Azailia going to say about this?" After parking the unit, I began a slow walk toward the house, trying to drum up some kind of explanation since she was as yet uninformed of my finalized decision of employment. As the walk continued, the kitchen door opened and there stood Azailia herself in person. I expected to hear an ear-splitting torrent of abuse, but not a word was uttered. She started crying instead. I came up to her and put my arms around her. Then I started crying, too. During this pitiful scene the boys came out the door one by one. When observation had been made that Mom and Dad were in this tear-jerking situation, they, each in turn from the oldest to the youngest, began a similar plaintive wail until reaching such a crescendo of howling, the likes of which are seldom heard in today's modern society. A funeral dirge could not have been more appropriate. During the entire process and while reaching a grand finale, I was desperately hoping that none of the neighbors would happen to drive by.

"What am I doing?" Good Self was asking. "Here I am, deserting wife and kids and 233 pigs (one more had died last night) to drive this miserable piece of junk way out to some hick town just to pick up a couple of bucks." At the same time, another thunderbolt was striking. Friday would be our second wedding anniversary and I wouldn't even be here. I tearfully told Azailia that I should have never signed that employment contract, but that it was too late now. Promises were made to her that Old Barney would be contacted to do the hog chores and that I would bring her a present from Tulsa, if I ever got back.

For the second night in a row there wasn't much sleep for my tired body what with all the tossing and turning, tortured mind regrets, and worrying about the trip tomorrow. Before going to bed a telephone call had been made to Old Barney, seeking his help to care for the hogs in my absence.

"Hello?"

"Barney?"

"Yep."

"How you doin'?"

"O.K., I reckon."

"Say, Barney, this is Myle. I have to be gone for a few days and am wondering if you can take care of the pigs while I am gone. There won't be much work to do. It won't take you long. Just about an hour morning and night. The wife can show you what to do."

"Well, I reckon I kin do 'em in the mornin's but the hired girl comes over at night to clean house."

"She comes over at night to clean house?"

"Yep."

"Couldn't she see better in the daytime?"

"It don't make no difference. That gal got eyes like a hawk. She can even can spot dust under the bed at midnight."

"Well, alright, Barney. It maybe would be O.K. if you would come over here early to do the chores, before she comes. Would that be alright?"

"I reckon so. Yep."

"Then, Barney, I'm counting on you. I'll do the chores tomorrow morning and then you come early tomorrow evening. And then work twice a day until I get back. I'll pay you the same as you charge all the other farmers for the work you do. Will that be enough?"

"Yep."

Somehow this telephone call seemed to seal my fate. There was no way to back out now. There was a hired man to do the chores. There was a motor home sitting in my yard. There were papers signed forcing me to go to Tulsa. There was a nagging conscience that was arguing back and forth. There was a boss at the office who would make sure I carried out the agreement.

So it came to pass that I was to begin a series of extraordinary excitement and adventure. The accomplishments would be measured by unlimited financial gain, inspirational highlights, enlargement of the borders of my world, crowning of victories, good fortune thrust forward, success delivered in galloping amounts, the bluebird of happiness would be perching on my shoulder, prosperity heaped upon my head, kisses given by the Goddess of Love, the Devil would take the hindmost, Lady Luck would sit on my doorstep, and Old Man Trouble would go in hiding. Not.

CHAPTER III

Journey to Relativity

The morning for my first trip had arrived! A swallow of breakfast was followed by a jaunt to the hog house to hopefully coax 232 pigs to survive through another day. The routine of feeding, watering, and cleaning out were the mainstays of the endeavor, completing the mission until Old Barney took charge later in the afternoon. A quick preparation for departure was made. I threw my clothes together in the travel case, crammed the satchel with essentials, and filled my jacket pockets with pork sandwiches. A glance at the clock revealed there wouldn't be enough time for a bath. Before leaving, I tiptoed up the stairs to kiss Azailia goodbye and touch the head of each sleeping boy.

With destiny sealed, and a tear in the eye, I bravely marched to my unit with head held high. Out of the driveway went the motor home, on to the gravel road, thence to the blacktop highway and from there to the great interstate, fifteen miles from my residence. Rolling down this great four-lane road provided an increasing sense of confidence and control. It was epitomizing an aura of serenity, joviality, and superiority. I was becoming King of the Road! My skill advanced so quickly that one-hand driving became the mode of conduct while locking firmly the cruise control. Momentous enjoyment was taking precedence while singing along with Willie Nelson at high blast on the radio. Waves of uplifting inspiration abounded forward in a supercillious manner while viewing the spectacular scenery of dead corn stalks, plowed black ground, treeless leaves, and leaden skies. Self-adulation swept over my thinking. This is really living! And to think I am getting paid for such an easy job as this. Dispelling all manner of defeatism, fearfulness, and worry was the outcome.

Except for the gas needle. It was causing trouble the first thing. It was moving swiftly in such a downward arc that monetary profits flying out of my pockets was easily visualized. How foolish it had been to believe that filling the gas tank at Otoonga would be sufficient. As the unit approached Bethany, Missouri, a fuel stop became mandatory. Carefully guiding the behemoth into the fueling area, I stopped alongside a pump situated between two other autos. Being tired, I stood up to stretch after unhooking my seat belt. A strange phenomenon began to occur. These same two autos seemed to be moving backward in unison at the same rate of speed. To my horror, discovery was made that instead of these cars moving backward, it was my own unit that was rolling forward. I quickly jumped back onto the seat, slammed on the brakes, and managed to stop just inches from the cement barricade surrounding the station. This was yet another time when nerves exploded, stomach churned, and eyes twitched. Fortunately, with mental agility and physical dexterity, I escaped disaster. My front end didn't get smashed and death once again was cheated. All this because the gear shift had been forgotten to be moved into "park."

Having escaped calamity for the second time on my very first trip, renewed confidence again was gained as the miles rolled by. Hair which had been standing on end began to straighten out, jumpy nerves restored to normality, and the shirt under my armpits was drying out. The sun broke through, birds were chirping, the highway widened out, speed moved up, and spirits once again were soaring. Lady Luck was making an appearance after all. I was coasting along in big-time style, laughing at all the farmers who were in their fields struggling to get the corn picked, beans combined, and plowing finished.

Cruising through the town of Pittsburgh, Kansas, two young girls were seen approaching the high school grounds. For some unexplainable reason, a brave and macho inclination caused an immediate honking of the horn and a waving of the hand. To my surprise, they both smiled and waved in return. Boy, did my chest rise! Bad Self had to go and spoil everything by muttering, "Yeah, they just waved because they thought you were some young hunk. They couldn't get a good look at your face to see how old you are." Then my chest slumped back into normal position.

How quickly the time passes when you are having fun! By the middle of the afternoon I had made such good time that the approach to the city of Albadoxin was at hand. This was the residence of cousin Bolivar and Delores. Both taught classes at the university located at the southern edge of the city. It would be a nice gesture to stop and say hello since their home was only two blocks off the highway. Good Self began an attempt at intervention, warning that trouble lay brewing. Bad Self wasn't paying any attention, and in retaliation mouthed the words, "How can an innocent little visit do any harm?"

Since Bad Self usually prevailed, a short time later found my index finger ringing the doorbell of a brick ranch type mansion, complete with manicured lawn, gushing fountain, and swimming pool in back. Good Self piped up, "Just hope no one is home." As it so happened, they had both returned from their classes at the end of the teaching day. Bolivar opened the door with a big grin on his face, but the grin on Delores looked more like a scowl.

"Myle, this is a surprise. Come on in. What brings you to our fair city?"

"Hi, Bolivar. I was passing through Albadoxin and thought I would stop a minute to say hello. I got a new job driving motor homes and I'm taking this one to Tulsa."

"That's great. But we can't let you by that easy, can we Delores? You must come in and have lunch with us. Right, Delores?"

Delores wasn't replying, but I managed to say, "Maybe I could come in and chat for a few minutes. I got a little time. This unit doesn't have to be delivered until tomorrow anyhow."

"If that is the case we are going to insist you spend the night with us. Right, Delores?"

Delores still wasn't replying so I did instead. "I sure hadn't planned to do that, Bolivar. But maybe I could this one time. I can sleep in the motor home, though, and won't have to get one of your beds dirty."

"Nonsense. We won't allow you to spend the night in that old tin trap. Right, Delores? We've got five guest rooms and you can take your pick."

Delores still wasn't replying all the while Bolivar was grabbing my arm, ushering me into the living room which boasted a thick white carpet, cathedral ceiling, and glass walls.

"This sure isn't necessary, Bolivar, but maybe I could make an exception this one little time."

As we were being seated, Delores finally replied. "We sometimes have our friends over for the night, but we don't make a practice of opening our doors to just anyone who comes along."

"I can certainly understand that. You two are sure doing real good, having this nice house and all. Do you both like the teaching profession?"

"We seem to get by," was her answer. "Tell us, is this how you are making your living, driving motor homes?"

"Well, no. I am actually in the farming business now. I quit college to farm Uncle Zeb's place. I've picked up this part-time driving job for when nothing else is going on."

Bolivar spoke again. "You're a farmer now? I didn't know that. I didn't know you went to college either. You didn't graduate?"

"No, I just lacked a few weeks," I lied. "Uncle Zeb begged me to farm his ground so that is what I'm doing."

"Delores and I are certainly glad you stopped in to visit. Aren't we, Delores?" Delores didn't reply. "You are in luck as the saying goes. After Delores fixes us a bite to eat, we will all go to the university theatre where the symphony orchestra is playing tonight. Guest conductor Abe Abromvitzkly is at the baton. He's that famous virtuoso from New York City. You came at a most opportune time."

"Sounds good to me," I answered. "I've never been to a symphony orchestra before, but am willing to try anything once." Bolivar and Delores just looked at each other.

Our conversation continued in small talk regarding relatives, the teaching profession, how my children were doing, and various affairs that govern our lives. Cousin Bolivar actually wasn't a cousin blood-wise. His mother and my step-mother were cousins so that meant Bolivar and myself were step-cousins, or cousins three times removed, or however it is figured out. It was far enough down the line that it caused Delores to shrug her shoulders every time my mouth opened.

Sometime later Bolivar escorted me to one of the bedrooms where I was to spend the night. It was a few minutes after he had left that trouble placed its curse upon me. Trouble so diabolical and heart-ending that suicide would have been my choice, had choice been available. After unpacking my bag, I opened the closet door on the opposite side of the room, intending to hang up my jacket. The problem was that it was a different kind of closet than what had been expected. There in full view sat Delores on the stool.

"Oh, I beg your pardon. I thought this was a clothes closet," was my embarrassed apology.

"I should have made sure the door was locked," she answered with a red face. "I thought Bolivar placed you in the south room. I didn't know you would be snooping in my bathroom."

"I'm sorry. It's my fault. I shouldn't have been opening doors that I don't know what was on the other side."

"No, don't blame yourself. I should have known something like this would happen when we open our doors to the first person that comes along."

"Well, I'm sure sorry that I saw you—. I mean it's too bad that you were—. What I meant to say is that I'll shut the door and you can keep on—."

The original grin on her face that had turned into a scowl was now advancing to one of deep disgust while her steel-blue eyes glared hostility.

I blundered on, "Yes, I'm sure sorry about this, but we can talk about it later."

Closing the door, I staggered to the bed and threw myself upon it. Shame, humiliation, and remorse swept over my prone carcass in overwhelming waves, causing a sucking of thumb while in a fetal position. How can such deplorable incidents force their intrusion upon innocent motor home drivers, depriving them of the will to even live? How long I lay in this comatose state one could not tell. It was only a rap at the door sometime later that broke the spell.

Bolivar gave a summons to lunch. We gathered around the kitchen table, the three of us. I sort of slumped down, depressed and defeated. Do you know what this lunch proved to be? Tuna sandwiches, lettuce with no dressing, and prune juice.

"We usually eat a light, healthful lunch in the evening for our stomach's sake. Health is the most important thing to consider," said Bolivar.

"Yeah, it sure is. I try to eat as much rabbit food as I can," I replied, but knew it was the wrong thing to have said the minute the words left my mouth.

Somehow the entire conversation seemed a little strained. My eyes never once glanced at Delores and I'm sure she was doing the same thing right back to me. The silent disapproval was radiating outward in an engulfing arc in a bitter retribution. I ate as swiftly as possible since nausea was causing the tuna to slosh around in chunks at the bottom of my stomach.

My humiliation only worsened when having to borrow a jacket, white shirt and bow tie from Bolivar, since I had no formal attire. Bolivar's pants were much too large for me, forcing me to wear my own, even though being a little worn in the place where I sat down. This didn't seem to matter because the coat was much too large as well, advantageously long enough to cover my shiny seat. Thankfully, each concert-goer was so absorbed with the music that my appearance was generally disregarded.

To this day I am unable to remember the name of the university where the symphony was held. It seemed like it had a connection to some church. It may have been Presbyterian or maybe Jewish, since they are so much alike. I was more concerned at the time that Bolivar's bow tie wouldn't slip too far down on my neck. Being a high-brow university professor, Bolivar was able to obtain tickets down front in center aisle. Delores entered the row, followed by Bolivar and then myself. The other seat next to mine was soon occupied by a woman who was wearing a low-cut gown, like most of the other women were wearing. Whether she was a single lady or one whose husband wouldn't come along, was an unanswered question. Her voice rang out in a silly quirk when she spoke to me, "Isn't this exciting? I just adore Mr. Abromvitzkly's music, don't you?"

"Yes," I said. "These kind of symphonies really turn me on."

During this time, I was deeply conscious of my appearance, that of a coat too large and shirt sleeves extending to the tip of my fingers. By keeping my elbows bent, chest expanded and shoulders stretched upward, no one seemed to notice. My eyes had never seen so many dark coats, black bow ties and low-cut evening dresses. I tried not to look too closely at the gal beside me, even when she spoke, for fear of seeing more than I intended. Other men with big Adam's apples had the same problem as myself. Their black bow ties would bob up and down when swallowing. To alleviate this condition I kept as much spit in my mouth as possible so that it wouldn't happen very often. During one episode of alleviation I choked, coughed and sputtered from too much accumulation, until acquiring bulging eyes and a red face. Boy, did that cause nervousness and consternation from Bolivar and Delores. It did me, too.

Rescue came and predicament forgotten when the orchestra began filing in and assembling on stage. Permeating instead were cacophonous augmentations, wild eruptions from all sorts of weird instruments and ear-splitting reverberations collecting together in a crazy melee of sound while the orchestra tuned. What a remarkable change to silence prevailed the moment Mr. Abromvitzkly approached the podium. The little mutt was only about four feet tall, was cross-eyed and displayed a rumpled, unkempt appearance that made me look like Prince Charles in comparison. With a flick of the baton the silence was broken, reversing the prior conditions into melodious refrains. The beautiful sounds proved to be uplifting and inspiring, even though I didn't recognize any of the pieces played. Not one of Willie Nelson's hits were played. None of Tanya Tucker's either. The music was extremely loud at times, especially from the flutes and xylophone...The applause was even louder, reaching a crescendo of hand clapping, whistles, cheers, including jumping up and down. Abe must have been doing a marvelous job, proven by the exclamations of bravo and hooray.

The concert droned on and on, but finally ended in a wild, standing ovation, waking me from a restless dozing. As the applause was ending, I beat a fast track to the exit, leaving Bolivar and Delores to greet their friends without having to introduce them to me. Of course my elbows were kept bent, chest expanded and shoulders extended while the mad rush was underway.

Conversation was kept to a low ebb during the short ride back to Bolivar's residence. The hushed discussion mostly related to the excellence of the orchestral direction and to the excited acceptance by those in the audience. Delores was in her glory, elaborating her explanation of the various movements of the arrangements Abe had conquered. This was made in an attempt to make great impression on one dumb farmer. (But it didn't.) The discussion did provide a certain calming effect on the three of us, however, but for me this calming didn't last. Trouble hadn't ended.

Upon arrival at Bolivar's home, I was told to enter the doorway first which proved to be my undoing. How was I to know the Siamese cat's tail would be sticking out from underneath the platform rocker? How was I to know that a ferocious uproar would ensue when shoe leather and cat tail came in contact? A terrible commotion was displayed as the injured animal sprang upward, forward and outward, temporarily resting on top of the drawstring drapery of the north picture window. The escape was only momentary because the drapery soon gave way to the clawing beast. This in turn caused the rapacious activity of ripping and tearing, scratching and mewing, and weeping and wailing, in a grand crescendo of agitation with the movement of cloth, fur and flesh. The ripping and tearing happened to the curtains, the scratching and mewing came from the cat, while the weeping and wailing came from Delores and me. Bolivar first stood there in amazement, then exploded in laughter.

"It wasn't my fault. This wouldn't have happened if that cat had his tail tucked around him like a normal cat should," I said, with tears in my eyes. "You won't have to worry none about the curtains. I'll send you some money to pay for them when I get back to Otoonga."

As Delores gathered the poor creature in her arms she was heard to be saying, "My poor little Poopsie." She repeated it over and over again. Bolivar said something about a fine kettle of fish, but I don't know if he meant cat food or me.

Sleeping was somewhat evasive for the third night in a row. This wasn't much of a surprise considering all the arguing taking place. A low, hushed rumble was proceeding from down the hall in one of the bedrooms. The other dialogue was bouncing from wall to wall in my room where Good Self was taunting, "I told you so," while the Bad Guy was replying, "So what?" Aggravating the situation was the dropping of a water glass on the ceramic tile floor in the bathroom at two o'clock in the morning. No way could it be glued back together since it was broken into a thousand shards.

That did it! This was all I could take! I decided to sneak out of this ugly place right away so Bolivar and Delores wouldn't have to kiss me goodbye. Tiptoeing out of my bedroom and across the living room floor revealed a fierce looking animal glaring at me with hatred in its eyes. He was lying near the fireplace in pitiful condition with tail wrapped in bandages. I left a note on the table thanking Bolivar and Delores for their hospitality. It ended with an invitation to visit my own home in Otoonga, if they were near that location at any time, which I hoped they wouldn't be. My mind was made up about one thing. I would never stop at this miserable mansion again. And I wouldn't go to any family reunions next Christmas either.

Why hadn't I listened to Good Self's warning? His intuition was usually reliable. Now I'm paying for it with remorse and humiliation. Recurrence of heart palpitations, peptic ulcers and gastric enteralgia, each contribute to the downward spiral toward degeneracy. Yes, dreadful consequences prevail when pursuing this obscene habit of driving motor homes. Can't you see what has already happened to me? And this is only my first trip. Yet this one isn't even over. Take caution, all of you out there in the journey of life. Care must be taken in order to avoid such terrible perils. Running into cement barricades, waving at high school girls, visiting relatives, attending symphonies, opening strange bathroom doors, torturing animals and breaking water glasses must all be avoided like the plague. The relativity relating to relative relations is another consideration.

Lest you may think there is no joy whatsoever in my travels, think again. For out there in the moonlight darkness was sitting the most beautiful, magnificent, dazzling vehicle yet seen. And it was waiting patiently just for me.

CHAPTER IV

Tarnished Victory

The final conquest was at hand! The dealer at Tulsa was to receive another beautiful, magnificent, dazzling vehicle, this time driven by the skillful hands of Myle Heyers. Perusal of the accompanying documents revealed a different location than what I expected. This unit's destiny was 150683 Cherry Boot Lane, Xyelothian, Oklahoma, seventeen miles southwest of Tulsa as the crow flies. Very few dealerships are located within the confines of a metropolitan area. Most likely a location would be found in the suburbs or in a smaller city nearby. There are several reasons for this. For one, it is next to impossible to find a parking place in a large congested city. If a buyer lived in a big city, chances are his lot wouldn't be large enough to contain it. His garage undoubtedly would be too small to park it inside without smashing in the roof of the motor home. Nor would it be advisable to park it in his own driveway because of jealous neighbors. More than one motor home has ended up in the junk pile because of vicious people who in a jealous frenzy smash in the windshield, slash the tires or scratch the sides with a sharp instrument.

It was no problem to exit the freeway called Oklahoma Bend, turn right on Elbow Valley Boulevard and to victoriously guide the unit into the dealer parking lot on Cherry Boot Lane. What a proud, victorious feeling enveloped this humble driver who had guided this huge apparatus six hundred miles from the factory in Otoonga. I parked it directly in front of the showcase window, gathered the papers of transfer, cleaned the inside up a bit, stepped out of this beautiful, magnificent, dazzling vehicle and sauntered haughtily to the doorway.

My expectations were that a warm, cordial greeting would commence, praising me for a job well done. Instead, to my dismay, I was completely ignored. They acted like I wasn't even there. No one came to ask the reason I had come in the door. A secretary sat typing at a desk, a salesman was attempting to persuade a potential buyer, a janitor listlessly swept the floor, while someone who could have been the manager was talking on the telephone. No one looked my way. Grouchy, angry and insulting people can sometimes be overlooked, but to be ignored is worse than a slap in the face. After a few minutes the customer exited the door, apparently not persuaded, leaving the salesman unattended. That's when I began a slow, hesitant approach toward him.

"What is your problem?" were his first words.

"Well, I drove this here thing down here like they told me to, and so there it is, sitting right out there."

"I'll go tell Mar to check it over to see if it is any good or not. Go back out to your unit. He will be out in a minute or two."

The few minutes turned out to be thirty nail-biting ones before Mar made an appearance, and then another thirty for his scrutinizing exam.

"This bugger's got a screw loose in the left visor, a bolt missing in the generator compartment, a crease in the driver's seat and is about the dirtiest one ever drove in here."

"None of that is my fault," I protested. "A big semi about run over me and splattered mud on it and scared me half to death."

"That's not my worry, Bub. You're the driver and responsible so that's the way I'm going to report it," was his sarcastic reply. "And I want you and Jake to get that ugly generator out of the toilet."

"I didn't put it in the toilet. I can't help it if it jiggled inside the door on the way down here."

It was another thirty nail-biting minutes before Jake came out of the work room to help me. Jake turned out to be a ninety-eight pound weakling who was a mechanic's helper during after-school hours. Somehow we were able to squeeze it out the entry door, carry it two hundred feet to the storage shed and to drop it on the cement floor without hitting our toes. While Mar was signing the release documents, I was making a quick change of clothes. Since my duties were now completed, I cautiously asked Mar if provision could be made to give me a ride to the Black Dog Bus Station in downtown Tulsa. His reply was in the negative. But he did tell me where I could go. If I would walk six blocks north and two west there was a city bus stop where a transit coach could be boarded for Tulsa. Carrying two heavy bags eight blocks was no easy task, yet no worse than lifting generators in and out of motor homes, nor cleaning out the hog barn back on the farm, for that matter.

After an hour of waiting in the cool autumnal Oklahoma breeze, sure enough, along came bus #386 to convey my remains to the Black Dog. It seemed to be an endless journey back and forth through the streets and alleys of both Xyelothian and Tulsa in zig-zag fashion. The route passed Oral Roberts University, a beautiful conglomerate of school buildings, campus and hospital. The question arose in my mind why a hospital was needed at all, since all Oral had to do was lay hands on people and they would be healed.

After two hours and thirteen minutes of bumping and jerking, the Black Dog Bus Station was reached. To purchase a ticket at the clerk's window, stepping over a few bodies lying on the floor was necessary. Derelicts most likely. They seem to enjoy bus stations, when their time isn't all taken up lying in the gutters. What a shock it was to purchase that one little old ticket back to Otoonga! This trip wasn't going to be very profitable having to pay for that high-priced fuel, recompensing Old Barney for his labor and buying all that expensive food at McDonald's. A decision was reached, after argumentation between Bad Self and Good, that there would be no more food eating on the way home. No pop or coffee either. By so doing, a profit from the trip could still be maintained. Azailia would just have to wait for a more convenient time to receive any anniversary present from me.

The next bus to Otoonga wasn't scheduled to leave for another two hours, allowing an opportunity to roam downtown Tulsa during that time. To my surprise, Tulsa didn't appear to be such a hick town after all. A few people, of the more baser sort, looked like they could be classified as hicks, but surprisingly enough, they were dressed as well as I was. It was a marvelous city of stateliness and grandeur. Structures of brick and glass, thousands of vehicles darting to and fro, milling pedestrians clogging the walkways, consumers consuming, buyers monopolizing the stores, skyscrapers that had no tops and streets paved with brick, cement and gold. It was almost more than a farm boy could take.

Time passed quickly and I soon found myself boarding a Black Dog at Gate Number Five. A vacant seat was located inside the coach four rows from the front, with an unoccupied adjoining seat. Leaving the driving to someone else might not be such a bad idea. This would be far better than pulling a little car behind the delivered unit, and then have to make that long return journey back to Otoonga in the car. This would be an excellent way to get some rest and catch up on that sleep which had been so evasive the past three nights. Wrong. While attempting to stretch out and make myself comfortable for the long night, coming into the bus was the biggest, ugliest black woman to be seen. She flopped herself down in the seat beside me. Now, I don't have any prejudice against black people. Some of my best friends are black. I don't look down on ugly people since there are a lot of us around. No feelings of superiority are imposed against any women because many of my female acquaintances are nearly my equal. But I am prejudiced against the seats being too narrow. It came to pass that I was squashed up against the side of the bus, barely able to move. Breathing became an effort. I was afraid to move my hands in fear of being accused of sexual harassment.

"My name is Josephine. What's yours?"

"Myle."

"That sure sounds like a white man's name alright."

"Yeah, I guess it does. I don't know any other race that has that name."

"Neither do I. I'm goin' to see my sister and bus ridin' is the cheapest way to get there. We gonna have a party once I get there, if she kin shake her kids long enough. She's got five little bratty kids and another one on the way."

"That's nice." (I wasn't about to tell her I was in the same condition.)

"She's in trouble again. Her second man just up and run off and left her with nothin'. And the gov'ment don't want to pay for no more kids. It's a hard world out there."

"It sure is," I said. "A person has to have two jobs to make a living anymore."

"Ain't that the truth? It makes a body sick the way the gov'ment don't want to pay for nothin' these days."

"It sure does."

"And all them big corp'rations want to pay is min'im wage. How's a body gonna live on that? They could pay a lot more but they just won't do it. All them fat cats are gettin' fatter all the time. It makes a body sick."

"It does me too." My breathing was becoming labored and my words were coming out in gasps.

"What you all doin' in this here town? You comin' or goin'?"

"I'm beginning to wonder about that myself, Josephine. I am on my way back home where I belong. Where does your sister live?" I was desparately hoping she wouldn't be going far. How would I get any sleep, sitting straight up and squashed against the side of the bus?

"I'm goin' to Crestfallen. The ticket man said I would be ridin' all night and wouldn't get there until tomorra evenin'. It's a long way but this ole bus better get me there."

Not Crestfallen! This can't be happening! Crestfallen is the next stop after Otoonga, which meant she would be on the bus the entire time I would be. What have I done to deserve this? How could survival be maintained while locked in a bone-crushing, body-squeezing vice, with only a five minute relief every three hours at rest stops, and this continuing for nineteen hours?

Though being inflicted with this painful body subjugation, my mind began running rampant in a free-fall. Before leaving Tulsa I had called Azailia to see how everything was going back home. Information was readily supplied that baby Ozzie was sick again, Doc Johansen was getting even richer through another office visit and that Azailia wasn't feeling too well herself, what with baby unknown kicking so hard on her ribs. To top it all off, twenty-nine of the two hundred and thirty-one pigs had crawled under the fence and rooted out Mrs. Lewis' flower garden and was she ever mad, and from her tone of voice I thought maybe Azailia was too. Old Barney had been drinking again, leaving her and Jack, our eldest, to chase in the hogs. They also had to do the feeding and watering during Barney's incapacitation.

It is with great remorse that I relate this tale of woe, a warning to those desiring of following my footsteps, if they are crazy enough. Surely you can see the horrible results that have already befallen me. Being ignored by those in authority, facing grouchy inspectors, carrying heavy generators, accused falsely and being crushed in dirty buses are problems that you face, along with sick kids and wife, rooting hogs and hired men on a toot back home.

Little did I realize that such ordeals would follow me to the grave. In spite of the horrible tricks that fate was playing upon me and even though heartache, pain and tragedy were riding on the seat beside me, yet I was left undaunted. I was getting hooked on driving after only one trip. You must understand, there is something diabolical about motor home driving, something sinister that grasps you in its tentacles, no matter how much foreseen ahead downward drop into oblivion might befall you. The excitement and adventure seem to position the negative approach into extreme necessarianism, nullifying a reverse of the reversal, you might say. This enigma is thus resolved through patience and stick-to-it-iveness acquired through systematic bull-headed perspicacity, tenaciousness and exceptional redundancy. Oh well, what difference does it make after the bus ride has been completed to Otoonga?

CHAPTER V

Sleeping My Way to Michigan

The next morning found one smashed, tired driver in a different field of endeavor. It really wasn't a field exactly…more like a hog house would be a better description. This certain driver was busily engrossed scooping out the hog house pens which hadn't been adequately cleaned due to the negligence of a certain hired hand. This unfinished work was still unfinished when a certain housewife named Azailia suddenly appeared at the hog house door with a startling announcement. It seems that a certain Otoonga Dispatch Office had called, asking that certain driver to take another trip.

"For Pete's sake," I said with a raspy voice. "That Hummer didn't give me much time off did he? I just got home. Already he wants me to take another trip? But if I want to keep this good driving job I'd best get out of this hog house right away, because business goes before pleasure."

His request, or rather commandment, was to go directly to his office as soon as possible, for there was a "hot" unit going to Muskegon, Michigan. "Hot" in Otoonga trailer language meant it had already been sold to some unsuspecting customer, sight unseen, and was to be driven there immediately. This command forced a hurried finish to the morning chores and cleaning out, a phone call to Old Barney for his services again (this in hopes that bottle tipping had temporarily ended), a quick change of clothes, cramming an extra pair of pants into my bag, and checking my blood pressure twice.

"What about little Ozzie?" Azailia asked while I was running out the door. "He still has that awful cough and isn't getting any better."

"Give him a good dose of vinegar and honey. If he isn't better in a couple of days, you'll have to take him in to see Doc Johansen again. Be sure to tell Doc to go easy on the bill." Ozzie was our youngest, eight months old, who usually entertained a cough and cold, along with a continual antagonistic attitude against his old man as well.

"How about Old Barney? He didn't do much work on your last trip. I had to do all the heavy feed carrying and it wasn't easy."

"I already gave Old Barney a good talking to. He'll do his share of the work this time for sure. But I didn't want to offend him. He's a good guy at heart, with a wonderful personality. I don't want to upset the apple cart." With this advice I gave her a goodbye kiss on the cheek, streaked for the car, and was on my way to another great adventure.

At the office, papers were quickly issued and instructions given. Mr. Hummer admonished, "Get this unit out there as fast as you can. It's already overdue. If you get tired you can sleep a few hours, but don't dawdle around."

The vehicle was stored out in Lot 65, Row 13. By this time I was an old pro at determining parking locations, so discovery was readily made. This unit was much larger than the first one driven, and was decorated with more elaborated designs, logos, and candy stripes, along with a greenish-tan background. The interior was more luxuriant also, exhibiting thick carpet floors, fancy oak cabinets, gold-rimmed glass mirrors hanging on the walls, overhead florescent lights, two generator-driven air conditioners, another motor air conditioner in the dash, venetian blinds, double bed in the rear that would hold three people, and a price tag that would make your head swim. After a quick check over, I assumed it was road worthy. This necessitated picking up a spare tire at the parts department, filling the gas tank with fuel, and I was on my way. Departing through the gate, who was it that my eyes should behold? Standing there with a forlorn expression on his face was my good friend Eddie.

"What are you doing here, Eddie? How did you get back so soon? Weren't you going to do some sight-seeing out in Oregon for a few days?" I remarked after parking the unit nearby.

"Well, I had a little accident on the way and never even got there."

"Oh, Eddie, what happened?"

"I was going across a bridge out in Laramie, Wyoming, when a big gust of wind sort of came up and kind of, well, just blew me into it."

"I'm sure sorry about that, Eddie. Did it do much damage?"

"No, not much. Just bent the front bumper around into a semi-circle, smashed the right fender, and put a dent all along one side, is all."

"That's sure too bad, Eddie."

"Yeah, and they gave me my walking papers, too. They're kind of a particular bunch around here. When I called back from Laramie, they ordered me to drive it all the way back here. Hummer acted sort of mad like. I guess I'll have to see if I can get my old job back at the rock quarry."

"Boy, they are touchy, aren't they? While you were on your way to Oregon, I came here, got hired, and have already had a trip to Tulsa and back."

"You've got all the luck, Myle."

"Seems like my luck has changed and I'm hittin' real good now. That trip to Tulsa paid off real good and I had a great time. But I can't waste my time talking to you all day. I'm taking this here baby to Michigan. I hope you have good goin' at the rock quarry. Good luck and don't work too hard." With these words I restarted the motor, gunned the accelerator, and spun off in a flash, leaving poor Eddie in an envious, stunned condition.

In an upbeat mood, I began my eastward journey while singing along with an old Beatles tune on the radio. The unit was purring smoothly and all seemed to be right with the world. This is what is called the good life, riding around in ritzy style, enjoying the colorful countryside, and scorning all the farmers and factory workers who had to work for a living. Looking at the map provided an easy preview of the highways on which to travel. Even the exact dealer location could be located, which was Michisota City, on the outskirts of Muskegon. Limited knowledge of the state of Michigan came from a history book in the fourth grade. If my remembrance is not faulty, it was a huge state surrounded by lofty mountain peaks with a great lake dividing it in the middle from east to west.

Interrupting the tranquillity was a suspicious, ominous sound which seemed to emanate from somewhere under the hood. This didn't cause a cessation in forward movement since nothing much seemed to be wrong. Except that the heat gauge was shooting up by a considerable amount once in a while. Whenever it became necessary to stop, the radiator would boil over. That didn't seem so bad, so I just kept merrily on my way. After driving another hundred miles, gasoline needed to be purchased, and that's when more water began boiling out in earnest. Asking the mechanic at the gas station didn't provide any satisfaction. He couldn't see anything wrong either, telling me to add some more water and antifreeze. By the time Snide, Illinois came into view, it appeared that all might not be well because huge clouds of steam were erupting from the most unlikely places. Stopping at another garage in Snide gave notice that a fan belt had broken. In fact, the entire belt had just disappeared into thin air. To replace the belt, the mechanic was required to remove the motor cover inside the unit to the right of the driver's seat, slouch down in awkward position, and at times to stand on his head. After laboring with different belts for nearly an hour, he reported that the correct size belt was unavailable in his collection, although there were thousands of odd-shaped belts hanging on his shop wall.

"We're going to have to take a little jaunt over to Abernathy where the Majority Rules Station has the correct belt, I just know," was his explanation. "Before that, I'm goin' to run down to the schoolhouse to pick up the kids. The Missus is away to Bloomington on a shopping spree. Do you wanna ride along?"

"Why not? it won't be much fun sitting in this dump waiting on you."

After we rode down to pick up the kids he said to me, "We gotta get somethin' to eat. You wanna come along?"

"Why not? It won't be much fun sitting in this dump waiting on you."

At the Snide Charcoal Cafe my burned hamburger was barely able to be choked down, what with nerves on edge, and watching his kids fighting back and forth across the table while in the process of sassing their father at each reprimand. The scene brought a lump to my throat, reminding me of the way things usually were back home.

From the cafe we bumped and jerked our way in his '67 Ford pickup to the town of Snarl where he obtained what he thought was the correct belt, only it wasn't and we had to bump and jerk our way back to Snarl before the correct size was found. When belt installation was finally completed, it was discovered that an oil spot was in evidence on the carpet near the motor cover. The soiled carpet was undoubtedly caused by the incompetence of the careless mechanic. This unit was supposed to have been delivered in record fast time and in number one condition. Instead there was a three-hour delay and a glistening spot on my interior. When such unnatural calamities collide head on in deviating circumstances, irrational abnormalities and bewildering fits of derision are the results. Good Self interjected, "Why don't you buy a bottle of vinegar when you get to Michisota City. Rub some of it on the oil spot because vinegar will cure anything. If that doesn't work, try placing a piece of cardboard over it. That might do the trick long enough for you to get out of there before the inspector sees it."

Once again the miles rolled by, darkness descended, the moon rose, and another curse of driving was initiated. Sleepiness. Suddenly I was fighting sleepiness with all my willpower. Being sleepy is a dreadful enemy, one that appears in a moment of time and at a most inopportune occasion. What a horrible force it is, attempting to wreck your vehicle in a split second and cause a new name to be written on a tombstone.

Two choices confronted me—to keep driving in spite of this awful threat or to stop at some convenient place for a couple hours of restful annihilation. In my condition, annihilation became the objective. In the city of Aurora, I began roaming the streets and alleys for some ideal place to complete this objective. To my dismay, the only safe and convenient place discovered was an all-night laundry. Parked at the far rear side, I became engrossed with the possibility of unconsciousness, with sleeping bag curled around me. Somehow things didn't work out very well. Immediately upon lying down I became wide awake. Too many people were coming and going in continual confusion, slamming doors, squealing tires, and yelling at each other. The bright lights from the laundromat shone in my face or reflected off the glass no matter which way I turned. Instead of a peaceful slumber, a tossing and turning, groaning and grumbling, squinting and staring added to the misfortune. Next, I found myself sitting straight up awkwardly in my sleeping bag, watching the good looking women carry their laundry in and out, and to observe the wild goings on at the restaurant across the street. Since sleep became an evasion, this miserable location was soon abandoned. Never again would my feet be found in the sleepless, disgusting city of Aurora, Illinois.

Driving once again preoccupied my time and actions in the middle of the night, all the while being spellbound by the white paint lines in the center of the pavement. While thus mesmerized, an awful thought struck me. Day after tomorrow would be Thanksgiving Day and I wouldn't yet be home! I had been absent on our anniversary, and now Thanksgiving too. A tear started down my left cheek, but by sheer willpower I stopped it half-way down. A veteran driver such as I wouldn't let mere sentiment get the best of him. I was becoming immune to all emotions, although the prospect of riding some bouncing Black Dog on Thanksgiving Day wasn't the most ideal situation.

After driving another grueling, death-defying forty minutes, you guessed it. Sleepiness. It was making another confident approach to my in-roads. What a hazard to your health drowsiness can be! Why is it that given the chance to sleep I can't, but when I can't, I can? It is easy to recognize the characteristics of sleepiness. When oncoming car lights are constantly switching from bright to dim, horns are honking as they drive by, and your own vehicle has been weaving all over the road, it is certain that dozing off has been on the increase. What an abominable condition to be enveloped in helplessness, overcome by lethargic, miserable sleepiness!

Thankfully, there are many successful ways to combat this dreadful monster. Through the admonition from my boss and Miss Missmossmus, from advice from other drivers, after reading Aunt Moriah's Health Book, and from little discoveries that I, myself have made in times of distress, tiredness and exhaustion can readily be overcome if a driver puts his mind to it.

One of the very first recommendations on everyone's list is to eat something. With this firmly in mind, my inclination was to withdraw from my lunch sack an apple and a dill pickle which were to be consumed simultaneously. Since swift fermentation in the stomach causes indigestion or heartburn, it's for sure you won't be falling asleep with misery like that. When this only helped for a few minutes, I then began devouring gobs of potato chips and red hot candy. Next came beef jerky and onion rings. In spite of all the belching and distress, my eyes would barely stay open after the last bite had been devoured.

Another sure-fire remedy is to drink a lot of liquids. At an all-night convenience store a purchase was made of a Thermos of coffee and three cans of pop which were then systematically ingested one after the other. This did delay drowsiness for a time, primarily because it caused numerous stops at other convenience and rest stops for the next forty-seven miles. As soon as this effect quickly wore off, the problem began to worsen.

At the forty-first mile a stop was initiated in which the process of running around the motor home one hundred and eight times really kept me awake, since this was the equivalent of two and one-half miles. Sorry to say, this didn't last. Re-entry into the unit allowed the warm air inside to stealthily contribute to increased drowsiness, once the physical activity had abated.

To sing aloud at the top of one's voice is a great help in finding a solution. As long as a person can keep singing, he would know he was awake. The difficulty of this endeavor is that after so long a time, one's voice will eventually give out, and who can sing with a given-out voice, and who can stay awake when not singing?

There is a method of overcoming drowsiness that is certain to bring success, yet it should only be used as a last resort. This discovery I have found myself. I highly recommend this method. To inflict pain upon oneself while driving is a certain cure. The more painful the pain, the better. Try slapping your hands on your legs for a starter. Whenever feeling an eyelid starting to close, I strike a hard blow to the top of my legs. This undertaking can only be withstood for an hour or two, with intervals between leg slaps varying time-wise, depending on the degree of sleepiness, and the combined ability of both hand and leg to comply with such gruesome ordeals. Trying an alternative method of reversing directions from left hand to right leg and then vice versa is helpful, but is somewhat complicated by having the wrong hand on the wrong place at the wrong time, such as when meeting a school bus on a narrow bridge or attempting to navigate a sharp curve on a high peak in the Rocky Mountains. When one of your hands becomes so tired that it falls asleep itself, this is a clear signal that some other remedy should be sought, especially if your legs are getting raw during the process.

A somewhat unusual system in using pain as a sleep deterrent is to pull hair. This, too, is only a temporary counteraction. Care must be taken not to overdo it. Hair can only stand so much animosity. Discovering a few left-over hairs between your fingers after each activity is a warning to cease operation in fear that baldness may be the next contention.

Hitting oneself with a rolled-up newspaper is another excellent way to keep awake and alert, more so if whacked directly in the face. However appealing this may be, it could be a dangerous device if one is particularly thin-skinned or prone to fits of extreme frustration. An unnatural ringing in the ears, spots before one's eyes, or blood trickling down the cheeks, are all indications that it would be far better to fall asleep and run in the ditch than to prolong the affliction unduly. Forcing pain upon oneself varies with each individual since some can withstand more injurious activity than others.

Dancing is another excellent means to deter unconsciousness at the wheel. I'm not inferring that to seek out a ballroom on each trip would provide an answer. No, advice is merely given that dancing one's feet up and down while driving, keeping time to the radio music could be the solution for many. This device is best appropriated while the cruise control is in operation, otherwise there is a constant jumping and jerking of the vehicle from too much or too little play on the accelerator. It is also wise not to prolong the action beyond reason. Getting tired, exhausted, and out of breath may counteract the design for which the operation was intended to accomplish in the first place.

There are multitudes of cures for the abominable curse of sleepiness. Turning on the radio at full blast, honking the horn continuously for miles at a time, driving at an extremely high rate of speed, darting dangerously in and out of heavy traffic, racing semis downhill, elimination of sleeping pill swallowing before driving, and wearing only a bathing suit in cold weather. My advice to each sleepy driver would be to try the many different methods that are available to his own consideration which would allow the discovery for which he was best suited.

It was almost unbelievable, but by the time each of these deterrents had been tried several times, a sign along the highway was the one that finally woke me up. The sign read: Muskegon 35 miles. Suddenly I was wide awake. One little sign did more to infuse alertness than all the other attempts put together. There was a pink tinge to the eastern sky by this time, a new day was to be faced, and a new adventure to confront. To think that I had driven the entire night without one wink of sleep! This was sure to be a record, and a first for all motor home drivers, who are usually considered a bunch of lazy louts.

The sun was peeking over the horizon as a "hot" unit was maneuvered into the dealer lot at Michisota City. While extricating myself from the seat belt, there was a surprising rap at the entry door.

"What do you think you're doing?" This curt introduction came from a big, rugged individual who seemed to have an aura of authority about him.

"The Otoonga Trailer Factory made me drive this thing down here to you. And here it is."

"Mister, you can take this thing back from where you got it. This unit had been on order for six weeks and there was a buyer for it. Since you didn't come and you didn't come, I cobbled up another unit and made it over to about what he ordered. He bought it but I could tell he wasn't satisfied. It cost me a lot of money to change it over to his liking, you can bet on that. Now you come driving in like a king and two weeks too late."

"This is unreal," I protested. "I don't know what to say. My boss ordered me to drive it down here real quick like. I drove it all night long without any sleep. So it isn't my fault."

"You can bet it isn't my fault, mister. I cancelled this order two weeks ago and now you show up."

"Nobody told me not to come here. I just drive where they tell me to go. And this is where they told me to go."

"Mister, I'm not going to buy this thing, that's for sure." After a considerable pause, he continued, "Tell you what I'm going to do. I'll call your factory to say that I will accept this unit for storage only."

"That's o.k. with me. Anything so I won't have to drive all night to take it back to Otoonga."

A telephone conversation later took place between Mr. Owlinface, the owner, and the Otoonga factory representative. The owner complained about the late arrival and that the order had been cancelled, and was allowed to sign a statement "for storage only." Often, unscrupulous dealers will use any excuse they can find to reject the unit and keep it for storage. In such arrangements no payments are required to be made, it may be kept interest free, and if they later sell the unit there may be extra profit. If I was boss at Otoonga, all the dealers would be fired and there would only be new ones that I'd do business with. After the telephone call, Mr. Owlinface gradually shed his belligerency, completely reversing his personality. Soon he became into such a jovial mood that he drove me to the bus station himself, more to get rid of me than anything.

The Black Dog in Muskegon was located twenty blocks from downtown, with no restaurant nearby, and with me sporting a growling stomach. Several other misfits were waiting for a bus and taking up space on hard benches. Three hours waiting for a bus proved to be a long wait in these cramped quarters with rain beginning to pelt down outside, with mean-looking females giving you the eye, and observing a pan handler working his way around the room. "Get a life," was my answer when he approached me. I'm not considered to be hard-nosed sort of guy, but it must have scared him off for he didn't come near me again.

It was an appealing aspect to consider the return trip to Otoonga by bus, mainly because it would be passing through the great city of Chicago with its tallest building in the world. To my regret, tiredness was so overwhelming that I slept through Chicago entirely. When nightfall fell I became rudely awake, mainly because the guy behind me took off his shoes and was periodically kicking me between the seats with his stinking feet. Such a rowdy bunch of passengers there were! All kinds of noise and commotion were made prominent, all because one little jerk had sneaked a bottle past the driver. They were having a high time, celebrating the Thanksgiving Holiday a little early. Loud snoring took precedence the last half of the night, and who can sleep under such conditions?

A twenty-minute bus rest stop was made in Rockford the next day, Thanksgiving. During a telephone conversation, my wife informed me that the family would be going to her mother's house for dinner. The menu was to consist of turkey and dressing, mashed potatoes and gravy, baked beans, cranberry salad, corn on the cob, and pumpkin pie with whipped cream. You know what my Thanksgiving dinner was? A bottle of pop and a baloney sandwich out of a vending machine. What did I have to be thankful for? It was times like these that made me wonder why I began driving motor homes in the first place.

One little thought crossed my mind that provided a little satisfaction anyway. Mr. Owlinface had accepted the unit without inspecting it. He got an oil spot on his carpet, so I had the last laugh after all. Ha ha.

Vehicles delivered in record fast time, all-night driving with no sleep, fan belts disappearing, overheated motors, inept mechanics, dirty carpets, unreasonable dealers, sleepiness, exhaustion, starvation, homesickness, dirty buses, drunken passengers, and stinking feet all contributed to the many obstacles, woes, and perils that face poor, misled drivers like myself. Yet during contemplation on the long homeward journey, thoughts were jockeying through my cranium between Bad Self and Good, trying to figure out how to get all my farm work done, induce 230 pigs to grow faster, placate wife and kids, and persuade Old Barney to do the chores, so I could get another motor home to drive as soon as possible.

Chapter VI

Reversal

"It's Mr. Hummer on the phone again," Azailia told me, with downcast eyes and a troubled look. We were finishing our morning coffee, after having discussed the hog and children situations. I had returned from the hog buying station where a truckload of fattened hogs had been sold. This should have brought a semblance of celebration, but a steep drop in sales price caused discouragement to reign instead. Ozzie and Baylan continued in cough specialization, causing contemplation about another visit to Doc Johansen, which could result in a deeper plunge below the poverty level. After a brief conversation with my boss, Azailia asked me, "Where to this time?"

"Shreveport, Louisiana," I replied, trying to keep too much jubilation from dropping out of my eyes.

"I don't know how much longer I can keep going like this, Myle. My stomach is getting bigger all the time, which makes it harder and harder to do all that cleaning out and carrying feed. I usually have to do most of the work with Old Barney being in that condition so much. And what little you are making from driving doesn't much more than pay his wages."

It seemed that she was getting a little hyper. "Honey, I admit a lot of bad luck happened during those first trips. I know this one to Shreveport will be a lot better. It would be a lot warmer down south too, and I'd sure hate to miss out on that." It had snowed two inches last night, attracting my thoughts toward a warmer clime, green grass, and sun-bathed skies.

"Myle, you know I'm sick a lot lately, too."

"Honey, I'm going to make sure the chores get done without you even going out to the hog house. I thought up a new idea. It's bound to work."

"You sure haven't had much influence on Old Barney so far."

"The trouble with Barney is that he is so busy watching that young gal do his housework that he forgets how to do the hog chores. This new idea was thought up in the middle of the night when I couldn't sleep."

"And what must this new idea be?"

"Why not hire his housekeeper to do part of the hog chores?"

"You mean to pay two people to do the job of one? This is the most idiotic idea yet."

"No, it isn't. Old Barney would be so busy showing off in front of that gal, he would do a good job. And she could help too. It would only take two people half as long, so wouldn't cost a penny more. Don't you think that is a good idea? This means no more worries for you and we will all be better off."

"This will never work. I've got bad feelings about it."

"Don't you worry, everything will come out fine. I'll give that gal, Jane Berkenholtzen, a call. I can't let the boss down, you know, and Louisiana will sure be a nice place to visit."

After two short telephone conversations, it was agreed by all parties, except Azailia, that Jane would help Old Barney do the farm chores while I was gone. A quick preparation for the journey was made. An extra pair of pants, a dress-up shirt, and two pairs of socks were hastily stuffed in my bag, perchance that my driving clothes should get dirty or wrinkled after several days of travel. Maybe it was just my imagination that Azailia had a tear in her eye when I kissed her goodbye.

At the Otoonga dispatch office, papers, keys, and instructions were issued. To my surprise and delight, a little van was assigned to my care, a welcome change from the larger, more cumbersome units usually provided. It contained no bathroom, table, or stove, but did have a rear seat that folded to make a bed. That was what mattered most. The van was called a conversion unit, was assembled in Detroit, shipped to Otoonga by rail, and changed over into whatever was salvageable. It would be sold to some Otoonga dealer by special order. Good Self remarked, "This will be great, Myle, almost like driving a car and less likely to face accidents or trouble." Much less was the chance of crashing into light poles, vision would be unobstructed, fewer trucks could go unseen when attempting to attack from the rear, and there would be a greater provision for a realistic sense of manipulation, unlike being perched twenty feet in the air as in a conventional motor home in which an eerie balance disoriented the equilibrium a driver should possess. If thoughts were not entertained about more hogs dying, the sales prices sinking lower and lower, and more kids getting sick, this trip held in promise a welcome relief from ice, snow, and cold winds, by jaunting down to a tropical paradise of palm trees, golden beaches, and bathing beauties. So I presumed.

To my utter dismay, a problem surfaced even before leaving the dispatch area. The transmission on the unit was a straight stick instead of the usual automatic, which should not have presented a problem, but it did. I was unable to shift the gear into reverse! Try as I might, pushing on the brake while pulling the shifting lever down with all my strength, it simply refused to back up. Going through this same procedure a hundred times proved to no avail. I just could not shift it into reverse gear. Why do things like this have to happen, when everything was so promising? Predicaments like this greatly improve the chances for heart to race and nerves to jangle. Dejectedly I climbed the long flight of three stairs back to the office where my circumstances were made known to Miss Missmossmus, who in turn made them known to Mr. Hummer. Inside his office, opportunity was provided to explain the situation.

"Drive the mother on to Shreveport," was the curt instruction. "We don't want to be bothered with it here. Just be careful you don't get into a place where you have to back up. Let the dealer worry about it. You know it's under warranty, don't you?"

"You mean for me to drive it down there with no reverse?"

"That's right. And don't goof up."

I stumbled out of the office, puzzled and stunned. How would it be possible to drive nine hundred miles without once backing up? All previous instructions to drivers were that each unit had to be in top-notch condition upon delivery, with no damages, and to be clean and spotless. Now the boss tells me this. Dreams of a worry-free journey to paradise were slipping down the drain, and the pleasant aspirations quickly evaporating.

Slowly down the driveway moved the reverse-less van, through the exit gate, on to the blacktop highway, and from there to the giant freeway heading south. Apprehension and misgivings were causing batting eyes, sweaty palms, and rising blood pressure. To my relief, the motor purred contentedly, the sun broke through the threatening clouds, and a tail wind promised good gas mileage. Good Self provided comforting stimulation with the encouraging words, "Ease off, Myle, everything is going to be alright."

From that time onward, whenever stopping became a necessity, I made certain there was ample room to make a forward advance with no requirement to back up. Running was smooth the first day, no trouble crossed my pathway, no backing up was needed, and fears were evaporating. Only two times during the entire journey did problems make an intrusion. Overnight parking at the Jolly Joplin Plaza near Joplin, Missouri found my unit parked at the far end of the plaza, away from any other vehicle that could pose a threat. Through wit and resourcefulness, I was able to disentangle myself from other negative potentialities. Stopping in Rogers, Arkansas did present one little difficulty after having stopped for morning coffee. A little Dodge Omni had deliberately parked in front of my van, even though there were a hundred other empty parking lanes. In spite of all the other empty spaces this little menace sat there in an arrogant manner in direct defiance. It was no telling how long it would remain, causing me to go into a fit of dramatic scheming. The first thought was to ram the little devil out of the way, bumper to bumper. At that very moment, Good Self made an intercessory appearance with the admonition, "Why don't you try pushing your van backwards by hand?" This was what I did, and it worked! By shifting the gears to neutral and using my muscles to shove it backward, it rolled so easily that an angel must have dropped out of a cloud to help. The other time of near heart failure occurred in the city of Texarkana while making a wrong turn which led to a dead end street. The perception of an incapacitated van being unable to turn around and no way out offered little encouragement, leading only to adverse perplexity, until wonderful Good Self once again interrupted with advice and wisdom unavailable to the average intellect, "Why not drive into the house yard on your right, cramp your wheels to the extreme left, make a big, wide turn, and you can make a complete getaway." This sage advice gave success (making huge ruts in the wet house yard), allowing for a reverse in direction without backing up. Very little damage was committed. Running over and ruining a clump of bushes left only a small amount of evidence with only a few twigs left sticking out of the radiator fins. This could easily be covered up by using a little twig plucking ingenuity. And I doubt if anyone could have read my number with all that mud slopped on the license plate.

Driving over the speed limit for only the second time in my life enabled the unit to arrive at the sales office before closing time. As the great metropolis of Shreveport loomed in the distance, a roadside arrow pointed to Sleezeharbor, which was the exact location of the Sludge RV dealer. While driving into the showroom lot, another round of apprehensive disposition engulfed my entire body, causing a reaction of shaky knees, trembling hands, and wiggling ears. What was the inspector going to say? Maybe I wouldn't tell them of the ailing conditon of the van at all and let them find out for themselves later. That might make them angry, causing them to report to Otoonga what a terrible crime had been committed. I could be fired from this lucrative position for insubordination and conspiracy to thrust on the public a defective product.

"How may I help you?" asked a young woman as she rose from her desk in the sales office.

"Well, I drove down a new van for you from Otoonga."

"For little ole me?" This was said with a toss of her curls and a twinkle in her eye. It seemed that she was trying to flirt with me until I realized she was looking over my shoulder, making eyes with the hunk mechanic in the next room.

"No, I'm sorry, it's for your boss, the dealer man, to sell to somebody that might want it."

"Oh, that's too bad. I was hoping for a new van for myself. Did it run alright? Is it damaged in any way or anything wrong?"

I knew my goose was cooked but answered, "It was the best running van I ever drove."

"That sounds great. I will notify Mr. Blakeforming, the manager. He will come out to take a look at it and sign your papers."

Mr. Bad Self then opened his trap and muttered, "I bet he will sign your papers."

Mr. Blakeforming proved to be a very pleasant individual, friendly and polite, unlike the majority of motor home dealers who won't give you the time of day. Maybe I could throw myself at his mercy without any violence or blood being shed. He shook my hand before asking, "How did it drive?"

"It drove real nice. The motor runs good. It didn't use a drop of oil. I didn't have any flat tires either."

Mr. Blakeforming then made a ritual inspection which took only a few minutes but during those few minutes my stomach was tying itself into a sailor's knot. He remarked, "I'll get behind the wheel and take it for a little drive. You say there is nothing wrong? Some drivers come in here with bent bumpers, cracked windshields, and low on oil. If they don't report it we are forced to write it up for the Otoonga office. It would have been better for them if they had been honest and reported it to us to begin with. While he continued speaking I made a sudden glance at the front of the vehicle, which revealed twigs still extending from the radiator grill. I had forgotten to remove them.

That did it. With downcast eyes and hangdog expression I told him, "Mr. Blakeforming, there is one little thing wrong."

"Yes? What is that?"

"Well, I can't get it to—, I mean it won't—, Mr. Blakeforming, what I mean to say is that it won't back up. I can't make it shift into reverse. But it's not my fault. That's the way it was put together back at the factory."

"It won't go into reverse? Why not?"

"I don't know. It just won't."

"I'll take it for a drive and see if it will work for me." He entered the van, seated himself, and started the motor. He moved the gears back and forth a few times which caused a great miracle to occur. It began backing up under its own power! I couldn't believe my eyes. What kind of magician was he? I had tried a thousand times to shift into reverse, yet he did it on the very first try. I didn't know whether to laugh or cry. Chagrin covered my countenance from head to foot.

"Wow! How did you do that? This is awesome!"

"Why didn't you try shifting it on the other side? The letter 'R' for reverse was installed on the wrong side. That's all that's the matter."

Come to find out, as Mr. Blakeforming had said, the letter "R" had been painted on the wrong side of the shifting lever from what it was supposed to have been. It hadn't entered my mind to try the opposite side to shift it. It wasn't my fault that some dummy at the factory had put in the wrong diagram. Anyhow, it was a great relief to be set free from such a humiliating, mortifying, degrading, disgraceful, exasperating situation. I had driven nine hundred miles in a nervous sweat, and the fear was all for nothing. So was the sweat.

It wasn't long until Mr. Blakeforming signed the delivery sheet, shook my hand, and called a taxi. As I stepped into the taxi, a dreadful scene was enveloping before my eyes. Behind the office windows were three characters, all of whom were in a state of uncontrollable laughter. I knew it was at my expense. It was none other than Mr. Blakeforming, his flirting secretary, and the hunk mechanic who were the culprits and I'll never forgive them.

Before boarding a bus at the Shreveport Black Dog, I placed a phone call to Azailia. "How are the hogs doing? Is Old Barney taking good care of everything? Are the kids getting over their colds? How are you feeling?"

"Things aren't so good, Myle. Jane got sick while doing Barney's housework. Barney wouldn't come over for chores because he had to take care of Jane. His words were slurred over the phone so you know what that means. Jack and I were somehow able to feed and water the pigs but it was just too much to do all that cleaning out. The pigs are up to their bellies in manure, but so far only one had died since you left."

"I'm sorry, Honey. But you can't blame Barney if Jane gets sick. One thing you might do if some of the smaller pigs get stuck in the muck and can't get out. You might try putting on my boots and wading in. Just grab a tail with one hand and an ear with the other. They will usually come out squealing up a storm. Be careful they don't shake themselves all over you. How are the boys? Are you getting over that morning sickness yet?"

"The boys are a little better. But I had to go to Doc Johansen's to get some antibiotics."

"You did? How much did that cost?"

"$29.95."

"$29.95? That Doc must think I'm made of money. One good thing is that we won't have to pay Barney and Jane, so that will make up for it. I'll have to hang up now or the phone bill will be getting too high.

Now don't work too hard at cleaning out. Remember, there's a baby on the way."

The bus ride home wasn't very pleasant either. With being mad at the Sleezeharbor Office and worried about the troubles back home, I was in a constant state of agitation and disrepair. As usual on the Black Dog, a wild bunch of hooligans were yelling and making noise which allowed nobody to sleep. Compounding the predicament was the sweet, sickening smell like somebody was doing drugs. The bus driver warned them, said they could be taken off the bus. They all laughed at him since he was such a little squirt and couldn't follow through on his threat.

On the ride home I did get a little mental revenge. Mr. Blakeforming never did see twigs sticking out of the radiator, so I had the last laugh. Ha, ha. Mulling the disgraceful situation over and over gave conclusions that when unreasonable bosses make unreasonable demands, when gear shifts won't shift, secretaries and mechanics make fun of you, hired help won't help, and the Black Dog bus smells like an opium den, then it's about time to quit driving motor homes and get a job at the rock quarry instead.

On the other hand, to contemplate the future, because of the call to Azailia, was indeed exciting and promising. My name was to be on the list on Monday for another trip. Being previewed were another wonderful chance for adventure, an opportunity to make a wad of money, removing myself from ice and snow, and freedom from pig chores for a few more days.

Heated arguments between Bad Self and Good were leading me to believe that hooked on motor home driving was what was happening, mainly because Bad Self was always declared the winner. If one had his mind made up beforehand, kept his eyes shut, and affirmed a hard set to the will, this prospect may not be as bad as it seemed. Maybe.

CHAPTER VII

On Top of Old Smoky

It was amazing that no problems occurred during the travel assignment to the southern city of Valdosta, Georgia; nor were there any upon the return trip as well. This indeed was an energizing, delightful and inspiring journey. Cooperating weather, road, and health concerns allowed for ease and pleasantry. The sun shone brightly each day while in this December excursion and light winds were advantageous helpers with a southward movement in evidence throughout. No attempted robberies or assaults, no beggars with menacing threats, nor any motor difficulties made an intrusion. The unit soared gracefully over hill and valley, reasonably priced gasoline insured a somewhat profitable conclusion, and a friendly dealer signed his name gratefully on the dotted line and provided a free ride to the bus station. The return by Black Dog presented no terrorizing incidents, no long waits during bus changes, and very few unsavory characters to cause alarm. A phone call home informed me that Old Barney had done his duties admirably, with a little help from Jane of course. Azailia had to clean out the hog house only once by herself, so things were looking up. Most of the boys were well again, except for Ozzie who kept up his dreadful whooping.

The route of travel guided the unit through the cities of Peoria, Evansville, Nashville, and Chattanooga. The first ten-hour driving period terminated at Danville, Illinois which allowed plenty of time for a steak dinner and period for rest in off-duty time. The second session of driving furnished a successful continuation, concluding at the vibrant city of Chattanooga, Tennessee. Since there was no truck stop available, a hotel parking lot had to suffice. The hotel clerks would assume you were occupying one of the high-priced rooms as long as you kept out of sight and didn't turn on any of the lights inside the unit.

Sad to say, it was in this same city of Chattanooga that trouble found a way to make an appearance. In fact, two troubles made an appearance. Three, if you want to get explicit. Nearing the city, skillfully placed billboards had attracted my attention. Each one spectacularly advertised the alluring resorts and entertainment of the surrounding areas. What particularly caught my eyes were the signs depicting rides to the top of Lookout Mountain by inclined railway. This was an appealing alternative to an unreasonable early retirement, since I am the kind of gung-ho guy who likes to take in every opportunity that comes his way. On top of Lookout Mountain were other enticements, including Ruby Falls, Point Park, and the Centennial Exhibits. Therefore, my intention was to drive to the inclined railway station, park my vehicle, and to take a thrilling, awe-inspiring ride to the top. My heart began to skip beats and the adrenalin to flow, with the prospect of a ride on the world's steepest passenger railroad. Making an exit off the Interstate Highway, I drove to a nearby gas station to ask directions where the depot might be located.

"You all see that there road off to the right?" drawled the attendant. "You all make a left right there and you all will run right to it."

"Thanks a lot, man," I replied.

I guided the unit to the road he mentioned, made a left turn, and proceeded with anticipation. This anticipation soon diverted into dismay, because the farther I drove, the less likely there would be any railway station whatsoever. The road made a gradual ascent originally, and then began turning abruptly upward. Awful truth was dawning—this was not the way to any railway station. This was the road that led to the top of the mountain! The station attendant evidently assumed that I wished to drive to the top and take the railway down, instead of the other way around.

Now the road leading to the top of Lookout Mountain is not dangerous in one's personal auto when caution is taken. But in a thirty-three foot home with a "scaredy-cat" driver at the wheel, that is a different story. You see, I am afraid of heights. Last summer, while helping neighbor Max shingle his barn roof, I was told to go home, since not many nails could be pounded while hanging on with both hands. So I did. (And that was only ten feet off the ground). Climbing this narrow, winding road was most terrifying! No place could be found to turn around, permitting only a forward advancement toward the top. Intense hoping was taking place that the brakes wouldn't fail, the motor was powerful enough to propel it all the way, the sides wouldn't scrape the jutting rocks, and that my composure would be sufficient to keep from going over the edge of the cliffs. I was clinging desperately to the steering wheel with white knuckles, bitten lips, and sweat pouring out of everywhere, constantly aware of the tremendous heights, yet trying not to look down. Lucky for me, the lane was on the inside while the poor guys on the outside were the ones facing an untimely demise. Bad Self chided all the way, "Now you've really done it, Myle. How are you going to drive this big thing to the top? And if you make it, how are you going to get back down?"

Good Self had no reply, leaving me with the frightening continuation to higher heights. Most of the cars buzzed swiftly past me, the drivers seemingly oblivious to any impending danger. Extreme terror became my constant companion as inch by slow inch the vehicle moved upward. Stomach acid also climbed upward, culminating in brain upheaval projecting mental impairment, if total destruction was somehow avoided. Seldom had fear been so dominant (except when about ten years old my sister and I threw eggs at a bees nest on the side of my uncle's barn, and the bees buzzed out, mad as hornets, taking their revenge by stinging the horses at the threshing machine, causing a runaway and overturning the oat bundle racks, and was my uncle ever mad, and were we scared at what his retaliation might be).

Fears were partially nullified when observing a sign pointing toward the summit only half a mile in the distance. With such an encouraging prospect, the expectation of survival became prominent. A few minutes later this expectation was realized as the vehicle rolled to a stop at the summit. Not in my wildest dreams could such a feat be accomplished by an old farm boy from the Midwest! And in a thirty-three foot motor home! Undoubtedly this had to be the highest peak in North America, and I had conquered it. How proud I was to descend from my unit, place my feet on this famous summit, and enjoy the tremendous view.

This great feeling of conviviality didn't last long. The appealing attractions were losing appeal, the luster being tarnished because Mr. Bad Self continued his harangue, "Remember, you've got to drive this thing back down."

Once again, he triumphed. How could it be possible to enjoy these famous sights while beleaguered with a constant bombardment of criticism, and with thoughts of a frightening retracement looming threateningly? Coming to my rescue was Other Self, uttering words of encouragement with a resounding rebuttal, "Don't worry so much, Myle. You drove all the way to the top, and you can get to the bottom one way or another."

With reproof ringing in my ears, the descent began. Gears were shifted to neutral, hands strangled the steering wheel, and brakes were applied all the way to the bottom. Large doses of quivering, nail biting, and hyperbulia were in evidence also. Dangerous curves were con-quered, ascending autos narrowly missed, and pedestrians avoided. What a sense of accomplishment! All the way to the top of Lookout Mountain and back down in one piece. No damage could be found on the unit, and myself having aged only ten years! It was worth it all to control the bragging rights to such an adventure, unequaled in scope and daring.

To add to the elation, the sun was still far above the horizon, causing Bad Self to make the inquiry, "Do you suppose that little old rail station could yet be found?" This caused a perking up of the ears, and a circling about in search of the desired depot. I stopped the unit long enough to roll down the window and yell at a passerby, "Can you tell me where the inclined railway is?"

"You all make two rights and a left and y'all be right there," was the quick retort.

"Thanks, man."

Strictly following his instructions, the unit was guided two lefts and a right. Strangely, no station could be found. Instead, the road led over what seemed to be familiar territory, changing into a gradual ascent and then turning abruptly upward. Awful truth was once again dawning for the second time in a row. I was on the way to the summit of Lookout Mountain!

"Now look what you've done. You're driving up the same road you were on before. How stupid can you get?" Bad Self was proud of himself.

How could this be happening to a nice guy like me? With no place to reverse directions, repeating the entire process was inevitable. I was frightened the other time, but was now petrified. A bitter tongue lashing prevailed as fainting continued as a constant threat, while up the narrow trail the unit powered forward. With incessant derision, Bad Self focused his unmerciful retaliation by prosecuting with a vengeance whatever Good Self could employ. Unprecedented vindictiveness permeated the struggle, allowing verbal indictment to indulge persuasively, permitting argumentative condemnation to excel, lapsing into extreme pseudopsia, leading to unconcilliatory degeneration, climaxing in suicidal aspirations. Constant threats advanced concepts of potential perishability once again during this second ascent, redefining terror until symptosis became a horrifying outcome.

"You blundering idiot," Bad Self again in vile condemnation. "How dumb can you be? Your head ought to be examined before it's too late." This simmering rebuke continued all the way to the summit. "Of all the crazy, senseless acts, this takes the cake. Such an imbecile. Without a brain in your head. You don't deserve one drop of pity. Driving up the same mountain twice in a row! It's time the white coats come and get you, don't you think?"

Somehow arrival at the summit once more became a reality. By my temerity and skillfullness, a successful ascension had been guaranteed before hand, despite all the castigation ringing in my ears. Being limp from exhaustion and light-headed from the altitude, I decided to immediately turn the vehicle around and drive back down. Desire had completely vanished to visit these falls, the rock piles, or the museums located nearby on top of this mountain resort. I didn't even get out of the vehicle this time.

With determined intent, once again the unit was sailing downward. So natural was the excessive height and so familiar the roadway, that one hand driving became customary while coasting down the tree line elevations. Speeds up to sixty miles an hour became common, even though the right rear dual hung out in space on some of the sharper curves. It was scary to look down when facing the steepest drop-offs. That's when I would close my eyes for a few seconds at a time, to shut out the fearful sights.

After safely reaching the bottom for the second time, pride welled within my breast in contemplation for the agility, capability, and pervasive determination myself had shown to the world under such harrowing conditions. Forever afterward, this great pinnacle of victorious victory will be remembered as a notorious accomplishment (permitting bragging rights to my children, future grandchildren, friends, acquaintances, neighbors, and even strangers who would listen), a stupendous attainment that undoubtedly has not henceforth been recorded, and probably will be a record never again to be broken. Nothing can defeat a died-in-the-wool motor home driver, that's for sure.

Halting for a few moments at the bottom of the mount, I glanced about to get my bearings. In an exhausted condition and with nerve endings still tingling, an awesome sight met my eyes—the railway embarkation point, and only a short distance away! Why couldn't I have seen it before? It was in plain view. Since the sun had not yet set, would it still be possible to get that desired ride to the top? Since Bad Self was urging me to go for it, and since curiosity had not yet departed, an affirmative declaration was readily advanced.

The unit was soon parked, a ticket was purchased, and a still- shaking driver found himself seated inside one of the railway cars. What an excellent view there would be seated in an open air car with nothing to block the view. The entire train was vacant except the car ahead which contained two couples. Honeymooners, oblivious to the scenery, were seated on the left, while opposite them was an elderly couple who were arguing so loudly that the loud speaker sound could not be heard. What a marvelous ride this was becoming! Upward toward heights sublime, spectacular scenery unfolding, and with no worries about driving, parking, or crashing to the bottom. Good fortune was my partner after all! Yet not for long. Only until nearing the midway point. Suddenly dark clouds invaded our domain in an envelopment of mist and fog. Our beautiful scenery was transformed into a gray wall. From that time on, all I could see were honeymooners with arms entwined and two old people with rapidly-moving mouths.

Accompanying the fog was a strong wind blowing icy cold, freezing the perspiration on my skin into tiny ice droplets. What a disgusting outcome this was becoming.

"You better enjoy it, Myle. This is what you came for, isn't it?" Bad Mouth sounding off again.

When the summit was reached and the ride ended, absolutely nothing could be seen. Other disappointments were also reigning. The attendants had shut off the water supply to Ruby Falls, the doors to Fairyland Caverns and Mother Goose Village had been padlocked, and at Point Park the guards stood with extended rifles so that no forced entry be allowed. All that I could investigate was the machine room where the giant gears and cables were located, but who wants to see giant gears and cables? Thoroughly disappointed, I once again placed myself in the railway car, hoping that the return ride would soon depart.

Falling asleep on the descent didn't make any difference. Nothing could be enjoyed under these despicable conditions. This entire episode, a three-time excursion up Lookout Mountain, proved to be a senseless waste of time. Nerves were shattered and ego beaten to a pulp. My hands shook for a week afterward. In fact they are still shaking, probably will continue shaking as long as this disgusting occupation is endured. This is yet another warning to the would-be motor home drivers of America. Can't you see the end result? Are you so dense that an out-of-body experience such as mine cannot change your thinking?

Inclinations favoring self-destruction intensify dramatically in certain situations. The status quo is greatly altered by a reconditioned outlook previously promoting sublime ambitions, nullifying the obligations required to portray a radiant face and a turning against evil potentialities, enhanced in uncanny persuasion by the forward set-backs imposed upon the innocent and gullible who are ensnared in traps indiscriminately forcing circumstances to impale victims on swords sharpened through outrageous acts of defamation, degradation, and disgrace. That's the way it was for me anyway. And it's all because of motor home driving.

CHAPTER VIII
California Dreamin'

"Wake up, Myle, there's somebody outside."

"Huh, what?" I was groggy with sleep. The clock read 2:00 A.M.

"I heard a car drive in the yard and a door slam. This scares me. Who could be out there this time of night?"

"I don't hear anything."

"Well, I do. There's a truck out in back by the hog house. I can see somebody moving around in the shadows." Azailia had crawled out of bed and was peering out the window.

"Maybe I better get out of bed and get dressed if you think you hear something. I'll go downstairs to get the rifle."

I then remembered that the rifle had been loaned to Jim Hodges to go skunk hunting. I was beginning to get frightened myself but knew these situations must be faced with a brave heart and calm spirit.

"What if there are hog thieves out there? Hog thieves were discovered at Dan Schnitze's last week, remember?" Azailia kept harping.

This was remembered all too well. Getting a grip on myself with a quick dose of bravery, I dressed, tiptoed down the stairs, and prepared to outwit any would-be robber. Armed with Jack's BB gun and a butcher knife, I sneaked out the back door, circled the house, crept along the grove of trees while staying in the shadows, and cautiously moved toward the hog house. From this vantage point could be seen a dark and sinister figure fumbling with the door latch.

"Stop thief," I yelled, while raising the knife over my head and lunging toward him.

"What?" said the dark and sinister figure.

To my surprise, it wasn't a hog thief after all. The dark and sinister figure was none other than Old Barney. I lowered the knife but said in exasperation, "Barney, what are you doing?"

"Hi, Myle. Did you get home?" He peered at me with half closed eyes. "I figured you was still in St. Louis."

"Not St. Louis. You mean Louisville. I've been home from that trip for three days."

"What's the diff? I came over to feed the hogs."

His slurred speech meant that he was soused again. "Barney, this is not the time to be doing chores. It's 2:00 o'clock in the morning." I took his arm and led him back to his pickup. "You go back home, Barney. Do you feel o.k. to drive?"

"Yep, sure. Nothin' wrong with me. I thought it was time to feed the hogs. I'll be fine soon as I get behind the wheel."

With a little help, Barney climbed back in his truck and headed for home while I made my way to the house, greatly relieved. Sleeplessness, however, dominated the rest of the night. This Barney episode nullified a good night's sleep, which was badly needed because another fantastic trip was on the agenda for today. Miss Missmossmus, in the absence of Mr. Hummer who was playing golf, had sought my services to drive a Homing Special to Los Angeles, California. I had spontaneously given an affirmative response, preparing to rise early this morning to carry out the request. Thinking about such a marvelous place to visit caused my mouth to water, the adrenalin to flow, and goose bumps to break out on the back of my neck. California! That great place of beauty where the rich and famous dwell, the sun always shines, and everybody lives the good life.

The Homing Special, a thirty-foot gleaming monster, proved to be in top notch condition, upon my scrupulous inspection. The unit was extremely luxurious with plush seats and carpets, superb fixtures and appliances, and elaborately furnished with excellent workmanship and design. So it was with a merry heart that a certain driver made careful preparation for the long excursion to the golden west.

Sitting on Cloud Nine! King of the Hill! Top of the Heap! All were accurate descriptions of the superior attitudes bouncing from wall to wall and from steering wheel to potty chair, as I proudly exited the dispatch area. Talk about adventure! This tops it all. Hard to believe such good fortune had come my way. Los Angeles—undoubtedly the most fabulous place in the good old USA and I was headed straight for it! A boastful self-agrandizement, accompanied by gobs of personal exultation, supremely dispelled considerations of impending doom, intensified internal emotions and highlighted potential conquests in superlative terms of magnified excess. The scare tactics provided by Old Barney's mistaken misdemeanor could not disperse this passionate celebration.

For a while.

It wasn't long until the tide began turning adversely. It began slowly, randomly helter-skelter with both subtle thought intrusions and physical intervention, climaxing with the utterances of that menace, Bad Self, who emphatically proclaimed, "You know you ain't there yet, Myle. All kinds of trouble could happen, you know, Myle."

These prophetic words were vividly etched mentally, contrasting dramatically with the vibrant endowment which formerly had been exquisitely applied. Even the sky began to take on a menacing appearance after the somber warning. The radio forecast had hinted at possible snow showers and rising winds, but with no great immediate impending alarm. Yet it wasn't long, while approaching the small town of Happenstance, Nebraska, that the first snow flake came pounding down. Soon another one struck. The third flake was as big as a fist, hindering visibility, for it landed on the driver's side of the windshield, trickling down in haphazard fashion. The next one hit on the roof directly above my head, sounding as if a rock had been thrown.

Miraculously, the large flakes began dissolving into thousands of tiny ones. Consternation and disorientation took charge, replacing former peace and anticipation. The wind began chiming in with a ferocious howl, slanting against my poor vehicle in a terrifying sideways pattern. Visibility thus caused driving to deteriorate from difficult to impossible in a matter of minutes.

Lucky for me, a sign appeared suddenly out of the gloom with notification that the city limits of Happenstance had been entered. The only alternative was to park the unit along the street and wait out the storm. What a miserable night it was. My sorry unit was rocking back and forth, with me in it, while snow pellets crashed down with great rapaciousness, along with nerve shattering, hair pulling and knee-knocking priority. That sneaking Miss Missmossmus is to blame for sending me out in a snowstorm like this. I was imprisoned within four walls, lying in a sleeping bag while trying to keep warm, directly across the hall from a bathroom I wasn't allowed to use. Nor could the motor be run because the gas was getting low and asphyxiation could result if snow clogged the vents or if too much oxygen seeped through the windows. My chilled, quivering body didn't get much rest that night.

When morning finally came, the snow had stopped falling, the wind had abated, and guess what? The sun was shining. Could it be that my luck had changed? Not really, because a huge snow drift had surrounded the unit, too large to drive through. My option was to walk six blocks in zero weather to where purchase could be made of a hand driven snow scoop, to return to the scene of disaster, and to make an attempt at rescue. Nearly an hour of back-breaking attempts were made before a wide enough path could be envisaged. Next, the motor wouldn't start. Because of the extreme cold, the battery had run down, allowing for nothing to happen. Another brisk walk downtown six blocks became necessary, hopefully to provide liberation via a jumpstart. Back at the unit, more nail biting was endured during the two-hour wait for a tow truck, or anything that would cause my vehicle to run again. At last, a life-saving truck did arrive, giving new life to my unit and ending the exasperating delay.

What a relief it was to again be moving down the highway, even when considering that my pocketbook was leaner by $54.67. Relief was cut short however, and my troubles had not yet ended. The pavement was covered with ice and snow, making travel slow and hazardous. About four miles west of Happenstance the car ahead began swerving, completely lost control, slammed on the brakes, causing a likewise performance from my carriage. The little auto managed to escape without mishap, while my unit had swerved so much to avoid collision that it slid into another drift on the shoulder of the road. Stuck again! Thankfully, I still held in possession the scoop purchased from the Benotly Hardware, allowing for new hope in the midst of catastrophe. Scooping and hopes weren't enough. The big unit was so far off the roadway that not enough traction could be applied, causing the wheels to spin in wild frenzy. Walking half a mile to the nearest farmhouse proved fruitless because the place didn't have a telephone, so the old hag told me. One and a half miles walking west was successful, a call for a tow truck was made. Rescue was embraced as a truck with a cable pulled my beautiful, magnificent, dazzling, mud-spattered vehicle onto the road. "This must be your lucky day," Bad Self whispered while I wrote out another check for $54.67.

These heart-breaking delays caused much consternation and indecision. How would I make it to Los Angeles by Friday? It was narrowed down to two law-breaking options: drive faster than the speed limit or throw away the logbook. Since always obeying the traffic laws of our government, a compromise was settled upon. I would do both. If you are breaking one law, you may as well be breaking two while you're at it.

Making this choice led to rushing through Wichita at rush hour, gunning it on the open highway, and scurrying through the smaller towns at a frenzied pace, since by this time the roads had melted off from the ice and snow. A few hours of such a rapid motion brought on another curse, one that had to be faced many times—I was getting sleepy. A red light flashing in my rear view mirror awakened me quickly from this stupor. They throw the book at out-of-state drivers, especially if they look rich and prosperous. I must have looked that way, driving a fancy motor home. My worst fears were coming to pass—confrontation with the law. The motorcycle gentleman with a helmet on his head uttered in a rough, uncouth voice, "Let me see your driver's license. Why were you weaving all over the road?"

"Sir, I was getting a little sleepy and was looking for a place to buy a cup of coffee."

After walking a chalk line, taking a breath test, and watching his fingers move before my eyes, his conclusion must have been that I wasn't drunk enough to get hauled in. "I'm going to let you go this time, but you better get over that sleepiness real quick. I don't want to be called up on the scanner and find out you are wrapped around a telephone pole and have to pick up your remains from between the stove and refrigerator."

"I'll be very careful, sir. It won't happen again. You won't have to worry about digging me out of the refrigerator."

By this time I was very, very wide awake. What a relief it was to see him drive away. That Smoky Joe didn't have enough smarts to ask about a log book, evidently surmising I owned this high-priced outfit. Wow, did I fool him! Too ignorant to notice the serial numbers and chalk marks on the windows. I was laughing out loud, realizing how lucky I was to have gone through that snow storm since the numbers had nearly been wiped out.

With new-found zest and zeal I proceeded to the prized objective— the great city of Los Angeles. On and on, driving continued, and hour after hour. Some of the Otoonga drivers boasted they could drive all the way to California, 1800 miles, without stopping to sleep. When quizzed how they got by doing this, the reply was that two log books were used and interchanged. I was one who always obeyed the traffic laws, come what may. I wouldn't resort to such underhanded tactics as that. Except for this one little time. This would be the only exception. "Laws were made to be broken," Bad Self asserted, being so vociferous that Good Guy remained silent.

By Thursday the Homing Special had passed through Albuquerque, Flagstaff, Kingman, and across the border into California. Sleep was undertaken very sparingly, while the endless cycle of stopping for gas, swallowing a sandwich, and keeping awake while driving were the main concerns. During the daylight hours spectacular mountain views featured indescribable majesty, towering in magnificence with each curve in the road. It wasn't long, however, when a dramatic change unfolded, causing an intervening attitude of depression. Perhaps a drastic change to desert locale was a contributing factor in this sensation. Mile upon mile of sand and desolation choked in upon me. No towns, farms or people to be seen. Except for the continued auto traffic along the roadway, one could believe he was a lone figure in the vast universe. This concept was overwhelming, along with a fear of the unknown. Such meditation caused all kinds of weird conjectures, hastened admirably by the words of You Know Who, "What will happen when you get to that big city of Los Angeles, Myle? You will be nothing but a little twerp in that big place."

Yes, I knew that very well. That was the trouble.

"How are you going to drive through all that traffic? How are you going to find the dealer location? What if the dealer man doesn't like you and gives a bad report? How are you going to get to the airport? You won't be able to even get on an airplane. You're afraid of flying don't you know, Myle?"

These nagging thoughts were my companions during the remainder of the journey. First, there were questions. Then came apprehension. Apprehension advanced to worry. Worry was climaxed by out and out fear. Anyone who sits behind the wheel of a motor vehicle knows what fear is all about, at one time or another. In my case, I knew what it was all about, all the time. Adding fear to the multitudes of other perils confronting every driver, and you have a good start to complete defeat. Before entering the door of any of today's modern horse-less carriages, one must be prepared for any eventuality, as I have told you previously. Many of the eventualities lead to horrible conclusions, cause untold anxiety and regret, plunge its victims into cauldrons of despair, and enhance the downward spiral to failure.

My fears began consummating gradually, the closer I came to the huge metropolis. Traffic congestion picked up noticeably. By the time the suburbs were entered, it was bumper to bumper motivation. Then fog descended. So did smog. So did nervousness and more fear. Another surprising turn of events took place as soon as each driver read the sign: SPEED LIMIT 45. Driver reaction remarkably caused speeds to increase, not decrease, as strange as this may seem. A quick peek at my speedometer revealed a reading of 70 miles an hour while trying to keep up with the flow of traffic. California drivers are certainly weird, to my estimation. If one were to slow his speed only slightly, it would cause horn honking, dirty looks, and thumbed noses. Hand waving also took place, evidenced by a closed fist, motioning in my direction. I can't understand the police reaction either. All of these vehicles travelling 25 miles an hour above the speed limit, and not one patrolman in sight. Should just one cop stop but one lane of traffic, he could write tickets to his heart's content, picking up a thousand bucks real quick like. Yet to think that out in Wyoming at three o'clock in the morning, you are liable to get pulled over and socked fifty bucks for driving sixty in a fifty-five mile an hour zone.

I found myself in the middle lane with a turn off at Hollywood X-rated Lane 25 ahead, where the dealer was located. Suddenly my luck changed for the good. A slow-moving truck in the right lane was going uphill, and miraculously my unit was able to work ahead of it. Making the exit and moving fifteen blocks to Hollywood X-rated Lane 25, and I was able to make a successful conclusion to this fantastic journey. Relief broke upon me for there it was—Hollywood X-rated RV Dealer of Los

Angeles! Permission was granted to wash the unit at the dealer's covered bay instead of having to search for a car wash large enough to accommodate my vehicle. The checking inspector was an amiable fellow who quickly checked the unit and signed the documents.

I had driven 1900 miles under dire circumstances, emerging as a conquering hero! What an accomplishment! I was on my way! "To where?" asked Good Self. With the signing of a paper, my bed was taken away and so was my means of travel. I was left standing alone on a strange street with only the clothes on my back and two large bags to carry. No one was there to protect me from these foreigners who at any given moment could slug, rob, or kill at their discretion. How would you like that, all you who think motor home driving is a piece of cake?

With extreme ingenuity I was able to escape all menacing threats. By walking two blocks to Hollywood X-rated Lane 27, 1 was permitted to board a city bus to a terminal in Watts, transfer to Manhattan Beach, and to once again transfer to a terminal near the airport. A van could then be entered which whisked my body to the airport berth of my choosing. By asking directions from fellow passengers, various bus drivers enroute, and by making a nuisance of myself, I completed the cycle in three hours and twenty-two minutes. Such economical transportation cost $3.50, while hiring a taxi would have amounted to nearly $60.00.

It was a proud, fortunate fellow who swaggered toward the Skyjack Airlines ticket counter. The LAX Airport was a madhouse of customers rushing about, hither and yon, with little seemingly purpose or intention. My happy feelings were soon diminished when forced to stand in an endless line waiting to buy a ticket. Being surrounded by impatient, ill-mannered ruffians contributed greatly by multiplying this diminishment. Nothing is worse than waiting. That's what I was doing, and plenty of it.

To make matters worse, fear was once more taking control. I was having very bad feelings about this upcoming flight. With my luck it was sure to crash. You see, I had never ridden a plane before now, and am afraid of heights. When climbing in the hay mow to survey the crops from the top window, I shrink back in fear. The worst case scenario would be crashing on some lofty mountain range where our bodies would never be found. Even that may not be so bad, for my memory would live on in infamy as a hero for the Otoonga Trailer Factory. There would be a picture of myself hanging along the hallway of the dispatch office, with words underneath describing how a valiant driver had given his life for the cause. My wife would shed a tear or two when contemplating all the mean things she had done to me. Old Barney would probably drown his sorrow during a couple of weeks of debilitating remorse. The boys would only miss me for a few days and the pigs may not miss me at all. There would be a big funeral at the church, making me famous in a glamorous light. In an airplane crash you wouldn't have to suffer long…it would be over in a matter of seconds. So it was needless to worry. But I did anyhow.

When my turn at the counter finally came, it was a rough, tough individual who waited on me. "How may I help you?" was her smug question.

"I would like to buy a ticket to Otoonga," was my stammering reply.

She answered with a smirk, "I'm sorry, but the last flight departed fifteen minutes ago. If you would care to get a hotel for the night there are vacancies on flight #3657 at 8:15 in the morning. Or if you care to wait for six hours there is a red eye flight #7563 at 1:00 A.M."

"The red eye flight sounds best for me." (This would nullify a high-priced hotel bill and I wouldn't have to see the ground by travelling under cover of darkness.)

"We need some means of identification and $296.75 for the ticket."

"Wow," said Good Self under his breath. "There cannot be much left after paying for this high priced ticket, for all the gas you bought, and to pay Old Barney and Jane."

Instead I said with haughty eyes and a nervous grin, "My credit card should handle it nicely, madam."

Waiting those six hours seemed boring and endless. Food was so expensive in the airport, I remained hungry. My cell mates at the gate were in the same condition as myself—bleary-eyed, sour-faced, unkempt, and with hair standing on end. Some were in a prone position, sprawled on the seats in disgraceful fashion. Others were lying flat on the floor. One young hoodlum displayed an array of chains hanging from his neck, shoulders, and waist, while sitting on the lap of his girl friend. Two little ladies with puffy eyes were arguing vehemently over a feature article in the Frequent Flyer Magazine. A mini-skirted young female was tossing her curls, flirting with old men, and exhibiting a bare midriff with hog rings in her navel. Some of the weirdos were reading paperback novels, others were slumped in contemplation, while many sat dejectedly with nodding heads and flustered expressions. Three little toddlers with runny noses were bawling up a storm while their mother slept, either uncaring or hard of hearing. Several well-dressed executive types sat with staring eyes, scowling faces, and hardened features, dismayed at all the noise and confusion. One eighty-ish old gal was dancing about, arms waving, skirt swirling, lips moving, attempting to attract attention, and she was doing a good job of it. What a shame that such obnoxious characters take control of our airports, bus stations and train depots. Such a motley bunch of humanity. And to think that I was one of them. This was worse than back home in Red's Tavern on a Saturday night. These are the elite of California?

At last, the red eye flight was announced by some mysterious voice coming out of the ceiling. It appeared that my destiny was destined, with no apparent means of escape.

As I walked down the loading ramp, a slight twinge could be felt under the eighth vertebra. It began in a wild encircling arc, penetrating the entire spinal column. The pain gradually progressed, causing a crying out of the mouth and a grabbing of the back by the hand. This provided a startling upward transmission extending to the cranial mass, where nerve waves went on general alert, sending outrageous messages throughout the body, reaching to the extreme points of the extremities. I was desperately hoping that heart palpitations would not ensue, along with angina, swooning, and unconsciousness.

Batting eyes and shaky-leg syndrome took precedence upon entering the plane itself. My seat was located next to the window, but that didn't mean I had to look down. Everyone was so engrossed in stuffing bags and cases into the overhead compartments that my nervousness went unnoticed. To remember what happened just three days ago on Flight #79835 out of this same airport, didn't help matters any. That plane had trouble at take-off, had made a nose dive into the bay snuffing out the lives of all 9,387 passengers, except for one lucky guy who was in the rest room when he wasn't supposed to be. He survived the disaster by using the toilet seat as a flotation device.

An elderly woman became the occupant of the seat next to mine. In spite of the lateness of the hour, she was prone to be talkative. "This should be an interesting flight," she observed. "I've not had the privilege to fly this time of night before. Isn't it exciting?"

"Yeah, this should be a real blast."

"I'm going to see my brother in Chicago. He will be 89 years old next Tuesday. He's the baby of the family," she giggled.

"That's nice."

"Where are you going? Do you fly much?"

"Yes, I'm forever flying here and there," I lied. "I'm an executive sales manager for the Otoonga Trailer Factory which means I've got to go on one plane after another to here and there all the time. I'm going back now to headquarters to report my recent findings."

"Sounds like you are leading an exciting life. I just love young men who are making their company great and famous."

"Yes, that's what we are doing alright."

Soon another mysterious voice told us to fasten our seat belts, and how to do it, but I already knew how, even though never having been on a plane before. Suddenly the big bird was rumbling down the runway at break-neck speed. Next came a thunderous roar and it was airborne, with only air between us and the ground.

"Can you get a good look at the city skyline? It is so beautiful at night with all the lights shining when we make the turn over the bay."

"Yes, it certainly is a beautiful sight," I answered while looking out the window with closed eyes.

Good Self then came to my rescue. "Shut her up! Tell her you are getting sleepy."

"I'm getting real sleepy all of a sudden. It must be time for my midnight nap."

Pretending sleep offered consolation in two ways. I didn't have to look down out the window, and talking to the woman beside me was put on hold. This pretension continued while the flight attendants were serving something to whoever was wake enough to slosh it down. A little later I was changing my position when an accidental peek out the window was made. A horrible sight met my eyes. The wing was wobbling. I mean up and down. This didn't provide much fear cancellation. What if that wing dropped off? Would the plane go down in circles in a spiral plunge, or make an abrupt nosedive straight down? Miraculously neither one happened! The plane kept purring like a kitten and didn't pay any attention to its wobbling wing.

Within a few hours I became a seasoned veteran at flying. My fears were beginning to subside. Except for the time when we hit an air pocket and everything flew to the ceiling, even the stewardess. Flying proved to be an excellent way to travel after all. I would sure be able to brag about it to all the neighborhood farmers, making them jealous like I used to be. It is silly for so many people to be afraid of flying. The only worry you have is crashing, and that would only happen once.

Little did I realize that hundreds of hours of flight time were to be on my agenda. It was nothing but cowardice to have been so afraid. Fear of flying was cancelled, had been completely conquered by my fifty-third flight. Nothing up there can scare me anymore. Fires in the cockpit, passengers being sucked out of windows, lightning striking the tail fins, geese sucked into the jet engines, renegades hijacking the plane to Cuba, air pockets causing drops of two or three miles, oxygen masks popping out of the ceiling, and little kids vomiting in my lap. I have become a hardened customer and nothing can faze me anymore. Even under the most dire circumstances, I keep on reading my newspaper, drinking my Coke, watching the good-looking gals across the aisle, or to quietly snooze the time away. This is not to imply there are no hazards to flying. But motor home driving is the cause. If it wasn't for motor home driving there would be no worries about hog thieves, snow storms in Nebraska, sliding off slippery roads, highway patrolmen, flashing red lights, horrendous traffic jams, sleepless nights in airports, and planes with wobbling wings.

"You shouldn't be driving motor homes anyway, Myle," said Good Self, emphatically.

"Oh, shut up and be quiet," was Bad Self's reply.

And you know which one I listened to.

CHAPTER IX

Birthing Instincts

As warmer spring weather approached, so did the time for the mother sows to give birth. This caused a disruption in driving plans. My report to Mr. Hummer was that a temporary halt in delivering vehicles was imperative. He was a very understanding person in spite of his gruff manners. When the first sows began to show signs of pregnancy distress, my driving was put on hold for a few weeks. Instead of traveling from one unknown destination to another, my duties were transformed into the "dumb farmer" syndrome again. Cleaning and disinfecting the far-rowing house, assembling and positioning the sow crates, and laying in store the necessary food and medical supplies, all became impending necessities. Manual labor wasn't easy after the lazy life of travel, but neither Old Barney or Azailia would assume responsibility for the farrowing. That left me holding the bag.

The first sows to give birth were to be placed in crates just inside the hog house door. Each sow was to be thus imprisoned from four to six weeks until their piglets were weaned. I had to force each potential mother to enter one of these individual crates. This task was best accomplished by placing food and water at the head of each crate, put-ting straw or other soft bedding on the floor to enhance their birthing instincts, and then to use extreme mental and physical ingenuity to guide each one to the proper destination. Each had to be persuaded individually by begging, enticing, commanding, or hypnotizing. If such attempts didn't provide adequate inducement, a good whacking over the nose would be the last resort.

The first two expectant mothers walked obediently to the stalls, allowing me to lower the gates behind them. The third one, however, decided that stubbornness was her objective. The remedy then was to give her a good whacking over the nose with a stick. This method also proved to be insufficient, for she stood in the alley chomping her jaws, frothing at the mouth, and with evil intent in her eyes. Who could blame her? How would you like it if some mean old codger whacked you over the nose a few hours before you were to give birth? Good Self rescued the situation by giving the sage advice, "Why don't you try to guide her by putting a basket over her head like Uncle Zeb used to do? Sows don't like baskets over their heads, you know Myle."

With many threats, yells, basket maneuverings, and bad words being said, the old girl backed herself into the stall, because sows don't like baskets over their heads. Now she was trapped and would just have to stew in her own juice for the next few weeks. Being installed in her stall backwards would cause a multitude of problems, for she would be messing in her feed and water pans and was apt to bite my leg each time I walked through the alley in front of her.

Many frenzied farrowing procedures such as this continued on unabated until all the pregnant animals were captured, birth accomplishments were completed, the little ones weaned and moved to growing pens, the mothers placed again in breeding facilities, and to continue each process over and over in an endless cycle. The trick was to decide which sow would be the first to give birth, because each one would try her best to hide her condition, and then to farrow an entire litter in the yuckiest mud hole they could find.

The very next day birth pains erupted in the first sow by the door. This was easily verified by squeezing one of her nipples which caused a line of milk to squirt across the alley into the open mouth of one of the tomcats that frequented the habitation, presumably to obtain a warm meal of one of the pigs born dead, or to wait patiently for more squirts of milk.

After finishing the evening chores, an array of ham sandwiches was presented for supper around the kitchen table. Then it was back to the farrowing house. Before my return, the first newborn had safely made it to the other side. You see, it is very advantageous for the herdsman to be present during birth because many of the piglets could be saved from being crushed by the mother, by wiping mucous from their mouths to prevent suffocation, and by helping the weaker ones to find a place to suckle. The farmer could place heat bulbs over the birthing area to keep the little ones warm and dry, clip the needle teeth of each one to prevent injury from fighting, to cut off and disinfect the navel cord, to dispose of the afterbirth, and to do a thousand other acts that go along with little pigs being born. This entire process was a most fascinating, awe-inspiring, wonderful, disgusting, horrible, miraculous event—the creation of a new life. Now I don't believe in evolution because pigs don't look anything like monkeys. Humans maybe do, but not pigs. No, I would much rather believe a Great Creator began all of this, rather than to consider what those stupid educated scientists tell us. Any dumb farmer knows more about creation than they do, and pigs sure weren't created by evolution.

But why do most of the pigs have to be created at night? Eighty-nine percent of all pigs are born at night, according to the Farmers Almanac. This means not enough sleep for the caretaker herdsman. In fact, there may not be a wink of sleep for this particular herdsman tonight. No sooner than the first sow had given birth to three pigs, than the second one began propelling. I kept darting from one crate to the next, doing whatever it was that I was supposed to be doing. It was not long until the first sow was straining and nothing was happening. I knew what this meant. Arming myself with a pail of warm water, pouring in antiseptic liquid, and soaping my arm and hand, I began the often attempted endeavor of pulling a pig. Usually I could reach inside the birth canal to grasp hold of a leg, tail, or head. Using this method and with the sow straining simultaneously, victory would be won, resulting in a new life being born. If this daring procedure proved unsuccessful, I would insert a wire hook to puncture a jaw, thus enabling a more forceful coercion. As a last resort a veterinary from Otoonga could be summoned, but this was so expensive one may as well let the entire litter die and hope for the best for the next sow.

With my right arm in the birth canal up to my shoulder, a noise was heard at the far end of the barn. The door opened and there stood little Jack.

"What are you doing out here this time of night, Jack? You should be in bed by now shouldn't you?" I could sense that something must be wrong.

"I was sleeping but Mamma woke me up. She made me come out here to tell you she has pains in her tummy."

Oh, no, this can't be happening! Azailia getting birth pains the same time the sows are! It must be another false alarm. The baby isn't due for another two weeks. Frantically grasping for a pig's foot in a birth canal while hearing such alarming news is indeed perplexing. Yet an answer suddenly sprang forth from my lips, "Jack, go back in the house and have Mamma call Old Barney. Ask him to come help us."

"What?"

"I said, go back in the house and have Mamma call Old Barney to come help us."

"O.K., Dad."

The sows were continuing their duties very nicely, competing against each other as to which one would have the largest litter. Moving from one farrowing crate to the next was keeping me awake. The spell was broken about midnight when the third mother, the grouchy one, decided she wasn't to be unnoticed, by quietly ejaculating her first pig. This tripled my concentration while attempting to give each pig a chance at survival, trying to comfort each mother in distress, and hoping to avoid being bitten on the leg or kicked in the jaw in the meantime.

My willpower was indeed sorely tested. What was keeping Old Barney? He was always dependable in times of emergency. It had been a considerable length of time since my instructions to Jack had been issued, yet Barney was still a no-show, even though he lived only a short distance away.

A few minutes later the barn door opened again. But instead of Old Barney, it was once again little Jack.

He spoke out in a high-pitched voice, "It's alright now, Dad. Barney took Mamma to the hospital."

Hearing these words was such a shock that the pig I was wiping off fell through my hands, bounced to the cement floor, and staggered off in utter confusion.

"What did you say, Jack?"

"I said, Barney took Mamma to the hospital."

"Oh, no, he hasn't done that, has he? I wanted him to come out here to help with the little pigs and I could be with Mamma."

"Yeah, but Mamma said her tummy hurt real bad, so Barney took her."

This isn't real! I should never started driving motor homes because something like this was bound to happen. Now fate was dealing me a revengeful blow, causing conflict between wife and pigs. What will Azailia think of me, allowing Old Barney to take her to the hospital when she might be starting labor? That Barney! I could ring his neck! To think that he was usurping my place of authority and leaving me here in this stinking hog house when my own baby was about to be born.

Quickly I washed my hands in the disinfected water, ran with Jack to the house where a quick change of clothes was hurriedly made, and then a dash to the garage, only to discover a flat tire on the car. And the pickup was in Otoonga, getting a brake job. This caused running to the house again to change clothes, changing the tire in the garage, and back to the house once more to change clothes, and back to the garage where a mad rush to the Otoonga Hospital was undertaken. These antics were accompanied by a considerable amount of nervousness, breathlessness, and freaking out.

A nurse at the Otoonga Blessed Light Hospital informed me that Azailia had not checked in. "Someone who must have been her husband drove to the Angel of Mercy Hospital in Crestfallen with her in the back seat. Her doctor was there overseeing another birth in progress."

I staggered out to the car. Racing another twenty miles to Crestfallen brought another bout of near hysteria to break forth. Poor Azailia, with that good for nothing Barney chauffeuring her around to who knows where. And the little pigs, what will happen to them with nobody to love them. Will they all die?

At the Angel of Mercy Hospital, sure enough, there sat Barney's beat-up 1961 Buick, slanting at an odd angle a few cars down the line. I rushed up the hospital walkway, there to find Old Barney himself, standing outside the entrance. He was chomping on a cigarette with a big, toothless grin on his face.

"You don't have a thing to worry about, Myle," he smirked. "I reckon I got everyting under control."

"Barney, I'm almost mad at you. I wanted you to be taking care of the little pigs. I was supposed to be taking Azailia to the hospital, not you."

"Well, I decided to bring her here, and she didn't object none since she knew you was busy out in the hog house, you know."

"No, Barney, you got it all wrong. But it's too late now. How is she doing? Is she really in labor, or is it just a false alarm?"

"She's doin' fine. I stayed with her in the labor room, too," he said proudly.

"You mean to tell me she is in the labor room already? Where is the labor room in this forsaken place?"

"No, Myle, they took her to the delivery place not long after we got here, you know."

"You're not saying she is in the delivery room now, are you Barney?"

"No, she's out of there by now."

That did it. I backed against the wall, slumping down so far that I ended up sitting on the floor. I was trying to faint but couldn't quite pull it off. Somehow words were gasped, "The baby hasn't been born yet, has it? Say it isn't so, Barney."

"Well sure. When the nurse brought him out of there she gave him to me to hold. She thought I was the father. He was bawling his head off, but quieted right down when I held him."

Of all the rotten, putrid luck, this takes the prize. From my comatose state Bad Self began harping, "What's Azailia going to say about this? Not being present at the birth of your sixth child. She will think you love the pigs more than you do her."

"Barney. Did you say HE? Isn't it a girl this time?"

"Nope. But he's the spittin' image of you."

"Not another boy. We were hoping for a girl."

Six boys. Good Self said, "It could have been worse. He could have been twins."

The nerve of that Barney. The nerve of him! Assuming the role I was to have played. He was supposed to have been in the hog barn. On the other hand, maybe it was good that he wasn't there. In his usual condition he could have clipped off their ears instead of their teeth. Barney is an expert at goofing things up. There will be a lot of little pigs dying because no one is present to save them. What will happen if they all die? Bankruptcy court is sure to get me.

Picking myself up from off the floor, a decision was made to go immediately back to the farm. Good Self intervened by admonishing, "Aren't you going to see your new little boy? Or Azailia either?"

This so shamed me that I began shuffling my way toward the nursery under the direction of Old Barney, of course, who knew the way very well. He had to be the one to point out which baby was mine. The baby didn't look a bit like me. He must have taken after Azailia's side of the family. His face was red as a beet and he was bald as an eagle. While I looked at him, his facial expression changed from angelic to angry (as if to say his father had been derelict in his duty). In my current disposition we could have started an argument between the two of us at once.

Old Barney also proudly led me to my wife's room. It took a few minutes to get up enough nerve to enter. Barney was ordered to stay outside. She was lying with her eyes closed, white as the sheet that covered her. There was a peaceful look on her face, which calmed my fears somewhat. Her eyes opened as I approached the bed.

"Honey, I'm so sorry I wasn't here when you needed me."

"It's over now. Someone had to be with the little pigs when they were born."

"I sure didn't intend for Barney to bring you here. He was supposed to be helping in the pig barn. I wanted to be here with you at a time like this."

"Maybe it came out better this way, Myle. You know how nervous and upset you got whenever the other boys were born."

Once again I realized what a wonderful person she was. Offering consolation to me when she should have been the one to receive it.

"Yeah, sometimes I do get a little upset when things go wrong. It is just as hard on me as it is you whenever one of the boys were born," I replied, with a little feeling of guilt afterward.

"Have you seen the baby yet?"

"I just came from the nursery. He had a lot of wrinkles and a red face. He looks a lot like you. It sure is disappointing not to get a girl this time. How are we going to manage with six boys? One good thing is that we won't have to buy a lot of clothes for a girl. The boys can all get by with hand-me-downs. What new clothes we have to buy we can get at the used clothing stores."

"Have you decided on a name for him yet, Myle? It is your turn since I named the last one."

"Yeah, I had a name all picked out. Charlotte. Guess we can't use that now." A little later I remarked, "One thing is for sure, we aren't going to name him Barney."

We bantered small talk for awhile, like how she was feeling, how I was holding up under this ordeal, and what the future might hold. Abruptly I said, "Maybe I should be getting back to the farm. Got to see how the sows and pigs are doing. And in a couple of hours somebody will have to get the boys some breakfast. I don't know how I'm going to manage without you. I hope they don't keep you long in this place. Tell the doctor you got work to do at home." While her eyes were closed I kissed her goodbye and tip-toed out the door.

Driving home, my mind became dulled by so much arguing between Bad Self and Good. Fate had dealt me a cruel blow—another boy! And him born under the watchful eye of Old Barney. Yet my suffering could have been multiplied if Old Barney had been drunk like he usually was and had a car wreck that would have left me wife-less with five or six boys to raise (depending whether the unborn baby would have lived through the accident or not), and I wouldn't have been able to drive any more of those motor homes that were always beautiful, magnificent and dazzling. Nor would I have any more fabulous adventures to experience, no more airplanes to ride, or any waitresses to serve my coffee. Instead of grumbling I should be counting my blessings, like the preacher says every Sunday. Hopefully, in a few days Azailia will be well enough to do the hog chores again whenever Barney is too sick to help. Life is full of trouble and woe, but once in awhile a ray of sunshine pokes through the dark clouds long enough to sunburn your nose. Yet when felicity becomes too powerful of an objective, one may discover it has been countermanded by instauration diabolical in nature, subverted through nihilism, and thwarted with perversity, giving way to miscalculation, perturbation, and vituperation, all because one has chosen not to abandon motor home driving.

Chapter X

Houston Debacle

As the warmer days of springtime began advancing, acceleration of farm activities were paramount, but were not so confining as the pig farrowing had been. Planting preparation, machinery repairs, and pig weaning took precedence, along with innumerable diaper changings in the upstairs bedroom. I sought for a convenient time to again place my name on the driving list compiled by Miss Missmossmus at the dispatch office. Another mouth to feed added to the burden of a heavy schedule. You must understand that it wasn't necessarily repulsive to be standing knee-deep in doo doo out in the barn, but to change one diaper after another sort of affected me in a negative manner, so to speak. Not that I did not welcome the new little guy, nor was there even one streak of laziness running up and down my spine. How can I best explain it? Perhaps becoming hooked on motor home driving had somewhat altered adversely the fact that diaper changing had somehow lost the appeal it formerly held.

Life took on new zest with interest sky-rocketing and spirits soaring in anticipation with each telephone ring. When at last a summons was issued, through the voice of Mr. Hummer, my ears tingled, heart leaped, and voice quaked.

"Since your name is back on the chart, it lines up with a unit going to Houston. Can you come in this afternoon to pick it up?"

"Sure, Mr. Hummer, that will be no problem," I heard my voice saying.

"The dealer wants it there by Thursday."

"I won't wait until this afternoon. I'll come right up."

Soon as the phone was placed on the cradle, second thoughts came rushing forward while Mr. Bad Self engaged his throttle, "What is Azailia going to say about leaving so soon after the baby is born? Will Old Barney be willing to take on the burden of caring for another 276 little pigs? Will Jane continue helping? What if the boys don't get over their colds and snotty noses? What if the baby keeps getting the bellyache?"

Not waiting for Good Self to reply, I cowardly yelled up the stairs to Azailia that Mr. Hummer was forcing me to take a trip to Houston and there was no possible way to get out of it. A quick call was made to Old Barney, supplies were thrown together, and a valiant jaunt to the dispatch office took place.

The unit waiting for me, a 34-foot Osporter Cruiser, was parked in the outpatient area in Lot 4, Row 96. It was a sleek, streamlined model with sloping front to pacify the opposing winds. Multi-colored zig-zag designs were installed along both sides. It contained two air conditioners, a television set in the bedroom, California mirrors, tinted side windows, fog lights, truck horns, and two sets of duals on each side in the rear. Four rooms graced the interior. Bedroom, bath, shower room, and a combination dining-living-driving room all in one. The bedroom contained a huge queen-sized bed, two closets, two ceiling lights, four wall lights, an oak night stand, Venetian blinds, a soft pink carpet, and a folding door that latched tightly at the end of the hallway. Positioned along one side was a shower room with pink ceramic tiled walls and floor, complete with sliding glass door. Across from the shower was a large closet with a drawer at the bottom. Directly across on the opposite side was the bathroom with a sparkling lavender tub on on end, separated by a stool and sink which were in deep violet hue, while the contrasting walls were embossed in a bright, glossy pink design. A gleaming mirror with golden frame hung over the purple enclosed shelves, brightening the decor in flashing charm. A ceiling exhaust fan purred softly at the flick of a switch. Directly ahead of the closet was the open kitchen, containing an orange four-burner stove, glossy pink microwave oven, glittering green sink, two-door yellow refrigerator, and a ceiling aerating fan. On the opposite side of the kitchen was an oak table with plush soft benches that would seat four. A combination interwoven purple-pink diagrammed fabric covered the benches. Behind the drivers seat was a bright yellow sofa that would make into a bed. This too was covered with the same colored material which dazzled the eyes. On the other side were two swivel chairs with matching color and fabric as the sofa. Along the side walls were walnut cabinets reaching to the ceiling, with spring loaded door latches that snapped open like a charm. The same fuzzy pink carpet extended from the bedroom to the living compartments, except that the kitchen floor was covered with lavender-hued ceramic tile.

It is next to impossible to remember all the attractive features that graced this awesome unit, since there were so many. Oh, yes, there was an electric stop that magically sprang forward whenever the side-entry door was opened. Gadgets, gauges, lights, buttons, horns, fans, and needles not only were manipulated from the dash and front, but were also randomly positioned from floor-to-ceiling in hard-to-find places. A driver's door, passenger door, and side entry allowed easy access or departure (if you knew which one you wanted). And wonder of wonders, a back-up television screen hung in the dash, showing what was on the road behind the vehicle, whenever the gears were shifted to reverse or the "on power" button was engaged while the motor was running.

These luxury models make all to wonder where all the money was coming from. Anyone able to purchase one of these outlandish machines must be wealthy, over his head in debt, or insane. A lot of rich guys are running around the country in one of these things, taking up more space on our crowded highways. This causes a pause for deep contemplation in consideration of the thousands of homeless people lying in the streets of our large cities, to see starving children begging for bread on every street corner, and to observe so many naked people standing in line at the welfare office. Since our country is broke with a five trillion debt draped over our shoulders by high-flying presidents and a mindless Congress, the average person would say, "What the heck, let's live a little."

Because they are "living a little" is why I am able to drive one of these luxury models now and then. But I've got an answer that would solve our country's problem. Since our good old USA is the only super power, why don't they pass a law that requires every man, woman, and child to pay our government a thousand dollars each, allowing our country to become debt free, and then Congress could go on a spending spree greater than ever. On the other hand, who am I to criticize our government when I am broke myself? The debt of $75,000 for machinery, hogs, household furniture, and baby doctors is only half as much as this Osporter Cruiser costs, it with a diesel engine even.

The trip itself was more or less a humdrum affair for the first four hundred miles. Good weather was encountered except for a pesky side wind that wanted me to drive in the opposing lane of traffic. Two-lane highways were prominent in southern Missouri and on through Arkansas, forcing cessation of one-hand driving and a more careful approach to the entire undertaking. A few large cities had to be conquered, encountering numerous traffic snarls in the process. When the Ozark Mountains hovered overhead, the condition of being half asleep at the wheel had to be abandoned. By skillful manipulation the sharp curves and narrow roadways were successfully subdued. The first day of journey climaxed near the town of Rogers, Arkansas where the Ark-Kan-Saw Multipurpose Truck Haven became my abode for the night.

This abode supplied provisions for food and drink, allowed purchases of fuel and travel needs, employed able mechanics for assistance in case of flat tires or motor failure, furnished shower facilities, and above all provided parking spaces for motor homes. During the eight hours off duty, I was able to eat an evening meal, found time to work on my log book, jogged a half mile for exercise, read the Rogers Daily Chronicle, spied on the gal parked just ahead, and crawled in my sleeping bag for a few hours of much needed rest.

Rays of sunlight split an eastern sky as departure was made from the busy plaza the next morning. Escaping the harsh weather from the north allowed for a pleasant day, enjoying the pleasure of traveling, and to experience self-fulfillment in the highest degree. Until heavy traffic, sharp curves, road detours, slow moving vehicles, one-lane bridges, and tailing trucks reversed the equanimity. I am constantly exasperated by the truck drivers that clog our roads, yet I consider them my buddies on the road, facing experiences many times worse than what I encounter. They are forced to drive in all kinds of bad weather and road conditions whereas I usually have a choice. My driving is only one way, while they are in perpetual motion. Most of their rigs are twice the size of mine, which multiplies the potential difficulties. Cargoes are picked up and delivered at all hours of the day or night, involving inspections from suppliers, delivery clerks, and highway commissions. So it is with deep admiration that my hat goes off to them, even though most drivers are mean, cantankerous, bossy, and big-bellied.

The second day dragged slowly by. A continuation of stop and go, passing semis, darting in and out, all can leave a scar on the nervous system. That night was spent in the parking lot of an all-night roadhouse where pop, potato chips, candy, hot dogs, and beer were on the listed menu.

My intention was to arrive early the third day at Nutsonville, the suburb of Houston which was the delivery point. It is expedient to arrive early in the morning if possible, permitting more chances for bus or plane departure. To accomplish this I was forced to drive through downtown Houston at 5:00 a.m. Apparently every other driver in Houston was doing the same—trying to beat the morning rush hour two hours early. A sigh of relief was uttered when the Nutsonville RV Center came into view. After such a harrowing trip, you can believe that many sighs of relief were uttered. Although the office had not yet opened, the night attendant showed me where to park and hose off this beautiful, magnificent, dazzling Osporter Cruiser. Ample time was thus provided to get the papers in order, pack my bags, change clothes, and to devour a light breakfast of steak and eggs, biscuits, fries, pancakes and coffee in the cafe across the street. I had dusted and cleaned the inside, washed off the dirt and grease spots on the exterior, and made everything a place of beauty, magnificence, and dazzle. So I thought.

The checker man, as we drivers call them, was a woman. She was big, stout, and towered over me like a giant sequoia. Did she ever inspect that unit! All the time she was very pleasant and courteous, however. That poor vehicle was scrutinized from top to bottom, from stem to stern, and from hood to spare tire. No scratches, dents, marks, or rock chips could be found. "Looks like y'all did a good thing of gettin' this ole baby down here," were her words of appraisal.

Wow, did that make me feel superior! To think that such an excellent job of driving and cleaning had been done! While the checker woman was inspecting the interior, I was basking in pride. To my dismay, this basking had not long to last. An angry outcry proceeded from inside. As she came out of the unit her face was contorted in rage. She didn't speak a word at first, just stared at me scornfully.

"Did you find something wrong? As far as I know, this baby is in number one excellent condition."

She kept staring, eyes blazing, and with pencil tapping spasmodically against her notepad holder.

"I sure don't know of anything wrong inside. Did you find something that is?" Uneasiness was beginning to take control.

"How did you think you could get by pulling a trick like that? If y'all don't clean it up, I'm going to reject this unit and y'all can drive it back to where it came from."

"I'm sorry, I don't know what you are talking about.

"Well, come inside and explain what you did in the bathroom."

We both went inside the vehicle. I cautiously opened the bathroom door but was unable to observe anything out of place, missing, or damaged.

"Look under the toilet seat, and don't act so innocent."

"I don't make a practice of looking under toilet seats, but I will if you say so," was my nervous reply.

Inside the stool was the awfullest mess seen by the eyes of man. We aren't allowed to use the bathroom but she must have thought I had broken the rules. I was aghast. All I could say was, "It wasn't me who did it. I didn't know it was even there. Somebody else did it. I don't know who it was."

"Don't y'all check these units before y'all drive them? What kind of a driver are y'all anyway?"

"I did check it over real good. How did I know somebody snuck in here and did something like that?"

"I tell y'all what. Y'all better clean up that mess or start drivin' back to Otoonga."

"Yes, Ma'am, I'll try to."

"Trying isn't good enough. You clean that mess up or else."

As she strutted out the entry door I began pondering what I could do since there was no water in the holding tank to flush it. Bad Self tried to offer condolence, "That old man Hummer, he's the one to blame, sending you out on the road with a full stool. You can give him a piece of your mind when you get back."

Evidently someone at the factory was the culprit. Either they were angry at their foreman and chose this way to get even, or they couldn't wait. From the looks of things, it might have been a conspiracy with several culprits involved.

Bad Self: "Now what are you going to do, Myle?"

Good Self: "Use your brain. You can surely think of something to get out of this predicament."

Luck was kind of with me in a way. A plastic spoon was still lodged in my pants pocket from the last foray at McDonalds. By the mechanics door sat an empty oil can. A few drops of water were squeezed from a garden hose lying nearby. A pair of pliers and a screwdriver were found in my satchel, both of which proved to be a big help in the upcoming endeavor. A handkerchief from my back pocket was another life saver. A clothespin from my overnight bag was a remedy to repulse fainting, when adequately applied over the nostrils.

What an arduous task it proved to be. I won't go into detail except to mention that a lot of gagging, spitting, and crying could have been observed. A difficult hour was endured by spooning and digging, scraping and scratching, wetting and wiping, and finally, disinfecting with my after-shave lotion. I was then able to rise a victor, having victimized the motor home's most modest interior.

Why did this have to happen to me? It spoiled the entire trip. I'll never come back to this smelly town of Houston again! How could such an overwhelming obstacle deliberately fly in my face? Yet somehow perseverance must be kept on, defeat must be conquered, giving up has to be given up, and continuation continued if success is to be found in this meaningful occupation. Going ballistic wasn't the answer, although the temptation was there. The results promoted a painful case of hemicrany, an acceleration of hypesthesia, and caused a dreadful onslaught of hystriciasis, nor was there any noticeable minimizing of liver spot enlargement. Yet completely losing my cool was verifiably unsubstantiated, even by the most nosy passerby glancing a look into the dealer's lot, where the battle had enraged. Proud was I that a commendable job of cover up had been covered up, although a cheerful outlook was somewhat negated thereby.

After another round of scrutinization by the checker woman, my papers were reluctantly signed, permitting one sorry driver to stagger through the doorway of the Uscarem Taxi. My intentions were to fly back to Otoonga but changed my mind when consideration was given of the high cost of taxi, the outrageous prices of food and fuel, and paying two people to do the work of one back home. Mental deterioration took place on the miserable bus ride, the entire one thousand miles. But I could hold my head high, having faced that dreadful encounter with bravery, efficiency, and an undaunted spirit. To avail oneself of life's opportunities, to climb the mountain of success, overcome the most devious of devil's plots, direct one's steps through the maze of despair, and to amble where angels fear to tread, one must be prepared for any eventuality, even if it means looking under toilet seats to get there.

CHAPTER XI

Moonstruck in Montreal

"Azailia! Mr. Hummer called while you were changing the baby. He gave me strict orders to come to the office right away. I am being forced to drive to Montreal."

Mr. Hummer had issued instructions for delivery, when it was to be dispatched, where the port of entry was located, and which Canadian broker was to be contacted regarding entry fees and permits. This delivery was to be to a foreign country, different from a normal business contract between two parties in the United States.

Hog priorities were soon cared for, Barney and Jane were contacted, the wife and kids were kissed goodbye, and a mad romp to the office took place. Awaiting in Row 274, Lot 5 was a flashy 29-foot bed-over-the-cab model which appeared to be in perfect running condition. In spite of all the unpleasantries one may encounter, weather imperfections threatening in a moment's notice, and confronting potential evils at each blink of an eye, this trip promised exciting adventure, causing extreme inspiration to abound. Anticipation swept over me even though I am a constant victim of pessimism regarding the future, both past and present. This would be the first time my feet can enter the great city of Montreal. The first time in Canada, or any foreign country for that matter. A provoking sensation creeped charismatically through each nerve ending, dismissing the previous set-backs in such cities as Chattanooga, Houston, and Tulsa. How many Midwestern farm boys have experienced such as an adventure as this? I fully intend never to boast or brag of my accomplishments, but this may prove to be an exception. Bad Self attempted an interjection, but he was hushed up with a smile.

Everything seemed to be going in my favor all the way to the Canadian border. The usual traffic snarl south of Chicago dissolved like a vapor. The highways through Indiana and Ohio were a pussy-cat, bypassing Toledo and Cleveland as if by magic. The toll roads dodging Buffalo and Rochester are so expensive that the rich can't afford to pass over, so traffic was minimal. Since the factory pays all our tolls, state-entry fees, and bridge crossings, we Otoonga drivers need only to worry about feeding the fuel tanks and our own mouths.

It wasn't difficult to make a great impression on myself by using the cruise control, turning the radio dial to some easy- listening music, drive with only one hand on the wheel, and to doze off a second or two when other vehicles weren't close by. Driving smart is my forte. Very few other drivers have learned this secret. You see, if the speed limit is 60, you can be sure 99% of other drivers are going 70 or better. My cruise control usually gets set at 65, which provides opportunity to sit back and relax with no worries about passing or jockeying for position. This enables me to enjoy the music, the scenery, and delicious snacks while the trucks and all other vehicles are in a tizzy trying to pass me and each other. You will find that the miniscule 1% that drive slow like I do, cause very few problems. You only see one of them about every half hour, so it doesn't cause much concentration. It pays big dividends to drive smart like I do. Driving smart means contending with only two or three bad accidents a year if I'm lucky.

The approach to the Canadian border occurred on the third day of driving. Several signs warned that a stop at customs check was essential. No inspection was required on the U.S. side where I was quickly waved forward. Stopping at the guard shack for the Canadian check was a different story. It was demanded that entry papers, manifests and other documents be presented. After I handed over the required packet of papers, shocking words came out of the official's mouth, "You don't have a shipping manifest in here. Where is it?"

Dumbfoundedness crept over me. "I don't know. It should be in there. Those are the only papers they gave me."

"If this is all you have, you don't have a shipping manifest. No manifest, no entry," was his sarcastic reply. "You can take this packet to your broker's office to see if they will let you in the country. Otherwise turn around and go back to where you came from."

"Can you tell me how to get to that office?" I was whimpering in dismay.

"To get to the broker's department you drive straight ahead for seven signal lights and then make a right turn. Go over the iron bridge, turn left at the next intersection and then drive 2 1/4 kilometers until you see three parking lots. Don't stop at the first two. The third one is where your broker is located. Park in the designated area and walk three or four blocks down the blue sidewalk that leads to a brick building where you go to the third door on your left or else the second on your right. Don't go wandering around. You don't have permission to go anywhere in Canada until you have a shipping manifest. Now move your big box out of here, you're holding up a line of cars waiting to go through."

"Yes sir."

By the time this colorful oration had come to a conclusion, a fast-diminishing confidence was gaining ground. How will it be possible to find my way around in this evil foreign country with such impossible instructions? Bad Self took command, "Now you're in trouble big time, Myle. Comin' all the way from Otoonga without a shipping manifest, you dummy! Why didn't you check your papers before starting out? You might be incarcerated in this place until Hummer sends the right documents."

My heart sank in fear as this agonizing prospect sprang forward. Envisioning being imprisoned in some underground dungeon on bread and water caused a drooping of the eyelids, a shaking of the hands, and a stammering of the tongue. They might accuse me of smuggling this motor home into the country without paying duty. That Hummer is going to get told a thing or two, sending me to Canada without a shipping manifest. If I ever get back. And that Missie-moss is going to hear it, too. She's the one that does the paper work.

After several wrong turns, reversals, and asking directions from the local foreigners, somehow the correct parking lot was discovered. I was able to squeeze in between two eighteen wheelers, both of whom were parked on my side of the paint marks, since that was the only space available. The next task was to follow the blue sidewalk to the correct office.

"To get to the broker's office you follow that alley between the red-frame building and the Office for the Canadian Blind. Go two blocks past the Sky Patrol House, turn a half block left past the Highway Black-top Shed, turn left again at the yellow brick Canadian Dept. of Eskimo Affairs until you come to an office with a red-striped door. Proceed through the hall, turn left at the open doorway at your right, go down four steps and turn right at the flashing yellow pole, go up twenty-nine steps to the fourth floor and go down the hall to your right until you come to an alcove surrounded by glass windows, turn right until you see door number 32. You can't miss it." These were the directions given by the guard in front of the Welfare Office for Displaced Americans. He had a bayonet sticking from the end of his rifle, too.

Sure enough, after twenty minutes of hall meandering, there it was—door number 32. Only I was somehow on the wrong floor. A reversal was made to the next hallway to door number 65 where ten steps led upward to the correct floor. Door number 32 contained a painted sign on the door reading, "Exenphilbilia and Jehoramed," Custom Brokers, the same names that were on my documents.

Timidly I approached the counter inside while grasping in my fingers the packet that contained all the important papers except a shipping manifest. "The customs officer guard told me I didn't have a shipping manifest for a motor home to be delivered to Montreal. He told me to come here to see if you can help me," I managed to utter.

"You're Mr. Heyers? Your office faxed the information we need. You may have a seat along the wall, please. We will have you on your way in fifteen minutes," said the most wonderful matron lady this side of the Arctic Circle.

Wow! Relief was pouring out of my skin all over. Instead of being imprisoned maybe 500 feet below ground in some Canadian dungeon for motor home smuggling, I would be free and on my way to Montreal in fifteen minutes! Suddenly in an exclamation of joy that knew no bounds, I foolishly blurted out, "You're such a wonderful person, I could just kiss you."

That was the wrong thing to have said, because the entire office immediately became stony silent. The typists paused and stared straight ahead, the pencil pushers held pencils in mid-air and the waiters-in-line from the States found their mouths flying open. You see, everything is taken seriously in Canada. There is no jesting, small talk, laughter, or even a handshake in this dreadful country. Eskimos can shake off their snow, Indians can ruffle their feathers, but let a State-side guy open his mouth the wrong way and he's had it. I could feel my countenance dropping to a new low. Very slowly things got back to normal. I stumbled my way over to a chair along the wall, slouching down beside a forty-ish man with a heavy black beard and with legs akimbo.

"How you doin' man?" I asked with a cracking voice.

"Don't ask me how I'm doing, Jake," he muttered, with anger in his voice and bitterness in his demeanor. "I been sittin' here for two hours waitin' on these numbskulls to get my paper work finished, and I'm about to tell them what I think again. I already told them once but it didn't do any good."

"They let me by quite easy," I replied. "That lady in the grey uniform said I'd be on my way in fifteen minutes."

"No, you won't. You're not gettin' ahead of me. I been sittin' here 'til the cows come home, and I'm ahead of you. Haven't had no smoke for all that time and I'm about to go bananas."

"As far as I'm concerned you can go ahead. No, what I mean is go ahead of me first. Not go bananas," I said, trying to cover up my chagrin.

But we both kept sitting there. Way past fifteen minutes. And kept on sitting. Realization of what was happening hit me with full force. We were being punished, Canadian style. We both had said the wrong thing in this office and were now paying for it.

Nearly an hour later my grouchy seat mate was called to the desk where his release papers were finally issued. As he passed through the doorway he muttered in a bitter complaint, with a few obscenities and profanities all mixed together. Immediately after he left the office, the matron lady in the grey uniform picked up the telephone. This meant more trouble for that poor, unfortunate victim, of this I was certain.

Shortly afterward, my name was called by this same lady who presented my release papers also. She also instructed me to proceed to the parking area. All during the time I was at her desk the entire office again became noiseless, presumably to discover if my threat to kiss her would be carried out.

While making my way to the parking area, I was appalled at the sight confronting me. Across the tarmac was the sorry spectacle revealing a man being punished by those in authority over him. Our instruction pamphlets gave the warning: BE VERY POLITE AND OBEY ALL ORDERS FROM FOREIGN INSPECTORS. Evidently this poor man had evoked their wrath, as that telephone call had proven. Mouthing off to authorities doesn't pay, as he was now finding out. Under pretext of a drug search, he was forced to unload his cargo, box by box. Each container of groceries had to be opened separately while the inspectors were presumably checking each one. In reality, they were lounging around, laughing, telling stories, and smoking cigarettes. This was the

Canadian way of getting even with some State-side complainer who over-stepped his limitations.

While feeling sorry for the guy, Bad Self pipes up, "What are you feeling sorry for him about? You better start feeling sorry for yourself. Don't you know you've got to wait until those inspectors finish checking his cargo before they can inspect yours?"

He was right. These same officials must be the ones to search my unit, leaving a long wait to endure. What a discouraging development. Another two hours passed before the canned vegetable cargo was released. By this time my fingernails had been chewed to the bone, holes had been worn in the bottom of my shoes, and my head was wobbling back and forth. Patience wasn't my main characteristic.

Finally, the driver was leaving, permitting me the expectation that the inspectors would come to my unit next. That wasn't happening. One of the officers hurriedly left the premises while the other one was stashing papers in a briefcase. I quickly ran over to where the stasher stood, saying, "I'm next in line. Would you like me to drive my motor home over here for you to inspect it now?"

"Sorry sir, it is past closing time already and we can't possibly handle any more inspections today. You will be first in line in the morning."

"You're not saying that I have to stay in this stinking—"

"You may leave your carriage parked where it is," he interrupted. "You aren't allowed to leave these premises but you may sleep in it here." He then disappeared inside the Customs Office, with the last word, "Cheerio."

Needless to say, I was flabbergasted. And horror stricken. This was unbelievable. After waiting six hours and fourteen minutes, still not allowed across the border? I rushed into the office to see if perchance some official could yet inspect it. The reply was negative, as I knew beforehand. I asked one of the clerks, "What am I going to do for the next fifteen hours, waiting for the office to open tomorrow morning? Isn't there a cafe around here someplace?"

"Sorry sir, no cafe. There are vending machines across the pavement."

This can't be happening! How much bad luck can one guy have? To top it off, the vending machines would only accommodate Canadian coins, allowing for hunger and starvation to set in. How would I get any sleep under such frustrating conditions? And the semis next door were roaring their motors all night long. How much more would I be forced to endure in this miserable occupation? To antagonize me, the Canadian full moon shone down with such ferocity, bouncing off the side windows and glancing from the mirrors, that being moonstruck could be the next problem. During this nerve-wracking ordeal, consternation was again prevalent, revoking a prior tendency toward hedonism, allowing monophobia to regain recusancy, and permitting an unbalanced psychosis to develop. The preacher last Sunday admonished our congregation to shut the door before the horse gets out, but what happens when the horse gallops away while you are still holding the bridle? You can be sure, nightmares of the baser sort were surging randomly throughout the entire night.

Hundreds of minutes later, dawn somehow broke, bringing with it a partial alleviation. When the eight o'clock bell chimed from my wristwatch, Canadian time (whatever that was), back on duty came the two officials. The fat one, with the British mustache, approached my unit and asked to view my papers. With a quick glance at the documents he uttered the most awful words I ever heard. "What were you doing staying here all night? Didn't you see the words stamped 'Approved for Entry'?"

"You mean I don't have to get this unit inspected? I stayed all night in this hole for nothing?"

"That's right," he smartly replied. "There was no reason for you to have remained here overnight. Your broker's office approved your entry and to make delivery to Montreal. We aren't required to inspect motor homes unless foul play is suspected."

"Why didn't you tell me that last night?"

"You didn't show us your papers. You asked us to inspect it. How could we tell that it had been released?"

"How did I know that?"

"Sorry for the inconvenience. Better luck next time. Cheerio." He ambled off.

Of all the troubles in motor home driving this tops them all! I was at the breaking point of complete hysteria. This was worse than having an accident, because an accident happens real fast and you don't have to wait around fifteen hours for it to happen.

Somehow I managed to maintain enough composure to drive out of that despicable place. Next came emotions of relief, hatred, and fear. Fear led the way because the morning rush hour into Montreal was the next obstacle to face. All road signs were printed in French, words that normal people have a difficult time deciphering. The imposing skyline soon loomed into view. The highway appeared to be leading in the opposite direction until straightening out by going over bridges and turn-arounds.

The dealership was located on the Rue de laPaloosa Parley Voo Boulevard, but how was it to be found in this weird foreign city? Who can you ask for directions when everyone speaks in some horrible foreign language? A stop had to be made at three different petrol stations before finding an attendant who could even speak sign language. He seemed to be saying to turn left at the third stop light, moving right at the second light thereafter, going backward one light, driving two kilometers down hill, turning right two blocks, whereupon the Parlay Voo Rec. Center was located, only seven more blocks to the left.

"Why are you so late? This unit was to have been here yesterday," said the gruff inspector with a French haircut, a French mustache, and who wore a French beret.

"Well sir, the Customs Office goofed everything up and wouldn't let me in the country like they were supposed to yesterday. It wasn't my fault."

"These delivery papers will be signed as being late." He was moody and sullen as most Frenchmen are in this obnoxious place.

To my credit, such an excellent job of driving and cleaning had taken place that he could find nothing amiss. This obligated him to release me with an otherwise good report. Surprisingly, the offer was made to transport my body to the airport, which I readily accepted. Hopes of conveyance by a uniformed driver in a stretch limousine were dashed when pulling up beside was a teen-aged mechanic's helper in a rusty '73 Dodge pickup. In spite of this odious chauffeuring, the jaunt to the Montreal Oak Leaf Airport was accomplished in record time, so how could one do much complaining?

Complaining came a little later. Another obstacle made an unwanted intrusion. No matter which ticket counter was approached, the same story was enumerated. There were no flights to Otoonga from this disgusting airport. There was no way to get there from here. I was stranded. A telephone call to the airport should have been made before coming out here. It probably wouldn't have done any good because I wouldn't have been able to talk over a French telephone anyway.

My next choice was to enlist a taxi to carry my debilitated carcass to the Canadian Black Dog Bus Station. This option was quickly abandoned when discovering the enormous cost of riding in a French taxi, especially since I was an American. Not only that, I still hadn't acquired any French play money to make recompense.

How disconcerting it was to walk the six kilometers from the airport to the Black Dog in downtown Montreal. How would you like to walk six kilometers down a foreign street, in a foreign country, and be surrounded by weird foreigners all that time? Not one person offered a kind word, even in French. It took nearly three hours (by Canadian time) to walk that long distance while carrying two heavy bags and trying not to cry. I had a great desire to see the fascinating city of Montreal. That desire came to pass. But not according to my intentions. What I did see was foreign motor cars, sullen and angry foreign people, and disjointed foreign buildings perched at cocked angles in haphazard array. Not a single Frenchman offered to give me a ride or to carry my bags. They could tell I was an American by my sallow look, limping gait, and smiling face. The French never smile. Canada sure does have a bunch of sour apples. The only way to find the Black Dog was to ask some American tourist.

How disheartening it was to learn that the next bus leaving for the U.S. didn't leave for another five hours. No place could be found to check my luggage since the baggage department had closed until morning. My time was wasted in the miserable bus station watching my bags so no foreigner could steal them. Instead of exploring the great city of Montreal, peering out a window at a blank brick wall had to suffice. My feet were so sore from the six kilometer walk that downtown sightseeing was out of the question anyhow. Travel brochures and tourist information portrayed the glamour, beauty, and fantasy of this metropolis, but how did I know? You can't prove it by me.

Darkness had fallen like a black curtain as the Black Dog Bus headed south toward stateside. A severe case of homesickness was developing along with an ordeal of lumps in the throat. Anything would have been given just to glimpse once more the smiling faces of Mr. Hummer and Miss Missmossmus. Old Barney and Jane would have looked like angels from Heaven. To anticipate seeing the lovely countenance of Azailia, to gather in my arms those six rowdy boys, and to feel the loving nuzzle of 296 little pigs and their 5 mothers, would have been paradise compared to the outrageous ordeals I had endured in this hateful country.

While immense rubber tires were churning an outward pass, hallucinations through horrifying dream sequences provided a ghoulish parade of fiendish apparitions, invoking curses of subliminal accusation, intensified by Bad Self interpolations. Such provocations left indelible marks upon my warped personality, which cannot be erased with a shrug of the shoulders or a negative reply. That's what a trip to Canada did to me. And the bus had to go through customs.

"Each of you must let me see your passport and other means of identification," stated the surly official who boarded our bus on the U.S. side of the border.

"I've got a passport at home but I don't have it with me, sir," was my reply when he approached me. "But I've got here a telephone number and a library card."

"You're saying you don't have a passport?"

"Yes, I said I got one but it is back home in Otoonga. I didn't need one to get out of the country so why should I need one to get back in?"

"You and all the rest of you people who don't have a proper identification will have to get off this coach. Follow me to that open door in the Custom House."

Starting again for me was another series of shaking and quaking. As I tottered out the door, Bad Self started in, "Now you are really in trouble. No passport. You can be incarcerated, don't you know? You ignoramus, why didn't you bring your passport?"

Coming to my rescue was the Other Guy who intervened with dignity and grace, "Don't worry, Myle. Show them your delivery documents and your driver's license. That will prove you are a U.S. citizen and will keep you out of jail."

All fellow passengers with questionable appearance and were young enough to be drug smugglers were required to be seated along the wall inside the station. What a motley, downcast bunch we all were. A yellow-skinned guy exiting Pakistan or Holland, two white guys with green hair, bare feet and nose rings, a short black man wearing a loin cloth and tattooed face, and a middle-aged woman in a red mini-skirt and purple bandana, all topped the list of undesirables, with me heading the list. (What I meant was, I was first in line.) The officials soon released me after viewing the delivery documents, but the others were led off to prison, weeping and wailing with tears in their eyes. To think that my fate could have been like that, caused a humble retrospect and a bowed head. How thankful I was that my birthplace was down in one of the lower forty-eight south of the border. A breath of fresh air greeted my lungs coming out of the customs building. It was a breath of freedom, even though it was awful close to the Canadian side.

I have a long time to count my blessings during the endless and bumpy ride back to Otoonga. Meeting all sorts of weird foreign people, waiting an endless twenty-one hours at the Montreal port of entry, walking three hours from airport to bus station amid cat-calls and stares, pleading valiantly in vain to unfeeling officials, riding forty-eight hours in crowded buses (changing four times, in Albany, Erie, Cleveland, Chicago, and St. Louis), barely overcoming starvation, and aging five years, all contributed to a backward retrospect into life's meaning but there didn't seem to be any. For sure, I'm never setting foot in that obnoxious city of Montreal where foreigners won't speak to you, ignore and insult, taking revenge with every attempt possible to throw you in jail. My decision was to remain forever at home on the farm the rest of my days and to find happiness with my pigs, wife, and boys. My driving days will have to end. There are just too many perils in motor home driving. Facing demeaning provocations was causing a fast increasing slowdown in attaining life's goals, as the rest of this story will prove.

CHAPTER XII

Kidnapped

Since diesel fuel was advertised eight cents cheaper at the Subterfuge Fuel Haven, it was natural that my unit abruptly exited the freeway and headed for the nearest fuel pump. Several other motorists evidently held the same conservative ideas, for there were extended waiting lines. The needle had registered near the empty mark, a very undesirable condition for a diesel-powered vehicle. It must have taken at least ten minutes to fill the empty tank. Meanwhile, inside the station were hot-dogs off the grill waiting to be devoured. The entire procedure must have taken nearly a half hour of time, an ample period for abnormal happenings to occur. The Spectacular Paradise unit under my supervision was indeed spectacular, with luxury dispensing from every joint and connection. It purred like a kitten when soaring down the open highways, but clattered like any old semi when idling or cruising at slow speed. The station was located off exit #379 on Interstate #4923, sixty miles east of Dallas. It was a warm April evening after sunset, the moon began showing its golden face over the eastern horizon, and it was a wonderful feeling to be absent from the chilly Midwest. The designated place of delivery was West Rattlesnake City, approximately two hundred miles south of Dallas.

After swallowing the smothered-in-onions hotdog and gulping down a can of green root-beer pop, I hopped back on to the drivers seat, energized and content. Things were going great, pigs and boys were free from illness and death, highways were wide and smooth, weather outlooks were in total cooperation, and all was right with the world. For awhile.

Such tranquillity was soon to be interrupted. While zipping along, relaxed and rejuvinated, and with the radio dial tuned to some sizzling Mexican music, an ominous sound could be heard coming from the rear. "You'll be in trouble big time, Myle, if something is wrong with this diesel motor," was the obtuse incantation Bad Self interjected. This became reason enough to shut off the rousing music, perk up my ears, and become alert. Maybe it was my imagination. These Spectacular Paradise units were equipped with motors in the rear and were called "pushers" by expert Otoonga analysts. Any noise from the rear aroused my negative, suspicious nature, causing lightning flashes to zigzag up and down my spine. Driving cautiously onward, ears protruding sharply upward, I waited for terror to strike. I didn't have to wait long. Again the noise was being heard. It was more like a bumping sound, rather than a motor discrepancy. Instead of alleviation to my fears, terror was striking, causing chills and sweat to break out simultaneously. Along with the bumping sounds, an audible voice was seemed to be heard.

"Oh, no. Get real! This can't be happening to a good guy like you, Myle. Somebody must be back there." Bad Self delighted in my misery. Do you suppose somebody was actually in the back of this motor home? If so, he must have sneaked on board while I was in the store paying for the gas and eating that delicious hotdog. My arms were going limp, the line of sweat on my brow was oozing down into my eyes, and losing control of the speeding vehicle was a distinct possibility. "Now what are you going to do?" Bad Self kept at his oration.

I continued driving, gripped with fright, knowing that at any time a hooded gunman could approach with a revolver pointed directly at me. He could force me to drive to a wooded area where my money would be stolen (which wasn't much because my billfold was nearly depleted from the enormous amount of fuel this machine had guzzled). He could shoot me dead, or stab me in the guts with a knife, or maybe just tease me along by shooting off my fingernails one by one until I bled to death. What a terrible mistake had been made by not locking the door after pumping fuel. Mr. Hummer and Miss Missmossmus had repeatedly warned us drivers, through office memos and verbal tongue-lashings, that we should always lock our doors when leaving our units. I had failed to obey, had disgracefully scorned their stern admonitions. What a fool I was. Now my life may be forfeited because of such carelessness.

Horrible thoughts were running pell-mell through my brain waves, interspersed with warnings from both Bad Self and Good. Should I ram this unit in the ditch, in hopes that the stowaway would be knocked unconscious? Should the brakes be suddenly applied so that the intruder would be thrown to the floor disoriented, and I could be a famous hero by overpowering him? Maybe I could bide my time, hoping he wouldn't make an appearance, and that I could deliver him and the unit together at the dealer's office?

Instead of following through on one of those options, the most foolish decision of all took place. I yelled out impulsively, "I know you're back there. You better come out and turn yourself in." Immediately I was disgusted at myself for being so foolish. What should have been done was to have turned off at the first exit, jumped out with keys in hand, ran inside the nearest store, called the police, and hid until rescued. Why hadn't I thought of this first?

I could hear the bedroom door slowly opening. Somebody was actually back there and approaching the front. It was becoming difficult to keep the vehicle on the road, being in the freaked-out condition I found myself. Out of the darkness came not one intruder, but two! They made their way slowly and cautiously to the front until they stood beside me. To my great astonishment, it was not hooded robbers that stood beside me. No, they were two small children who were almost as frightened as I was. What a relief came over me! A death experience appeared to be evaporating. My tears changed into smiles and I nearly cried for joy.

Good Self then asked the question, "What are those kids doing in your vehicle?"

"What are you kids doing in my vehicle?" An act of rigid authority was being assumed.

The children appeared to be no more than eight or ten years old. The boy, who was the oldest replied, "We came in here when you were in the gas station."

"That's just what I thought. You kids snuck in here when my back was turned. I can have you both put in jail for this, don't you know that?"

"No, you can't," said the little wisp of a girl, standing defiantly with arms crossed.

"Yes, I can."

"No, you can't."

"Yes, I can."

"No, you can't."

"Yes, I can."

"No, you can't."

"Why can't I?"

"Because Mamma said you couldn't."

"Your mother didn't tell you no such thing."

"Yes, she did."

"No, she didn't."

"Yes, she did."

"No, she didn't."

"Yes, she did."

"No, she didn't."

"Yes, she did."

"Well, I know your mother didn't tell you anything like that. You're running away from home, aren't you?"

"Yes, but she told us to."

"No, she didn't."

"Yes, she did."

"No, she didn't."

"Yes, she did."

"No, she didn't."

"Yes, she did."

"Well I know she didn't. What I'm going to do is to stop at the next town and take you to the police station. I'll tell them you have run away from home and they will put you in jail until your mother gets you out. Then we shall see who is right."

"No, you won't."

"Yes, I will."

"No, you won't."

"Yes, I will."

"No, you won't."

"Yes, I will."

"No, you won't."

The boy was the one who carried on the argument. "Because you are going to take us to our grandmother's house in Dallas."

"Oh, no I won't. That's the last thing I'll ever do."

"Oh, yes you will."

"Oh, no I won't."

"Oh, yes you will."

"Oh, no I won't."

"Oh, yes you will."

"Oh, no I won't take you to your gramma's house and you can't make me."

"Oh, yes we can."

"Oh, no you can't."

"Oh, yes we can."

"Oh, no you can't."

"Oh, yes we can."

"Oh, no you can't."

"Oh, yes we can."

By this time I was getting perturbed with these two upstarts. Two little kids causing all this aggravation. Who did they think they were? I decided to call their bluff with the question, "How are you little brats going to make me take you to Dallas?"

The boy answered, "Because we will tell the police you kidnapped us."

"No, you won't."

"Yes, we will."

"No, you won't."

"Yes, we will."

"No, you won't"

"Yes, we will."

With these threatening words that old nemesis of fear began inching its way up my spinal column. Bad Self sounded off, "Don't tell me, Myle, that you're being outsmarted by two little kids?"

Ignoring this insinuation I spoke out resolutely once more, "Then I'm going to fool you. I won't take you to the police station. I'll pull off the road and throw you both out of here. And you can walk home. You won't be so smart then."

"No, you won't."

"Yes, I will."

"No, you won't."

"Yes, I will."

"No, you won't."

"Yes, I will."

"No, you won't."

"Tell me, why ain't I going to throw you both out of here?"

The boy continued his role of spokesman. "Because Mamma wrote down your license plate number and she will report to the police that you kidnapped us if you don't take us to Grandma's house."

This sent shock waves multiplying throughout my nervous system, culminating in another round of trembling hands and sweating brow. I almost lost control of the vehicle. These ornery brats were really threatening me. Me, a motor home driver, being threatened by two little kids! If these menaces were carried out, I would end up being overcome by two children and an unknown mother. The children were too well coached to be bluffing. If their mother reported my license plate number to the police, my days of freedom would be over. It would be my words against the three of them, and the police wouldn't believe the words of a broken down motor home driver. Kidnapping is a terrible offense, worse than cocaine conviction. They would lock me in solitary and throw away the key. Stressed out degeneracy again overcame me, causing an accidental honking of the horn, bumping of my head on the sun visor, twisting and tangling my right arm in the shoulder harness, knocking my elbow against the steering wheel, and weaving from one side of the road to the other.

"How do you get in such a mess, Myle? You're in trouble now," Bad Self said accusingly.

So it came to pass that it was me, Myle Heyers, who was the one being kidnapped, not the children. This was the first time I had been kidnapped, although my father threatened to let that happen many times when I was a little boy. At the first main highway heading west, my unit made a right turn toward Dallas, fifty miles in the distance. What the outcome would be, was a mystery. Perhaps this was merely a hoax. The grandmother might turn me over to the police for having the children forced on her. Anything can happen when you are being held hostage.

"O.K., kids, you win. Why are you making me go to Dallas? What are your names?"

"My name is Jolene."

"And my name is Jonathan, but they call me Than for short," said the boy. "Mamma is having us go to Grandma's house to get away from Daddy."

"Why are you leaving your Daddy's house?"

"Because he is mean to us. He beats us. He beats Mamma, too."

"Why does your father beat you?"

"He comes home drunk and gets angry at us for no reason."

A closer look at the children under the dome light revealed a big welt on the boy's left cheek while the little girl had black swollen eyes, one of which was almost shut. For the first time, it looked like being kidnapped might turn into a good deed.

"Where does your grandmother live in Dallas?"

"At 3546 Stolen Child Lane," said Than.

"Where is that? I've not been on Stolen Child Lane before."

"We know the way. I'll tell how you get there when we get there," said Than.

On we rode toward the city of Dallas. The farther we traveled the more jovial the kids became. They were laughing and playing, no more afraid of me than of a fly. That mother must have been quite a conspirator to have devised such a plan as this.

About an hour later the lights of Dallas shown prominently in the western sky while the eyes of the children seemed to sparkle almost as brightly under the ceiling lights. Through the suburbs of Texasville and Rodeo City we passed. Hushed anticipation was evident as Than instructed where to exit the highway and which streets to follow. All at once Jolene screamed, "There it is, Grandma's house!"

I parked the unit across the street from where Jolene was pointing. The house was an old dilapidated two-story frame structure with an open front porch. On the porch sat an elderly woman in a rocking chair.

"It's Grandma!" they both yelled as out the door they ran. Grandma swept them into her arms with hugs and kisses. I bashfully strode across the street to meet the woman who was partly responsible for this intrusion into my life.

"Thank the good Lord," she cried. "I was so worried what might become of the children when Doris thought up a scheme like this. Thank you for helping us. You're such a nice man to bring the children here."

"It wasn't much trouble," I lied. "Anybody would be glad to help such wonderful grandchildren like you have."

"We can't thank you enough. I'm going inside this minute to call Doris and let her know that the children have arrived safely so she won't have to call the police."

"You mean she would have called the police if I hadn't brought them?"

"She certainly would have. But we're glad she didn't have to because you're such a nice man."

"Yes, I know," was my shy reply.

I didn't linger with them long. Jolene gave me a kiss on the cheek, Than offered me a thumbs-up, while the grandmother gave a warm embrace. Then I was out of there, only too glad to be away from the harmful potentialities that could have befallen me from this dysfunctional family.

Once again on the road toward West Rattlesnake City, numerous and jumbled thoughts were bouncing off the walls and ceiling of the Spectacular Paradise. Thoughts both evil and sublime. I was glad and mad, proud and embarrassed, heroic and cowardly. Arrogance welled up within me about this fulfilled courageous deed. How praiseworthy, exemplary, commendable, and honorable it was! Such a distinguished act might qualify me to be a kingpin in Heaven someday in the next life. This wonderful accomplishment would not result in a monetary reward, yet eternal memories of this admirable achievement would be reward enough, ceaseless in self-praise, locked in my heart forever, exemplifying goodness in a magnanimous overture.

Yet on the other side of the equation, I was thoroughly disgusted that this disgraceful episode had been thrust upon me. A wellspring of distrust against my fellow man left an indelible impression upon my nerve endings. Who knew but what an early demise from Alzheimer's, Ebola, or insanity could be the outcome. This experience has been the most humiliating experience that I've experienced. To think that two little kids had held me hostage! If this happens to me again sometime, I'm not going to pussy-foot, beat around the bush, or be such an easy pushover. It would have been better if they were robbers instead of those miserable little brats. I would have lost only money if they had been robbers. This way I lost my pride and self-worth, not to mention all the money it cost me to buy extra diesel fuel because of the extra hundred miles of driving. I was intensely hoping that Hummer wouldn't find out about the extra miles driven. Termination was a certainty for allowing your beautiful, magnificent, dazzling motor home get kidnapped by two little kids.

CHAPTER XIII

I and The Cab Driver

It was extremely hot, not an uncommon condition in central Florida in September. The drive down had been most pleasant except for the heavy congestion in Nashville, where perseverance required a slow crawl, mile after mile. Termination of the journey was at Flora Village to a car dealership, where motor homes were sold as a sideline. I was allowed to wash the unit in an open carport structure. This was quickly accomplished since three flunkies helped me. The inspector was a hard-nosed guy, but polite. Although he examined the unit thoroughly, no discrepancies could be found. He asked several point-blank questions as to how it ran, if there were any unusual vibrations, if the cruise control and air conditioner worked properly, if there were any marks on the furniture, and on and on. I gave accurate answers, never once telling a falsehood. He accepted my replies, signed the papers, and I was released. His only undesirable trait was that the company, under any circumstances, would not give rides to the airport. He asked me if he should call a cab and I reluctantly said yes.

Soon appearing was a black and white Yellow Taxi, operated by a tousled-haired younger man who opened the door for me and placed my bags in the trunk. He seemed at first to be a congenial fellow, accommodating and friendly. We swiftly headed for the airport in admirable compliance. Like the taxi, his mouth was fast running, an unusual habit for a cabbie. Most of his accomplices were sullen, sour-faced individuals who said very few audible words to their customers.

This guy gave a detailed interpretation of the Orlando scenario and of the alluring enticements for living in this area. He informed me of the many tourist attractions nearby, including the famous Disney World, Epcot Center, Universal Studios and many others. I told him I had visited all these places before and don't like to go to those places where all the senior citizens are taking all the rides and shows while the kids were in school. He continued spewing an oration about Orlando had more hotels and motels than anywhere in the world, perfect weather here was the norm, and that the greatest place to have fun was right here under my nose. Soon he changed the conversation by questioning my personal life, where I lived, how much the company paid me for travel, and if I had any rich relatives nearby. I told him that was a big joke, and then turned the tables on him by asking him a question, one that should have been asked prior to entering the cab.

"How far is it to the airport? How much is this ride going to cost?"

His answer was, "It's only about twenty-five minutes. We go over two toll roads, seven bridges, three highways, and zippo, we're there."

"Twenty-five minutes?" I said in shock, knowing that this wasn't going to be a mere ten or twenty dollar expense. The meter was already reading eight dollars and we had only traveled three minutes.

"It will only cost you about seventy bucks. This is the only way to go, man."

"Seventy bucks? I thought the airport was close to Flora Village. There's an airplane emblem on the map that shows like it was."

"That airplane mark on the map shows where the local airport training center is located. The Orlando airport is way to heck and gone, southeast of Orlando."

"It is? Wow, I might not have enough cash to pay your fare. But I've got a credit card though."

"Listen, Mac, the law says you got to pay your fare in cash money. I'm not a credit card bureau you know."

"Well, I don't mean you had to take my credit card. I meant that if I could get to a bank, I could get some more money. But don't worry, I think there is enough in my billfold to pay you off." I had been counting it, and there was at least seventy dollars, but very little more.

Soon after I had spoken, he changed streets and in about ten more minutes we parked in front of a convenience store. (This tipped me off that his scheme was to be charging me even more than seventy dollars.) Of course the meter was running all the time, even when I was inside the store, getting money from the teller machine. After getting back into the cab I realized that we were running over the same streets we were on before. Many warnings had I heard previously about how unscrupulous taxi drivers would cheat their customers, driving out of the way at the slightest pretext, thus enlarging their fares. Tales were told how some drivers would go in circles cheating innocent unsuspecting customers. Looking back, it wasn't difficult to understand that his deception was a well-practiced work of art.

"You're really socking it to me, aren't you?" These words were spoken with a twinge in my voice.

This seemed to rile him up for some reason. "Listen, Mac, I didn't ask to go for more money, you did. Now you're calling me a thief. You can call me what you want to, but the law is on my side. A rider has got to pay his fare. That's the law, Mac."

"I didn't tell you to go get more money. I just said IF I could go to a bank."

"You said you might not have enough money to pay me off. And you did not object none when we went to the teller machine."

"I had counted my money and I told you myself that I had enough money to pay you. I never once told you to go to a bank or anywhere else. I know what you're doing. You're pulling a fast one on me."

"We can just see about that," he said with bitterness and an angry look. "We will stop our little ride right here and now and go call the sheriff. Then you can learn what the law says. And the law is on my side.

Us drivers is due our fare. You're calling me a thief and a liar, and I don't take that lightly."

"I never once called you a thief. I only said you were socking it to me, that's all I said."

"We can stop our little ride and you can pay me off. Then you won't have to ride with a thief and a robber no more. The meter only reads $68.50. So if you want to pay me off now you can walk the rest of the way."

His offer didn't seem to be very appealing, being miles from nowhere, miserable traffic, and with alligators and snakes sneaking along the road. So I meekly replied, "No, we've come this far, we might as well finish the job."

He had me and I knew it. This sort of scheme had undoubtedly been played out many times before. At the first hint of changing courses for any reason, he could smoothly drive blocks and miles out of the way. The rest of the ride toward the airport came a loud tirade of people not knowing what they want, about riders trying to cheat him, his being called a thief, rich guys lording over poor cab drivers, and on and on. I was overwhelmingly defeated. For the rest of the ride, my lips were sealed shut, letting him rattle on. It has been said that a soft answer turns away wrath. If that be true, no answer to his harangue would end the fiasco.

During the last few miles, he too became silent. As we stopped in front of the Skyjack Airlines entry door, the meter read $108.75. I could barely extricate myself from the cab, I was shaking so badly.

There goes another trip's profit. What had I done to deserve this? In humble humility I said, "Here's your money. And I apologize."

He was so stunned upon hearing these kind words that his head slumped to his chest in shame and dishonor. This was like feeding your enemy. Good Self then whispered to me in adulation, "What a worthy, commendable act you have dome, Myle, to pay this outlandish fare and humiliate yourself before him. You're really a swell guy, Myle." And you know, Bad Self echoed the sentiments. When those two are an the same wavelength, I sit up and take notice. I had paid a thief money he shouldn't have received, portraying myself an unassuming hero to the world. How proud of myself I was. And in the confusion of it all I was able to get a little revenge—I didn't give him a tip, not one dime. This was posterior revenge committed in an unlikely manner.

Through it all you can easily see another warning to motor home drivers. Never, ever ride in a taxicab, no matter what. That crook made more money in thirty minutes than I did in three days, two hours and six and one-half minutes of driving to get down to this lousy place. It is far better to miss your heart doctor appointment, arrive at the airport five minutes after your plane took off, or to get to your daughter's wedding an hour late, than to ride in some foul-smelling taxi, where you are insulted, ostracized, and cheated by some low life who is out to grab his share of a crooked pie before you do.

I was mad, too. After such a demeaning, demoralizing condescension, my outlook on life was severely damaged. Such irrational conflicts disturb the sleeping giant in my subconsciousness, affecting a tendency toward future misconducts which exacerbate misappropriation in the highest degree while completely dispelling equanimity in sequential irregularities, and absorbing cynicism in a belligerent manner. The outcome of it all is continued health failure, perpetuated and accented by mydriasis of the eyes, myelitis of the spine, squeamishness of the stomach, mesognathous of the jaws, instability of the hair line, and a relentless abrogation of metabolic dependency. I'm never going back to that disgusting city of Orlando again. It harbors criminals, some of whom can be discovered lurking in taxicabs.

Good Self said during the plane ride back to Otoonga, "And you better quit driving motor homes altogether, Myle."

CHAPTER XIV

Left it Won't Go

About twenty-four miles east of downtown Indianapolis on highway 6397, the gas needle was fast approaching the empty mark. I was driving a used 33-foot Luxury Mobile which had been in an accident, having crashed into a cement viaduct, was repaired in the Otoonga Trailer repair shop, and was assigned to myself who was ordered to return it to Pittsburgh where its rightful owner lived. The most intelligent undertaking would be to pour in gas at the East 500 Truckstop located at the next exit. My intention was to turn left since the East 500 Truckstop was not located on the right side. This intention, however, was unrealized. This most beautiful, magnificent, dazzling vehicle, with no prior warning, refused to turn left. Every other attempt during this journey had been accomplished with grace and charm. But not this time. I cramped the steering wheel to the left with all my strength, but it simply refused the invitation. There was no other recourse but to coast through the intersection and to continue on to the entrance ramp on the other side. It was headed for a steep embankment, which if not navigated properly, offered destruction and death to everyone involved. Since I was the lone occupant, a single-grave plot would be all that was necessary, but this didn't provide any consolation at the time. By using all the skill and ingenuity at my disposal, I was able to concoct a most reasonable rationale. I slammed on the brakes! By so doing, destruction and death were circumnavigated. The unit was left precariously perched at the top of the embankment, just inches from oblivion, since it was nearly three feet to the bottom.

"Now what are you going to do, Myle?" Bad Self began harping.

Though the monster wouldn't turn to the left, it would turn right. By backing to the right, then going forward, backing again to the right, and once more going forward, it was finally parked off the roadway on the right side of the ramp. There we sat, the motor home and I, inoperative. And it was raining cats and dogs. And it was dark. And it was six o'clock in the morning. Orders from the Otoonga office permitted absolutely no telephone calls to headquarters unless being involved in an accident. Since this had not yet evolved into accident incident, I was left high and dry. High maybe, but not dry.

In desperation, yet not quite in the throes of freaking out, I found my flashlight, draped a jacket about my upper torso, and squeezed out the doorway, with hopes of crawling under the vehicle to discover what was wrong. That was a laugh. I am undoubtedly the most unhandy handy-man employed by Otoonga, and should not be driving motor homes for that reason alone, not to mention all the other reasons. While departing the unit, the rain seemed to be coming down harder than ever, as if in pent-up vindictiveness. Easing myself under the vehicle and using my flashlight was only adequate enough to reveal a profusion of rods, pipes, nuts, bolts, wires, hoses, shafts, steel frames, axles, and dead animals. When lying on my back, the motor kept the rain off the upper part of my body, but my feet and legs were getting soaked. The constant drip, drip was soon getting the rest of me in the same condition. I tried valiantly to find something wrong, but it was a useless attempt. When such ostentatious confugalties occur, it causes an explosion of degenerating apprehension, self-debasement in epic procurement, graduating into biological upheaval, evolving toward a destructive desuetude, which leads to opinionated desultory formative speculation involving wild forms of schizophrenia, and to a paralyzing obliquity, deviating primarily into unnatural conditions of irrational naumachia, and advancing toward psychopathic maturation, defeated outlook, along with intensifying, heterocyclic mesogastrium bordering on an unintentional spasmodic coercion ending up in a bad case of cranial atrophy.

In spite of such horrible circumstances, I was indeed fortunate because less than six hundred feet away was the desired truck stop, complete with breakfast bar, showers, and television room. To reach this desired objective, a short-cut was made. I locked the doors of the broken-down jalopy, scaled a barbwire fence, dodged the raindrops, and made my way to security in the lighted sepulcher. Sorry to say, the mud puddle by the fence was too large and the barbwire fence was too high. The result was a good soaking from the continuing rain, mud up to my knees from the puddle, and a rip in my pants from the barbwire fence.

Since I couldn't call the office for two more hours to register my complaint, a bite of breakfast seemed opportune. Being soaking wet, wearing mucky shoes, and displaying a hole in the seat of my pants didn't make any difference in a truck stop since all the other truckers were in the same condition. As long as you are wearing a shirt and shoes you pass inspection. No mention on the signs about pants. Sloshing nonchalantly up to the breakfast bar, I soon decided that the menu was not conducive to a fast-fading appetite. My stomach was already churning from shot nerves, and to see the bacon crawling around the gleaming shells in the scrambled eggs proved to be more than I could stand. Attention was instead directed to the fountain bar where devouring a hotdog and a cup of bitter coffee was endured.

For the next two hours my sole occupation was watching reruns of "Andy Griffith" and "I Love Lucy," while being perched uncomfortably on a bar stool in the television room. This endless waiting was far worse than the comparable two hours spent in Doc Johansen's office last summer after having been bitten by a mouse, wondering if it was rabid or not.

At the hour of eight a call was made to the Otoonga office where contact and response would be given from one of the unsavory characters in the breakdown department. Instead it was the booming voice of one Mr. Hummer who belched out the advisement to call back at nine which resulted in more television watching. A call back at nine said to call back at ten resulting in more television watching and more suspense. Another call at ten answered by Miss Missmossmus gave information that Mr. Hummer (who by that time was out playing golf with an important client) had commanded I should call a tow truck for a pull to the Moron Garage on the west side of Indianapolis, some twenty miles to the west. The tow truck girl reported that the truck would be a little late, allowing for still more television watching, including Lucy getting hit in the face three times with pies.

At eleven forty-nine I proceeded back to the stalled vehicle, trying to dodge the raindrops which by this time had stopped, wading through the mud hole that by now was drying up, and again crossing the barb-wire fence with the same result as before. The tow truck should have been here by now. This was not the case. It wasn't until twelve-thirty by my water-soaked watch that a huge truck arrived. Two of its wheels weren't even touching the ground, why I don't know. It was quite understandable why an extra large truck was needed, since the big baby I was driving was so large. Just any old truck would never do. After a considerable amount of hand wringing by myself, a few vivid cuss words by the tow truck man, and wow, connection was made. The next thing I knew was that the motor home had its front end off the ground. Would you believe that driver backed up the entire alignment sixty feet to the intersection, turned it completely around, and proceeded in the opposite direction while dodging through a whirl of traffic, and missing signs, guard rails, and pedestrians in so doing? While I sat bug-eyed in astonishment, he propelled the entire entourage through downtown Indianapolis at speeds exceeding sixty-five miles an hour!

At the repair shop destination he backed the unit into a narrow bay on the first try with only a blink of his eye, but it took several blinks from me. He did so directly through the middle of parked cars sitting in helter-skelter fashion, without so much as a scratch on a fender. I would have been scared to death to back into that narrow door like he had done, even if my life depended upon it. Which it probably does, because I'll be lucky to drive out of this awful place alive. The service manager reported a capable mechanic would work on it immediately, that there was a customer lounge on the door to the right, and there was a small diner down the street if I was hungry, which by this time I didn't know if I was or not. The diner proved to be another one of those fast food places where as many hotdogs and hamburgers could be devoured as one's heart and stomach desired. Looking at a greasy hamburger that some other idiot had ordered, caused me to opt for a hotdog instead. This wasn't a very good choice, for the hotdog too was smothered in grease. Two hotdogs in one day might cause stomach tumult. Which happened. The coffee was perhaps more bitter than the one drunk this morning, if that were possible…and it was.

Upon returning from the diner, I noticed the front end of the motor home had been lowered. This was a good sign that repairs had been made, causing my hopes to mount. Instead of repairs already made maybe they had given up on it altogether. I found a seat in the customer lounge, feeling certain that someone would soon be reporting a verdict of complete recovery. My heart skipped a beat in anticipation at every door opening, each telephone ring, and every noisy footstep on the carpet. No one came near me. Impatiently I waited in the room along with two other disgruntled gentlemen, one of whom kept crossing and uncrossing his legs, while the other kept uncrossing and crossing his. Man, does the time go slow sitting and waiting, with nothing to read, no "I Love Lucy" shows to watch, and with only a brief glimpse, of the good-looking office girls across the hall now and then. The girls weren't exactly beautiful but were a great improvement than gawking at the greasy mechanics on the opposite side of the hall.

After an hour of miserable waiting, I became fed up. Not just from the distasteful hotdog, but from boredom and disgust as well. I bravely approached one of the office janitors to ask where the repair shop office was located. He told me where I could go. With much trepidation the repair office clerk was contacted, fearful as to what his verdict might be.

"Oh, are you Mr. Heyers? Your vehicle has been repaired, It was finished about an hour ago." Now he tells me.

"Great," I replied. "Was there much wrong with it?"

"Nothing serious. A plate around the left gizmo had slipped, interfering with the movement of the power-steering cylinder. It caused discombobulation of the dflincle, loosening up the dardowitz, allowing the madeojunk elbow to drop down on the rotnstuff diaphragm, preventing motion of the left tie-rod. You're a lucky man. If that plate had slipped a quarter of an inch more while you were driving, it would have caused your vehicle to do a somersault in the air. It would have landed on its roof and you would have been food for the vultures."

"Wow! How lucky can I get?" I managed to utter while grabbing the edge of the counter to keep from falling down.

"Another lucky thing for you is that you are only obligated to pay $75 for use of the customer lounge. The entire bill was $394.85 but that will be paid by the owner."

While carefully driving out of the Moron service shed and heading-for Pittsburgh, I was grateful to be alive and not food for vultures. Units that won't turn left proves once again that there are many hazards to motor home driving. My advice to every purchaser or driver of a motor home is to carefully check each steering wheel to see if it will turn to the left before starting out on any long journey. If there is the least bit of suspicion in your mind that it would not do so, an immediate evacuation of the motor home is essential before trouble starts. It would be far, far better to leave the unit in a stationary position to corrode and rust away, than to stubbornly go against your better judgement where your ending could be food for vultures, like mine almost was.

CHAPTER XV

Scalped In Rockstrewn

When one was first employed by the Otoonga Trailer Factory the dispatch offered excellent accomodations to the new drivers in all phases of jurisdiction. Taken into consideration were the decision of each individual driver regarding desired destinations, size of unit, times of departure, and paper work being smoothed out to advantage. Whenever feasible the employers made attempts to please. As time went by, however, the office personnel could easily know when a driver was hooked, so to speak. From that time forward, a noticeable deterioration in driver influence could be noted. Each clerk began to give less and less consideration to a driver's concerns, even in trivial matters. The dispatchers became more sullen, pay checks became later and later in issuance, and orders were more pronounced and direct. Excellent trips were provided in my behalf early on. Destinations to such admirable cities as San Francisco, Tampa, New York and Niagra Falls were within my repertoire during the first year of driving. New Orleans, Key West, Corpus Christi, and Portland were names appearing on my delivery sheets.

Slowly but surely things began to change. Instead of the above mentioned cities to deliver a unit, orders were being given to drive to Elephant Lake, Kansas, Broken Hearted Valley, Montana, to Bent Elbow, New Mexico or to Two Faced Alley, Vermont. Most all of Otoonga drivers detested driving to Canada, not necessarily because the Canadian people were so reprehensible. No, it was because of the cold and uncooperative weather, too much time was taken to cross the border, and prices of food and fuel were at times intolerable. Such destinations were popping up on my delivery sheets too often for my liking.

Rockstrewn, Alberta was dubiously one of the least desirable places to visit. There was no airport in Rockstrewn, the closest being in Edmonton some 210 kilometers to the east. Only one bus left the thriving city each day, that being twelve o'clock midnight. The people of Rockstrewn were not bad people for the most part, but the good ones were usually invisible. The recreational vehicle dealership, local tavern and cafe, grocery store, gas station, bus depot, and church were all conveniently located under one roof and ownership. The population of the city was 47, serving the surrounding suburbs and rural areas for a diameter of 85 kilometers. You can imagine my chagrin upon arriving the 15th of July to find walking the streets of the city only took 15 minutes, and what was I going to do for 14 hours? Big Chief Thundercloud had checked in my unit leaving me free to do as I pleased until bus departure at midnight. Yet what was there to do? It was highly undesirable to venture outside this time of the morning what with a howling wind driving the icy flakes of snow, some of which was piling up inside my parka. It was useless to read a book in the park or to climb up to the glacier in the adjoining mountains.

My first decision was to enter the local cafe and tavern to buy a drink. Coke, of course. There were no waitresses, so it was Big Chief Thundercloud who managed to skip over from the RV garage to serve the $3.00 Coke to the table where I sat. Dust had to be wiped off the bottle and the lid pried off with a wrecking bar. To my surprise, the Coke was found to be fermented. Intoxication would have been desirable, but my decision was not to imbibe, perchance one of Hummer's spy henchmen might be lurking in a corner. I managed to dawdle over that Coke for some 45 wasted minutes or more, pouring a little at a time down a rat hole in the wooden floor. When this became extremely boring, I decided to buy a magazine at the news stand in the self-service department. Except that there wasn't any self-service department, nor any news stand either. One issue of "Modern Logging" was in a rack, but it was a 1966 issue. The only other occupants in the cafe were two gentlemen seated in a booth on the opposite side. Since it seemed good to be friendly with the local populace, I cautiously sauntered to where they were seated, my tennis shoes making horrible little squeaking sounds while so doing. Trying to make a good impression, an attempt at conversation was initiated, an act that I would have never done under ordinary circumstances, since bashfulness and backwardness were two of my most exemplary traits.

"Hi, fellas, what's new in Rockstrewn?" My face was covered with a sour smile during the introduction.

Quizzing looks, icy stares, and expressionless frowns were their replies. Since one was a Chinese and the other an Indian, my state-side twang was evidently not understood.

"Velly solly, we no know what you speakee," one finally replied who must have been the Chinese. They were playing cribbage and drinking beer. The Chinaman wore long red underwear which was sticking out of his shirt sleeves, above his shirt collar, protruding under his pant legs, and over the top of his boots. The other gentleman was attired in a buckskin short sleeved shirt, khaki shorts, and pheasant feather in his black hair.

"It's really a nice day out isn't it? I bet there's sunshine above those snow clouds, don't you?"

"Velly solly, me only speak Canadian."

This put an end to the abbreviated conversation. My words weren't understood by them, and vice versa, since the Canadian language couldn't be perceived by any normal person. It was so boring in the cafe that I decided to pace the streets of Rockstrewn again. To my surprise, the snow had ceased and the sun was seeking deliverance from behind the dark clouds. Perhaps my time in Rockstrewn held promise after all. Five hundred feet in any direction was the extent of my walk. Not a person was seen during all this perambulating, yet I could just feel those 88 pairs of eyes on my every movement. The billboard on the south entrance listed a population mixture of 29 Indians, 17 Chinese, and 1 Russian. Big Chief Thundercloud had told me at check-in there were only three women in the city, and they were all pregnant. The altitude at this location was approximately 7200 feet, causing me to wonder how cold it must be in the mountains to the west, the highest of which extended to a height of 10 miles.

In contrast to the multi-purpose establishments owned by the Chief, only one other business concern was operating in the city. It was a craft and flea market enterprise, owned and operated by the lone Russian, a huge 297-pound hulk of a man who evidently was able to hold his own with the 46 other antagonists. It was obviously a gung-ho type of enterprise, and with swarms of people coming from all directions by horse and buggy, snow sleighs, and riding the backs of St. Bernard dogs. Time was plenty, so I entered the building with a sheepish grin on my face, trying not to attract too much attention. The inside was packed with people, attracted to many strange objects hanging on the walls, jammed in jars on the floor, protruding from open drawers, and extending from the ceiling and swishing in your face when not ducking. Doing my best to act interested in the various objects displayed, I carefully moved about the cramped quarters, excusing myself whenever stepping on someone's bare toes. Most of the toes were attached to some mighty big feet, so it wasn't prudent to do too much aggravating.

One of the items for sale took my special attention, mainly because I couldn't figure out what it was. It was a long piece of woolen material with buttons along the entire length and small holes at each end. Inquisitively I asked the Russian proprietor about this object. He answered with a look of contemptible scorn.

"Don't you know what that is?" He asked this in querulous sarcasm.

"No, I don't believe so. What is it?"

"And you're one of those wise-mouthed state-side guys and you don't know what you're looking at?"

"I'm sure not wise-mouthed, but I don't know what it is either."

"Why, this here is a snake sweater, can't you tell that?" This was uttered in such a disdainful manner, as if he considered me a complete ignoramus.

"You mean a sweater for a real live snake?"

"Of course, Uncle Sam, haven't you seen one of these before?"

"No, for some reason I haven't before had the privilege."

"Let me clue you in, jungle boy. There's a lot of snakes around these parts. So we gots lots of snake sweaters. Some of the sweaters are the cheapie kind like you might buy. And others may be elaborate like, with bright colors, fur-trimmed collars, and little neckties in front. About every household has got a pet snake in their igloo and ever'body that's anybody at all makes sure his snake is comfortable. It gets perty cold in these parts in the winter and them poor snakes got to have some kind of pertekshun don't they?"

"Yeah, I guess you're right. Snakes do look awful naked."

"I myself has got me a pet rattler of my own. He is my pride and joy—a genuine diamondback. If you pick him up, be real gentle. He don't take to strangers."

A quick glance to the corner revealed that he spoke honestly. In a wicker basket was a complete snake sweater, with beady eyes peering out one end and rattles moving restlessly at the other.

My next reply was, "No, I think I'll go for a walk now. It's getting a little crowded in here."

It didn't take long to remove my presence from the threatening atmosphere and to start pacing the dirt streets once again. When the monotonous pacing had drug on for nearly four hours, I was beginning to feel tired and was holding a considerable amount of apprehension at the thought of those 88 pair of eyes following my every movement. What if a civil war broke out and I was caught in the middle of it? What if some bow and arrow hunters decided to use me for target practice? Or what if some jealous male thought I was searching for his pregnant girl friend and did away with me before I found her?

My next expedition was back into the cafe and tavern to purchase another $3.00 Coke. This time I drank it all, fermented or not. This caused a new and varied look to the great adventure being experienced. Next I was journeying into the bus station part of the building located inside the adjoining wall, only ten linear feet from where I drank the fermented Coke. Big Chief skipped in the twenty paces from the garage where he was changing the wheel on a covered wagon.

"Did you want to buy another bus ticket?"

"No, sir. I was wondering if you would allow me to rest awhile in the station. Maybe take a little nap?"

"You bettum your boots, Whitescalp. But the station closes at 5:00."

"How long does the restaurant stay open?"

"Until 8:00 sharp."

"By the way, Chief, who is it that buys all the motor homes from your recreational department?"

"It's the Amish. Them's the ones, mostly. They um got a paved road leading to their farms in the valley to the east. The Amish's Pope, he ordered a paved road to be built out there and they um got dozens of motor homes sitting alongs their um horse buggies, just waitin' to take off for Alaska this winter."

After he left, I found myself staring at the blank wall for a couple of hours while squeezed into the iron bus seat trying to catch a few winks which didn't happen because being mesmerized and freaked out had taken over. Going back nine feet into the cafe and tavern was my next endeavor, to order an evening meal. In marched Big Chief to be my waiter and cook. I was the sole occupant of the room.

"What is on the menu tonight, Chief?" This was asked while a spasm of uneasiness crawled up and down my esophagus.

When he answered I knew the uneasiness was justified. "We got dead buffalo steak, buffalo mountain oysters, and rattlesnake burgers."

With a churning stomach my reply was, "I'll try the buffalo steak if the meat is fresh."

"It um been dead for awhile, but it um sure to be fresh."

"What do you mean by that?"

"You see um, me and my hired man, Little Gutless, we um pulled this buffalo down the mountain only last week. It um sure to be fresh."

"You pulled the buffalo down the mountain?"

"You bet um, white man. We pulled it down the mountain. You um got to know whenever a buffalo dies in these mountains, it um freezes right up good and solid. That meat um as good and fresh as if we um killed it this morning. Me and Little Gutless rode Old Paint up um Mt. Toronto and found us an um good and tasty animal that um was buried in snow last Spring, and it um wasn't no job at all to bring it here. Little Gutless himself am um the one who cut it up with um the sharp arrows out of his quiver. I um guarantee it um plenty good and tasty."

"If it is all the same to you I'll try the rattlesnake burger instead. Be sure it is well done and all the rattles are cut off."

I sat waiting for my meal on the barstool at the counter, hoping my stomach would quit churning. It didn't. No sooner had Thundercloud gone to the kitchen to prepare the meal than the attack began. A marauding troop marched in to where I was sitting. Right down front and center. Cockroaches. Big ones. A large herd of them. They evidently were self-trained and on cue to strike whenever a patron was present and due to be served. Good Self cried out in alarm, "Don't let them get the best of you, Myle and don't retreat." With this advice ringing in my ears, I struck first. In one full swoop I swooped them off onto the floor with my arm as fast as they came. I watched in glee as they scurried along the cracks in the floor, trying to find a means of escape. It'll be a cold day in Rockstrewn before cockroaches get the best of me.

When the burger was finally served, an entire snake (minus rattles) could be observed curled within the confines of a sesame seed bun. It was steaming and well done, with head still intact and dead eyes staring straight ahead. Just a few bites were all that could be endured, and that with much squeamishness and indigestion. Nor could the stale dandelion greens or the side dish of garlic offer much in the way of stomach pacification. A maligning nasal persuasion was intensified from the odoriferous aroma proceeding from the kitchen, accompanied by the visual scenes of Big Chief Thundercloud stripped down to a loin cloth and moccasins, while meal preparation took place. Physical well being and mental stability were surreptitiously endangered during this ordeal, along with declining self-esteem. How the greens and garlic were swallowed at all remains a mystery, not to mention choking on the rattlesnake eyes. Now in Las Vegas one could expect such procedures to be in vogue, but in Rockstrewn?

Somehow I managed to linger over the meal until closing time. That left four more hours to waste. The only place not yet entered was the church. This was located on the north side of the building by exiting the tavern and turning right five paces. Above the church entry was the sign: OPEN 24 HOURS FOR PRAYER AND MEDITATION. NO VANDALISM ALLOWED. Underneath were the signatures of Big Chief Thundercloud, Minister; Big Chief Thundercloud, Chief of Police; and Big Chief Thundercloud, Mayor. Actually the signatures behind each title were nothing more than three fancy scrawled "X"s. Well, I didn't commit much vandalism once inside, but not much praying was done either. (Except for asking to get out of this fearful city alive.) Disgust, terror, and exasperation were reigning instead.

And the bus was an hour late. Wending its way southward, the bus became stuck in a snowdrift only two miles out of Rockstrewn. This caused another two-hour delay while men of the village awakened their sleeping horses in bed. It took three teams of six horses each to pull out the stalled bus. All during this time, my cap earflaps were pulled down as far as possible, hoping that would be an added incentive for scalp preservation, since all five bus companions were Indian.

So, dear friends, this eventful digression provides further insight to the many dangers that plague the pathway of motor home drivers. Isn't it awful? Killing time in dirty towns, walking deserted streets where villains lurked behind drawn curtains, being threatened with snake bite and then having to eat the slimy things, gagging on buffalo oysters, driving thousands of miles in bleak, foreboding lands to get to where you are going, sitting in cold, threatening churches, fighting insects that are trying to steal your food, and being stalled in a snow bank in threatening atmosphere while freezing to death, are all conditions that to me are abhorrent. Those two nincompoops, Mr. Hummer and Miss Missmossmus, are to blame. I'll never come back to that stinking town of Rockstrewn again. They can just fire me for all I care.

CHAPTER XVI
Churches I Shouldn't Have Gone To

When I was but a small lad my step-grandmother admonished me with the words, "If you want to go to heaven when you die, you got to go to church every Sunday and do what the preacher says." Grandma lived to be 100. Grandpa never darkened a church door and died at 33. That ought to prove something. Since Grandma seemed to know everything, following her advice became one of my objectives. Almost every Sunday, from youth on up, I could be found in church. This continued even while driving motor homes. No matter what the situation, interruption of driving plans took place. Not that my attendance was 100%, but then nobody is perfect. My feet have entered a church of about every denomination imaginable, with the exception of Jewish and Muslim ones. From what I hear, those churches don't appreciate our kind of believers. Baptist, Catholic, Lutheran, Methodist, Episcopal, Pentecostal, Mormon, and about everything else considered. Yet New Age Movement Tabernacles are difficult to find while Atheist Temples are few and far between. All my relatives were Protestant, except for a few who married Catholics and were never seen again.

One fine Sunday morning in the month of May while on my way to Atlanta, Georgia, a stop was made for gasoline and coffee in the town of Aploongonia, Indiana. Across the street was a huge Catholic church.

The church sign read: MASS 8:30. Since it was 8:20 what better opportunity for church attendance could be found? After parking the unit, I marched in line with other worshipers through the entrance. It is doubtful if anyone could tell the difference but what I belonged there. The sanctuary was extremely impressive with sparkling stained glass windows, polished statues, attractive Stations of the Cross, beautiful paintings and artwork, and shining floor. It was a remarkable contrast to most Protestant churches that have leaking roofs, dirty walls, cluttered pews, and noisy people.

It is sad to report that while walking down the aisle a little trouble overtook me. I was gawking around and gazing upward to the lovely paintings and engraved ceilings when all at once the lady ahead stooped to kneel before entering the pew. It is almost too embarrassing to report, but I, well, I fell right over her. Somehow I was able to leapfrog over the top, landing on one knee just as she was doing. I ended up directly across the pew in front of her. Was my face red! Luckily, very few fellow parishioners would have seen the disgraceful act, for they were entering and kneeling like we were. As far as could be told, excommunication wasn't an immediate threat, unless the priest might have seen it happen. I was glad he didn't have me thrown out of there by a couple of altar boys.

There isn't a lot of difficulty in attending a Catholic church. I have learned the secret to stand when everyone else stands, sit when everyone else sits, and kneel when everyone else is doing likewise. It is easy to follow along in the service by using the prayer book, unless the priest skips a few lines, reverses direction, or turns two pages at once. I didn't attempt going up to the altar for communion, hoping that no one would notice, but did remain seated until other parishioners had done so. It was amusing to notice that one elderly gentleman snored through the entire service. He was wide awake at communion time, however, walking up to the altar three times for the wine.

A proud man was I while leaving the vestibule. I had carried out my pledge to go to church once again. No one reprimanded me for my accident either. I could almost sense the approval from Grandma up above, even though she was a died-in-the-wool Methodist.

* * * * * * * * * * * *

To save money when returning from a trip to Portland, Oregon, I decided to ride the bus rather than fly, even though it would take at least forty hours to do so. Instead of sailing in comfort among the clouds, I found myself bouncing along the rough highways in a battered Black Dog bus. At that time the Black Dog Company was offering unlimited travel for one month at the unheard of price of one hundred and fifty dollars. Since those were the days when money was scarce, I was attempting to make as many trips as possible in that length of time. This was accomplished in hopes that Barney and Jane would comply and that Azailia wouldn't divorce me for desertion.

Changing buses in Salt Lake City was imperative. It coincidentally so happened that it was on a Sunday morning. As I departed the bus at Salt Lake, Good Self was heard to be exclaiming, "Wow, You don't suppose, do you, Myle, that you could go hear the Mormon Tabernacle choir sing?"

With this sort of prompting, I decided to investigate. A locker was found in the station in which to store my luggage, shaggy whiskers were quickly removed in the men's room, and an egg sandwich was hastily swallowed at a nearby McDonalds.

The Mormon complex was located a short distance away, providing an excellent opportunity to hear the choir. A ticket change to a later bus had to be conducted, but that was a small sacrifice to make if I was able to hear that famous Mormon choir. To my regret I should not have eaten the egg sandwich, because when reaching the Tabernacle entrance I found the door was closed and locked. The doors had been shut ten minutes ago, according to a nearby attendant. Seeing the look of dejection and disappointment upon my face, the attendant relented by saying, "If you follow the sidewalk to your left you will find a door that leads to a sound proof room where mothers care for their babies during the morning service. No one is allowed to enter the main auditorium when the singing has started. The service is being broadcast and there can be no interruptions. In the nursery you can both see and hear the choir. But it won't be the same as being in the sanctuary."

"That's fine with me. I don't mind sitting with the babies if I can hear the choir sing."

I was dismayed, upon entering the room, that the seats were nearly all taken. There were countless mothers and babies along with a number of other visitors like myself who must have had the same idea. Two or three seats were vacant in the back row. I gingerly made my way to the rear, trying not to step on any babies crawling on the floor or knock any of the mother's hats off. From this back row advantage I was able to both see and hear. But not always what I wanted to. From this point could be seen nearly half of the choir, the tenors and sopranos, provided one made the effort of leaning forward on the edge of his seat and tilt one's head at a ninety degree angle. It was very discouraging to discover that each time a choir member's lips moved, so did the babies'. Occasionally a spectacular melodious sound came forth but I couldn't tell where it was coming from. Another disappointment was that it only lasted five more minutes because the radio broadcast was a fifteen-minute segment.

It was one depressed motor home driver who walked back to the Black Dog to wait six hours for the next bus. Yet I know that Grandma would have been proud of me going to church, even if it was only for five minutes, and to a church with a different creed. I don't know what Mormons believe except that one of the Smith brothers found a pair of magic spectacles out in the forest, and ever since, Mormons having been looking at the world through rose-colored glasses. It was frustrating to have been inside the Tabernacle yet only seeing half the choir and hearing a mixture of angelic refrains and babies bawling. I hear enough babies bawling at home without having to drive 2000 miles to Salt Lake City to hear more of the same.

How does one know what to expect when attending these different places of worship? Some of them are very strange. Not that one faith is superior to another necessarily. I intend not to expostulate very much when arguments are made over religious matters. Anything is preferable to being an atheist. They believe you die like a dog, but I've seen more than one dog die—like the time I ran over Spot with the tractor. I thought he was dead right on the spot, but he got up and ran to the house howling all the way with his tail between his legs, but Azailia brushed him off the porch because he was tracking blood and he moaned and died on the spot after all. I really do feel sorry for atheists for they have no hope in the afterlife. Strangely enough, they seem happy and content, so who am I to persuade them to abandon their faith in nothing, even if they haven't got a prayer.

* * * * * * * * * * * *

A sign approaching Ujailem, Pennsylvania gave notice: UJAILEM PRESBYTERIAN CHURCH MORNING WORSHIP 11:00 3 BLOCKS RIGHT. The brakes were immediately applied and a turn to the right was instigated. The thirty-six foot FREE SPIRIT was parked near the church, taking up the spaces for three compact cars. This trip was destiny bound for Albany, New York. The previous day had been filled with frustration. Travelling had been difficult in Ohio and Pennsylvania because the wind was blowing a gale, rain had made visibility arduous, and my mood was definitely not in the realm of hilarity.

A well-dressed young man ushered me into the sanctuary with courtesy and aplomb. I was intimidated to see the service had already started and that seats were at a premium. He led me to a seventh row pew from the front, revealing an open space in the middle. No one rose to allow my entrance, causing me to squeeze in front of an old fat couple and then across a mother and her young son.

"Excuse me please," I whispered while knocking knees with the old fat couple. As I was easing past the boy, he doubled up his fist, hitting me as hard as he could with a blow to the stomach. The pain was so intense that I stumbled, landing precariously on the lap of his mother.

"Oh, I beg your pardon," I gasped, while clutching my stomach in agony. Suppressed titters of laughter emanated from the rows behind us while icy stares came from those in front, who were craning their necks in astonishment. It caused the minister to pause momentarily, but he soon composed himself to drone on about the upcoming roller skating party for teenagers. The wind was knocked out of me and I was out of breath, not to mention a reddening of the face. To extricate myself from the woman's lap was a serious effort, for who can do much extricating when breathing came laboriously? Along the row we sat: the old fat couple, the little boy, myself, and three other parishioners on the other side.

While I was catching my breath, the organ began playing, a number was announced, and we were asked to sing "Amazing Grace," number 576 in the green hymnal. The congregation was enraptured with the song, but my attempt at singing came out as short wheezes. While we were standing and still singing, the boy crawled past his mother and positioned himself directly beside me. As we were sitting down after the song was over, a rude awakening befell me once more. The boy had placed three hymn books underneath me and I landed on top of them. There was no room to slide to either side which left me with no other option than to slump down somewhat so I wouldn't be so noticeable. I managed a glance at the mother with pleading in my eyes for help. She stared back at me with a grim set line in her lips as if to say, "You got just what you deserved."

As the ushers were coming down the aisle to collect the morning offering, I made an attempt to reach the billfold in my back pocket. This caused a regaining in height, with more whispers and titters from those seated behind us. Also, the little brat wasn't finished with me yet. As the offering plate was passed in our row, he tipped the plate enough to allow some of the coins to spill to the floor beneath me. I was bending over, barely able to reach the floor from my lofty perch, attempting to retrieve the spilled coins and replace them in plate. More gasps, icy stares, and guffaws.

Next came a prayer by the minister who, to my great relief, requested the congregation to stand once more. While everyone else was praying, I was able to remove the books and replace them in the rack. It soon came to my attention that the little monster had more ideas how to inflict torture. Still seated, he began swinging his legs back and forth, each time connecting to the back of mine. I was so disgusted by this time that I grabbed one of those swinging legs and gave it a big pinch. This caused him to holler out a loud "ouch." A glare of hatred emanated from the mother's eyes, who had ceased from prayer long enough to see my retaliation. The outcry even caused the minister to stumble in his prayer in astonishment. Naturally what followed were open eyes, more evil stares, and hands over the mouths. I have been in many embarrassing situations while attending churches across the land, but this was one of the most aggravating of all.

The end of the fiasco had not yet come. The little devil had more work to do. After being reseated, and while the choir was screaming in glorious harmony, he began poking me with the point of a pencil. First in the arm, then in my side, and next in my leg. Mamma only looked the other way. I was becoming irate. No decent, upstanding motor home driver should have to tolerate a church where child abuse goes unchecked. I decided to leave this unwholesome atmosphere immediately, no matter what anyone thought. Easing out of the pew, I gave an extremely hard kick to ornery boy's leg, stepped unmercifully on the toes of the demonic mother, and gave a special vindictive knock on the knees to the old fat couple. All eyes were on me as I pushed the usher out of my path and defiantly left the open-mouthed congregation. Not one word did I hear

Churches I Shouldn't Have Gone To

of the pastor's sermon. The sermon title listed in the bulletin was "Children in a World Gone Mad." And I didn't want to hear anything that would put new ideas in my head.

Church going is supposed to make you a better person. Not me. I was angry, disgusted, and full of distrust for my fellow men(and boys). And glad of it. I was certainly glad to be getting out of this awful place. Only I couldn't. Little compact cars had parked ahead, behind and to each side of my unit, leaving no means of escape until the service ended. And longer than that. Much longer. A potluck dinner was held in the fellowship hall after the morning message. While the happy parishioners were eating and having a good time, inside a certain motor home was someone fuming, starving, and falling to pieces.

Much later, a certain motor home could be seen driving out of a certain church parking lot, following in line behind swarms of compact cars. To the shock and surprise of a certain driver inside the motor home, it wasn't a Presbyterian Church that he attended after all. No, the driver had pulled into the wrong church driveway on the opposite side of the street. The church he worshipped in was "New Life and Clear Conscience Tabernacle of St. Elmo the Devine." Now I know why this happened to me! I had gone to some weirdo church, one that didn't keep their naughty brats under control. Next time I go to church I am going to make sure the right one is entered. It isn't much wonder church attendance has fallen off so drastically these last few years, with such criminal acts performed right in the service itself. I Just hope the speculation isn't true that people in Heaven can look down and see what we're doing. If that be true, Grandma is probably disgusted at me for the way I acted in church. On the other hand, Grandma can't accuse me of not going to church, even if it was an off brand. If I hadn't been driving motor homes none of this would have happened, and none of these dreadful churches would have had to be gone to.

* * * * * * * * * * * *

It wasn't a Sunday morning but the option was obvious: attend this motivating service tonight or forget about attending any church this week. Tomorrow, Sunday, bus riding would be my occupation. The marquee sign of the Civic Center in Quasuquasneria was lighted with flashing colored lights announcing: TRUE LIFE CITY WIDE CRUSADE 7:30 PM. Dinner having already been eaten at the Green Crab Cafe, and with consideration given that the Black Dog bus didn't leave until 11:05, what was a body to do with his time for another four hours and fourteen minutes in a city of 11,007 citizens? The bars were supposedly off limits to Otoonga drivers, no athletic events were taking place in this berg on a Saturday night, and the shopping stores had already closed their doors. I had worked both sides of Main Street, several times, attempting to uncover something entertaining, but with no luck. Until now.

Delivered to the fairgrounds in the city of Quasuquasneria was a Super Ranch Exquisite, one of the 33-foot top of the lines Exquisites, to the exposition site for recreational vehicle display. Mr. Hummer had ordered this rare Saturday delivery with the intent to get the jump on other RV companies exhibiting their wares in a melee of extreme competition. After making the delivery, one of the exposition attendants drove me to the bus station, and I had been wandering around in a daze ever since. Old Barney, Jane, Azailia, and even little Jack had all been willing and eager to take care of the pigs in my absence (I hoped), so things had worked out to good advantage. Not much trouble had overtaken me driving from the factory except for three flat tires, the dimmer switch quit working, the cruise control bumped and jerked when flipped to the on position, and a violent west wind had repeatedly swerved the unit back and forth.

Trying to keep Grandma's commandment to attend church every Sunday would have to be broken slightly. A Saturday night would have to suffice instead. Also, a city-wide crusade might prove to be very enlightening and appealing. Healing the sick, snake- handling, and walking on fire may make any motor home driver sit up and take notice. Two choices faced me: attend a religious meeting where miracles might take place, or sit for four hours in a dirty bus station watching the low-lifes, druggies, drunks, wife beaters, child molesters, and evil ruffians come and go. It was hard to tell which might offer the most interesting show, but I opted for the crusade after deep contemplation.

Through the huge auditorium doors I entered. But something was wrong—there were no people. It was 7:25, the place should have been crowded out by this time. It would have been if Jimmie Swaggart was preaching anyway. The auditorium was dark and destitute. On the opposite side of the foyer was a janitor sweeping the floor. Approaching him I asked, "Isn't some kind of religious meeting supposed to be going on?"

"Yes, sir, there is," was the reply. "It's up on the second floor. Door number twelve." He kept sweeping.

With gradually increasing uneasiness, I proceeded up the stairs and reluctantly opened door number twelve. As few as fifty people were scattered about the one room enclosure, most of whom wore a different-colored skin than mine was. The room was medium- sized, with a platform, pulpit, organ, and only folding chairs for seats. A hubbub was going on, with a lot of laughter and boisterousness. Everything soon quieted down when a white man and a black woman seated themselves on the rostrum. At the left side of the platform sat a young man behind a keyboard, playing the most weird sounds imaginable, with no tune or logic. The chords sent shivers up and down my spine.

"You may be seated anywhere you like," said an elderly attendant.

I chose a seat toward the rear, one where I could get a panoramic view of the situation, and where it was possible to make a quick escape if conditions warranted. The chords were interrupted by the black lady who announced numbers for congregational singing. None of the songs were recognizable to my ears. My response was to mumble along in a monotone which was hopefully inaudible. The more we sang, the more spontaneous became the reaction. Conditions were getting impulsive and frenzied, with hand waving, yelling, and jumping up and downs.

After a half hour of such goings on, the black lady led a prayer, which quieted the crowd somewhat. After the prayer came a short sermon, offering quick prosperity and fame to all who were willing to give generously as the plates were passed. Another song brought the congregation to life once again, causing an intensifying eruption of hand clapping, back slapping, shouts of glory, handkerchief waving, dancing, and foot stomping. Increased hilarity and jubilation abounded throughout the room, except for where I was sitting. I tried my best to get in the same mood, but it was a useless attempt. Somehow this glorious feeling had escaped me.

Soon the white minister took control. His oration could convince anyone they were guilty of murder. Since stealing, lying, and cheating were my main misdemeanors, adding murder to it didn't alleviate my outlook a whit. As his stupendous declarations unfolded, other remarkable acts were committed. One dear sister emerged from the audience, wended her way down the aisle while in a screaming and moaning mode of operation. With one tumultuous outcry, she collapsed to the floor in front of the pulpit. Though falling into a state of unconsciousness, she was able to conveniently land on a mattress placed there. Also, conveniently, a good brother immediately covered her with a bright-colored blanket. Other good sisters soon followed her example in the same format. One by one they danced to the front, falling to the floor in ecstasy. Each one in turn was covered with a spread to protect their modesty.

How long these good ladies remained berserk I will never know. Such tumult was overpowering to skeptical motor home drivers. Good Self cautioned, "You better get out of here fast, Myle. You don't want some preacher getting spontaneous jurisdiction over your unconscious body. Especially that white preacher. He had an avaricious look in his eyes."

These words of warning almost caused a mental collapse, but I was able to gain enough composure to make a mad rush for the door.

During the grand conflict, I doubted if anyone noticed my hasty exit. If anyone did, their reaction must have been, "Good riddance."

Grandma would have been pleased to know I went to church, even if it was a little bizarre, and on a Saturday night. This was the fastest I left any church since being ten years old. Some kid had yelled out "fire" when everyone but the preacher had been asleep. It was very disappointing not to have seen miracles, like snake handling or raising the dead. Yet collapsing unconscious to the floor on a well-placed air mattress is just as mysterious and miraculous. But I'm never going to any religious crusade again. Unless it is to hear Billy Graham. And I'd make sure he didn't have any snake handlers on the platform with him.

Three hours remained before the scheduled bus departure. The only establishment still open in this hick town was a bar located two blocks from the bus station in a seedy part of town. Ten minutes after church attendance I found myself seated in a bar, drinking...Cokes, of course. For the next two hours and ten minutes drinking Cokes was my obsession. That, and watching the dancing girls. Care had to be taken, because wife Azailia could read my mind from a thousand miles away. Realizing this, I moved my chair behind a pole so the dancing girls could no longer be seen. The beautiful and melodious rap music could be enjoyed, and was it ever cool.

Boarding the coach at 11:45 couldn't be called an exhilarating experience. How was I to know that the same bunch of hooligans that were in the bus station at seven o'clock would be my fellow bus passengers? How darkened my countenance became upon discovering these same characters would be riding with me all the way to Otoonga. How even worse it was to know that they were also fellow Otoonga drivers who had also driven a unit to the Quasuquasneria exposition! What a bunch of bums they were! How remarkably odious it was. These ruffians were companion employees and were my peers. Maybe I'm not such a high brow after all. Such discordant realization caused worry lines to crease my cheeks, eyes to become sunken, and mental acumen to go in hiding.

Delivering motor home on Saturday, pacing the streets of a forsaken town, attending religious meetings, facing threatening preachers, observing awe- inspiring miracles, drinking a belly-full of Cokes, being scorned by dancing girls, and being trapped in sleazy buses with evil companions is altogether an awful, demoralizing exercise in futility. And motor home driving is to be blamed.

* * * * * * * * * * * *

Methodists are the most friendly people you can find. They are polite, cordial, and friendly. If you go to their churches they give you things. Free. Like pens etched with the Apostle's Creed, or maybe a notebook with a smiley face, or even a lapel pin with the words: UNITED METHODISTS UNITE. Attending a Methodist service one time, a loaf of bread was given to all the visitors. Can you imagine that, a complete bread loaf, fresh out of the church bakery? I was munching on it all day, not needing to buy any lunch…or dinner either.

Yet Methodists have the most boring preachers in the country, bar none. Their parishioners don't take them seriously. They laugh during the sermons. One time, in the Gladness Methodist Church in Slippery Elm, Arkansas (which was a suburb of Little Rock), I was trying to nod off but couldn't because so much laughter was waking me up. Either the preacher was constantly telling jokes or the congregation didn't believe a word he was saying. Think about it.

Sorry to say, one occasion of Methodist church attending almost spelled disaster. With a capital "D." It came to pass in a large church in Rockemville, Ohio. At the time, I couldn't remember the church name but remember it had the word Evil in its nomenclature. Being the eager-beaver sort of extrovert person that I am, a swagger and a proud look prevailed while entering the vestibule. It was 10:00 a.m., time for service, my unit was parked under the shade of a giant cactus, and there was a large crowd of people pushing and shoving to enter. Deep disappointment came when I entered the sanctuary. An usher told me that it was time for Sunday School, not the morning preaching service. He also revealed that if I went to the basement below to door number four, there would be a class for my kind of people.

Cautiously descending the steps to door number four, I entered the classroom only to find it empty. This allowed a wandering about of the room, looking at the drawings on the wall, staring out the window, and snooping on the teacher's desk. A few moments later could be heard a low rumbling sound which grew louder and louder, reaching a climax of crashing footsteps, noisy giggling, and hoarse yelling. To my amazement, the door opened and thirty or more galloping boys and girls rushed inside. While they were fighting for seats, one frail little girl came to the front where I was standing and asked, "Are you our new teacher?"

"Well, I—"

"He's the new teacher, he's the new teacher," they all began shouting.

I was being overwhelmed by this ovation and my meager protests were drowned out completely. Until shouting myself in reprisal. I yelled louder than they, "If you kids don't shut up and take your seats I'll tell the preacher on you all."

You could have heard a pin drop. From chaos to solemnity in five seconds. They obediently took their seats and order was restored. This was the only time so many people paid any attention to what I said, except when having to recite "The Night Before Christmas" when I was a wee little lad in kindergarten myself. That preacher must be a mean old man to instill so much awe and fear into thirty snotty-nosed second graders.

A timid little lad raised his hand and asked, "Are you going to tell us a Bible story?"

"Yes, tell us a Bible story, tell us a Bible story," they all chimed in.

"Shut up," I again yelled. While pondering my discomfort, Bad Self took center stage, "After reading the entire Bible through ten times, Myle, you can't remember even one little Bible story?"

I was believing that my entrance had been made to the wrong class-room. My heart was in my mouth, perspiration crossed my brow, my mind was blank, and I was in a quandary once more. Until a flash of intellectual ingenuity broke forth through the saving words of Mr. Good Self, "Change the subject. Ask them a riddle."

"I'm not going to tell you a story, but I've got a riddle for you."

"What is it, what is it?" they were yelling again.

"Where was Moses when the lights went out?"

"That's easy," said one little fellow with his necktie stuck inside his trousers. "He was in the ark in the dark."

"Yeah, he was in the ark in the dark," they all bellowed.

"Ha, ha, that's where I outsmarted all of you. It wasn't Moses in the ark at all."

"Then who was it?" asked one little man who was holding a puppy.

"It was…uh…it was…uh…Samson, that's who it was," I answered.

"No, no, no," came a defiant chorus.

"Yes it was."

"No, no, no," they kept shouting.

"Yes, it was Samson. I remember it all now. Samson was a big, strong ox of a man who built an ark in forty days and forty nights. He put ani-mals on that boat and then towed it out to sea by himself. A big storm came up and all the animals got sick and vomited all over the place and he got sick too and went to the side of the boat to heave, but instead he got heaved overboard into the open mouth of a big blue shark. As he was clawing his way out of the shark's stomach………………"

I was interrupted when a thirty-ish woman with a big nose barged through the door.

"This is wonderful of you, helping out as teacher. I discovered a hole in my nylons and went back home to change. You're a darling man to be taking charge."

"This is a privilege to be helping out. It was the righteous thing to do. Anybody could teach this well-behaved class."

"We won't impose upon you any longer. But I know the class, and especially myself, are asking you to remain with us and add a few comments. You may pull up a chair and sit here beside me at the desk."

I found myself seated close beside her, too close in fact. She had placed her chair near mine, and we were almost knocking knees under the desk. Every now and then she would give me a quick glance and a toss of her head, seemingly flirting with me in front of sixty pairs of eyes. What a poor example I was to the children. My squirming and fidgeting was worse than the class was doing. She droned on and on, something about Elijah and the bull-rushes. I thought the session would never end.

When a bell finally sounded from a distance, the children roared out, the same as they had roared in. That was a signal to do likewise, but the signal, to my sorrow, was subverted. "It has been nice meeting you madam," I told her. "I've kept my commitment to attend church today and I must be on my way."

"Oh, no. This was just Sunday School. The morning service will soon be starting. I will escort you up to the auditorium, since you're new here."

"I thought this was the morning service," I lied. "I've got to be on my way. I've wasted enough time here already."

"Nonsense, you can't leave now. You must hear our pastor speak. His topic this morning is love and marriage."

"No, I really can't. You see I've got to deliver a—"

She grabbed my arm firmly with her two powerful hands and began forcing me upstairs to the sanctuary. The foyer was a mad house, filled with a sedate throng, each of whom was trying to force his way ahead of the others. As we came through, the crowd seemed to fall back, allowing us to pass unscathed. To my chagrin, she dragged me to the front, depositing my body in the second row. How humiliating! Everyone was staring at some strange stranger sitting in front alone. A few moments later, the same woman entered the pew from the opposite side with another woman who must have been her mother. She pranced all the way across the pew and sat down close beside me, so close that we were now rubbing shoulders. This was getting out of hand. And me a married man. A sensation was sweeping over me that a gradual extension of increasing progression toward the downsizing of my equilibrium was at hand.

The choir marched in, followed by two distinguished-looking gentlemen, with the pastor trailing the solemn procession in a purple polka-dot robe. The pastor looked at me and, for some unknown reason, smiled. We stood for the hymn sing, prayer, and inspiration time. When we sat down, the gal was closer to me than before. I tried to crowd the pew end barrier, but to avail. It wouldn't budge. One of the distinguished gentlemen directed the choir in a beautiful rendition of "Lullaby of Palm Trees." The other one announced the announcements, and at last the preacher began his sermon. As if on cue, the congregation began to snicker, giggle, and laugh. A few quick jokes about Solomon's 500 concubines really brought the house down. Robust guffaws were reverberating off the cathedral ceiling. When he tried to get serious, it made no difference. Smiles enlightened countenances throughout the sanctuary, even those dozing in hopeful obscurity. The way he explained love and marriage, I was wishing I had remained single. Since my favorite pastime of sleeping in church was circumvented, chewing my fingernails, biting my lip, and wiggling my ears had to suffice.

Good Self came to my rescue, "Not to worry, Myle. You can get out of here alive if you play your cards right." Taking his advice, I began relaxing. The wisdom of Hare Krishna began to twist my thoughts into the stoicism of Yoga. And it worked! I had no more than fallen into a trance when the sermon came to a conclusion.

Good Self assured me, "See, everything is going to come out alright."

Bad Self replied, "You're not out of the woods yet, Myle."

And I wasn't, but I thought I was. The aisles quickly flooded, blocking my quick intentioned exit. Surprising me greatly and to my relief, the gal beside me evaporated without a word of goodbye. She and the other woman exited from the other side of the pew. I was free from her after all! It didn't matter how long it took to get out of here as long as she had left. No matter how much scuffling in the vestibule would have to be endured, the pursuit by some weird Sunday School teacher had ended. In the foyer the minister was shaking hands with each departing attendant. When my turn finally came I looked him directly in the eyes and said, "That was the most wonderful sermon I have ever heard."

"Glad you liked it. You're a stranger here and alone aren't you?"

"Yes. I'm driving on to—"

"Well, you're going to be a stranger no longer if I have anything to say about it. Dinner is cooking at home and I'm issuing you an invitation. Any visitor that goes through our church doors gets invited to dinner by some member of the congregation. It isn't our turn, but when we saw you sitting in our pew, looking so lost and forlorn, we decided to change places with the Higgenbottoms. So we are taking you home with us to partake of the bounty."

"No, that would be impossible. I must be moving on. I got to drive—"

"Rubbish. You must come with us. A delicious meal has been planned."

"No, really. I can't come. I've got to drive a big—"

He interrupted again. We absolutely insist that you come and won't take no for an answer."

"But I—"

"Say no more. You're coming with us."

While he was speaking, I noticed that his foot was firmly planted on one of my untied shoelaces. I was being overcome by a minister who ripped off his polka-dot robe and threw it in a corner. Grasping my arm firmly, he led me out to his waiting Mercedes and shoved me inside. It was overwhelming! Was this the way you get converted in a Methodist church? To my horror, on the other side of the back seat sat someone previously met. My Sunday School teacher.

"Hello again," were her words of greeting. "This is a surprise." (I bet it was.) "Coincidences really happen, don't they?"

"Yeah, I guess they do," was my choking reply.

As we sped off, the Reverend spoke again, "By the way, we haven't introduced ourselves, have we? My name is Robert Hitumguud. This is my wife, Eugenia, sitting beside me. The fun-loving girl back there with you is our daughter, Hermione."

"Glad to know you all," I managed to utter.

A warning light began to flash in my brain by Good Self's prompting. They think I'm not married because my wedding ring isn't on my finger.

My finger hurts and swells up when driving twenty hours a day in the hot summertime. The ring had been removed from my finger at Branson, Missouri, and placed in my coin purse for safekeeping. That's about the safest place since there is rarely anything in it. This dinner was a trap to get me interested in the daughter. I could see through their little scheme.

"How you gonna get out of this, Myle?" Bad Self again.

At the moment there didn't seem to be any means of escape. The Mercedes was being driven too fast to jump out the door. A leg could get fractured or a brain concussed. Maybe that wouldn't be a bad circumstance, under the circumstances.

Rev. Hitumguud continued, "We have yet to hear the mention of your name."

"My name is Heyer Miles. No, no, I sometimes get mixed up. My name is Liar Hiles. No, I'm forever getting my tongue tangled when I'm with strangers. My real name is Myle Heyers."

"Myle, what a beautiful name," spoke a voice from the back seat across from where I was sitting.

"Yeah, it is. My mother thought so anyway." In embarrassment my voice box blundered on, "Folks down south call me Mol. Yeah, down there they call me Mol Haaaars, with a soft "r" and kind of a drawl like."

Soon the big Mercedes was being turned to the right into a long driveway lined with coconut palms and orange groves. At the end of the lane was the largest mansion I had ever seen. As the auto came to a stop, a uniformed livery man opened the door for us. Ten granite pillars lined the open front porch of the dwelling. Golden angels with wings extending above the roof level were perched solemnly on the top of each pillar.

Servants greeted us warmly as we entered the palace, leading us across the marble floor into the seventy-foot long dining room. We were seated on one end of a sixty-foot mahogany table where Bob offered the prayer "Now I Lay Me Down to Sleep" and we were served fillet of mutton chops, rice smothered in onion broth, green-eyed peas, lemon ice crystal salad, lobster breasts covered in sweet and sour sauce, and blueberry pie smashed with cream cheese. Wow! Methodist preachers must really be rich. They have caring, loving congregations. Either that or the preacher and the church treasurer have a good thing going, swindling the widows out of their Social Security. How a sorry-looking motor home driver was able to choke down his meal remains a mystery after dropping his napkin on the floor three times, spilling gravy on his tie, gargling on the green-eyed peas, choking on his mutton, and knocking over his glass of ale.

"When we thought you might be coming, the girls bid the servants and cooks to remain over the noon, although Sunday is their usual day off," Bob said to me as the meal was completed. "Come, let us retire to the den where Miranda will serve us coffee."

We retired to the den which contained moose and tiger heads protruding from the walls, buffalo and tiger hides lying on the hardwood floor, and stained glass situated in bay windows that provided a marvelous view of the ocean, and where Miranda brought us coffee. While Miranda was pouring Bob said, "I'm getting sleepy. I'll drink my coffee later. If you need me for any reason I'll be in the left wing on the second door on the right side of the middle hallway on the sixth floor." As he was speaking, I caught him winking at his wife and she meekly followed behind him.

Hermione and I were left alone. For the fifth time in my life I felt faint. One other time was when I was a wee lad and went to a funeral of a neighbor who died from colliding with a bull. My sister and I got separated from our parents because there wasn't enough room in their pew and the ushers put us in a row come to find out was in the relatives' section. In those days, relatives went out of the church last when the funeral was over and so did my sister and me. As we filed past the casket to pay our last respects, we let the relatives have a good cry, which they did, and so did my sister and me, only we were crying harder than the relatives.

Hermione and I sat thus in embarrassment, immobilized and preoccupied in nervous self-consciousness, when Bad Self began shouting whispers into my ears, "Now you're in a real life muddle, aren't you, Myle? They think you are some lone wolf intruding into the real imagined fantasies of this woman, some Don Juan coming from out of nowhere to rescue her from spinsterhood. I bet they'll try to get you hitched before nightfall. The preacher is here already in case he's needed, you know. Maybe that wouldn't be a bad idea. Think how rich she is qoing to be when her old man finally kicks off. Yet it would cause you to be a bigamist, Myle. But you know what you could do? You could become a Mormon, or maybe a Muslim, 'cause them kinds of religions let you have all the wives you want."

For the first time I was able to get a good look at Hermione, enlightening my understanding why she was an old maid. Only the wicked witch from the Wizard of Oz could have been uglier than she was. Black bags hung under her eyes, her ears looked like spoiled apricots, pock marks covered her cheeks, stringy hair trickled half way down her back, a nervous twitch wobbled her head in a sideways motion, and her nose was as big as, well I couldn't really tell how big her nose was, but it was big. How she was chosen to be a Sunday School teacher was not understandable, unless her old man pulled a few strings at the monthly board meetings.

This paralyzing condition continued unabated, allowing extreme desperation to become more intrusive. When the ardors of love take control, anything is liable to happen, permitting blissfulness, felicity and supreme happiness to emerge, hopefully resulting in masculinity appropriation which may provide a distinctive articulation of the sublime, a modification of irresponsible irrationality nullifying ostracism, instead accelerating the cultivation of a cul-de-sac, which in opposition cursorily downgraded infatuation by infusing innocuous innuendoes, climaxing in the propagation of spontaneous exhibits of improper indulgences. Yes, cataloging of catastrophies was going to get the best of me. Cataplexy began to negatively affect the physical in unmanageable methods of circumvolution with surprising attacks of tingling sensations near base of the sternum in desperate manueveuring, while simultaneously forcing a methodical agony as internal repercussions ran pell-mell throughout the nerve networks while infiltrating the bloodstream in rapidly incredible switchbacks, theoretically utilizing a grasp of uncompromising urorrhagia in torment and anguish, causing a stench to enter the nose membranes, neutralizing the pacification of momentary relief whenever any potential indication of indecorous behavior escorted the desecration of natural functioning.

Breaking the silence I stood and solemnly proclaimed, "I've got to go to the bathroom. Do you know where there is one in this place?"

With a flushed face, Hermione instructed, "The closest one is just off the alcove of the anteroom after you pass through the sitting room balcony on the second floor. You make a left at the third doorway and go up two more flights past the sun room and it's the second door on your right. You can't miss it."

"Oh, yes I can." It was muttered under my breath. Audibly I said, "Thank you so much. You don't know what this means to me."

While exiting her presence another slight whisper rang out, "Make a run for it. Get out of here." Good Self was making a valiant effort for my self-preservation.

Following this advice, a change in direction was advanced. Tiptoeing across the seventy-foot dining room, shuffling past the sixty-foot table, and quietly promenading along the marble floor to the vestibule helped advance the cause of freedom. A cautious, silent turning of the doorknob would advance it still further. The door was locked.

Good Self again screamed silently, "Do what you gotta do before it's too late."

One of the hanging moose heads was yanked from the wall and was used as ammunition to smash the side window of the foyer into a million pieces. A tear in the seat of the pants was the result of crawling through the shattered aperture, but that was the least of my worries. If neighbors were alert they could have seen one frightened motor home driver dashing madly back to the church parking lot in five minutes flat. All nineteen blocks.

Sitting parked was the most beautiful, magnificent, dazzling vehicle my eyes could behold, still partially shaded by the giant cactus. Even in my haste, another quick glance at the church sign revealed the church's name—Reject Evil Methods Church. This must not have been a bonafide Methodist Church after all!

No other beautiful, magnificent, dazzling vehicle could have been propelled out of the city of Rockemville, Ohio any faster than this one was. Being pursued by a speeding Mercedes with three angry- looking people in the front seat may have been a contributing factor. The little Mercedes was no match for my high- powered Honda motor home. I poured on the gas and they faded into obscurity. Out-distancing them was no problem. Flying down the freeway at high speeds became an obsession, providing a vast relief which was magnified into a glowing exhaltation, engulfing this poor country boy to shouts of joy, unheard of heretofore in the present- day modem of ordinary articulation. In realms of predictable presentation, onlookers could mumble in their beer, "That lucky guy escaped from a horrible fate." And I did. Free as a bird. No two wives after all. However, in the escape, the chance of acquiring unfathomable riches crumbled in the dust. Yet it was worth it to realize the Reject Evil Methods Church would never be my place of worship.

Don't these church-going events once more prove to you skeptics what horrible confrontations we motor home drivers face? Are you too blind to see? Is your understanding still darkened? Impossible situations face us at each bend in the road, at the descent from every hill, at each acceleration of the gas pedal, and under every church steeple. All drivers passing through the doors of the Otoonga Trailer Factory constantly face worse conditions than that, magnified many times over. It becomes especially notorious when you are parked at a church somewhere when Miss Missmossmus thinks you are easing on down the road. If I get to Heaven, Grandma is going to get told a thing or two why drivers shouldn't have to go to church every Sunday. Church going combined with motor home driving creates too many hazards to suit me.

Chapter XVII
Leaving Las Vegas

Burning up the road for two strenuous days placed myself, and the thirty-three foot Excel Excapade surrounding it, in the Las Vantage Truck Plaza in Los Gambel, Nevada, one hundred and forty miles from destination. The most exciting resort in North America would soon be conquered. This conquest, however, shouldn't be happening because my corn needed cultivating. The weeds were higher than the corn. It was more enthralling to heed the beckoning call from Mr. Hummer than to be crossing the fields a hundred times to eliminate a few growing plants that had sprouted life according to Mother Nature's designated order. Crossing the western half of the United States could be done in a comparable amount of time, and while chomping on a few Wendy's hamburgers in so doing. I did the smart thing—leaving the cultivating in the hands of Azailia, since she was a capable tractor operator. By now, the baby was old enough to be fed and cared for by his brothers, and Old Barney had become more and more skillful in watching Jane feed the hogs. So it came about that I was enabled to move on down the road, and get ready to conquer that exotic city…Las Vegas.

A pleasant journey it was, with bright sunshine most of the way, warm gentle breezes lifting one's ego, and stupendous views of mountain and plain. Wheat harvest in Kansas was in full swing with giant combines swathing through the ripened fields. The Excapade was a driver's delight, easy to manipulate, energized with power, and hovered over the pathway in impressive domination. The pavement was smooth as glass, no earthquakes were erupting, and nature shone forth her love to all earth's transgressors who held high their heads.

I was holding high my head early the next morning, awakening before sunrise, eager to deliver another beautiful, magnificent, dazzling vehicle to its new owner, and to discover the wonderment which was to soon appear before my widened eyes. Before my eyes were widened, however, an intrusion into my life took place. On a two-lane short cut out of New Trails, Nevada a stranger made an invasion. Up ahead, an auto stopped long enough for someone to exit, and immediately drove on. A lone figure was left standing as my vehicle approached. To my surprise, it was a woman with her thumb sticking out, leading me to believe she was wanting a ride. Now the one great cardinal rule proclaimed from the Otoonga Dispatch Office was: NEVER PICK UP HITCHHIKERS. This rule was emblazoned on the office walls, across the entry gates, and over the urinals in the rest rooms. But how could one pass by a woman in need, in desperate condition, and begging for help with pleading eyes? Especially a woman who was young and beautiful?

"Do you need a ride?" was my first question after the unit had stopped beside her.

"Oh, yes. I need a ride to Reno to visit my mother." Whereupon she quickly opened the passenger door, and was inside before I could give it a second thought.

"I'm not going to Reno," was my protest. "I'm headed for Las Vegas."

"That's close enough," she replied while seating herself in the passenger seat beside me and tossing her bags into the hallway behind.

"Why would you want to go to Las Vegas if you want to see mother in Reno?"

"Glad you asked. My mother doesn't know I'm coming, and since there is a chance to go to Las Vegas first, that's what I'll do."

"What's a pretty thing like you doing hitchhiking along the road? And why did you get out of that car just now?"

"That dirty snake tried to get fresh with me. I told him to let me out and he did."

"You're smart to get away from a guy like that. You don't have to worry about me. I don't get fresh with anybody. I don't even dare get fresh with my wife."

A loud unnatural laugh proceeded from her lips and I noticed her voice was extremely husky.

"Doesn't it frighten a good-looking gal to be hitchhiking all by yourself, all alone with no protection?"

"I can take care of myself, don't you worry."

"I'm not really worried. Just thought I'd ask."

As we rode along, a little uneasiness crept through my brain waves. Something aroused my suspicious nature before Good Self issued a warning, "She's probably got a gun hidden and you will end up meat for the vultures."

A quick glance revealed what appeared to be a five o'clock shadow on her face and unusually big arm muscles for a woman. Another glance at her legs (which I really shouldn't have been looking at) revealed dark hairs.

Bad Self added intervention, "What if, under all that make-up and girlish figure, she is a man, or something even worse?"

After such an appalling question and since the conversation was starting to lag, I decided to give her a test. "The radio has a lot of static right now but I feel like a little music should be heard, don't you? I'd like to sing a song while we drive, wouldn't you?"

"Sorry, big boy, I'm not much of a singer. Besides, I've got laryngitis."

Her reply alleviated my fears not a bit. A few more glances at her caused me to blurt out, "You're not a woman at all. You're a man!"

"What gives you that silly notion? I'm as female as I'll ever be."

"I can see through that phony get-up. You're not a woman in spite of that lipstick and yellow hair and breast implants. And you got a phony voice, too."

"How can you tell?" She finally admitted that my fears were justified.

"Because anyone with that much hair on her legs and man's voice, has got to be a man."

"You're right mister. I am a man. But I almost fooled you, didn't I?"

"Yeah, you had me fooled at first. What are you doing, travelling around like this, dressed as a woman? Oh, I bet you're gay."

"No, I'm not gay. I dress like this to get a free ride. Nobody will pick up a hitch-hiking man, but for a woman, nearly every car will stop."

"You mean you dress like a woman to get a free ride? Now I've heard everything."

"That's right. I get by cheap and go wherever I want. The worst trouble is that all the men that give me a ride expect favors in return."

"Then what happens?"

"I either tell them I am a man or else get out of the car. They don't get far with me, especially when they find out I'm not the gal they think I am. I've taken karate lessons and no man has got the best of me yet, even if I am little."

Discovering that he really was a man didn't calm my nerves any. The farther we traveled, the more my fears penetrated. Bad Self began whimpering, "Now that she is a man, this makes it even worse. You might be able to overpower a woman if she tried to rob you, but what about a man with big karate muscles sticking out all over him?"

Good Self also advised, "Think of some way to get rid of him."

I thoughtlessly blurted out, "I suppose you got a knife hidden under your dress and will slit my throat at the first red light?"

"Naw, I wouldn't do a thing like that. I only want a free ride. I don't have any mother in Reno. Las Vegas is a hotter spot anyhow."

"Nothing surprises me any more. Since you aren't going to stick a knife in my back you can stay on board. We should be in Las Vegas in a couple of hours."

And you know, we had the best conversation, laughing and joking all the way. He was a student at Ohio University but during the summer months he was a roving vagabond, hitchhiking everywhere he wanted to go. He dressed as a woman, short skirt and all, which permitted ride catching to be a successful venture. This was his way to see the country and he was doing a good job of it. He was twenty-nine years of age and a professional student through previous military service, loans, grants, and a little help along the way from his dear old dad. As we talked and drove, an odd question jogged through my mind causing me to ask, "Tell me, what rest rooms do you go in?"

"Curiosity got the best of you, huh? Usually when I get to a place I want to stay for awhile, I try to find a deserted building to change back into men's clothes. Whenever I'm unable to do this, I am forced to use the ladies rest room. But what's the big deal? Nobody knows the difference."

On and on he spoke, explaining this and that, elaborating of the exciting places and adventures encountered. That guy had been all over the country, and he didn't have to drive a motor home to do it either. As we neared the city, I told him we must part company because my delivery was at West 1658th Lane which was miles out of the way from downtown.

"That's fine, I'll get there somehow. What I really came to see was the Strip anyway. I sure want to thank you for the ride, Mac. Not many fellows find out that I'm a man."

"Maybe I'll see you on the Strip. I plan to go there after making delivery of this baby anyway."

His last words to me were, "If at any time during your travels you see a hitch-hiking woman, be sure to stop because it will probably be me."

While driving away, the rearview mirror reflected back a remarkable sight. Standing at the curb was a young woman in a mini-skirt, clutching two bags in one hand and with a thumb pointed out of the other. The first automobile that drove by made a sudden stop, the girl hopped inside, and off they drove. I laughed to myself all the way to the dealer's office. You can be sure of one thing—she was the best-looking man my eyes had yet seen.

Delivery of the Excel Excapade went smoothly and quickly, leaving ample time to embark on another exciting adventure. My ego was high in anticipation of visiting the fabulous Strip. Since my return plane reservation wasn't until 10:00 at night, boarding a city bus in front of the dealer's driveway was an easy method of fulfilling my intentions.

Downtown Las Vegas is wildly spectacular but the Strip is even more so. You have to see it to believe it and even then you probably wouldn't. Huge hotels, cities in themselves, sit in glorious and imposing array along the broad avenues. Each contain extraordinary diversities of robbing its customers in a multitude of schemes. From hotel to hotel can be found bustling casinos, towers, actual waterfalls, space needles, moving ships, bungee jumps, simulated volcanoes, pyramids, statues, glass walls, bridges, circus acts, rousing night clubs, reveling dance halls, restaurants, show acts, wedding parlors, divorce courts, shopping stores, movie houses, sports arenas, live animals, and dissatisfied people. Pleasure palaces of every description provided excitement, entertainment, and satisfaction to all who succumbed to temptation.

Few places on earth could be found such happiness, joy, and complete fulfillment. Wondrous beauty is displayed through nature's majesty where gigantic palm tress emerge out of the cement, giant cactuses protrude from the water ponds, where exotic flowers bloom profusely, shrubs and hedges grow unhindered, and where displayed were man's glorious achievements fashioned in wood, cement, brick, stone, and precious jewels...leading the gullible to the gates of paradise. Each casino was nearly a city in itself competing against rivals with cafes, bars, floor shows, shopping malls, game rooms, souvenir shops, clothing stores, beauty parlors, recreation areas, children's playrooms, smoke shops, liquor stores, and gambling halls dominating in splendor. The top pinnacle of delight, that which superseded all other riotous activity, the objective of every patron's desires was, of course, to gamble and get rich. This was the ultimate climax!

No other pleasure could surpass the fantastic thrill of grasping something for nothing. No doubt each customer leaving this great city had won a fortune, had embraced ecstasy without measure, and enjoyed a new high and a wild blast in so doing. Far be it from me, a plain old country boy, to explain discovery of the paths, roads, and alleys leading to the streets of gold. Entering these pathways brought untold riches and notoriety. How else could one explain why crowds clogged the streets, surrounded the gaming tables, collected in bars, massed in dance halls, and express themselves in a mad frenzy of enjoyment? When enthralled by the golden streets or when beholding rainbows at sunset extending from golden pots at each end, the sun rays were forced to hunker down in shame and futility at the city's beauty surpassing them.

You ought to see the city at night! The moon hides its face; a mere masquerade in comparison to the myriad glories abounding in lighted explosions of magnificence and splendor. A phantasmagloria of colored fantasy beyond description. Heaven is sure going to be a disappointment after seeing this. Beauties beyond imagination, excelling wonder in expressions of metaphoric felicity. Lights of glory flashed from all directions. Beacons, revolving spotlights, multi-colored illuminations, lighted torches, reflectors, signs, hued emblems, miles of flashing colors, dazzling luminaries, and countless florescent wonders all glittered in decorative emblazonry from the largest revelation to the single beckoning red bulb over an open doorway. A thousand Fourth of Julys rolled into one.

Never mind a few disgraceful acts in the midst of revelry. Such can easily be dismissed in the quest for riches and pleasure. Now and then a drunk stumbled to the ground in a stupor, but this was of little concern to multitudes stepping over him. Beggars with open palms were easily pushed aside while entering the gleaming palaces. Unaccompanied ladies strolled nonchalantly along the boulevard yet only minor notice was afforded them. (Maybe most of them were wives who let their husbands stay home to baby sit. How do I know? I ordinarily wasn't one to ask.)

My time in Las Vegas consisted of wandering in a daze, hither and yon, back and forth, here and there, up and down, going in circles, pacing the sidewalks, deeply involved in the pursuit of who knows what. Perambulating the Strip fortuitously from one end to the other like a zombie brought no real satisfaction. Evidently the bird of paradise flew in the opposite direction. The more noisy, boisterous, and attractive each amusement produced, the more disinterested I became. My only chance at riches came upon discovering a silver dollar lying under a slot machine in Caesar's Palace. How could the free acts at Circus Circus be enjoyed when eyes were swollen shut from so much gawking and staring, feet were burning from incessant walking, and ears constantly ringing from the endless mayhem? I must be immune to pleasure. Even the nasal twangs from Texas Joe and the Mustang Cowboys beating out a number in the Tropicana couldn't persuade my ear canal to respond favorably. Good Self summed it up accurately with the question, "Wouldn't it be more enjoyable, Myle, to be back home in Otoonga sitting on the porch swing with Azailia, tucking the boys in bed at night, and to be scratching a sow's ear when she was in labor, than having fun in this artificial environment, a sacrilege to the real meaning of life?"

You can have Las Vegas. Oh, it has a few mountain-top attractions. Somehow I was unable to climb a high enough hill to find where they were. Advancing to the highest peak brought to me only a slippery slope, a quick slide to the bottom of disappointment and despair and vanity. It saddened me to see that well-dressed couple, she in high heels and fur coat and he with white shirt and tie, standing along the freeway entrance, begging for a ride. And there were hundreds of other couples following in their footsteps. How appalling it was to see thousands of street derelicts lying in gutters and to be trapped by the Gay Rights activists marching in a parade at midnight.

Do you know what was the most amazing sight of all on the Strip that night? It came at the end of this wonderful visit to Las Vegas. Just before entering the taxi that would whisk my body to the airport, I happened to glance to my left, there to behold the most beautiful girl my eyes had ever seen. She was hanging on the arm of a First Lieutenant as they exited the Excalibar. What a shock it was to hear her speaking in husky tones, to see bulging arm muscles, and to observe (what I really shouldn't have been looking at) dark hair on her bare legs. Just how many surprises can a motor home driver be expected to endure?

CHAPTER XVIII
Baltimore Interlude

The pair came mincing their way along the outer fringes of the Neanderthal parking lot, seemingly with no urgency or meaningful motivation, but rather with a "who cares" attitude, not what would be expected from persons needing help or information. Pausing in front of a big Peterbilt, one of them stepped upon the immense running board, but no apparent response came forth from inside. They continued a nonchalant meandering along the concrete walkway directly in front of a line of parked semis. The same procedure was carried out once more, this time at the cab of a trailer loaded with Chevrolet automobiles. A window was rolled down, a brief discussion was held, whereupon the sauntering continued, this time approaching my vehicle since it was next in line.

You see, my unit was resting at the Neanderthal Plaza after concluding a day of driving the Purple Flash toward the city of Baltimore, Maryland. The Dundalk ship yards was the destination of this unit, where it would be herded on board the Atlantic Wave bound for Germany, and from there to Oslo, Norway, according to the information on the packing list held in my possession. Several other vehicles had found harbor in this same location in prior times and under different conditions, each being guided there by my capable hands. On each occasion my hopes were for some kind of miracle to happen, and that I would be allowed to accompany the vehicle to its European appointment, or that somehow I could be a stowaway under the bed or in the toilet to fulfill my desired mission.

No such luck ever took place. It would have been a great adventure to cross the wild waters of the Atlantic and to visit those enticing lands of Europe. Such hopes were once again reduced to idle dreaming.

As in previous itineraries, before even delivering the unit to the docks, I was duty bound to drive four miles beyond the docks on a busy, narrow street to a fuel station, from there to a car wash, and then reversing once again to the dock-loading area. The episode at the car wash was nerve-wracking and spine-tingling. Somewhere in this humongous city of Baltimore there surely must be existing a car bath large enough to accommodate a big vehicle such as this. But not this car wash. The bays were much too low to make entrance without smashing in the roof. Instead, I was forced to place the unit close to the entrance, extend the wash gun as far as possible, and to squirt from long distance. I would wash one side and the front by this method, jump back inside to turn the vehicle around as quickly as possible, and to cleanse the opposite and rear next, attempting to complete the entire process all for $1.75 time slot (which was an impossibility, of course).

This was done with the hope that there would be no scraping of the sides of the unit on the concrete walls, knocking over the wiper stands could be avoided, and smashing the vacuum cleaners with my rear end wouldn't take place. The jaunt back to the docks could then be consummated, providing one didn't get lost in the maze of traffic, didn't run over the Toyota autos ahead, and nerves didn't completely get out of control at the dock area. This caused a considerable amount of nail biting also. I was required to reverse the vehicle into a fifty-foot long bay marked faintly with orange paint marks. No scratching the side on the adjacent barb wire fence was to be allowed either. After parking, cleaning up the unit inside, and gathering my wits about me, standing in line at a dock office for an endless period of time had to be endured while holding tightly in my fingers the embarkation sheets to keep the ocean breeze from sailing them out to sea. Waiting for the indolent, sullen, insulting, cocky, foul-talking office workers to process the papers for shipment wasn't exactly a piece of cake either. They acted like it was much ado about nothing or maybe less than that.

What an exhilarating thrill it was, what a huge lump came to my throat, watching the skilled dockmen drive the unit up the long gangplank for the sea voyage! What a deep sense of inspirational patriotism overwhelmed this humble motor home driver, knowing that he had been instrumental in assisting some rich man in a foreign country to acquire his heart's desire, even though deep down inside you knew he was being taken for a sucker.

Finally, with signed papers in hand, I was free to move on! At the doorway some sneaky character could usually be seen lurking who boasted he would drive you to the airport for less than half what a taxi ride would cost. It was a big lie, I had found out previously. This time I fooled him completely by carrying my bags four blocks to a city bus stand where after an hour of waiting, a coach wended its way downtown to the Black Dog Bus.

At the station, a ticket could be purchased that would save many dollars instead of flying, providing you were willing to wait seven hours and ride another thirty-three.

It came to pass, however, that the savings only amounted to twenty-five cents because of a little interlude mixed in. Offhand, it would appear not worthwhile. But thinking it over, it was. For only six blocks from the bus station was the illustrious Camden Yards where the famous Baltimore Orioles played. To this day, Azailia has not been told of this diversion, for she would not have thought it worthwhile to spend $29.00 to see a bunch of ball throwers, even if their names were Cal Ripken, Roberto Alomar, and Brooks Robinson.

To me, interminable waiting in line at dock-shipping offices, slouching on iron seats at bus stations, and acquiring ringing ears from yelling spectators are direct causes of agitation. It sensationally interferes with the brain waves, conveying a sense of discouragement to the brain fibers themselves, which send messages to all parts of the body and originates motion. Neuradynamia criss-crosses this network, inserting incongruous innuendoes in inappropriate places, nullifying complacency with a good case of folderol, and castigating encouragement from Good Self with bellicose indictments, snatching defeat from victory, deliberately deleting sublime conjecture, and replacing the entire mess with supercilious reprimands.

At the Neanderthal Plaza it became apparent the next stop for the two meandering figures would be my motor home. I could easily be seen under the low ceiling lights. I was faithfully working on my logbook, drawing lines and entering numbers, attempting to fool the dispatch clerks in the Otoonga office. What could these two approaching figures be doing in the darkening gloom of evening? This was a cause for concern if they stopped at my door. I didn't want to be a victim of robbery, swindle or assault. The windshield could easily be broken with a club, an axe could smash through the walls, or a bullet could be fired which might penetrate the brain, lodge in the logbook and leave its victim with an incoherent babble, and the logbook torn to shreds.

What a great relief it was to discover my fears were without basis. Instead of threatening characters disrupting my life, closer sight revealed merely two young girls ambling about. What harm could two innocent young girls cause? Not only were they young, but very good looking as well, with mini-skirts, high heels, red fingernail polish, and piled up hair. Rolling down my window I said to them, "You gals having car trouble? Flat tire maybe? And you needing help and no one gentleman enough to help you?"

Immediately they burst forth in fits of giggling and laughter. While they continued laughing, I asked them another question. "Do your mammas know you gals are out here this time of evening? It's getting dark and you should be home instead of a place like this."

This really broke them up. They bent over in convulsions of uncontrolled laughter as if I had told the funniest story ever heard. I wasn't going to let my warnings go unheeded. "Don't you know that a truck stop is a bad place for you gals? You can't be too careful in a place like this. Some of these truck drivers can't be trusted. Your mammas should have told you not to be here this time of night."

By this time tears were running down their faces, arms were entwined about each other to keep from falling down, and they were tiring themselves out with laughter. The blonde eventually composed herself to reply, "You got it all wrong mister. We're only here looking for our brother." The other girl was black and both were better looking than the other one.

"Well, you are looking in a dangerous place. Your mamma should have warned you. There might be some criminal around here just waiting to take advantage of gals like you."

In the middle of another round of hilarity, the blonde answered, "I told you once, we're trying to find our brother. What's wrong with that? Go mind your own business."

With arms around each other they began limping away toward the line of trucks sitting on the opposite side of my unit. The black girl turned her head toward me and gave one parting shot, "We don't do no truckin' with Sunday School boys." Whatever that meant.

Watching them leave, I thought to myself that they were asking for trouble. The motor was running on the third truck down the line which appeared to be their next objective. To my surprise, the door opened and both made a hasty entrance. Was this remarkable, or what? Could it be they found their brother that easily? What a coincidence that would be! If so, that would mean he was a half-breed, to be a brother to both of them. Yet, stranger things are happening every day and this must be one of them.

A considerable amount of apprehension was felt for these girls, even if they were fortunate enough to find their brother. To be out in a dangerous truck stop, where there is little self-control in eating and pop drinking, isn't the place for innocent young girls. There is little discipline in the home these days. It seems like anything is tolerated with kids running the streets rampant, and the parents don't care. It isn't much wonder there are so many thefts, murders, violence, and cheating on school tests when mothers don't make the kids mind, and maybe don't even know where they are. Look what happens—chaos and foul talk. Many troubles and dangers face young people and motor home drivers in the day in which we live, and these two lonely girls searching for their brother is just one more example.

I desperately hoped no harm would come to them, or their brother either, and that they would soon be out of this dangerous place and back home in their mothers' care. You can't pick up a newspaper or turn on the TV anymore but what you see more disastrous results of some young person in a terrible predicament, and probably have to stay after school in detention for a night a two. Yes, my heart goes out to the youth today, and motor home drivers like myself too, for the world is no longer a safe place anymore, not like in the war years when I grew up, and everyone lived in peace with his neighbor. This was only one more situation of desperation, watching two lovely, innocent girls cutting across the corner of a truck stop parking lot in hopes of finding a relative, and in a hurry to arrive back to their places of abode, and soon to be safely tucked in bed.

CHAPTER XIX

Espionage and Intrigue

People hate motor home drivers. Other drivers hate motor home drivers. Some hate us because they think we are rich, arrogant, and self-serving. Some accuse us of being bragga-docious, egotistical, and high fallutin'. Semi drivers hate us most of all. We drive a little slower than they do which works them into a frenzy. It may take a semi up to fifteen minutes to pass a motor home on a level stretch. Then comes an uphill advance where we go around them in two minutes, only to go downhill once again which requires us to apply the brakes to keep from rear-ending them. We have to accelerate at each upturn to pass the trucks, they reciprocate when going down. On and on it goes, a never-ending cycle of frustration and anger.

I remember the time when a big Freightliner kept passing me and vice versa in the mountains of Colorado. This kept up for more than an hour, causing a back up of traffic for nearly three miles, since neither one was completely able to persevere over the other. I tried counting how many times a Jolly Walloper Superbelly eighteen-wheeler passed by, but lost track after the 837th pass. Truckers tailgate us, trying to get even. Some get as close as 10 inches from our rear bumper while going 70 miles an hour. But they don't scare me any. If one gets too careless and smashes into my unit, it would be his fault. His insurance company would be required to pay for all the repairs, the hospital bill, and for death benefits for widow and child support. I would have the last laugh after all. A lot of good it would do them to try a trick like that.

Another reason truck drivers hate us is because we park in the slots for trucks at truck stops and rest areas. Most of the motor homes are too large to park in car spaces, forcing us to use the truck lanes. Our units require half the space of a semi, but it keeps them out of a parking lane, and does that ever make them antagonistic. They try to run us off the road at every opportunity, but I have discovered that if you hold your ground, most of them lose their nerve. The ones that don't will be sorry for it afterwards. No matter how much espionage and intrigue they use against us, they come out on the short end.

Espionage and intrigue are used against motor home driver in many other methods also. Advantage is taken against delivery drivers. We get short-changed, cheated, lied about, and made fun of. Hitchhikers appear from everywhere, trying to get rides. At the dispatch office you will find moochers wanting a ride to Chicago, Los Angeles, or Death Valley.

The company orders state that no hitchhikers may be picked up, but should such a one appear at the office in a beggar-like mood, you can be sure that Hummer or Missmossmus would get his signature on a piece of paper, forcing us to give them a ride in the direction we were going.

One sunny morning in September my delivery documents gave information that Biloxi, Mississippi was due a visit. I had finished examining the twenty-four foot bed-over-the-cab model, had signed the inspection sheet, and was ready to launch out. Suddenly appearing before me was a huge elderly woman with a notice in her hand that would allow her to accompany me as far as Nashville. Can you believe that? Would they allow a fat old lady to ride with me to Nashville? Surely Miss Missmossmus must have thought she was a man, since she looked like a man, talked like a man, and acted like a man. But I could tell she was a woman by the hair growing out of a mole on her cheek. Or was Miss Missmossmus getting even with me for all the underhanded tricks I had pulled, attempting to climb the ladder of success and higher esteem in the eyes of my superiors? Azailia would kill me if she knew there was to be a woman on board, even if she was old and obese.

"I'm not leaving until tomorrow morning," I told the woman, thinking that would put an end to the whole affair. Affair?

"That will be fine with me," was her answer. "You tell me where and when to be, and that's where and when I'll be. I'll have a forty dollar bill with me to help pay for your trouble."

"That will be no trouble," I said after learning that she would be a paying customer instead of just another moocher. "I'm leaving bright and early at four A.M. at Third and Yarley."

"That will be a nice time to start. I'll be there."

She proceeded to explain why she wanted to go to Nashville, what her plans were, and what a nice guy I was to be taking her along. She kept up a constant chatter until I was forced to excuse myself to get away. Sure enough, at four A.M. the next morning at Third and Yarley stood a woman under a lamp-post. She said good morning, opened the entry door, tossed her bags in the hall, and chose a seat behind the refrigerator where I couldn't see her from the driver's seat. This seemed strange, since she had been so forward and outspoken the morning before.

It wasn't until stopping for gas at Teardrop Hill, Missouri that I was able to get a good look at her. Something wasn't right. This wasn't the same woman at all. She was an imposter. She was fat alright, had grey hair alright, but everything else wasn't right. Her apparent credentials were: bright red fingernails, high heels, a grey-haired wig, and fat with pregnancy. I had been hoodwinked! This must be another case of espionage and intrigue.

"Hey, you aren't the gal I talked to yesterday."

"No, but I am her daughter."

"What are you doing in here?"

"I need a ride to Nashville."

"What kind of a set up is this, anyway? I could be in deep trouble for taking the wrong person. How old are you?"

"I'll be seventeen next month."

"Seventeen? And I bet you don't have a husband at all, do you?"

"Not yet. But I'm gonna get one when I get to Nashville."

With this abbreviated conversation only, I could tell that old nemesis of mine was making a comeback…fear. Now, I am ordinarily an extremely brave person and don't get scared very often, but this wasn't one of those times. Driving across state lines with an under-aged female on board wasn't conducive to a pleasant outlook. I might be charged with being a white slaver, and no judge would have pity on a white slaver. My eyes started to twitch, knuckles were turning white, toes began tingling, and sweat lined my brow.

"I'll give you three choices. You can get off this unit right now. Or, you can go in the bathroom, lock the door, and sit on the stool all the way to Nashville. Or, you can crawl under the bed, stay there, and don't let out a peep. And if a patrolman stops me to search this place, my number will be up. And so will yours, because your throat will have ten deep finger marks on it before you get a chance to escape."

"I'll crawl under the bed."

"And I don't want you telling anyone that I am the father of your child either."

The farther I drove, the deeper I fell into the cauldron of depression, agonizing over the implications of impropriety, irrationality, and deception, which were encumbered with other thought-provoking interventions of drastic descending speculations while emitting questions regarding irregularities enumerated and delivered in escalating momentum, applicable to the plunge into surrealism in but a twinkle of the eye.

So, the farther I drove, the faster I went—intentions being that the farther I drove and the faster I went, the quicker I would get there, and that it wouldn't be too soon. Little did I know that it not being too soon wouldn't be soon enough. Disaster was about to strike again.

Disaster struck first about 100 miles northeast of Nashville, perhaps still in Kentucky. I was doing about 85 miles an hour when I first heard it. It came in the form of moans and groans coming from underneath the bed.

"I told you not to let out a peep," I yelled back.

The moans ceased for a few minutes and then began again in earnest.

"If you don't shut up, a passing patrolman will hear you, make me stop this vehicle, and our numbers will be up. Try to hold out a little longer. We'll be in Nashville in a couple of hours. You can hunt up a restroom then."

In spite of my warnings, the moans and groans grew louder and more intense, causing me to increase my speed by another 15 miles an hour. All at once the groans reached a high crescendo, and then silence! Silence didn't last long however. In place of silence came the most horrible outcry that I ever have heard. Being a farmer, I have heard thousands of outcries. Most of them came from the mouths of little pigs being born. Now this wasn't the outcry of a little pig being born but there was a somewhat similarity. It was so similar that my speed automatically increased another 15 miles per hour and the hairs on my head stood straight up.

The vehicle was moving so fast that I almost missed the sign "Sisters of Mercy Hospital, 5 blocks right." The brakes were applied so forcefully that the driver nearly went through the windshield.

During the five-block drive, Bad Self began taunting, "Don't tell me, Myle, that you have started using a motor home as a hospital room. What will one Mr. Hummer say about that?"

At the Emergency Hospital Entrance, one scared driver ran furiously to the admittance desk, explaining that he thought a baby had just been born. Soon four white-masked men trotted out to the vehicle carrying a stretcher and who knows what else. Sure enough, they soon retreated holding a bawling baby, a bawling mother, and a bawling motor home driver followed them toward the hospital. The bawling motor home driver managed to ask the bawling mother why she didn't tell me she was having a baby. "You told me not to let out a peep," she answered.

Before entering the door, the head white-masked man said, "We will take this woman to an emergency room. You go over to the desk to register and fill out insurance forms. That's when Good Self came to my rescue. "Don't do it! You're not responsible. Get out of here before they make you sign on the dotted line that you are the father."

Seldom have such welcome words reached my ears. While they took the bawling baby and the bawling mother to the emergency room, I took off on the run for my waiting unit. That unit took off so fast that it did wheelies the entire five blocks back to the interstate. I had escaped! I sure did not want to be the father of another baby. I got enough kids of my own.

Tears of joy, untwitching eyes, and smiling frowns were the consequences of this escape. I sure fooled that hospital. It takes a cold day in Nashville to get the best of Myle Heyers. It must have been all that bouncing and jolting while lying on the floor that brought on the labor. How were they to know who I was? They couldn't pin anything on me, especially a diaper.

"What will you tell Hummer when you get back?" said Bad Self.

"Don't tell him anything. How is he to know a baby was born on one of his motor homes?" answered Good Self.

The result was that I didn't tell Hummer what happened. I didn't tell Missmossmus what happened. And I didn't tell the dealer in Biloxi what happened either. Let them find it out for themselves. The Biloxi inspector didn't think to look under the bed, so how would he know a baby had been born there?

Each driver must be prepared for any eventuality when delivering motor homes, as you have been told. In the midst of deviating circumstances and fly-in-your-face obstacles, one must be firm and unsentimental. That's what I am anyway. The next time a pregnant woman sets foot in one of my motor homes, I am going to check her due date, because I don't like the outcome from these kinds of situations. And I don't like espionage and intrigue between and mother, a daughter, and a baby to interfere in this lucrative position of delivering motor homes either.

Criminal activity is a never-ending threat to drivers such as me. Either there is a temptation to commit a crime yourself, or else one is being committed against you. The impending danger of evil action hangs over one's head like the Sword of Damocles. Law violation against us is a continued menace, more so since the word has gotten out that it is a bunch of dumb Midwestern white boys that do most of the driving out of Otoonga. Lately, however, an immigration of roughneck California thugs have been muscling in on our turf. Disturbing consequences result, since most of them are high on drugs all hours of the day or night. They attempt to upset our apple carts through robbery, theft, stealing, and taking something that doesn't belong to them through threats of knives, guns, or muscle flexing. Apple carts are easily upset when you are susceptible to being a pushover, and the more susceptible you are, the more likely it is that you will be.

I try not to be a pushover but that doesn't always occur. Like the time I headed for Pittshead, Pennsylvania with my hands guiding a thirty-three foot Tiger Lille, the one that has a motor in the rear and you must remember to fill with diesel instead of gasoline. This Tiger Lille was a well-equipped aggravation, costing an untold amount of dollars (the management formerly listed the suggested retail price in the window, but with wild inflationary tendencies in today's pricing, the practice is no longer carried out, leaving the price unknown until some panting buyer has signed on the dotted line).

Before leaving the factory yards I was commanded by Miss Missmossmus to pick up a carburetor at the parts department building between the tail light shed and the nut and bolt building. I was carrying out the order with fastidiousness and agility by grasping the carburetor by its tentacles when a booming voice halted my advancement, "Here is a satchel and a book of instructions that goes along with it, you know, Jake." Strange, nothing was mentioned in my orders about anything else to take along. A note on the satchel was marked "Urgent", and around the container inside was a band of tape enclosing the words "Do not Open."

Before starting for Pittshead, I drove to the farm to kiss Azailia good-bye, gave a hug to the boys, and slipped out to the hog house to see how Old Barney was doing. Only he wasn't. He was still in his pickup, fast asleep. I rapped on the window to awaken him.

"Barney, are you O.K.? Jane isn't here yet."

"Well, I reckon I would come over early so I wouldn't be late."

"Go ahead and finish your nap. But when she comes, be sure to go out and help her. And I don't want you forking manure into the feed bin. Throw it out the door, not in the feed bin."

"O.K., Myle, I gotcha."

He immediately fell asleep, allowing a quick departure for myself.

I was off to Pittshead, with hope springing eternal in my breast. A strong headwind was my opponent for the first 400 miles. A traffic snarl at Gary, Indiana also slowed my progress. By nightfall the wind had abated considerably, allowing for a smooth sailing from then onward.

My vehicle was parked for the night at a service area along the Interstate in Indiana. During the night I suddenly awoke, thinking the rest room was calling me. I scrambled out of my sleeping bag, staggered aimlessly toward the front in search of my clothes, and stumbled over the carburetor lying in the hallway. The carburetor bounced across the aisle, puncturing a hole in the satchel. After returning from the rest room at the service plaza, a further survey was made of the damage I had done to the satchel. Lying by the satchel was a pile of salt-like substance which had trickled out of the hole. I tasted a little of it, to see if it really was salt or not. A sharp jolt of pain hit the back of my neck with such force that I nearly fell over backward. A jolt of disturbing revelation struck my brain shortly thereafter also. It caused a mental oscillation to reverberate with extemporaneous agility, culminating in a primary observation that Bad Self declared, "You're in big time trouble now, Myle. That must be smuggled dope in that satchel!"

What a shock that statement was! In my possession was a satchel containing a granulated substance. My mind began running rampant as it often does, prodded on by the confusion between Bad Self and Good. Probably coke, meth, marijuana, opium, or a vaccine for AIDS was in that container, being smuggled by unknown gangsters while using me as the fall guy. Most likely a big black sedan was following me and probably parked in this very same service area, just waiting to attack. At any moment they could burst into this vehicle, shoot me dead, cut my heart out, burn up the motor home to destroy evidence, and make a fast getaway with the prized satchel worth millions of dollars. How could I have been so stupid? And I bet Hummer and Missmossmus were in on the whole idea from the start.

Further sleeping was out of the question because of tearful eyes, shaking limbs, and a rapidly-exploding heartbeat. This wakefulness, as nerve wracking as it was, allowed an intricate plan of defense to be devised. More than one can play at this game. It would be one lone driver against the mob. Just how many thugs were involved in this venture was unknown, but it could have been several. Maybe many. Perhaps they had a fleet of vehicles to run me down, with evil intentions.

My incredible plan was to make an escape at daybreak, before they had time to reorganize. As soon as it would begin to get light, my motor would be revved up, my foot be sticking to the gas pedal, my fingers were to be grasping tightly to the steering wheel, and with an alert mind tuned to action. I would outrun this evil bunch or die trying! Tears then came to my eyes. I don't want to die yet. What if I never again get to see those little eyes staring up at me so trustingly from the hog house? Or what if Azailia's lovely countenance was never again beheld. And those six boys—they need a father to watch over them. If I get out of this awful predicament I promise never to spank those boys again.

True to my word, at the first crack of dawn, that Tiger Lille sped out of that parking yard so fast it would make your head swim. The motor was gunned so high that a race car couldn't catch it. So far, so good.

No black sedan with armed thugs could be seen for the first few miles. I made sure no vehicle passed me except for O.J. Simpson's limousine, and even his driver barely made it. By using such accelerated speed, no rear attack could be made. I had completely given them the slip. You have to get up pretty early in the morning to get ahead of Myle Heyers!

By motivating the monster eight hours straight, allowing no vehicles to pass me or get close to my rear, and making certain no black sedans darted near me from entrance ramps, I was able to make it all the way to Pittshead with absolutely no threat whatsoever. The fuel needle registered empty for the last 95 miles, but I made it anyway. It was a happy driver that guided a huge, cumbersome conveyance into the dealer's yard in Pittshead. Smiles broke out all over his face, sweat ceased from trickling down his brow, tears in his eyes dried up as if in a dust storm, and shaking limbs desisted from counter activity. Bounding up the office stairs with extreme confidence was followed by a burst into the manager's office with the thought-provoking exclamation, "I made it!"

"I see you have," said the manager. "But is this any way to be delivering your unit, Heyers, with mud slopped all over it, the tires smoking, and the radiator boiling over antifreeze?"

"But sir," I answered. "I have saved my life and maybe yours and maybe saved the whole Otoonga corporation from a terrible fate!"

"Just what have you saved? In the condition your unit is in, I think everything is lost."

"No, you don't understand. I kept from getting myself killed and maybe you too. And I got here before them robbers could get their hands on the satchel. You see, there's a bag out there in the unit that is filled with some kind of dope and I escaped from four guys in a black sedan that might have been following me and I got it here safely and now we can turn it over to the police and we'll all be heroes."

"Now just calm down a little, Heyers. Where is that bag of dope you are talking about?"

"Right out there in my unit. It's lying in the hall with dope leaking out of it. I already tasted it and it sure isn't salt, that's for sure."

"If that be so, then we'll go down to your unit and have a look-see."

We entered the entry door and both kneeled to the floor where the satchel was located. Examining the contents for a short time brought heart-rending results. He broke out into a hideous laugh!

"What's the matter? Why are you laughing?" My confidence was slipping.

"This isn't dope."

"It isn't?"

"Of course not."

"Then what is it?"

"Why, this is a new degreaser that our Otoonga engineers have invented. It is in pellet form and under experimentation while being tried out by all the dealers. It is being kept secret by the factory. If it is a success the stock price of Otoonga will skyrocket. Those of us who are smart enough to get in on the ground floor will make a killing."

"You mean it isn't drugs?"

"No."

"Not any of it?"

"None whatsoever. Otoonga certainly has a lot of ignoramuses doing the driving lately."

I was abashed and shamed beyond measure. I was sure that dope was in that satchel. A few minutes later found a dejected driver washing the unit with a hose and a long-handled brush. He couldn't help but notice that several office personnel were looking out the window. All were in throes of laughter and finger pointing. I had given my best, even to the pouring out of my life's blood, and this is my reward—complete humiliation. As each brush stroke went back and forth over the surface, the lips of Mr. Bad Self seemed to keep time in harmony. Shame and reproach poured out in copious amounts by his sneering mockery. "You dumb idiot, can't you get anything right? How could you pull such a foolish stunt? Mistaking degreaser for dope! Dope alright, but it's you instead. You, a grown motor home driver. You should smoke a few joints to find out what dope really is. You might as well quit driving and go back to farming, like all the other dopes are doing."

Even Good Self deserted me with his own concurrence, "You know, he's right, isn't he?"

Disgrace and dismay once again dumped their load of condemnation upon my head. A shameful burning sensation expedited this physical misery, developing a ravishing pythogenic appropriation while ritually postponing a positive recovery, and in conjunction persistently structured an adverse postulation, and advancing night time floccillation with devilish adherence.

As Skyjack Flight #38972 took off from the runway at the Pittshead Airport, a downcast, disconcerted, and angry fellow remarked to the gentleman seated beside him, "At least I didn't get my head shot off, my heart wasn't cut out, and I didn't get burned alive."

"That's right," said the gentleman in astonishment while buckling his seat belt.

CHAPTER XX

Sleepless in Seattle

"We're assigning you a trip to Seattle." The domineering voice of Mr. Hummer pounded in my ears in a threatening manner. "Can you handle that, Heyers? I want that unit delivered by Friday. I advise you to accompany the Makoneys in a three-vehicle convoy. They each have units bound for the same dealer. They are a husband and wife team who will be towing a car to drive back. They agreed you could return with them as a paying rider. It would save you an airplane ticket and would help them in their return expense as well."

"That's fine with me, Mr. Hummer. I'll be glad to come back with them." What had I said? Seattle is a fantastic city, my favorite large city in fact. But in the winter time? Over treacherous mountain roads covered with ice and snow, and with cliffs of 4000-foot drop-offs? And with Azailia most likely hyper and throwing a tantrum because the pipes to the barn were frozen underground requiring stretching a hose from the house to the barn to water the pigs which are growing faster all the time and demanding more feed and toilet concerns and besides this, finding the baby had tonsillitis and stayed awaked all night bawling and Beckley with the diarrhea and Zachary in trouble at school from putting a dead mouse in the teacher's desk and someone had to drive every afternoon to school in town to get him because of his detention?

While hanging up the receiver I told Azailia, "They are sending me on a trip to Seattle and there is no possible way for me to get out of it. I'll be back as soon as possible. I'll make sure Old Barney does all of the chores."

She answered that Barney was complaining about a sore back and indigestion…but it was actually laziness and intoxication. She also remarked how difficult it was to keep the boys under control and that she was afraid she was slipping into a state of depression.

"It's only a case of postnatal blues, Azailia," I answered. "You'll soon get over it. A few mornings out in the cold winter air helping Barney do the chores will snap you out of it, I know. Barney is going to be told in no uncertain terms he's got to do his share. And Jane can help do some of the housework. It is my obligated duty to take this trip. Mr. Hummer has been so good to assign me these wonderful trips. It puts food on the table, you know." I was a firm believer in being firm since I was the head of the house, according to our preacher.

Five o'clock the next morning found one scared driver behind the wheel of a 29-foot Blue Spring, meeting the Makoneys at the intersection of highway 93 and route 1861 three miles north of Otoonga, and fearing doom was certain. In my dreams the previous night we were scaling a tremendous 15,000 foot peak, on a road so steep and slick with ice that I became light headed under the covers over my head. When the road was ultimately navigated over the extreme top, it disappeared into thin air, which catapulted my vehicle into a 15,000 foot free fall that woke me up in a sweat, even though it was freezing cold in our bedroom since the thermostat had been turned low to save on fuel. Mr. and Mrs. Makoney, with first names Pat and Mike, were eager to be moving out. After a brief discussion, it was decided they would lead the way and I would bring up the tail end. My problem was that I couldn't tell which was which. Was Pat the he and Mike the she, or was Pat the she and Mike the he? Was it Patrick and Michelle, or Patricia and Michael? They must have had a pact to keep fooling me. Both had deep voices so I couldn't tell which one was talking. When asking Pat a question, I think Mike answered, and so it went. Thus it came to pass that our convoy of three began the arduous journey, more or less like in the covered wagon days of the Wild West. What a good feeling it was to be in the rear. If one of the other units slid off a cliff I would hopefully be able to stop in time to prevent a similar fate.

Before embarking, we had devised a remarkable scheme by which if anyone became hungry, needed gasoline, or desired to go rest room hunting, whoever was guilty would pass in front of the others and ultimately turn off at the next exit. The problem was no one had to do the same thing at the same time as the others, which meant passing and exiting for the most trivial causes. We were progressing at a snail's pace. This plot, therefore, as remarkable as it was, had to be abandoned. Because it was impossible to discern which one had to do what, or if they might have already done it or not, I would ask Pat or Mike what the solution should be, and the other person would more than likely reply. The person that answered, it must be concluded, must have been the right one to have done it, but if not it was up to the other one. To me, this seemed somewhat confusing but worked famously as long as too much time was not wasted trying to figure out the right one after the answer was given, if it really was that one or not, or if it was the other one.

Surprisingly, the first day of migration provided excellent travel conditions, in spite of the limited beginning. No ice, snow, or howling winds impeded our pathway. With weather and road in our favor, we were able to traverse the entire state of South Dakota. A truck stop at Belle Fourche became our nesting place for the night, accomplished by driving the complete ten hours of allotted time. There had been no head-on collisions, flat tires, dented fenders, or one drop of oil used in any of the units. We synchronized our log books to keep Hummer out of our hair. A hearty meal was devoured at the Ranchero Cafe. For the first time in months, I was able to get a good night's sleep, primarily because Mike or Pat was in charge of the alarm clock operation.

Unbelievable as it is to believe, the second day of transportation was a carbon copy of the first, with crystal clear skies, light winds, and with Old Devil Trouble vanishing from our presence. The western foothills rolled by like a dream while the larger mountains beckoned our challenge with gentle persuasion. The three motor homes scored gigantic victories over the rough terrain, roaring upward and onward with little effort. We made camp that night in Butte. Bozeman Pass had been a pussycat while the mountain ranges surrounding Butte glided by like mounds of marshmallows with the towering cumulous clouds viewed as a whip cream topping.

By evening of the third day, Seattle was within striking distance, some hundred and fifty miles to the west. This was unheard of, coasting through the coastal ranges in the dead of winter with no interruptions whatsoever. Pat and Mike both were uttering extraordinary comments regarding the placable conditions during this epic journey, vanishing all fears and greatly altering the formerly negative outlook. A measure of optimism surged jubilantly through my veins at the prospect of successful delivery of these vehicles, of the economical method of return, and of coins once again ringing joyfully in my pocket. Light-hearted conviviality swept away cobwebs of anxiety, holocaust reversed into celebration, fretfulness dissolved into levity, and confidence reigned over defeat. The third night found our party camped in a parking area for trucks near Ellensburg after another day under clear blue skies. The nights were cool but what can you expect in January?

Our triumphant entry into Seattle resembled somewhat the great victory of King David fighting the battle of Jericho or Napoleon conquering Waterloo. The dealer man in Seattle embraced us with open arms, a pat on the back, and a kiss to the cheek. Why shouldn't he, for all the dough he will make when selling these contraptions? Our delivery papers were signed with a flourish while Pat or Mike unhooked the car that he or she had been towing. We were free spirits, victors of a great mission, heroes of the Otoonga world, successors over calamity! Almost.

The long return back to Otoonga remained to be retraced. That should provide no problem for three skillful drivers as we taking turns at the helm. Happy moods caused a celebration to be our first objective. Mike, or maybe Pat, concocted the idea, "Why don't we eat out in a fancy restaurant and get hotel rooms for the night in this fabulous city? We can have a little fun for a change instead of beating our brains out on the highway every day. We deserve it."

Pat or Mike readily concurred, "Yeah, I'm getting sick of those hamburgers we eat at McDonald's morning, noon, and night."

A few ribald jokes were bandied back and forth, sealing a mutual agreement to secure rooms at the Cauliflower Hotel in downtown Seattle. Pat and his wife or her husband were together in one room on the seventh floor, while my adjoining room was one door farther down the hall. Before retiring, we strolled through the streets of downtown, sightseeing and seeking a dining establishment. Charlie's Lobster Pot was chosen. It was an exquisite place to satisfy hunger. That restaurant had everything. So that's what we ordered. Pink shrimp, blue oysters, red lobster, fin of whale, leg of alligator, and a few wiggling scallops thrown in. It was an effort to walk back to the hotel, being in such a stuffed condition. This was living high on the hog, as they say in Otoonga. I laughed to myself of how much bragging could be done when we get back home. Poor Eddie, he's going to be so jealous when he hears about this, while pounding rocks in the quarry.

Once settled in our rooms, a spectacular view could be seen from our windows. With only a turn of the head could be offered scenes of Mt. Ranier, the sprawling bay with an incessant parade of liners and ferries, a super colossal skyline revealing towering structures climbing to the heights, the gigantic space needle left over from the World's Fair, and the awe-inspiring Olympic Mountains to the west. Seattle has it all. Sky-blue lakes, cascading rivers, trees and foliage of utmost beauty, colorful parks, and the hum of congestion, all within the city limits. Contributing valiantly was the rumble of train and motor vehicles, the moving sounds from both bay and sky, and the incessant jumble of milling pedestrians. This was undoubtedly my favorite American city, unsurpassed in beauty, attractiveness, and awe-inspiring magnificence. Up to now.

In my room, time was spent watching the television news, indulging in an exhilarating shower, fifteen glorious minutes in the hot tub, and the gratification of clean sheets and pillow. Sleep was fast coming although it didn't last long.

I was awakened by a faint bumping noise. It was at first dismissed as a dream sequence or my imagination. Gradually the sound became louder and more prominent. It was coming from the wall adjacent to Makoney's room. It was intermittent but forceful. If the Makoneys were in trouble it would seem they would have called me. Unless something bad had taken place.

After struggling into my clothes, I quickly made my way to their room where a ring of the bell brought no response. Neither did a knock on the door. With my ear pressed to the door, the bumping sound could be heard, growing progressively louder. This convinced me that something definitely was wrong with the Makoney's room. I quickly called the desk clerk from my own room. A house detective soon appeared who slowly unlocked the door while holding a revolver. I was right about wrong. Pat and Mike were bound hand and foot with gags in their mouths and wearing not a stitch of clothes. Pat or Mike the woman was lying on the bed tied to the bed post, while Pat or Mike the man was lying on the floor along the wall adjoining my room. The man had inched himself across the floor and, even though being tied by his ankles, had raised both feet high enough to strike them against the wall, hopefully to attract my attention. The detective removed his gag and began untying him. This left myself to untie Pat or Mike the woman.

My first act was to remove her gag and throw a sheet over her. A pitiful wail of complaint was heard.

"Two guys came in, stole our money and luggage, tied us up, and made us take off our clothes," she cried. "I thought we would be killed." She shook with weeping and trembling.

"Boy, I'm sure sorry about this." I was trying to offer consolation.

As the security man untied Mr. Makoney, he asked many questions. "What went on in here? Why did you let them in your room?"

Through fits of sniffling and shaking, man Makoney replied, "A ring sounded on our buzzer. Through the door I asked what they wanted. Someone said they had a message for us from the desk. That's where I made a terrible mistake. Soon as I unlocked the door, in rushed two masked men with guns pointed at us. It was horrible."

"Had you seen these men before?"

The woman replied in a quivering voice, "No, they were complete strangers. They took everything we had, even our clothes, and tied us up."

While moaning and groaning continued, I was trying to untie Mike or Pat, whoever it was. Have you ever tried untying a naked lady with her hands tied behind her back? Since it was unsuccessful with a sheet covering her, I threw caution to the winds and tossed the sheet aside.

"I'll keep my eyes closed as much as possible," I said in embarrassment.

"I don't care anymore," she whimpered. "Just get me loose."

By struggling heroically and only peeking once in a while, I was able to soon release her. By this time Mr. Makoney had been freed by the security agent as well. They wrapped themselves in the bed clothes for a covering.

Shortly thereafter, four city policemen barged through the door, each one with a swaggering gait and authoritative look, while holding billy clubs, fingering revolvers strapped to their sides, and wearing hats at a cocked angle. The policemen huddled together with the security detective for a time before coming to the other side of the room where we were. A barrage of questions spewed forth, leaving the Makoneys in a hopeless daze. This continued for half an hour, leaving the Makoneys shaking under their sheets, while I was doing likewise under my clothes. Again the group gathered together in a corner for a brief period of time. The Chief (or someone who thought he was) gave us an informative disclosure.

"What we have here is a robbery, pure and simple. It appears you Makoneys got robbed. Who the unknown robbers were, we don't know. But we will shake these city streets until we get to the bottom of this. You can mark it down, these theives won't get away with this. Crime never pays! We want you Makoneys and Heyers to remember this. If this ever happens to you again here you can count on us to get to the bottom of it! These perpetrators will be brought to justice! You can mark it down."

Strolling about the room, his tirade continued, "We come up with a consensus here. You two Makoneys, we're going to require you to remain here in your rooms overnight. Tomorrow you will be run through the suspect lines to see if you can make any identifications. All your expenses will be paid. We'll ask the Salvation Army to outfit you with clothes and send you through their food lines for the homeless. We're going to get to the bottom of this. You can mark it down. But be sure and lock your door. We don't want to get another call in the middle of the night from this same room number."

After giving the shaking Makoneys orders, he came over to where I was shaking, getting right in my face. "You, Heyers, what do you know about this robbery?"

"Nothing sir. I was asleep when I heard—"

"That don't make no difference. This might be an inside job and you look a little suspicious to me. You're the only one that knew the Makoneys, ain't you?"

"Yes, but officer, I—"

"That don't make no difference."

"But officer, I came all the way from Otoonga with the Makoneys. We were driving—"

"That don't make no difference. This might be an inside job."

"But officer, I don't know anything about this robbery and I—"

"That don't make no difference in a court of law. We got to see things in black and white and right now you got a big black question mark hanging over your head."

"But officer, just ask the Makoneys. I came all the way with them to—"

"That don't make no difference. I think we're going to have what you call a little interrogation."

Pat or Mike said, "We can vouch for him, officer. He's as honest as the day is long. He wouldn't—"

"That don't make no difference. The days got a lot shorter this winter, and for all we know he might be in the middle of an inside job."

"But officer, I—"

While my protests continued, a pair of handcuffs was slipped on my wrists, leg irons encased my legs, and my mouth was gagged. I was led out the door, up the hall, down the elevator, and into the squad car on the street. The squad car raced through downtown with lights flashing and sirens screaming. At headquarters I was blindfolded, a spotlight was shone in my face, and I was what you call interrogated. The first question asked my name, rank, and serial number. One poor unfortunate motor home driver was suffering with head swimming, perspiration running down his cheeks and spine slipping out of place. No matter how much interrogation took place, it didn't do them any good. I was like George Washington and the cherry tree, or like another well-known president in the Oval Office, I couldn't tell a lie.

Nearly an hour of what you call interrogation had gone by before the chief investigator said to me, "You are a very suspicious character, Heyers, but we haven't got any goods on you yet. What we have here is a robbery by some unknown hoodlums and you may or may not be one of them. But you can mark it down, we'll get to the bottom of this. Those perpetrators will be brought to justice. It don't pay to rob people, even if they are sneaky out-of-towners, in this town. Maybe the Makoneys will shed some light on the subject when we what you call interrogate them again tomorrow. But you can know, if we find out that what the Makoneys confess involves you, I will personally in person drive my squad car out to that so-called hillbilly town of Otoonga and bring you to justice. Since we haven't got any goods on you yet, you can go free. Any questions, Heyers?"

"Just two, sir."

"And what might they be?"

"Why didn't you let me have a lawyer?"

"You didn't ask for one, robber boy. So it's your own fault. Ha ha. What's the other one?"

"When you interrogate the Makoneys again tomorrow would you please try to find out if Pat is the man and Mike is the woman, or if Pat is the woman and Mike is the man?"

With that question rudely unanswered I was briskly ushered out of the office and on to the street. I was given my two bags but no transportation or even a kiss goodbye. What a horrible change of events had befallen me. From felicity to disaster in but a few hours. Pat and Mike, or Mike and Pat would get their expenses paid, would receive free food from the Salvation Army, free hotel from the Police Department, their name published in newspapers and maybe their pictures on television, and still had a car to drive home. Where did that leave me? Out in the cold street, that's where it left me. All I got out of it was a tendency toward suicide. There goes my cheap ride home. Loneliness, heartbreak, and high expenses were the replacement.

I decided to leave this miserable city as soon as possible. From a nearby pay phone I called a cab, hoping to catch the late Red Eye flight from SeaTac Airport. Fate once again intervened, raising its ugly head in mockery. A game was played at the Skydome and, even at this late hour, traffic was stalled to a standstill. Arrival at the terminal revealed the flight had left thirty minutes ago.

How is some dead-beat guy supposed to outsmart Lady Luck when She deserts him, taunts him, and laughs at his misfortune? By this time of night, Pat and his wife or her husband would be cozying down, snug in a warm water bed in that fancy hotel room. I had been humiliated, ostracized, frustrated, and wrongly accused all the while a bombardment from the lips of Mr. Bad Self echoed the same sentiments in not too nice of a manner throughout the airport confinement. His constant harangue made it impossible to get one wink of sleep. Slouched in a straight-back chair wasn't conducive to sleep, but I was too proud to lay on the floor like some of the other victims were doing. How revolting this was! I'll never drive another motor home to this repugnant, miserable city again. Inside its walls dwell robbers, insulting policemen, slow taxi drivers, and snoring, uncaring passengers. It is during such awful times that the principles of well-being degenerate into systematic myodynamics, slowly mutating until all parts of one's body are entangled, accentuating hemiopia of the eyesight, slowing the acceleration of super-charged ego, perpetuating infallibility loss, compounding the degeneracy of favorable decorum, and multiplying the deficiency of successful attainment into a bankruptcy of hopelessness, despair, regret and defeat. That's what driving a motor home to Seattle will do to you.

Chapter XXI

Drivers' Room

"Do you know what old man Hummer has thought up now?"

"No, what?"

"He wrote up an order to make all of us drivers take another driving test."

"You mean after drivin' for forty years, he's gonna have some eighteen-year-old yokel see if I know how to drive or not?"

"That's exactly right. It makes my blood boil."

"I ain't goin' to do it."

"Me neither. If they make us take another driving test, I'm walkin' out this door and never comin' back."

"You can't believe what all they think up for us to do. This is the most chicken outfit in the whole U.S.A."

"And the price of gas has gone up again. But do you think they will pay us any more expense money? That's a joke. After this trip I'm walkin' out this door and never comin' back."

The guy with the bald head, mustache, and ponytail added, "That ain't all, men. When we get to the dealers, we got to have them sign a paper sayin' there was no damage on the unit. And it has to be clean as snow. Next thing, they'll make us wax the tires."

"It's almost that way already. Some of them dealers have a spittin' fit if they find a speck of grease on the whitewalls, after us driving over two thousand miles to get there," said the driver in striped overalls.

"Yeah, and a couple of weeks ago on a trip to Spokane I had me a little accident. The right front fender got dented in only one inch. And Hummer tried to blame me. Even when some crazy lobo had run into a road sign and bending it over into my lane and made me run into it. It makes me so mad."

"That's nothin'," said the skinny twerp wearing a yellow cap with earflaps. "I was runnin' behind a snowplow out in Wyoming last month, and the joker sudden like dodged left, leavin' a big pile of snow in my lane. This all ended up with me runnin' into it instead. That snow bank was so hard it bent my bumper back six inches. And Hummer said it was my fault. I had to dig up $75 deductible, 'cause he said it was my fault that I ran into a snow bank the snowplow wouldn't plow. Can you believe that? I'm never takin' another cotton-pickin' trip for these yo-yos."

We five drivers were sitting in the Otoonga drivers' waiting room, waiting for our papers for another trip. Some of the units may have had a mechanical deficiency and were being repaired. Perhaps the delivery sheets were not yet prepared, the office personnel were out on a three-hour lunch break, or maybe they were just testing our endurance. This was the place where gripes continually sprang forth, each driver attempting to impress others, and extensive exasperation was the order of the day.

Some of the tales being recounted actually happened. It was sometimes difficult to separate a true rendition from a false account unless shifty eyes gave the offender away. The room was approximately twenty-by-twenty, lined with folding chairs scattered about in disarray. Contained therein was a badly worn folding table, a large hanging wall clock, a bulletin board tacked with notes and orders, two waste baskets, and vending machines dispensing coffee, pop, and candy. My own unit was sent back to the service department because the cruise control wasn't working properly. Most of the units were squeaky-clean new, yet it was amazing what all could go wrong after driving a short distance or even before leaving the dispatch lot. If the unit malfunctioned on the road, it was up to the driver to have it repaired at a garage maintained by the chassis service dealer of the make of unit he was driving. By the time we had driven a unit for hundreds or thousands of miles, it had to be in perfect shape for the sales office to which it was being delivered.

This was the room where tales were told, disgust was spewed forth with venom, envies were issued when one driver was issued a better trip than another, vile criticism of Otoonga construction was discussed, and dirty stories were occupational therapy. I'm not going to repeat any of those stories, any pornographic language, or obscene imprecations in case some young person under the age of twenty-eight should get a copy of this. I was content to listen to the renditions and complaints, and interrupting occasionally.

The green-eyed fellow with a red jacket started in, "You guys talk about snow piles, man. You ain't seen nothin'. I just got back from Ebony River, Montana. Talk about snow piles! The road was blocked at Bismark with drifts thirty feet high. The plows couldn't get through at all. But before you knew it, some of the little compact cars started drivin' over the top of the banks, they were so hard. It weren't long before pickups were drivin' over. That's when I says to myself, 'Greg, if those guys kin go over the top, so kin you. I revved up the motor on my twenty-two foot Blue Moon, and took off followin' in line with all the other bozos. And I made it all the way to Bismark on one drift five miles long and thirty feet high in places."

"This is one whale of a tale," said Striped Overalls.

"Well, it's gospel truth, believe it or not."

"I've heard everything there is to hear."

"There be only one car that didn't make it through. A little Dodge Orani hit a soft spot and sunk down and got wedged in. But did that stop the rest of us? No way. Ever'body else drove right over the top of him. Lucky for him, he sank down far enough to where it didn't do much damage.

The poor little bugger got an awful smashed roof though."

"I, myself, believe every word," said Striped Overalls with a wink toward me.

"You guys think snow drifts are bad. That's nothing compared to what I went through last week," said skinny guy with yellow ear flaps (which by this time one of the flaps had come loose and was dangling by his chin).

"What did poor little you get back from?" taunted Red Jacket.

"Floods in Oregon."

"Floods in Oregon, is it now?"

"Yeah, I never seen nothin' before like it before in my life."

"I suppose you're going to say the floods floated your tin can down the river and out to the ocean."

"It was almost that bad. The current was strong over the road at Ocean City, so I stopped to call Hummer to see if I should chance going through or not. He said go ahead, if I didn't drown. He makes me so mad. First he tells you one thing and then another. I'm goin' to quit this lousy job and never comin' back."

"Looks like you made it back, little man. What did you do, sprout water wings?"

Yellow Cap took a deep breath and retorted, "If you're so smart, why didn't you tell me before I started out, and I would have."

"Calm down, Joker. Just give me the rest of your sob story before I yawn and go to sleep."

"Give me a chance will you, and keep interruptin' and you won't know a thing what happened. 'Anyway, I drove on like he told me, right into the water. It was so deep, it was over my hood. I kept the wheels cramped hard to the right as far as they would go for over two miles to get over it. Goin' around the curves was real bad. The front wheels were skidding all the way. But I was what you call real lucky. The spark plugs worked OK, even under water. I had the motor roaring which made the radiator fan run fast, and it sort of created a vacuum around the plugs and they never missed once. I made it across the two miles and got my unit washed besides."

We were all so stunned that no one spoke a word for several minutes. Pony Tail finally broke the silence. "I can believe what you said about those vacuums. They are powerful stuff. I drove into one by Mobile last year, and lived to tell about it."

"You did? What do you mean by that?" asked Red jacket.

"I was goin' south and had crossed the Mason Dixon line in the road when the bluegrass music was interrupted by a tornado warning. It was for regions north of Mobile along highway 37C. When I saw the next road sign, sure enough, it was 37C. I was purrin' along about 60 when all at once the wind starts blowing crazy like and my old Lizzie starts joltin' back and forth like it was keepin' time to rock and roll instead of bluegrass. It was three o'clock in the afternoon but it was gettin' dark as blazes. All at once, in a flash of lightnin', I saw it."

"What was it you seen?"

"You really want to know? It was the biggest, blackest twister tail I ever saw, and it was wigglin' right toward me. I asked myself what I was goin' to do but there wasn't time to answer. There I saw a haystack in the field across the other side of the road. Since there wasn't time to get my thinkin' cap on, I quick drove into the ditch, endin' up on the north side of the haystack. Lucky there wasn't any fence, 'cause if there had a been it wouldn't have made any difference."

"Did the haystack protect you," someone asked.

"You bet it did. My life was saved and there was nary a scratch on my unit. A few straws got drove into the roof and was stickin' out all over, just like in a miracle. Like was said, that vacuum sucked up them straws and deposited them every which way, leavin' me barefaced and awe struck. All the buildings on the farm across the road blew away but that tail skipped right over top of me. But I blame Hummer for sending me down to Mobile when he knew good and well there might be tornado warnings down there. Them big haunchos in Otoonga, they don't care nothin' about us drivers.

I'm going to do the same as you guys are going to do. After this next trip, I'm walkin' out the door and never comin' back."

While such expressive orations were reverberating around the room, I decided to retaliate. "You fellows are threatening to quit driving and never coming back to this place again. Then why are you all sitting here, waiting for another trip? Why don't you quit right now? The truth of the matter is that you are a bunch of freaking addicts, like I am. Motor home driving is in your blood and quitting is impossible for each one of you."

My outburst shut them up for a little while. The skinny guy with yellow cap ear flaps (one of which was now swinging back and forth beneath his chin) replied, "You're probably right, Myle. But I'm not going to put up with much more of this abuse. The only reason I'm hangin' around here is that my name has come up for San Diego and I can't miss out on that."

Red Jacket added, "Yeah, I'm due for 'Frisco and I like that place. Those California gals are 'A Number One.' But I swear this is it. I can't take this rough life much longer. Anything is better than deliverin' motor homes."

Pony Tail echoed the sentiments, "I thought Vietnam was bad with them Gooks shootin' at yer head ever' minute. That was a piece of cake compared to this. When I get back from this trip to Miami, my papers are gettin' turned in and I'm goin' In-Cog-Nito, man, for sure."

The longer we waited for release of our units, the more impatient and disgruntled each one became, and the more surly became our attitudes. Bitter criticism abounded, much of which was directed to the boss and his secretary. The room was becoming blue with cigarette smoke, Coke cans were kicked across the floor, and it was all we could do to restrain Striped Overalls from knocking his head against the wall.

I decided to assert my wisdom once again, "You all better think twice before quitting your jobs. Remember, you always got a roof over your head when driving motor homes. Where would you find a better job than this around this town? The only openings right now are down at the rock quarry. Even driving is better than that."

"Yeah, but I'm gettin' sick of that prissy Missie Missmossmus, she is a pain if there ever was one," broke in Pony Tail again. "Her with her demands and political correctness and high fallutin' airs. I hope she ends up in a nursing home where she belongs. Then she could dispatch wheel chairs instead of motor homes."

Yellow Cap kept up the argument. "I'm not worried about finding a job. I used to have a job as milk tester and that is one job always in demand."

"Man, there ain't no cows around them parts anymore. How you goin' to test milk when there are no cows around?" asked Striped Overalls.

"There's plenty of cows around here. You just gotta know where to look, that's all."

"I ain't seen no cows around hereabouts for goin' on two years. All the farmers sold their cows when milk prices got so low."

"Like I said, there's plenty of cows, everywhere you look, almost. On my last trip to Fort Worth I almost hit one. There was a whole herd of them walkin' big as you please right down the freeway. I had to do a nifty piece of drivin' to keep from hittin' 'em. One of them swished her tail when I was dodgin' past her, and you could see the cut imprint of it on the windshield even after I got to the dealers office. It wouldn't wash off neither. If you don't believe me, ask the checker man down there."

"Whew! I hope my unit gets released pretty soon," spoke Striped Overalls. "These tales about cow tails are makin' me sick."

Detailed inaccuracy swept forcefully from each mouth, completely disregarding reasonable explanations or plausible persuasion. Stories of driver escapades continued unabated until detraction and unbelief would get the upper hand. On the other hand, how could you tell truth from fiction? If each tale was right on, or if each one was attempting to out do his peers?

"I'm getting tired of all this bragging," Striped Overalls continued. What happened to me on a little jaunt to Phoenix is as true as any preacher's sermon. My unit caught on fire by Las Cruces, and it was caused by an animal."

"Hear, hear! We've heard about everything, so I guess an animal playing with matches isn't too much to stretch a preacher's imagination," said Pony Tail in derision.

"Laugh all you want to. The unit really did catch on fire. I was parked at a rest area by Santa Rosa because I was getting sleepy. No sooner had I lain down on the sofa when I smelled smoke."

"I bet it was a human animal that caused it—you. Next you're goin' to say the tires caught on fire from drivin' so fast."

Striped Overalls was undaunted. "Scoff and make fun. My nose smelled smoke alright, and it wasn't long until my eyes saw it coming from under the hood. As I ran out the door, a squirrel ran out from under the front end, racing for the nearest tree. The funny part was…he didn't have any tail."

"First it was cow tails swishing and now it is squirrel tails disappearing, is that it?"

"That's right, he didn't have any tail. He must have crawled up by the motor to get warm when I stopped driving. And you know what? When I opened the hood, there was his tail caught in the radiator fan. Every time the fan went around, so did his tail. And his tail circled so many times that it caught on fire and burnt up all the spark plug wires, and man, was I disturbed. Yet I couldn't help but laugh at that crazy squirrel with no backside coverin'."

All other drivers laughed, too, but most likely in mockery.

"In spite of it all, I was a lucky guy. I had me some heavy cord string from my drawstring longjohns. I cut the cord in eight pieces, poured some Pepsi on each piece, and tied 'em to the spark plugs. It worked like a charm. I made it all the way to Phoenix using those strings for plug wires. The motor missed now and then but that there Pepsi was a good conductor of electricity for sure."

"This sounds more like a fish story than a squirrel story to me. But you fellas talkin' about cow tails and squirrel tails messin' things up. What happened to me on my last trip to Billings would make any animal's tail stand on end." Red Jacket was taking his turn.

"Listen to him would you?" was a scornful reply. "This will top them all, according to my calculations."

"If you don't believe me, that is your right. What happened to me puts you all to shame."

"Speak on then, but you better have good proof and a lot of shame to go along with it."

"I was hit by a skunk."

"Hit by a skunk? Must have been a giant one then. Are you telling us it smashed your unit all to pieces?"

"No, but it would have been better if it had, the way everything got stunk up."

"I can picture you hittin' a skunk but not a skunk hittin' you. What, did you stop in the middle of the road and wait until he attacked?"

"Just keep on needling. No, I was parkin' along highway 439 and only doin' the speed limit or maybe a little bit more. I was following an Atlas moving van, when all at once I saw this skunk run out from nowhere and he got nicked by a rear wheel of the van. That caused him to jump high in the air and he ended up landin' on my radiator grill. It wasn't long 'til the biggest stink ever stunk started stinkin'. I cracked the brakes right away and stopped. By that time my eyes were waterin' and my mouth could hardly breathe. After I ran outside I could see that skunk was wedged good and tight between the braces of the grill. I tried pullin' him out by the tail but it didn't do no good. Next I attempted to pry him loose with a tree branch but that didn't do no good neither, his body bein' stuck so tight. So I went back inside my unit and got my big sledgehammer from out of the tool box. I pounded on that grill for five minutes until one of the braces snapped in two. Down fell that stinkin' skunk right at my feet. And he wasn't even dead yet. He ambled off through a fence and into the forest, but not before squirtin' one big squirt at me. It made me so sick I had to lay down along side my unit for a few minutes. Seein' me layin' there all comatose caused a few cars to stop but as soon as they opened the doors they would take off like a shot, not waitin' to find out if I was dead or not. There sure are a lot of dirty cowards in this world.

Striped Overalls said, while scratching his head and rolling his eyes, "I believe every word so far, but what did you do to get rid of that stink before you got to the dealer at Billings?"

"That was the problem. I couldn't."

"What did the dealer man say?"

"I'm not finished yet, man. After wakin' up from my coma, I drug myself back inside the unit, only to find that it smelled worse inside than it did out. I held my nose with one hand and grabbed my last can of deodorant out of my bag. I sprayed that entire can of dope over everything but it didn't do much good. Next I opened a can of Mountain Dew and sprinkled it on all the furniture, but that didn't do much good either. It just popped and flizzed but the stink kept stinkin' on, worse than Uncle Harry's outhouse. As a last resort I slapped a piece of Scotch tape over my nose, put on my colored glasses on backwards, and drove on to Billings. Whenever stoppin' for gas at them self service stations, the cashiers wouldn't let me inside to pay for it. So I got by real cheap all the way to the sales office."

"I'm askin' you again, what did the dealer man say to you after you drove that stinking thing in his lot?"

"When I got there, everybody was too chicken to come outside and check it over and sign the papers. What did I do? I forged the dealer man's signature and left the papers on the dash. I unhooked my tow car that I was pulling behind my unit and headed back to Otoonga. The stink wasn't stinkin' quite as bad in my own car but my clothes were smelling so rotten that I took them off, threw' em in a ditch, and drove home in my underwear. I got by real cheap on the way home too, 'cause nobody would let me inside the stations to pay for the gas because of my smelly underwear."

"Didn't Hummer fire you when he found out you forged the name?"

"Surprising to say, he left me off OK. He said it wasn't my fault if some stinkin' skunk had stunk up the motor home. He didn't chew me out or deduct any pay. In fact, he gave me extra bonus for hazardous duty."

"You mean you got by leaving a motor home stinking like a skunk for some dealer to try to sell?"

"The last I saw of the dealer man, he was shakin' his fist at me through the office window but was too much of a sissy to come out to challenge me. I think that in a couple years time the smell would be mostly gone and that somebody with nasal trouble would buy it by then."

Pony Tail shook his head, expectorated a mouthful of tobacco juice into a nearby spittoon, wiped his chin, and began speaking his piece. "You jokers and your cows and squirrels and skunks. None of that can compare to the dangers I faced when wild animals tried to derail me on my last trip to Boise. You would have to hang your heads in shame."

"Wild animals causin' dangers? Spiders and mice, I bet. Will you be telling us you got lost and ended up in a zoo?" Striped Overalls was conceding nothing.

"It was a lot worse than that. My troubles started out in South Dakota, being run over by a herd of buffalo. Cow tails can't hold a candle to buffalo tails. Squirrel tails either. I was drivin' a 34-foot Wild Dasher, the model with three television sets, seven wall clocks, two potty chairs, and a can opener. Everything was going great, buzzing down the road 75 miles east of Rapid City when all at once I saw a big cloud of dust. It looked like a whirlwind at first, but it was headed right toward me. When I found out what it was, I stopped my unit dead still, hoping they would head off in another direction. The lead buffalo, who must have been the ring leader, dodged to the right, just missing my mirror. The next old boy dodged to the left. The rest of the herd came stampeding straight ahead and was packed so tight together that all they could do was jump. I swear, some of them critters can really jump. Four or five of them sailed clean over my unit without so much as scraping their hooves on the roof. But I wasn't so lucky when the last straggler came along. He plowed into my bumper with his knees, smashed the hood with his chest, and poked holes on each side of the windshield with his horns. This detoured his jump enough that he landed on the roof with all of his four feet. There were four giant dents in that roof where he landed."

"This is the sorriest story I ever heard. Did Hummer make you drive it back to the factory?"

"Man, you must be jokin'. That wasn't the last of what happened. Drivin' on through Utah more trouble struck."

"You might as well continue impressing us," I said.

"You know, when crossing the state line at Big Feather Heights, the first sign is 'Eagles on the Road.' It don't say there might be eagles on the road, it just says 'Eagles on the Road.' I never pay any attention to road warning signs, 'cause you never see anything happen that they warn you about. And I didn't see even one eagle on the road. Instead, there were millions of eagles in the air flyin' around everywhere, and they up and attacked. There were little splotches of meat on the roof where the buffalo had skinned his knees and if them eagles didn't swoop down and began fightin' over them meat scraps and blood, right when I was drivin' on down the highway. They pecked and pecked and made hundreds of little holes in the roof with their beaks and talons. You might know, it started raining after the last one had got his meal. With the roof top bein' like a sieve, it wasn't long until I was soaking wet sittin' behind the steering wheel. You ought to have seen the bedroom, the way rain came pourin' in. The bed was so wet you would have thought some two-year-old had been sleepin' in it. And so much water ran down the wall into the sink that you could have washed your hands without turning on the spigot."

"After all that trouble, did you call back to Hummer to tell what happened?"

"Yeah, I did, but Missie-Prissie said he was out playing golf. That made me so disgusted I decided to keep this thing movin' all the way to the dealer office, no matter what kind of condition it was in. So I did, and that dealer man out in Boisie had to worry about it, not me."

"We see you made it back home. How did you get by leaving that unit smashed up and rain soaked at the dealer sales office for him to sell?"

"Man, that wasn't the end of my troubles with wild animals. But you won't believe me when I tell you anyway."

Striped Overalls sarcastically replied, "Say on, story teller. We're sure to believe anything liars tell us in this office."

"No rampagin' buffalo or starved, pecking eagles could stop me from delivering this unit. Anyway, it was so wet inside I couldn't sleep, so I kept drivin' on. West of Salt Lake, a strange sight met my eyes. Not wanting to be stopped by a patrolman (what with my motor home all banged up), I drove on a two-lane instead of the freeway. The twilight was settin' in when I saw it. Something like a great big ball was rollin' down the highway, comin' straight for my unit. I tried to dodge it, but it struck my left front tire. I kept on drivin' until the tire sudden like went flat. The tire needed to be changed, of course, no matter if it was pourin' rain or not. I got soaked even more than inside from the leaking roof. The strangest thing of all was that the tire had little gashes on it that looked like tooth marks. And you know what?"

"What?"

"It was tooth marks for sure. According to the Salt Lake Journal was a story warning to be on the look out for boa constrictor on the loose. The report was that the snake had gotten sick and slimmed down so much that it was able to squeeze through his cage bars, and high-tailed it up to the mountains. The article stated the boa constrictor was so hungry by that time and had swallowed a big horn sheep in the mountains and then was so stuffed it had curled into a ball and rolled back on down the mountain side. When the snake-ball hit the road, it had smooth sailing on the rain slick pavement, and it bit my tire when it rolled by on the other lane."

We sat in stunned silence for several minutes until Red Jacket got enough courage to say, "I can believe each word you're sayin' but am wondering what happened when you finally checked in at the dealer office. Didn't the inspector reject your unit and make you drive it back to Otoonga?"

"That's the best part of it all. I didn't have to see any inspector at all. I pulled a fast one on them. I went to the desk of the reception gal and told her I just found out my mother was dyin' of cancer, and I had to get home as soon as possible. I gave her such a sob story that it got her cryin' so bad that she went ahead and signed my papers without checking what it looked like and she even hired a taxi for me to get to the airport and paid for the taxi herself. I sure pulled the wool over that dealer's eyes. I do pity the poor guy that buys that unit. He's not going to get what he bargained for."

Yellow Cap with Ear Flaps uttered in scornful reply, "All these lies and fabrications turn me off. Why can't you guys speak the truth in an honest manner for once. I'm goin' to be honest myself and confess a little bit about what scares me. It happens to me on every trip, and I ain't likin' it one bit."

"And what might that be?" Sarcasm was oozing out of Red Jacket's mouth.

"You dummies won't believe me but I know I'm right. Everyone of those motor homes I drive is haunted."

"Haunted motor homes! Have you boys heard anything sillier than that?"

"I'm here to tell you them motor homes is haunted. Every night you drive you can hear the most awful spooky sounds comin' out of the walls, screeching from the dash, and even out of the radio whether it is turned on or not. It about scares me to death."

"Listen up, men. This poor little boy is scared of his own shadow." Pony Tail taunting again.

"Laugh if you want to. I swear before a judge, them things is haunted. You can hear the most blood-curdling sounds… 'Whoooooooo' comin' from under the hood when you drive at night, and it ain't from no blown motor gasket."

"Next you'll tell us that you see ghosts and goblins flying in the windows and vampires sneaking in from under the toilet lids."

"Well, I pity the poor suckers that buy these haunted motor homes. They're going to get plenty of scares in the middle of the night like I have. It's worse on a cloudy and dark night when the wind is blowin' strong. It sure brings a lot of mournful sounds. And when the road goes by those cemeteries that are parked along it, all the spirits see these big things travellin' along and it makes a good place to hitch a ride and they can get in easily through the big bars in the grill and radiator fins." Yellow Cap couldn't be silenced even when both of his ear flaps came undone and he was gentleman enough to stop and tie them back up.

"I never heard anything so idiot like," scoffed Striped Overalls. "That sound you hear is only the wind howlin' through the grill when you drive at certain angles. It ain't no ghosts. How crazy you talk."

"I'm telling you, no wind could make such a scary sound like that. Not only that, but you can hear a rattling noise like skeleton bones shakin' and it comes directly out of the stoves."

"Why man, don't you know what that noise is?" Pony Tail was asking in exasperation. "Every motor home has that same noise problem. It's only the stove cover jigglin' around. It looks like those stupid big-wigs at the factory could figure out a way to make the stove lids fit better so they won't rattle every time you hit a bump. Looks like they could fit rubber cushions under them or something?"

"What, and let the whole place catch on fire? Rubber cushions would burn up the whole motor home. That idea is more stupid than believing in ghosts."

Yellow Cap with Ear Flaps continued his complaint by adding, "What scares me the most is those awful sounds comin' out of the walls. There are screeches and moans and groans and scratches all night long. It scares me, man. That's why I drive mostly in the daytime."

Pony Tail lit another cigarette, stroked his beard, and tossed his mane before replying in teasing mockery, "What a fraidy cat you are. Don't you know that all motor homes have noises like that. They are built that way on purpose. When the noises get so bad you can't stand it, that's when you go out and buy another motor home and trade the old one in. Them bigwigs ain't so dumb. The more motor homes they sell, the more money they make. Any fool like you ought to know that much."

"You can say all you want to, I know them motor homes are haunted. Even the radios sometimes howl and whistle and sometimes it is more like a high screech and it scares me half to death when I'm drivin' alone at midnight all by myself. It gets so bad that I hardly ever turn on a radio at night anymore."

Red jacket began a reprisal, partially to nullify his colleague's complaint while introducing one of his own. "Ghost noises don't scare me, animals don't scare me, and weather don't scare me neither. But there are things that scare me, no matter where you drive."

"Now it's Braveheart, is it? What be these things that scare such a courageous gentleman as you?"

"People."

"Hear that fellas? People scare him. Now don't get too close to him or he'll throw a tantrum and run away and hide."

"People do scare me. They try to rob you, pick your pocket, or to cheat you everywhere you go. Just go to any gas station, you'll find out. Them big oil companies got their station men so trained that they can always cheat you when making change for the gas you bought. I lose a couple of bucks ever' time, and sometimes it is as much as a fiver."

"Didn't you go to school at all? It don't take much brains to figure out change."

"Yeah but those guys are so slick with it you don't know the difference, and you think you made a good deal and are being glad to get out of there. And there are robbers lurking around, just waiting to take advantage. One night about 11:00 PM in El Dorado I was accosted by a masked man with a gun in one hand and a knife in the other. He attacked me right in front of a convenience store after I had stepped out of my unit. He said my money or my life, but I fooled him by saying I had only $2.29 and that's when he started slashing with his knife but I fooled him one more time.

"Fools are always good at foolin', aren't they boys?" said Pony Tail in attempt to more provocation.

"When he started slashin', I started duckin'. I yelled at him that he better watch out, my buddy was comin' behind him. Course I didn't have a buddy but how was he to know if I did or not? When he glanced back over his shoulder, that's when I swung my fist and knocked him over backwards. I jumped back into my unit and took off quicker than a flash, but not before he fired a bullet through my back window, just missing my head and ending up in the left sun visor. And Hummer made me pay the deductible for the window glass. I should have quit drivin' right then and there but for some reason I didn't. But when I get back from this trip to California, I'm goin' in that office and tell Hummer and Missie where they can go, and then I'm goin' out the door and never comin' back."

Striped Overalls ended the story told by Yellow Cap, and decided it was his turn at oration. "You cowards and all your bragging. None of that stuff scares me, animals, robbers, storms or anything else. I've gone through all kinds of scares and none Of it scares me. I've been there, done that. More than once. But what I'm goin' to tell you now will curl all your hairs."

"Let's hear it then. Boasters got to have their say, right boys? But don't let us hear anythin' about you goin' to some beauty shop to get your hair curled, right boys?"

"I was headin' out to Alamagordo in a 28-foot Alphonse Reliable and stopped for gas at Ratgut Junction, Colorado when it happened."

"Next he's goin' tell us Ratgut is the center of the universe, right boys?"

"Make fun. That's your privilege. That's where it all happened, just the same."

"And just what is it that makes Ratgut so famous?" asked Red Jacket, with a look of scorn trickling down his face.

"Well, what happened was partly my own fault. But bein' an honest man and not like some of the liars around here, I'm goin' to admit it. Like I said, I stopped in Ratgut to plug in gas. The tank held 55 gallons and I decided to fill it, since the price was a little cheaper."

"Isn't this exciting? My hairs are curlin' up perty good already."

"Just keep pesterin', little darlin'. But, as I was saying before being so rudely interrupted, after fillin' the tank I went into the station to pay for it, grabbed a candy bar, and hopped back into my baby and took off. That's when the trouble started. As I drove off, there was a terrible explosion and fire like you wouldn't believe."

"What did you do, stick a lighted match down the hose nozzle?"

"Worse than that. That's what I am ashamed of. I sort of forgot to take the qas nozzle out of my gas tank, and when I drove off, it sort of, well…pulled up the pump by the roots and all. There I was, headin' for the driveway with hose and gas pump and the whole works dragging behind."

Yellow Cap with Ear Flaps teased, "If it were me, I wouldn't be bragging about something as bad as that. Sounds like this was an inside job done by an imbecile."

"Just keep smartin' off. But I was the hero in spite of what you guys say. When that gas pump hole exploded there was a commotion around there makin' you think the world was comin' to an end. Flames and smoke were shootin' sky high in the air. People were yellin' and screamin' like a touchdown had been made. Ever'body was runnin' back and forth and tryin' to move their cars out of there before the fire got to them and it was a disaster. The station men were fit to be tied and ready to faint, not knowing what to do. But I took charge and stepped in and saved the day."

"You saved the day? Sounds like you lost the day, if you ask me."

"I saved the day, no matter what you say. When I saw flames engulfing ever'where, I jumped out of my unit, grabbed my fire extinguisher with one hand. I yelled at the station men to shut off all the gas pipes. I ran up to those roarin' flames, endangerin' my life, and started to squirt away with my little ol' fire extinguisher. You know what? That fire immediately shut down, as if by command. I saved a lot of lives and property while ever'body else was a coward and tryin' to run away. I could have been burnt to a crisp, but by puttin' my life on the line, no tellin' how many lives were saved by my bravery. If those flames had jumped over to the station building, the whole town of Ratgut would have probably burned up, what with the east wind blowing the ways it does this side of the Divide.

"Ever'body was so proud of me savin' the town that they passed the hat for a collection to give to such a brave man as myself. And you know, I found out later that there is a plaque hangin' in the mayor's office in Ratgut Junction, and it has my name on it. That plaque is hangin' there among others of heroes of bygone days. So it is a proud man I am to be a hero in Ratgut."

We were all speechless for a few moments until someone piped up, "I always wanted to meet an honest to goodness liar and this is my day."

Striped Overalls added to his rendition, "One little thing I am sorry about was that in all the excitement and hullabaloo,I forgot and drove out of that place with the pump still draggin' behind me. By the time I got to Baldface City, I realized the noise I been hearin' was the pump scrapin' on the highway. When I stopped to unhook the crazy thing, you know, there was still enough gas in it to fill my gas tank again. I really feel proud of myself for savin' so many lives. How man lives have you guys saved, answer me that?"

Applause broke out from the other four drivers, including myself, as his oration came to a conclusion. Whether or not his story was true, I have no way of knowing. It is beyond my comprehension to judge my peers because worse things than this are continually happening when-ever I place my body behind one of those steering wheels. Trying to stay out of trouble is the main objective of any motor home driver. One's life is constantly in danger, and fear is a constant companion, as I have told you on occasions previously. Youth of America have been warned many times to flee from such a defeated life style. Motor home driving sup-posedly leads to fame, fortune, and happiness if you can get it all together. I can't find anyone who did.

While we were all in a petrified state of contemplation, and before correct words of rebuttal were found, out of the dispatch office came Miss Missmossmus with our release papers. As usual, she waited until just before closing time to do so, obviously just to make us squirm. Yellow Cap with Ear Flaps got his papers for San Diego, Red jacket to San Francisco, Pony Tail to Miami, and Striped Overalls to Corpus Christi. And guess where they sent Myle Heyers? Potbelly Island, Missouri! Yes, Potbelly Island, Missouri, can you believe that? The other drivers were destined for exotic places, but I will end up in Potbelly Island, after waiting 3 hours and 12 1/4 minutes in the Drivers' Room.

This caused me to be so disgruntled that a decision, like the other drivers, was made spontaneously and with malice aforethought. I was going to turn in my papers, walk out that door, and never come back. That's what the other drivers threatened to do, and I had much more reason than they.

After making the trip to Potbelly, I was quitting for sure. No amount of mind changing by Mr. Bad Self was going to change my decision.

Do you want to know what did actually happen? I meekly completed the trip to Potbelly, rode the Black Dog, worked on the farm for two days, spent three more cleaning out the hog house, and then went begging for another trip, ending up in the same drivers' room, this time in company of One Eye, Three Fingers, and Little Joe. It must be that I am hooked on driving. Once it gets in your blood, it is too late for a transfusion. How exciting it is to drive some beautiful, magnificent, dazzling vehicle, even if the destination is Potbelly Island, Missouri and if you are compelled to sit in that awful drivers room for three hours and 12 1/4 minutes to do so. It is worth it all to have such glamorous adventures as I constantly enjoy.

Yet, a constant hope which dangles to my heartstrings is that each of you, especially you younger ones, will be able to understand and to have enough common sense not to fall into the same dangerous trap into which I have been entangled. Heartache, despair, and ruin are yours for the taking. Don't, I beg you, take them. You might end up in Potbelly Island like I did. Hazards await from all directions and waiting in the drivers' room is another one to add to the list.

CHAPTER XXII

Contrary Contradictions

Regarding health and survival of your dear children, many previous warnings have been proclaimed. Many lives could be preserved from dishonor, disappointment, and poverty if only the temptation to drive motor homes could be curtailed. Advice has been primarily directed toward delivery drivers, but owners of these diabolical machines are in dire need of counseling as well. I am not digressing from previous admonition so eloquently presented and, in fact, am well able to provide even more credible evidence for substantiation by the intricate tabulation of ignominy heaped upon my own head. Though such deviation has been thoroughly accentuated, there appears to be a concentrated opposition which permits each owner to do his own thing, not being encumbered by what your children may think, nor regarding how much scorn can be applied by their sneering accusations. Acceptance of this line of thought allowed each owner further exploration of the world's marvels while provoking his offspring to fits of derision. It would also help to insure abandonment of following in the parental footsteps.

Do you understand what you are being told? What the idea is meant to be? To make certain of a stress-free conclusion, a mind made up before hand is a good thing to have in store. This implies firm action will be implemented and an after the fact resolution shall remain firm to the bitter end, mattering not the scathing rebukes, icy stares, and thumbed noses, this all from your own family. Taking the bull by the horns while being resolute in one's assertions, even during periods of vacillation, are successful approaches to pie-in-the-sky generalizations. To be thus minded partially nullifies the sneering remarks made behind one's back during times of extreme opposition. To decide otherwise is but self-deception when considering the accusations concocted by the scornful as they decry the horrible mistakes committed.

No matter how bitter the pills being swallowed, how deeply one has plunged into the cauldrons of despair, nor how quickly the feet have sunk into quicksands of desperation, yet there is hope. Hope can best be exemplified in simple phrases, condemnation be thrust aside, and perspiration wiped from the brow, if perchance an about face is pursued and a mind set of defeat is converted into faith, hope, and limited doubt. Declarations of inspiration, if attention is caught, can turn night into day, overturn obstacles of surrender, and offer bright promise for tomorrow by providing silver lining to every dark cloud and cause the sun to break through on a stormy day.

Go for it! That's what I've been trying to pound through your thick skulls all this time. What are you ashamed of, you owners? A motor home driver need not be ashamed! Driving is one of the most honorable pastimes one can pursue. You are the cream of the crop, don't you realize? Nearly everyone in the entire world would gladly change places with you. Riding some hump back camel in the Gobi Desert or perched on an elephant in the jungles of Swahili has little appeal in comparison to driving a beautiful, magnificent, dazzling vehicle on a Los Angeles freeway, you know. No need to wear that hang-dog expression, to slink behind the bushes when meeting your neighbor, nor to pull the covers over your head when your wife walks into the bedroom. Stand our ground, don't give an inch, never take a back seat to anyone. That philosophy has worked well for me. Motor home driving can be considered the most praise worthy time waster invented, surpassed only by the romantic adventures of the rich and famous. Jealousy is the main ingredient of this philosophy when applied in copious amounts, flaunting the superiority you portray. What difference in your life style it would make if these observations can be accurately preserved. Making a good impression, flaunting wealth, and strutting your stuff, that's what its all about to a motor home driver.

To make a good impression, many are the avenues to pursue. Acquiring the art of ostentatiously lording it over friends and neighbors, is an act most people would give their right arm for. Driving the highest-priced vehicle the Otoonga Trailer Factory constructs is a prominent method to attain fulfillment. Boy, does that make them green with envy! To humbly display a boastful look, to act the part, and dress the part are skills not readily discounted when accompanied by presumptuous arrogance.

To avariciously dress the part is the mainstay of the performance.

What is more provocative than to watch a beautiful woman descending the steps of an elegant motor home, clad in a short mini-skirt and tossing her curls (even if she is sixty years of age and two hundred pounds in weight)? Clothed in expensive apparel exacerbates the enhancement, inciting contentious envy from other women of like sex. Covering the haughty look with a humble smile is a cause for having the same affect. High heels and diamonds and painting the toe nails a deep dark green contribute valiantly to a worshipful sense of awe.

You men are not exempt from envious adulation from your peers. To fastidiously display a striped ascot around the neck will do for a start. Huge shiny belt buckles, three earrings in the left ear, and ruby rings on the pinkie fingers are other fine examples. Wearing overalls while driving is another slick method to provoke covetousness. This must be done with stylish acumen, not just your common run-of-the-mill barnyard type. Stripes are the rage with the younger set, so why not make a similar application to your situation? Tact must play a prominent role in any such venture. Its inculcation should be perfected with the consideration that envious onlookers are looking on. Stripes in a zigzag angle from right to left are more to be desired than a sideways pattern, promoting avariciousness in a stylish manner.   It is imperative to have golden suspender buttons polished to a high sheen. A matching engineer's cap is a must to convey distinction while implementing the implication. Nothing is too good for a motor home driver, especially an owner. Just a casual tie and jacket will never do. In fact, a tie should never be worn. Injecting superiority in a blatant manner is undesirable. Only in an underhanded manner can this be accomplished. One should only assert superiority in an aspect of subtlety, rather than flagrant advertisement. That could bring more contempt than adoration, whether by a nose in the air approach, or a more humbly crawling in the dust. Significant approbation is the desired result, intensified by showing off in a behavior not too obtrusive nor prominently offensive, yet done in wily provocation causing your peers to eat their hearts out. Encumbrances encountered in opportune objectivism become a hindrance actively negating successful crossing the goal in supererogation, further enhancing a devil-may-care attitude imposing directly upon the unwary, even when the unwary are not as unwary as they pretend.

Not only in persuasion to dress the part, but most importantly, one is advised to act the part. Ignoring this imperative betrays the cause best exemplified by the old saying, "putting the cart before the horse," or as a dumb farmer might declare, "hitching up the wrong mules to the manure spreader." This transmits into uncompromising failure, showing little concern for others who may be struck speechless by your callous disregard. If your misdemeanors are published on the front page of the Otoonga Journal, the weekly paper for the local jet set, don't blame me if your name is at the top of the list. As hinted previously, a nose-in-the air approach might be a chief sticking point, pretending you don't see your next door neighbor at the fireman's ball. Completely ignoring cousin Howard is best emphasized with a holier-than-thou attitude. Associating only with the elite of the community is also a feather in the cap, multiplying further inducements toward fame and notoriety.

As previously stated, purchasing one of those high-priced vehicles creates an aura of respect, diminishes verbal criticism, and promotes the worshipping of the ground you walk on, causing a bowed head and a lowering of the eyes whenever your shadow strikes the envious. Use your imagination. Numerous are the methods of affirming authority and promoting jealousy, that far be it from me to compute all the answers. Sauntering along the sidewalk in a swaggering gait, being tardy at the Amalgamated Driver's Association monthly meeting each week, tipping the waiter a ten dollar bill at Gloria's Stakehouse Sooper Shed, all contribute to the desired intent. (With a quick hand you can remove the bill as you leave the cafe if no one is looking.)

Opposing the previous stipulated advice, I now pause to give warning. Be careful. Don't fall into the trap of overdoing it, of spreading it on too thick. Bitter ramifications may befall you if subordinates are thrust beneath you too forcefully. Fate has a strange way of intervention, you know. Illness may strike at any moment, slapping your face in retaliation if your haughtiness is too pronounced. Pride goeth before a fall, remember. Cancer may strike you down by the ultraviolet rays magnified through the huge drivers windshield, wreaking havoc with one's blood cells when turning a corner the wrong way. Radon could become a menace. It creeps from underneath those basement model motor homes, and could utterly incapacitate. That's right.

If your pride is too stuck-up, look out. Nature contains a law of the jungle that punishes those who overstep its boundary. Stomach upset, bloating, diarrhea, and hemorrhagic septemia are penalties resulting from direct proportion to the amount of time spent driving when your hat is cocked at too much of an angle. Constant bouncing and jerking is bound to cause something to happen. Digesting a bowl of chili for breakfast, swallowing a greasy hamburger for lunch, and downing a slice of pizza and plate of lasagna during the afternoon driving break bring punishment also. Bloodshot eye syndrome infects proud drivers in need of sleep. Likewise, dry eye and a weepy tear duct proves you should have taken advantage of beddie-bye time instead of the all-night roadhouse celebration. Heart arrythymia may afflict braggarts who lord it over the unfortunate wretches who are found lacking a silver spoon in the mouth at birthing time. Flat tires at midnight, dented fenders from criss-crossing mopeds, and smashed rear ends from doing wheelies in 52-foot motor homes, are reasons enough for vindictive retaliation from Mother Fate. It's your own fault when the door of opportunity slams in your face, driver. Maybe it's time to crawl in the basement window. The old adage, a stitch in time saves nine, but how can this be applied when driving down Interstate 95 with no needle and thread? Again my warning is repeated: Don't inflict excessive castigation upon those of inferior status. The trick is to artfully baffle those admirers with a suffocating glob of suspicion, undertaken simultaneously with a sly wink and robust smile.

One great discovery that opens wide the door to jealousy from your peers can be summed up on one word—effervescence! Yes, effervescence. Aiding flagrant amounts of effervescence combined with wit and charm provides enhancement to the objectives which cannot easily be deposed, even by those who distrust your motives and superciliousness. They're just jealous, you know. Once more is the repetition given— don't overdo the effervescence! Brushing the cat's hair the wrong way is not recommended. Your intentions must not be mistaken by using effervescence as the final yardstick of measurement. Using cautionary subtlety in intimidation is not likely to thwart motives if misunderstanding isn't advanced too vigorously.

This advice is not for the ultra rich, the Richie Rich types. Their assumption is that they are so far advanced above the average motor home driver in comparison, that it cannot be compared. The filthy rich look down their noses at we drivers. They wouldn't be caught dead in one of our machines. Oh no, they must be chauffeured around in some taxi, airport van, horse-drawn carriage, or stretch limousine. They can just look elsewhere for advice for all I care.

Wake up, drivers! Hair-brained ideology, in an attempt to nullify your opponents' criticism, places the blame squarely on our shoulders. This is indeed regrettable, advancing a diabolical conspiracy against those of us who are in the upper crust of society. Yet, our opinions must not be quelled! To dream the impossible dream is our dream, to reach the unreachable star can be reached if we put our shoulder to the wheel (no, not the motor home, you dummy) and feet to our prayers. Press forward in the struggle until the whipped pup comes home with his tail between his legs, the last dog has died, Old Paint has gone to the last roundup in the sky, or the calico cat has gone belly-up in his ninth life. If you think this is mere pseudaesthesia, think again. Improvident improvision must be carefully administered and each deviation accounted for. Unite behind the cause, advance our intentions of advancement, effectively promote the agenda. And not in a no-win situation either.

Non-essential conjecture is in continual bombardment against reaching an impossible decision. It is not always the final result, but suggests that an affirmative outlook cannot be forever maintained, especially when confronted with controversial disinformation, interfering with our road to progress. It's a sad commentary when motor home drivers are ostracized, reviled, condemned, and spit upon. Perhaps this over emphasizes our plight, but the fact remains that havoc has been reeked, victory nullified, and mayhem fulfilled. Devastation has taken an uppermost position, and it hasn't yet been made clear just what.

CHAPTER XXIII

Ups and Downs

The days, months, and years pass swiftly for those hooked on motor home driving, mattering not whether owner, renter, or deliveryman of one of these strange objects. It is an exceptional experience, evoking a sense of wonder and exhilaration, to be the honcho manipulating such a spectacular species of creation—a full-blown motor home. Oh, to be sure, there are ups and downs to be faced now and then, so to speak. Trouble may strike without warning, when least expected, and when most inconvenient. In spite of many incommodious situations, I seldom complained or felt sorry for myself when formidable obstacles intruded and jeopardized the status quo, more or less, you might say. Expressions of irritation were sometimes expressed now and then, notably during problems of extreme severity where incredulous life-threatening dangers existed, where extinction was feasible, and worst of all—cessation of driving was a distinct possibility. Since such demonic threats happened only occasionally, my direct response was to continue a self-centered intention of delivering these vehicles.

The pleading of advisors to ease off went unheeded. Even when unexplainable retribution exploded in my face, each onslaught was systematically overcome by the conjecture of high expectations, the accumulation of great profits, and the prospects of Shangrila escapism. Friends, neighbors, the religious, the jealous, and any street derelict who might be concerned for my welfare, were emphatically in disapproval of this infatuation. All manners of psychology, invocation, mysticism and sorcery were thrust upon my unwilling nature…but to no avail. Nothing could thwart my determination. It was a vain attempt. Azailia continued her disapproval with overwhelming entreaty. The growing boys echoed this complaint with the exuberance of childhood expression. Old Barney and Jane came before me, warning about the strangulating curse. Even the preacher gave a stunning Oration to hopefully deliver me from this recusancy. Nothing worked, pleadings were meaningless. I was hooked.

This is not to declare that triteness, insanity, or incapacitation had taken complete control. No, this is merely a repetition of prior warnings previously disclosed, specifically revealing through holophrasis of the dangers of ruining one's life forever, if not properly controlled. Which, of course, mine wasn't and I didn't want it to be. Nothing could detract from the prospect of adventure. None of the appeals could prevent my perseverance, forceful words of intervention were ignored, and menacing threats were cast aside. Persistence in driving promised delightful and uplifting advantages, along with monetary benefits which, if accumulated enough, would add proverbial feathers to the cap, contributing to the betterment of wife, children, and employees, all of whom had their hand in my pocket during such times.

As previously mentioned, a few ups and downs kept cropping up. None of them would get the best of me. My stated determination of overcoming the most diabolical circumstances devised by the mind of man was unwavering. Even the most infernal of all—the mechanical breakdown. You might ask the question, why would a high-priced new motor home ever break down? Well, why does anything new break down? New cars fall to pieces just a mile or two from the place of purchase, new tractors and combines fall apart before the first ear of corn has been picked, new manure spreaders fly to pieces when the drive gear heads one way and the manure another. Haven't you women cussed each time a new can opener wouldn't work, a light fixture blows out, or a new dress was found to have a hole in it? Well, you can say the same cuss words when a new motor home breaks down from no fault of our own.

Like the time when purring victoriously toward the resort city of Virginia Beach, Virginia in a twenty-nine foot bed-over-the-cab Pretty Blue Baby. Stopping for gas at Peoria, a noticeable smell of grease could be smelled. This was no concern of mine until farther down the road a jerky pause began, intermittently at first, and then gradually becoming more and more pronounced. Bad Self told me it wasn't anything to worry about and to keep on going. Suddenly there was a bumping and scraping noise underneath, ending in a loud "bang." The unit was slowing down fast even though the motor was still running at a fast slow-down. If it wasn't for my courageous nature, fainting spells would have ensued when descending from the vehicle and peering underneath. Seldom have been seen such blood-curdling sights. A portion of the drive chain had come loose and was rotating violently underneath the unit. The knuckle and part of the shaft were bouncing up and down on the pavement while still red hot, and completely disconnected from the rear portion of the transmission.

So it came to pass that I was once again stranded in the awful state of Illinois, alone and in the dark. Traffic whizzed by, caring nothing for my dire predicament. I could sense their smug and complacent attitudes while mentally reading their lips, "Too bad for you, buddy". It was hopeless to wait for a patrolman to come to my rescue, for such appearances are only made when speeding tickets need to be written. I ask what you would have done when confronting such a terrible condition? You want to know what I did? Being so thoroughly disgusted, I unrolled my sleeping bag, crawled inside, and erupted into complete oblivion. What did I care how much traffic passed by; let them go their merry way. My flashers were on, so what did it matter?

It may have been fifteen minutes or perhaps six hours before oblivion was interrupted by a knock at the entry door. Making an appearance was a young man in a turtle neck sweater who asked if I was having car trouble.

My disgruntled reply to the obvious was that this wasn't a car, along with a subtle hint for a call to a tow truck. He said he would be glad to make a call but I didn't think he would, resulting in another foray into oblivion via the sleeping bag routine.

It may have been another fifteen minutes or six hours when, to my complete surprise, a tow truck actually did arrive. The unit, complete with dragging drive chain, was quickly towed into Champaign to a car dealer lot who sold other chassis comparable to what I was driving. The remainder of the night was spent in miserable conditions caused by worry, sleeplessness, and an attitude of cynicism against the world in general but most pointedly at the Otoonga Trailer Factory where one of the workmen hadn't properly tightened the grease plug for the transmission. Above and beyond these miserable conditions a few uplifting thoughts surged randomly regarding the fact that there yet remain a few good people (although they are hard to find), such as this young man who had gone out of his way to spend twenty-five cents to make a call to help out a broken-down motor home driver.

Morning finally came, revealing a vehicle parked in a crummy car dealer lot, surrounded by limousines, compacts, pickup trucks, and four-wheelers. According to the instructions from the dispatch office, should a unit (heaven forbid) become incapacitated, it should be secured at a chassis dealer where a healing process could be initiated. That's what was trying to happen according to my intentions, providing cooperation from the mechanics would be forthcoming. This cooperation was delayed after an examination of the patient's condition had been diagnosed. In fact, the mechanics were in a state of agitation, anger, and censoriousness, and spelled it out in no uncertain terms bordering on pornography. According to their explanation, the prospect of resuscitating an infirm motor home was not an appealing endeavor.

"Don't you check the gear plugs to see if they are tight before driving?" was the sarcastic question spoken by the head honcho.

Is that what caused the trouble? I'm only a driver. Crawling underneath to check the gear plugs isn't in my job description."

After a few more grumblings, finger pointings, and bad words being said, they told me where I could go. According from the instructions Mr. Hummer had given, I left the unit in their care, gathering the papers to take back to Dispatch. Since asking for a ride was out of the question, I began walking toward the Black Dog Station, carrying along my two heavy bags. Carefully scrutinizing the disgusting situation, a developing obtuseness penetrating the cobwebs of the cranium took place. The entire predicament, was caused by the departure of the gear plug which had come off during transition, allowing the grease to drain out. Burning up of the gears and knuckle was the natural result. Some careless factory worker had failed to tighten the plug (unintentionally or otherwise), and I was left holding the bag. He had opened up a Pandora's Box, leaving me in humiliation, repugnance and remorse.

The long bus ride back to Otoonga left me in a state of withdrawal and anti-hedonism. Yet I considered it to be worth it all, for this means I will get to drive another beautiful, magnificent, dazzling vehicle just that much sooner.

Yes, there were many ups and downs durinq my part-time occupation. Ups and down were both good and bad, more or less, so to speak. Problems were continually cropping up now and then. When first employed, one of the most prominent difficulties was that gas line filters plugged up. Filters were faulty, dirty gas was installed, or the gas tank itself had not been freed of paint and shavings. This would cause the vehicle to jump and jerk wildly, if not stall out completely. Whenever confronted by this kind of odious situation, a multiplication of emotional aberrations controlling the nerve-ending faculties would suddenly explode into dictatorial behavior in a series of irrational consequences, climaxing into fits of uncontrolled irrationality, with accompanying tremors promoted thereby.

Overcoming the obstacle of plugged filters could be accomplished in a variety of methods. Using my own tool kit was useless, mainly because filter locations are impossible to find. Hoping that a highway patrolman would come to the rescue was wishful thinking. Calling for a tow truck was another option. As a last resort,(the one I usually resorted to) one could jump and jerk along, hoping to coax the behemoth to its destination before the motor conked out completely.

For example: On August 14th a jaunt to Jettison City was instigated in a Flashline Special. Near Toledo, Ohio the calm was awesomely interrupted with a pop and a bang as the unit slowed gradually until finally enveloped in a state of absolute futility. I was stopped dead in my tracks, as the old saying goes. The location was on a busy freeway swarming with moving objects during the period just before rush hour, which is always the worst. While sitting in stunned sorrow, Good Self came to my rescue. "Why don't you turn the key to see if it might start again?" So I did, and it did also. From doom to joy in two seconds of time! Confidently I barged once more into the stream of moving objects, speeding along with a new-found aura of hopefulness. All at once it happened again—slowing to a complete halt. By waiting a few minutes it would restart, and then stall after a few miles of driving. How it ran at all is a mystery to this day. I heard later that the gas line filter was 90% plugged. By starting and stopping, starting and stopping, the beast was maneuvered all the way to Jettison City. And through the humongous city of Cleveland during rush hour. While so doing, it may have caused a little aggravation to other drivers, in whose lane my unit held priority. Seldom has there been seen so much fist shaking, red faces, and bulging eves. How glad was I to see the sign "Chico Stein's Recreational Vehicles." Coasting the last ten miles to the dealership with a dead motor was possible since it was downhill all the way.

"This unit appears to be in number one shape," remarked the inspector. "Did you have any trouble while driving here?"

"It drove just fine as long as I kept moving," was my truthful reply. "I made a few stops along the way, though. That's why I am two hours late."

The inspector started the motor, and of course it ran perfectly while idling. He was so happy to acquire the desired unit which was sold sight unseen, that he generously drove me to the airport in his Rolls Royce. We were both happy. I've often wondered since what happened to the unfortunate purchaser after he had confidently driven out of the dealer's lot, only to be stalled a few miles down the road. Thankfully, that was not my worry.

I had enough worry getting it there in the first place. Plugged filters are just one more in a series of hazards to motor home driving, adding to malapropos misfortune, procrusteanizing profligacy, and malevolent maladjustment, the conclusion of which is somewhat clouded over in veiled revelation.

It is a falsification to proclaim there weren't any ups and downs. A lot of good ups were happening as well as bad downs, I'll have you know. So many good things happened while I was driving that it would be almost impossible to present a complete list. When approaching some famous landmark, scenic view, or historical attraction, a few minutes stop was usually undertaken. However, problems could arise while attempting to park a thirty-eight foot conveyance in a space marked out for compact cars. How difficult it was to enjoy the scenery while fearing the outcome would be fender scraping and dented bumpers and nasty confrontation with menacing motorcycle officers.

Exhilarating it was to suspend driving for a couple of hours at an attractive resort, state park, or lakeside where cares could be cast aside and pleasure pursued. Rest, diversion, and relaxation were great remedies for a tired driver against exhaustion. Parking along a rushing mountain stream enhanced the possibilities of fish jumping for a baited hook, until remembering that my fishing pole wouldn't fit in a suitcase. Swimming in a beautiful lake surrounded by pine, aspen, and fir was number one in priority. Unfortunately, during such times, a bathing suit was most likely forgotten to be brought along, causing much embarrassment while making a mad dash for the water in one's underwear. A lot of blushing accompanied such a venture, when realizing that wet undershorts were almost transparent, especially when well worn like most of mine were.

Yes, many were the good things and many were the bad during my days of travel. Why did the bad always win out, I ask? Not only were gas line filters plugging up during the early days of driving, but many other awful problems took precedence much too often. Fans belt breaking caused a lot of agitation. Nowadays such catastrophies seldom take place. New belt inventions now defy reason—combinations of woven plastic, unbreakable polyesters, spring-loaded hard-bodies, steel-lined cotton, and rubber-band indestructibles. Belt breaking alone isn't all that perplexing, but when the entire fan drive housing shatters, that is a different story.

Passing through the town of Hyper Falls, Minnesota at high noon was a difficult time for all involved, particularly when being all alone. As the noon whistle was sounding, another sound of rattling, banging, crashing, and screeching came from under the hood of the Yellow Daze. A horrible opportunity for freaking out was thereby provided. Peering under the hood was a terrifying experience. The fan, arm, and housing attachments were still revolving at break-neck speed, although completely severed from the motor. Gradually the motion ground to a halt, somehow doing no damage to the radiator or hoses. I pulled the entire contraption out of its nest and brought it up to the cabin area. Fortunately, a chassis dealer was located in Hyper Falls, allowing a reversal of directions and permitting a motor home with no fan to be propelled into the chassis service lot. A telephone call to the Otoonga dispatch office explained the dreadful predicament involving both the Yellow Daze and myself. Miss Missmossmus, after hearing my plaintive wail of complaint, replied, "Mr. Hummer is out playing golf but in this kind of situation, you know what must be done. Leave your unit at the chassis garage. Tell them to repair the damage as soon as possible, since it is covered by warranty. Bring home all your papers but leave the keys with them."

Argumentative snarls proceeded from the mechanics' mouths, but I stuck to my guns, followed her instructions, and left the obstinate vehicle in their loving care. Another abhorrent obstacle was to be faced when discovering that no Black Dog bus would leave Hyper Falls for another twenty-three hours. What should I do? Stay at some flea-bitten expensive hotel? Sleep in the streets? Bad Self and Good then began an unlimited argument. The consensus ultimately climaxed in words loudly proclaimed, "Hitchhike a ride." Hitchhike? When you come right down to it, perhaps hitchhiking may not be a bad idea. A lot of money would be kept, depriving those rich hotel keepers from receiving any satisfaction. Many people are begging for rides in this day and age. Hitchhikers can be observed everywhere you go. You see thumbs sticking out from bums on hills, curves, exit ramps, and street corners. Each beggar was intensively jockeying for position and fighting each other for rides to who knows where.

From downtown Hyper Falls I slowly wended my way to the east side of the city, carrying a sleeping bag in one hand and a travel case in the other. At a fork in the road where two highways met, I began a desperate maneuver. A shameful act of sticking out a thumb was instigated, along with mouthing the word, "Help" to each passing vehicle. Having read the latest issue of "Poor People's Travel Magazine" and hearing the advice of countless drifters, I was able to hold my head high with pride and confidence all the while reproachfully begging for a ride. Only in my situation it didn't seem to be working out very well. In one-half hour of time my arm was getting tired and my thumb was sore. Hopes were swiftly degenerating toward a pathway of perturbation, feelings of desperation led to desultory expressions, and frustrated tendencies advanced to uncontrollable exasperation.

Besides this, a scare tactic from Mother Nature promoted a sky tendency toward darkness with the approach of storm cloud formations in the atmosphere which predicted an unfavorable outcome—getting soaking wet. And it came to pass. Cars just whizzed on by. What do they care? Nobody to give a hoot whether or not some old bum got soaked. Doesn't he know enough to come out of the rain?

In the midst of this incongruous incident rescue came. An angel made a miraculous appearance, personified in the form of a gruff old man in a rickety pickup truck. As it slowed to a halt beside me, the window was rolled down, permitting a sarcastic query issued in a hoarse, husky voice, "Hey, bud, do you need a ride?"

"You bet," was the answer. Thereby another adventure entered closure, only to open to one more. What a saving outcome this became. Only not quite what had been expected.

"Where you headin' bud?"

"To Otoonga," I replied after placing my bags and myself inside his rescue device.

"How far is that?"

"About 120 miles due west, but if you can get me to a motel, that would be fine, no matter how much it costs."

"I ain't goin' to no Otoonga, but I kin get you part way, bud."

"Anything to be getting out of this cursed place."

It wasn't long until the storm path had been eclipsed completely and the sun began peeking from behind the dark clouds. While the sun was breaking through, so did the fire. Yes, actual fire in the pickup…somewhere under the hood. We both abandoned the flaming inferno with amazing swiftness. We threw handfuls of dirt on the smoking motor, causing the flames to gradually subside. Our actions were in vain, for the truck was rendered inoperable. The wiring, hoses, and belts were ruined, just like our good intentions. What else could go wrong on this trip? Had some devilish fiend excogitated a new method for my ruination? Burning to a crisp or being struck by lightning could have ended

life as I know it. I can see the handwriting on the wall. I should not have
started driving motor homes in the first place. I should have gone to
work in the rock quarry like Eddie. Then I would be living like a king
too, and not be stranded along this miserable highway with a fallen
angel in a burning pickup. Yet Good Self said I had to be thankful. My
wet clothes had been dried by the fire, the two bags were only scorched
on one side, and my head was still intact somewhere on my shoulders.

"This ole piece of junk was gettin' about old enough to trade in anyway," the angel said. "If we kin git to a phone somewhere, I'll call up the
Missus and have her pick us up in my new Caddy I bought las' week."

One great adventure had just ended but another was looming in the
distance. We were soon to be rescued by more angels in disguise. Amish
farmers. Yes, Amish farmers, including horses and buggies with lanterns
hanging from their rear ends. A whole convoy in fact. In proud authority
did they beckon us to desert our stalled piece of junk and to board a
surefire way to travel. The spokesman for the group made the most gra-
cious offer one could imagine. We were offered a bed for the night. Can
you believe that? Offering a bed to a couple ruffian strangers?

Upon arrival at their settlement we were served a delicious home-
cooked meal of bread and milk. Shortly thereafter, the old man and
myself were separated. One of the bearded gentlemen led me by candle-
light to a small shack, several hundred feet from the town hall. A quick
glimpse of this one room hotel revealed a small cot with single coverlet,
a straight-back wooden chair, and a dirt floor. While leaving, he closed
the door with a loud squeaking sound that could have been heard
throughout the entire compound. Thus was I abandoned. It was almost
like being in prison (in solitary confinement) with no electricity,
telephone, television, or even a candle. Being deprived of necessities,
climbing into bed became the next mode of operation.

It wasn't long, since sleep was an evasion, until another function
began crying for attention. I found myself groping along the wall in
attempt to find some sort of toilet outlet, with no luck whatsoever.

Opening that screeching door was out of the question because I didn't wish to awaken the entire village. Some other means of satisfaction needed to be sought. Sliding the straight-back chair across the dirt floor noiselessly, I placed it directly under the narrow window. I was able to squirm and squeeze my body through the aperture until landing on the ground below, head first. To my chagrin, sauntering past my prone carcass and having seen the disgraceful procedure, was one of the female Amish farmers who had apparently already discovered a toilet outlet of her liking. My appearance was somewhat demeaned by underwear, bare feet, and red face.

It was a mystery how survival throughout the frightful night was attained when one's ears were tuned to the howling of hyenas, growling of wolves, mourning of coyotes, and roaring of mountain lions. Other threats were spiders, mice, possums, and bed bugs which all ceremoniously made a visit through the habitation. Oh, what a tangled web we weave when driving motor homes.

The morning calm was broken by a summons to breakfast at the communal kitchen. Fried goose eggs, sour buttermilk, and a hunk of grizzly bear were on the menu. Females of all sizes were the servers of the feast. Men with beards, teenagers with fuzzy cheeks, and little boys with few whiskers at all were the supplicants of the meal, as well as two foreign ruffians who tried to keep their eyes closed through the long preliminary prayers. The two ruffians thanked these kind and generous people over and over for their hospitality.

Another thrilling buggy ride back to Hyper Falls was provided, passing the still smoldering truck on the way. We were deposited at the welcoming doors of the Black Dog Station. An attempt was made to pay these kind gentlemen for their trouble but to no avail. While waiting three more hours for a coach that was intended for me yesterday, I watched a bright red Cadillac whisk away my ruffian angel friend. It was driven by his Missus, a young gal in a mini-skirt and high heels.

As I told you before, when a driver wends his way out of the Otoonga dispatch yards, he has no way of telling what will happen from that moment onward. That's what happened to me lots of times. Inclement weather, atrocious break downs, and physical impairments are omnipresent. Motor explosions, rain storms, burning vehicles, frightening buggy rides, and dirty hotel rooms are continuing hazards, along with intimidating visitations of Amish outhouses in the dead of night.

During the many years of my employment at the Otoonga Trailer Factory, many ups and downs took place, as you already have known. Unexplainable events inauspiciously controlled my life, resulting in health endangerment and mental slippage. Such events occurred at random but were too often repeated to be merely happenstance. This allowed for a disgruntled mindset against the world to get the upper hand.

A disgruntled mindset took control in the city of Winnipeg, Manitoba after arrival by bus from the vehicle delivery point of Albatross Corners, a suburb of the noble city of Regina, Saskatchewan. Upon arrival at the Canadian Black Dog Bus Station in Winnipeg, a gut-wrenching disappointment asserted itself, for a seven-hour interruption in homeward travel was my reward. Waiting for transportation was one of the most difficult of perils, plunging this driver into moods of insurrection, nullifying successful outcome, and intensifying the incurable ravages of homesickness. This left my feet in a dangerous foreign city known for its crime and law breaking.

My completed excursion to Albatross Corners had brought unbridled smugness, for there had been no flat tires, motor disruptions, or near-death experiences. The delivered conversion van ran like a top, consumed minimal amounts of fuel (compared to its gargantuan brothers), and was easily controlled over hill and valley. Bisected were the states of North and South Dakota and Minnesota which offered a natural route to the provinces of Manitoba and Saskatchewan. No extreme agitation or distress had plagued my pathway, so it was a satisfied driver who drove into the Albatross RV Center in Albatross Corners.

Upon my arrival, the manager himself stepped out of his office, asking me to wash the unit in a car wash across the street.

"Be glad to, sir," was my congenial reply.

Congeniality, however, didn't last long for under his watchful eye, I proceeded to turn the unit around, but in so doing I backed into a light pole. The rear bumper was horribly bent and the right rear corner received a crack extending for three feet, seven and 14 inches! How could this have happened, after driving one thousand, three hundred and twenty-one and one-half miles without a scratch? In two seconds of time I blew the whole thing! Not only was the vehicle damaged, but so was my brain, leaving an eternal scar on the memory membrane. I could not blame the weather, traffic, or anything else, for the manager was present at the scene of the crime and had seen the entire episode.

At the moment, all I could think of was to carry out his orders to wash the unit across the street. Another dreadful mishap occurred while washing it. With hose valve turned on high volume, a sudden movement to the side of the unit caused me to jerk the stream in that direction. The full force of the flow splashed directly into the face of the RV manager who had followed the unit to the car wash on foot to inspect the damaged bumper. His dark suit and purple necktie were completely soaked. Self-accusation set in, a verbal tongue lashing from Mr. Bad Self, with no response from the opposing party. Proceeding from my lips was a stammering apology, along with hand wringing and tears, and with a solemn promise not to do such a thing again. Lucky for me, this guy was a saint. Not just a good guy, a saint! Of the most divine sort. He wasn't even angry. In fact, he laughed. While he was laughing, I was crying.

After the deplorable incident had reached its climax, I drove the unit back to the dealer lot and presented myself before him. This saint of a dealer signed my release papers with no complaints, explaining that insurance would cover the accident since it happened on his property. This same saint personally drove to the Black Dog in Regina, with me on board. This was a distance of twenty-two and one half kilometers from Albatross Corners. Another round of apologies sprang from the tongue, along with a few "I'm Sorrys" and other adjectives that were silently issued from Bad Self to Good.

I was a happy person, getting out of the hair of that dealer man. Only I didn't. After purchasing a bus ticket back to Otoonga via Winnipeg, Fargo, and Minneapolis, I was settling down into the comfort of the soft metal chairs the station provided for its customers, when who would make an appearance but Mr. Dealer Man. This sight caused my heart to flutter and go in hiding. Bad Self gave warning, "Now you've had it, Myle. Prepare for a hospital visit. He's going to make a retaliatory response after reconsidering the awful crimes you committed."

The dealer man, with suit yet not dry from the soaking I gave it, approached my shaking form. Instead of retaliation, he brought back the packing slip because I had signed it on the wrong place. He had driven back from Albatross Corners, all twenty-two and one half kilometers to insure the delivery forms were in proper order. Can you believe this? He had retraced his drive back through the vast complex of Regina streets in spite of all the trouble I had caused. That's why I call him a saint.

Nevertheless, I was enveloped in a state of hugger-mugger humiliation which weaved its way through my subconscious, dampening the hope of natural rejuvenation.

After an all-night bus ride from Regina to Winnipeg, that dangerous foreign city of international crime and espionage, I found myself with seven hours with nothing to do and nowhere to go. Until noticing the bulletin board in the station, that is. Listed were places to dine, hotels in which to commit luxury, entertainment to endure, athletic events to attend, and nightclubs where you could really have a blast. Since seven hours was a long time, I decided to go for it and take in the whole works.

The first temptation to which I succumbed was to go swimming. A pool was located only four blocks from the bus station. It would be real cool to go swimming in Canada in the middle of winter, even if it was indoors with heated water. Since the temperature was ten below at twelve noon, it would be something to brag about when getting back to Otoonga. Luckily for me, my bathing suit had been remembered to bring along. Once inside the locker room the process of stripping and showering began in earnest. To my vexation, several pairs of little eyes followed my every movement. Worse yet, the eyes belonged not to little boys, but to girls! Of all the nerve of these fathers to bring their daughters into men's locker rooms! Unprincipled Canadian fathers sure have some weird ways, allowing these apprehensible sexual practices to take place. I was desperately tugging on my bathing suit, acutely aware of every eyeball movement. I skittered along the pool approach and plunged into the water, submerging myself up to the nose holes, in hopes that no new discoveries could be made. This was so unnerving that swimming cessation was soon forthcoming. How could one enjoy oneself when the same unnatural forces would he endured again while dressing? In less than ten minutes I was out of there, thankful that such gruesome ordeals would no longer be endured.

Canadians sure are a backward lot, allowing such abominable sexual conditions to prevail, reverting to the olden days when civilization was on its threshold, when evolution was in its prime, and before Darwin had discovered his own species. Even if the little girls were only one-year-old.

After the ten-minute swimming episode, six hours and twenty-three minutes yet remained before departure could take place from this demoralizing city. What could be done to make the time go faster? One listing on the bulletin board took my fancy, so to speak, even though being considered questionable entertainment. Since my location was in a foreign country and no one from Otoonga would ever know, why not go for it? No self-respecting farmer in his right mind would be caught dead in such a despicable place as advertised on the lighted marquee. No, it was not a girlee show…not ordinarily identified as such anyway.

Yet my curiosity was sufficiently aroused, prodding my determination to purchase a ticket to…the ballet.

Into the Canadian Civility Center I trod, falling in line with other like creatures waiting to be seated. Most of the other creatures were exorbitantly dressed, except for a few slouches like myself who managed to evade detection no matter how they were dressed. The attendants weren't paying attention and were seating all customers who held tickets in outstretched hands. Ushers couldn't tell if I was an American or not, as long as I kept my mouth shut.

When the curtain rose, out came an entire troop dancing on their toes, just as pictured. The entire performance wasn't very impressive, to my way of thinking. Too dull, unimaginative, and sissy-like. It must be admitted that extremely strong toe muscles were needed to maneuver about the stage without stumbling or falling, which happened later during the feature act. By the sound of all the hand clapping and cheers, an excellent job must have been performed. To me, the program was a complete waste of time, despite all the verbal acclamations and newspaper praises. Yet, this waste of time was much more desirable than sitting forlornly in a foreign bus station, or haunting the streets of this forbidden city while one's life was in jeopardy…if discovery was made known that my nationality was Yankee. One distinguishing scene during the performance brought laughter and applause, even from myself. Two dancers suddenly acted like they couldn't dance any longer, bumping into each other, falling down in heaps, and making complete fools of themselves. This proved to be a redeeming quality for the whole production, some of the best comedy available anywhere. It just goes to show you can find good in anything if you look long enough.

By the time the acts were over, the skies were darkening, even though my watch read three in the afternoon. Only six hours of daylight can be expected here in the winter time, and on a cloudy day you can't see your hand in front of your face at noon. It was next to impossible to get a decent meal in Winnipeg. The feature attractions at the eating establishments were bear hams, elk gizzards, eagle drumsticks, and wolf tails. I went hungry.

The three remaining hours dragged by interminably but somehow time for bus departure arrived. To think I would be back home with all the pigs, Azailia, and the boys in twenty-three more hours caused a lump to the throat and a tear to the eye. Jubilation overcame me when crossing the border. What a wonderful sight—the good old U.S.A. So what if it is a little dirtier on this side of the line? And what difference is it if you see more drunks, dope pushers, pimps, racists, child molesters, and gun-toting teenagers south of the border? America is the land of the free, you know.

During customs examination I was required to present my passport, driver's license, and birth certificate. All those documents didn't satisfy one of the examiners, who acted as if I was a smuggler of some kind. Rescue came from another officer with a Spanish accent and a snow-white beard. "We see these American jokers passing through all the time, Ralph," he stated. "Let him across like all the rest. I couldn't find anything dirty in his travel bags, so he must be clean."

Trips to Canada prove how hazardous it is to drive motor homes. Lots of ups and downs. It's always worse in Canada, no matter how straight-laced they are. Predictions cannot be made just when the next hazard will strike, where it will take place, and what will be the outcome. That's what happens to me all the time. If you parents are determined to let your kids drive motor homes, shame on you. You can't blame me. I have given plenty of warnings. Do you want them to end up in a freaked-out condition like I'm in?

CHAPTER XXIV
Downs and Ups

How perplexing it is to decipher the results of all my travelling.

"Were there more ups than downs, or more downs than ups?" asks Good Self while scrutinizing the troubling considerations to satisfaction. "Does it really pay off in time and money, Myle?" he asks. With no computer to figure the conclusion, one's brain power seems unequal to the task and is somewhat disadvantaged thereby. Not everything worthwhile can be valued in dollars and cents, yet too often this becomes the primary consideration. Like the old saying, "Money isn't everything, but what else is there?" The financial riches that accrue through delivery are many times overshadowed by an exalting enlightenment in conjunction therewith, which doesn't necessarily impose prominence at the cashing of a paycheck.

In other words, to enjoy life as it is experienced becomes a more satisfactory illusion at the beginning of the termination of living, than to accumulate the millions that most delivery drivers acquire enroute. To explain myself in a more admirable manner, and to articulate the response when questioning the pros and cons concerning financial rewards which hopefully prevail over the more negative qualities which snowball into adversity, one is at a loss for words. Accurately applying situation ethics by various modes of forthright acknowledgements may result in mind-boggling conclusions, permitting desperation to enthrone the final outcome and causing the negative approach to be more successful in getting the upper hand.

Yes, ups and downs are definitely prominent, but downs are to be avoided whenever possible. Topping the list is avoiding husband abuse. Not lingering over that second cup of coffee at breakfast, deserting the bedroom for the hog house when the baby's diaper needs changing, and paying attention to the signs of the Zodiac foretelling disaster are all methods of escape. A great advantage is to dispel the derogatory and to explicitly assert the absolute. But motor-home driving had already taken its toll before I could pull this off. To erase the tendency toward despondency, self-portrayal as a gung-ho stereotype, rather than an inferior shrinking violet like myself, is a necessity. Insinuations and unfounded allegations constantly oppose we poor drivers, along with all the other disturbing disinformation flung across our pathway. Bizarre opposition interrupts the flow of imaginative counter action, downgrading an affirmative outlook when comparison is derived in minute detail rather than in a sloppy, haphazard, happy-go-lucky measurement that exacerbates the whole mess. When facing those old wives tales handed down from generation to generation (and bandied about helter-skelter), thumb sucking on my mother's lap should have been abandoned when it was time to go potty chair.

Another down syndrome to consider is that people don't have much respect for motor home drivers either. Our mail boxes get vandalized, little boys tie strings across our sidewalks to trip us, tacks are placed on our garage driveways, and April Fool's jokes are played throughout the year. But I've had a good life. I'm glad the doctor let me live instead of being aborted like most everybody else is these days. Nowadays, murderers would kill you right while you are being born. They wouldn't have dared try that on me from what I know now. It's a cruel world out there.

They can just have their wars, political fights, and those X-rated movies…see if I care. Contentment and bliss would be mine if only able to stay home with pigs, wife, and boys, and never again be compelled to darken the door of the Otoonga Trailer Factory.

On the other hand...what is more satisfying than to coast down the highway in the most excellent means of transportation conceived by the mind of man? Sports, games, hobbies, toys, and entertainment all come out on the short end. For example: (1) The hobby of fishing trails far in the distance as an appealing option. Sitting in a mosquito atmosphere on hard boards with sun beating down unmercifully waiting for nothing to happen isn't my idea of hilarity; (2) the sport skiing is also a miserable failure in comparison. Dressing in multiple layers of clothing to slide from terrifying heights into a nose-running collapse into frozen white stuff is foolhardy at best, most likely terminating with broken bones at the bottom of the mountain; (3) attending some boring ball game when the outcome is known before hand becomes worthless in comparison to the great adventures of travel; (4) what gratification can be grasped while stroking innocent little balls high in the air in hopes they will descend into dark holes? (5) sitting in the scorching heat, pouring rain, or freezing cold to watch different shaped balls being smashed, tossed about, or thrown into some target isn't what life is all about; (6) failing the test also are saddling up on a sweating animal to travel at a snail's pace, mounting a two- wheeled monster in death defying arrogance, or sailing above the clouds in a tin container with destructive intent; (7) to sit in a dark hall watching secondhand the lifeless movements of spineless characters is considered fanciful, a time waster, and purposeless.

Contrarily, how can you measure the thrill of the open road, fantastic scenery, provision for comfort and relaxation, and having a blast in such pursuit? High regard is given to those thus engaged, jealousies are provoked, and deep admiration is propagated even from the wealthy and famous.

A driver is at the top of the list, the most respected of the disrespectful, and causes a stir whenever another distinguishing mark has been created.

"Why not use discretion when trying to solve the meaning of life? Make a combination of life's pleasures when travelling, Myle. Then you got it made." Good Self was asserting noble advice. Following his admonition was totally appropriate. A billboard along the highway may read, "County Fair Today thru Friday," or "Cubs vs. Bears 8:00 Tonite." That's the time to ease off and grab a little gusto. Maybe the radio blared an ad about a Mexican Fiesta in progress, a car race on a two-mile track, or Cowboy Phil is in country concert tonight. Beckoning signals ask for your attendance at school plays, concerts, theatre productions, and tournaments in local auditoriums. Football, soccer, basketball, and tennis events are at your fingertips when riding in a motor home. If such opportunities are scorned, you may as well check in to the nursing home around the corner.

Many are the events taking place in unexpected locations. Ostrich races in Hot Springs, sword swallowers tournament in San Jose, dart-throwing contests in Kalamazoo, snake hunting in Boston, sky diving in New Haven, butterfly catching in Philadelphia, and shark fishing in Las Cruces. It has been my privilege to dip toes in the Atlantic, climb the rock strewn cliffs of Nebraska, attend a mud-wrestling contest in Minneapolis, cheer a bull fight in Newark, and watch a lipstick smearing fight in Wichita while a beard growing contest was going on in Louisville. I also got to wade across the whale-infested waters of the mighty Rio Grande.

My bragging will never cease about attending four world fairs in Spokane, New Orleans, Vancouver, New York, and Seattle. You may argue that the Spokane fair was only an exhibition, but what does that matter when located in a beautiful location, with exploding attractions, and issuing gourmet delights? Prominent was my involvement in one of the free acts going on. Well, it wasn't exactly a free act but they didn't charge admission. To the group of onlookers it may have been advertisement more than entertainment. Standing at the edge of the group with a blank look on my face may have been the reason why I was chosen to participate.

A sales representative of a prominent automobile manufacturer asked my help in a demonstration. I was to be the central figure in how a car bag would explode in an accident. While in the process of saying no, he grabbed my arm, led me to the opened car door, and forcibly crammed my unwilling body into the fearful passenger seat and closed the doors. My horror stricken ears heard, and my fearful eyes watched while the salesman articulated in artful persuasion the multiple advantages of owning a car bag in your car. Proper usage and installation would save thousands of lives annually, prevent untold injuries, and make America a safe place to live...so he said.

His oration continued for several minutes, creating a sense of anticipation and awe to the crowd, and a discernment of impending catastrophe to me. Shortly thereafter, when least expecting it, even though it was expected, it happened. A great jolt, a muffled noise, and a puff of exploding air enveloped my body in a ghastly seizure. An actual car wreck would have been preferable to that abominable simulation. I stumbled out the door with knocking knees, a frightened look, and a torn pant leg. Needless to say, I have never worn a car bag in my car to this day. Running out of that dreadful environment as fast as my wobbly legs would carry me provoked heckles, boos, and catcalls from the audience who were suddenly turning violent. For some reason, this episode left a taste in my mouth, and it wasn't from eating too much lasagna either. I'll not be seen in another Spokane Exposition ever again.

The New Orleans Fair was my favorite. Ignorant commentators labeled it a failure. Being located in a very small region, comparatively so, probably caused these negative assertions. One lone country boy hastily visited many of the attractions and gorged himself at the food booths. Multiple stage locations allowed enjoyment of musical delights of all kinds.

Lively bands caught my fancy while strolling through the grounds. Rock, Dixieland, Mexican, country western, religious, bluegrass, and Cajun melodies blared forth, all competing in a cacophony of rhythm.

The fair, in its entirety, could best be described as a down to earth experience…an American apple pie affair. Participation left me stuffed with jambalaya and crawfish pie, bug-eyed from show entertainment, and a ringing ear syndrome from the loud combo music.

The fairgrounds were situated on the banks of the Mississippi, only a tightrope walk away from the Latin quarter, and but a few blocks from the fabulous downtown. Impressionable farmers like myself were overwhelmed by the frenzied activity and hubbub. Beggars, drunks, and addicts makes their presence known at each attraction, in a quest for appetite appeasement. Delivering a 34-foot vehicle to the suburb of Metairie made this visit to the fair possible. The short city bus ride allowed for an exhilarating climax, spending the entire day and half the night within the confines of the fair grounds. I was sorry to leave this man-made chaos, however a bus ride was on the docket. A scary walk of nine blocks to the Black Dog was undertaken, with apprehension occurring at each step. Whenever accosted by one of the lurking riff-raff, I broke into a wild run, surprising the would-be attackers who had not seen such daring-do before in this conservative, staid, sedate city of New Orleans.

Vancouver, British Columbia! What a world's fair took place! I didn't like it. You want to know why? Too many people. People everywhere. Long lines where starvation initiates, where legs give out before seating was found, and where bladders leak before comfort stations were discovered. Being pushed around by women and children was very disconcerting, resulting in bruises, pinched nerves, swollen feet, sagging jowls, bleary eyes, and torn fingernails. Fighting back against the gregarious roughnecks was a losing battle, belying the principle of mutual friendship between nationalities. The location of the extravaganza was in a glorious setting, curving around the bay in domineering prominence, with the skyline of downtown Vancouver imposing in stately array in the distance. Hundreds of buildings were constructed for this event, and what entertainment and allurements each provided! Yet in opposition, several detestable circumstances prevented enjoyment thereof.

I would wander from one long line of people to another, in hopes that Utopia might be found. Shuffling along inch by inch brought only disappointment when at the end of the line it was discovered that only rolls of toilet paper were being handed out. I was at wits end trying to have fun, hoping my gusto wouldn't give out. Waiting in line to see King Tut's sarcophagus, with maybe him in it, meant two hours lost. Falling in a line that led to the hemisphere was another disappointment for the door was slammed shut for cleaning before I could enter. I would meander from line to line, hoping to grab a thread of levity, as hour after hour of futility rolled by. Failure was erupting, forcing me to settle for the mediocre. Since the crowds were so unruly and cantankerous while blocking my pathway, I decided to watch the free acts along the concourses. Knife-juggling acrobats, sword-swallowing Asians, fire-eating magicians, and strolling Eskimo musicians were on my agenda. Dismay wasn't unconquerable, for at a far corner location I was able to enjoy myself at last. A steel drum band from Jamaica was pounding furiously on thirty-gallon oil barrels, and from these clamorous antics came the most melodious sounds this side of Gloria Estefan. Not only was the music enrapturing, but seats were available, and that's what mattered most, even if they were only single boards with no back rest. This calypso claptrap was so enthralling that my countenance was uplifted, my spirits soared, and my metabolism reverted back to normal. I stayed over and watched the same act three times in a row.

Gradually, closing time approached, gates were shut, and continued festivities were permitted only to the younger set. A heavy-metal bunch of rowdies were taking center stage, hammering away at guitars and drums, bare-chested even. I fooled the gate keepers big time by purchasing a mustache-and-glasses disguise, along with an artificial nose ring, and they didn't know but what I was one of the young ones, providing my shirt collar was buttoned up so my turkey neck wasn't exposed. This frenzied activity continued until two o'clock in the morning, along with mood-altering music in a rock beat. When the music ended, I was compelled to leave by huge park policemen since I had no partner lying on the ground beside me.

From this place of rapturous fantasy, I sought my way through the threatening darkened streets to a staging area where vans provided by the fair authorities whisked waiting individuals to another staging area where, after a thirty-minute wait (if one were fortunate), one was enabled to mount a city coach that bounced through the deserted streets of Vancouver to another staging area where, after yet another thirty-minute wait (if one were fortunate), still another bus ride would deposit one's body to the very airport berth of his choosing. The city of Vancouver went all out to provide a stupendous worldwide celebration to its welcomed revelers, but for some reason the ecstasy didn't penetrate through my skin. Perhaps the average farmer doesn't appreciate the finer things of life. Toes being stepped on, police swinging billy clubs, panhandlers panhandling, and weirdos pushing and shoving all contribute to a defeatist attitude with a revenge motivation still in tact.

Going to world fairs, attending sports events of all kinds, and indulging in all forms of entertainment provide excellent means of lifting one's self up by the bootstraps unless the bootstraps weren't already worn out from previous endeavors. Yet these luxuries cannot compensate for the dangers, threats, and perils encountered along the way. I must admit, but not with a whining voice, there certainly are a lot of downs when attending world fairs, particularly so when one drives a motor home to get there.

When downs come, they come in gobs. Like the time I was going to get my clock cleaned in Butte, Montana. That's what the man said would happen when he broke into a rage, over nothing, actually. A gasoline advertisement had beckoned my unit to take advantage of unlimited service and cheaper prices. In fact, many billboards had listed the same message several times for the past forty miles past Bozeman. An abrupt halt at this well-publicized target was done with anticipation, and pumping gas from one of the thirty pumps was the result. While parking at the pump, I failed to notice a semi that was slowly reversing. While at the pumps, the semi driver stopped his truck when directly in line with my unit. With a scowl on his face he yelled out the window, "Hey, you, don't you know you should never pull behind a backing semi?"

"What backing semi?" I retorted.

"This here rig right here, can't you see?"

"Why, I wasn't anywhere near your back end, so what's the beef?"

"I repeat, Mac, so's you can get the message. You NEVER pull up behind a backing semi."

I turned my back on him and continued filling the tank while his harangue continued.

"Are you hard of hearing, Mac? I said you NEVER pull behind a backing semi. As soon as I park this rig I'm comin' over and clean your clock. Maybe then you kin understand."

He commenced to maneuver his huge vehicle backward into a space between two other like rigs and it wasn't taking him long to do it. His veiled threat caused my nerve endings to arouse from slumber while my Bad Self interjected, "You're going to be in awful shape if your clock gets cleaned, Myle."

Good Self attempted rescue, "Get out of here fast. He's a great big mountain of a man and has a lot of muscles to go with it."

When Bad Self and Good are both on the same wavelength, I start paying attention. I immediately quit pumping gas, although the tank was only half full. Sprinting into the store, I quickly paid the bill while removing my yellow seed corn jacket and throwing it in the trash can.

When Mr. Mad entered the front door, I ran out the back.

He was searching for some smart aleck nerd with a yellow jacket, but did he get fooled!

All he discovered were other slouchy truck drivers like himself, for old Yellow Jacket had vamoosed!

Laughter was running rampantly out of the corners of my mouth while driving out of truck stop and heading toward Missoula. I had sure pulled a fast one on that big ox. Only to soon find out that I hadn't. Within just a few miles, a slow-moving semi was running in my lane, forcing entry into the left lane to pass. Much to my dismay, another rig appeared out of nowhere travelling in the left lane, making it impossible to pass. By looking in the mirror I could see another eighteen- wheeler rapidly approaching from the rear. I was hemmed in, the way ahead blocked. How fast the word gets around to your buddies by CB radios. I was kept awake by speeds up to eighty miles an hour around dangerous mountain curves, slow downs to forty-five on level territory, and inter- mittent loud blasts from air horns. It was awful! All I could see ahead of me was a large letter "R" in Bimbo's Transport. Three feet separated my unit from the rig in front. Three feet separated my unit from the rig in back. Three feet separated my unit from the unit to the left. I was con- voyed all the way to Missoula, when the rig ahead speeded up, so did I. When the rig in back speeded up, so did I.

Miraculously, the entire flock disappeared at the fifth Missoula exit. This ride left me soaked in perspiration, shaking with fear, and with brain matter sloshing around. Mr. Mad had triumphed after all, when his buddies took control. The shameful admission was made that my clock really did get cleaned. I promise never to drive in the pathway of a reversing semi that was backing up, ever again.

Rational explanations to unanswered questions usually cannot be flippantly summarized with a simple yes or no reply. Sarcastic as this may sound, argumentation can be applied more frequently by the knowledgeable intelligentsia than by a crackpot bunch of morons who attempt sinister subjection of those a little lower on the social ladder. A veritable groping in the dark, a telepathic outburst in an otherwise objective response, and an unattainable escape from introspection must be used in finalizing the assumptions in measurement of encompassing considerations (which, if your reaction is prone to dissatisfaction), resulting in a more or less disingenuous ingenuity, so to speak. To further complicate an already unwarranted identification, a butting in of the nose leads only to a bitter climax, an unquickened spirit, a defeatist attitude, and perhaps a slap in the face from a lady of virtue. It isn't difficult to understand the vortex of such ramifications and, if improperly applied, supplants the preponderous surveillance of inadequate supplementation. A cart-wheeling free-fall into perplexity would be the evident simplification to the unanswered question, to such an extent that a satisfactory solution would be somewhat occluded. It can then be readily assumed that there are just as many downs than ups when driving motor homes.

CHAPTER XXV

Intermission

Tomorrow will be my 95th birthday. Just think, if this was only leap year I would have another day to live. These are my golden years, so everyone says. A lot of water has run over the dam. Many rewarding hours are now spent in melancholy nostalgia, reminiscing about the days gone by. I've had a good life. There have been a lot of ups and downs, as you have been told before. Most of my days have been wasted behind some wheel or another, either bouncing from fence row to fence row, or parading around the country in some beautiful, magnificent, dazzling vehicle. Memories haunt me continually about the good old days gone by when my wife was still here and the kids were growing up. A person does not appreciate the good times along the way. That's what I was told when growing up as a kid myself, but who would believe it then? How shocking it is to realize how fast your life flies by, and how intense was the desire to be a successful, happy person. How this proved to be so elusive is a mystery indeed.

My life expectancy is now on the downhill climb, probably no more than forty years left at best, and it could even be less. Since Judgement Day will soon be here, all my debts must soon be paid, all cheating on income tax made right, and all lies confessed. This is a rebuttal to all young people who think they have the merry old world by the tail and thumb their noses at us old duffers, thinking they have forever ahead of them. A concerted effort is somehow diffused by the nay-sayers who don't give respect when it is due. A lot of these young twerps think they have everything figured out after it happens. About all that is achieved is a short-sighted myopia in their detraction of the endeavors of those who have a few years advantage.

My uncle rented the farm out from underneath me last fall. He said I was getting too old. A lot he knows about it, lying on the beach every day in Fort Lauderdale. He got rich from the crop share that I worked so hard for. If he ever dies, he is going to will his farms to his young nurse, so he told me. My own chance at riches goes flying out the window with no inheritance from him. So what do I care?

Farming was a wonderful way of life, one of hard work and accomplishment. Farming allowed me to be my own boss and to enjoy the wonders of nature so miraculously created. Time was ample enough to enjoy life with wife and family after a long day's work, and to cast aside the cares and worries that invade and disrupt so easily. How pleasing it was to play with the dog under the apple tree, to watch the boys walk down the lane from the school bus, and to lie on your back in the hog pen with a straw between one's teeth watching the cumulous clouds build up overhead while the pigs were gently nosing at your side. An especially happy time it was when the boys were old enough to do the hog chores, chop the weeds, and plow the corn. This enabled me to sit on the porch in the shade reading a newspaper, smell the pot roast cooking through the open window, and watch the wife washing clothes on the scrub board. Farming gave witness to the amazing cycle of life drift before your eyes, ever-changing, ever-challenging. It was a procedure supernatural to behold, unexplainable to explain. I believe a Great Creator made all of this, regardless what those stupid educators tell us about how we all crawled out of a swamp somewhere a billion years ago.

To say that I miss farming and farm life is a great understatement. Working out in the fields, planting the crops, harvesting the bounty, and hauling the manure were all at the top of the list. It about breaks my heart to think that there are no little pigs to care for anymore. Pigs were so innocent and trustworthy. Their little eyes would look up at you in a thought- provoking manner whenever you would clamp a ring in their nose, give them a needle shot, cut off their tails, or provide castration service. Some of the more friendly ones were just like one of the family. That may be a crude statement, but when more time is spent with the pigs than with your own offspring, what else can you expect? What a sorry, tear-jerking time it was when time came to load them on the truck for the slaughter house. To this day, I find it difficult to eat pickled pigs feet, minced ham, pork chops, or roast, thinking some of it may have come from Porky, Hammy, or Penelope. The heart-rending squeals coming out of their little pink mouths were enough to cause even the most callous herdsman to hunker in shame and remorse. My attempts were to inflict as little pain as possible and to make gentleness one of my more desirable traits. Besides this, it isn't advantageous to get in trouble with a bunch of "Prevent Cruelty to Animals" organizations, for you could end up in court real quick like with that kind of confrontation. Only during times of extreme stress do I utter a harsh words to my pigs, or to get angry and violent with them. If one's temper gets out of control, that's when most of the pain gets inflicted. Like when they would crawl under the fence and ruin a patch of corn with all that rooting, or when they refused to go up   the loading chute and into the truck. That's where I would draw the line and go beserk. I wasn't responsible at a time like that. No telling how many went to market with bruised hams, bloody noses, and cracked ribs.

Not only were the good times of farming remembered, but also the marvelous get-togethers with friends drinking coffee at the Uptight Farmers Cafe, meeting the acquaintances at church, and to be with the brothers in the drivers room at the factory. It was a special time being with my best friend Eddie, who is still working at the rock quarry. He started drawing his Social Security check thirty years ago, but enjoyed busting up rocks so much that he kept on doing it. He saved his money and is now so rich he can afford a trailer house in the west part of Otoonga, across the tracks.

If I had only worked there instead of delivering motor homes, wealth would now be my companion too. Eddie got so he wouldn't speak to me the last forty years. He would sit across the aisle in church and he wouldn't say hello or look my way. So I did the same thing right back to him. He was jealous of all my travels and wonderful adventures. He still has a wife to care for him when he gets old, while mine is gone forever. He has the last laugh on me after all.

I do miss all the loved ones who have gone on before. Where they ended up, I don't know. All of the boys are out of school now. None of them got married except Jack, the oldest one. He told me I would be a grandfather for the first time in ten months. How wonderful it will be to have a little grandson jumping on my knees to comfort me when I get old. Buzzy was a slow learner and never made it out of the eighth grade. Like Eddie, he works in the rock quarry, enjoying the hard work and outdoor world. Nicholas got a job in the trailer factory building motor homes that I used to drive. Jack had a lot of smarts, living in the big city and employed at a pickle factory. Zachary is unemployed again. His trouble was that he liked to tip the bottle too much, but he is a good boy at heart. I only had to bail him out of jail twice. We are all proud of Beckley. He graduated from college with a degree in insect biology. He's now working on a project intended to keep beetles from multiplying so rapidly. I can't remember offhand just what the two youngest boys are doing. Or where they are living either. To tell the truth, I can't even remember their names, but it will come to me in a minute. Azailia could remember them if she was still with us. She was always good at keeping things straight right up to the very last. When you get to be my age, all you can remember are things that happened long ago. They say you become forgetful and can't remember what happened yesterday. But I can still remember what happened yesterday, and a few days before that.

I'll never forget Old Barney. He was a true friend if there ever was one, always willing to help out whenever he was needed. Azailia didn't have to work quite so hard whenever he was around and it freed me up to go driving down the highway. Poor Barney, rest his soul. He was dealt a low blow when Jane Berkenholtzen ran off with that eighteen-year-old son of a butcher from Max and Mark's Meat Market at 110 North Main in Crestfallen. Barney never got over that. And you know, the situation deteriorated so much that none of the other young women would come out to clean his house because he was so morose and grouchy. When they couldn't get at his money they would up and quit. The only house-keepers he was able to hire were the old widows who hoped they could trap him in marriage, but he was too smart for that. Old Barney isn't with us anymore. He bought a cemetery plot on a side hill on the out-skirts of Crestfallen. It's sort of a dreary place to my estimation, with weeds growing up around the tombstones and vines crawling along the entry gate. It was just like Barney to choose a place like that for his final resting place. Some of the older stones have fallen over in disgraceful fashion. His own gravestone has been vandalized with yellow paint splattered all over it. He's going to be really mad when he finds out about it. You see, after Jane left him he moved to Las Vegas, but he comes home each summer to check on his farms. Rumor has it that he has given up drinking for the Black Jack tables and chasing women.

Of course many fond memories remain of the remarkable days driv-ing for the Otoonga Trailer Factory. A lot of wonderful times, exciting experiences, and glorious opportunities came from that place of employment. What a thrill it was to meander across the country to some new destination in a brand new motor home with no cares or worries, and with a new adventure beckoning. To have seen the great beauties of our country and to have enjoyed to utmost the opportunity which was created by one's own ingenuity in moving certain movable objects from one place to another, resulting in happiness for your fellow men, in spite of the degradation forced on one's self by so doing, was in itself a remarkable achievement.

Remarkable achievements, however, led to frustrating conclusions of pain, suffering, and sorrow, as has been previously reported. The frustrating conclusions have been explained in detail to warn those who desire to follow in my footsteps, that they abandon such intentions and to pause in contemplation. If such warnings are heeded, perhaps my life has not been lived in vain, nor is it a complete failure. Hopefully these exhortations, uttered in humility, have had profound effect on the listening ear, and thereby have saved themselves from an early grave. To the thousands who did not allow these words to change your intentions, you ought to be ashamed. It's nobody's fault but your own. There may yet he time to rectify your position. It's never too late 'til it's over.

Of course, there are many fond memories of the wonderful people at the Otoonga Trailer Factory. How kind and thoughtful were Mr. Hummer and Miss Missmossmus. How lovable were the fellow drivers such as Red Jacket, Striped Overalls, One Eye, and Pony Tail. What characters they proved to be. Some were gentle and forbearing, others grouchy and angry, while many were silly and nonplussed. Hummer, you see, was both hot and cold, at times helpful, while at others, a pain in the assinine way he expressed himself. He finally got what he deserved. He got caught by the authorities for embezzling the company out of $450,000.07. He should have known that subtracting 10¢ from each pay check would some day be found out. His court case was delayed so often by his lawyers and spin doctors that all the money was spent on wine, women, and motor homes before they caught him. And that Miss Missmossmus! Did she come up in the world! She is now the head dispatcher, taking place of Mr. Hummer. By marrying one of the single drivers who hung around her desk once too often, she is no longer an old maid. She kept her maiden name, however, thinking it would provide much more authority than the name Smith.

This is a sad way to close my career. Yet it could have been worse. Many drivers experienced a more horrible fate than my own. Some ended in drunkard graves. Some turned to chain smoking. Still others were unable to withstand the rigors of driving, the nervous apprehension, and the jail sentences from so much law breaking. Some of the more fortunate drivers divorced the old hags they were married to, and found new ones in some bus station, airport, or all-night tavern. Other drivers faced a horrible final destiny in a state asylum, incoherent of speech, with featureless expressions, and twisted resolve. Sorry to report, there were many of the less fortunate who acquired eye twitches, nervous tics, shaking hands, and unable to live out a normal life, ending up as vassals of the state. The worst cases were forced to rely on Medicare to bail them out. These are the results of which I have been warning you about. What more can I say? Doesn't anyone pay attention?

Tragically, tragedy has struck my own home as well. In the pursuit of one more trip after another, one more little harmless adventure, ful-fillment of yet another dream…my life's bubble has burst. My happi-ness has ended. Between each trip lately, I could observe a gradual deterioration in Azailia's condition. All this travelling, leaving her with the farm responsibility for days at a time, well, it sort of broke down her health. She lost her zeal for living. I could see it gradually coming on but there wasn't much I could do about it. Little by little, her condition worsened until she was no longer her radiant self. She wandered about listlessly as erosion of her mental faculties and physical abilities com-bined to envelop her in a deadly embrace. Just working in the hog barn for an hour seemed to impair her appearance. Debate continued between Bad Self and Good whether to place her in a nursing facility or let nature take its course. Asking the pastor for advice proved worthless, for a mild shrug of the shoulders and a bewildered look were all he could offer. My predicament was heading for a climax when I began noticing she was losing the ability to grasp a pitchfork properly, and that her shoulders were sagging lower and lower while carrying buckets of feed from the shed to the hog house. Her assiduous nagging became less and less, a sure sign of obtuseness and degeneration. My heart was breaking from these observations. I was trying not to feel sorry for myself, but the realization was dawning…I would soon be left alone.

Lying on my bed at night in the wee hours of the morning in deep contemplation left me in a state of deep despondency. I was facing the awful prospect of cooking my own meals, making my own bed, and sewing on buttons. My luck was running out. The day of her departure was nearing and I had yet to buy a cemetery plot.

Then one day it happened. Well, it really wasn't in the day; it was more like in the middle of the night. Maybe not in the middle of the night. More like 2:00 A.M. I remember it well because I had just came back from a jolly trip to Syracuse and had driven my car home from the Otoonga airport. I had spent a couple hours at Red's Tavern drinking Cokes, and so the best of recollection put the time of my arrival home somewhere between 1:30 and 2:30. That Syracuse State Fair was one of the best I ever attended. I took in the grandstand acts and a few of the side shows. Boy, did they ever have good eats at the fair. I stuffed myself with hamburgers, pizza, onion rings, turkey legs, funnel cakes, corn on the cob, watermelon, and ice cream sandwiches. That Snoozetime Hotel was real fancy, too. Because the fair was so enjoyable, I couldn't help myself from staying over two extra nights, instead of rushing right back.

The minute I arrived home from the airport I could sense something was wrong. A sense of foreboding swept over me, a deep feeling in the pit of my stomach like it might be heartburn, only worse. Like a prediction of doom, a haunting echo of fear swept over me, a portent of fate, so to speak. The dog was glad to see me, so I played with him for thirty minutes under the apple tree. Yet this feeling of dread continued. Could it be that Azalia had already gone to her reward?

Entering the back door and kicking the cat out of my path, only led to a deeper feeling of despondency. Each step up the stairs to our bedroom caused my heart to sink and pulse to diminish. It took a lot of courage to open the bedroom door. To my surprise, the bed was empty. But on the nightstand was a note written in a shaky hand. It read: "Dear Myle. I can't take this any longer. I am going home to mother. Love,

Azailia." There was a P.S. "I didn't feed the hogs today. They can starve to death for all I care."

And I never saw her again. Rumor has it that she and her mother left the country. Brazil probably. That's where most fugitives go who never want to be seen again.

So it is with saddened heart that I make my final plea. Dear friend, whoever you are, never, ever start driving motor homes. You have seen what happened to me. My pigs and wife are gone forever. I now have to fend for myself and sew on my own buttons. My own boys won't speak to me anymore. Why should they when they found out I cut them out of any inheritance? Since there won't be anything to inherit anyway, they won't be speaking to me twice.

But I still have my health. It is said, if you have good health, you have everything. So that's what I got—everything. A lot there is to be thankful for. The golden years beckon to me. Promises of ease and splendor came upon me in overwhelming waves while peering out the window of my upstairs rented room at 465 Nuttsonville Avenue in Otoonga. Retirement found me far from the rigorous demands of the farm where weeds in the corn exceeded their environment, where pigs kept up that dreadful oinking, and snow piled higher than the barn windows in April. It instilled within me a new appreciation for life, a new awareness of our awesome world, and preserved a sense of reverence for the finer things of life. And it all came about because of the fantastic invitation received this morning. It came in the form of a telephone call.

"Hello?" I said.

"Is this Myle?"

"Yes."

"We have a 34-foot Extravaganzz Excellor ready to go to Hartford, Connecticut. Can you come in this afternoon to drive it out?"

"Sure, no problem, Ms. Missmossmus. I'll be right up as soon as eat my hot dog and beans."

Epilogue

Do you readers recall all the warnings I have given about not driving motor homes? You do? I thought so. Well, forget about it. Don't believe a word I said. I was lying through my teeth. Motor home travel is the most wonderful experience you can undertake. I ought to know. I've been driving one for eighty-five years.

Myle Heyers